The Tales of Arturo Vivante

The Tales of Arturo Vivante

Selected and with an Introduction by
Mary Kinzie

The Sheep Meadow Press
Riverdale-on-Hudson, New York

To my grandchild

All inquiries and permission requests should be addressed to:
The Sheep Meadow Press
P.O. Box 1345
Riverdale-on-Hudson, New York 10471

Distributed by:
Consortium Book Sales & Distribution, Inc.
287 East 6th Street, Suite 365
St. Paul, Minnesota 55101

Cover design by S.M.
Book design and typesetting by Keystrokes, Lenox, Massachusetts
Printed by Princeton University Press, Lawrenceville, New Jersey

Library of Congress Cataloging-in-Publication Data:

Vivante, Arturo.
[Selections. 1990]
The tales of Arturo Vivante / selected and with an introduction by Mary Kinzie.
p. cm.
ISBN 0-935296-95-6. — ISBN 0-935296-91-3 (pbk.)
I. Kinzie, Mary. II. Title
PS3572.I85A6 1990
813′.54—dc20 90-30053
CIP

Contents

Acknowledgments

Twenty-five of these thirty-five tales originally appeared in *The New Yorker:* from Part I, all but "Fioretta" and "The Angel"; of the selections in Part II, *The New Yorker* has published all but the uncollected stories listed below and the two excerpts from *A Goodly Babe* called "Mrs. Lee" and "Thistledown." Two parts of the excerpt from *Doctor Giovanni* here called "The Tower" have previously appeared in different form: "The Snake" (*The Manchester Guardian,* 1955), and "The Broken Holiday" (*The New Yorker,* 1959).

Many chapters of Mr. Vivante's two novels have also appeared as short stories. In three cases, "Fioretta" (*Massachusetts Review,* 1988) "The Short Cut" (*The New Yorker,* 1960), and "Fisherman's Terrace" (*The New Yorker,* 1961), the serial publication versions are used. In all the other cases of dual publication, the book versions appear here.

Stories have appeared as follows in the novels and previous collections:

A Goodly Babe, novel (1966): "Mrs. Lee," "Thistledown," "The Short Cut," "Fisherman's Terrace"

The French Girls of Killíni, stories (1967): "The Sound of the Cicadas," "Last Rites," "The Prince," "The Nightingale," "The Binoculars," "Radicofani"

Doctor Giovanni, novel (1969): "Fioretta," "The Tower"

English Stories (1975): "The Lighthouse," "The Holborn," "A Gift of Joy"

Run to the Waterfall, stories (1979): "The Conversationalist," "The Orchard," "Of Love and Friendship," "The Soft Core," "The Bell," "A Place in Italy," "A Game of Light and Shade"

Stories previously uncollected include "Gypsies" (*The New Yorker,* 1979), "The Angel" (*TriQuarterly,* 1982), "A Moment" (*The New Yorker,* 1968), "By the Bedside" (*The New Yorker,* 1980), "A Gallery of Women" (*The New Yorker,* 1978), "Beppa" (*Antaeus,* 1979), "The Emergency"

(*The New Yorker,* 1972), "The Art Teacher" (*Formations,* 1987), "Luca" (*Canto,* 1977), "Night in the Piazza" (*Agni Review,* 1987), "At the Caffè Greco" (*The New York Times,* July 13, 1986), "'Tarocchi, Cavoli, Belle Cavolelle, Donne, Oh!'" (*The New York Times,* November 10, 1979).

"The Last Kiss" is published here for the first time.

Introduction

ON THE TALES OF ARTURO VIVANTE

by Mary Kinzie

I. Fleeing Home

Although Arturo Vivante has written all his fiction in English and lived for most of the past thirty years in the United States, his tales about his Italian past form the heart of his *oeuvre.* Despite the variety of protagonists named Giacomo, Livio, Ferruccio, Lorenzo, Cosimo, Damiano, Bruno, and Giovanni, the characters bear a transparent likeness to each other—not least in the resemblances between their parents. While few fathers in literature have been as coolly exacting as the ubiquitous, wiry, philosopher-father (who summons from his family such extremes of devotion), few ambivalent sons can have been as reverential as this author toward an ageing patriarch—nor as adoring of his mother, the witty yet modest spirit who clearly taught Vivante how to see and relish the natural world.

As a result both of his father's devotion to books and of his painter-mother's inclination toward visual intelligence, the episodes of family and childhood are inevitably anchored in his father's and mother's land—the Italy of ports, walls, writers, and painters; but also the Italy of river, rock, vineyard, and clay, of woods and lichens and glorious wild plants like the *ginestra* (broom), beloved by the poet Leopardi as well. In a significant number of his tales, Vivante's protagonist lights out, traversing the country (usually in some broken-down vehicle) in a state of perpetual wonderment. In the background the Apennines, with their forbidding rocky passes, sheer outlooks, and proud, isolated towns, divide the country in all directions. Often the most pleasing intensity derives from the least welcoming vistas—like the one near

Radicofani on the ancient Via Cassia, which long familiarity from their trips moves Vivante to call "the road of my childhood":

> Most of the land is barren, but here and there, where the mountain isn't too steep, it is plowed for wheat. The harvests are scanty, for the clay sheds the rain, and, with no trees to hold it, the water rushes to the valley, carrying seeds with it and carving great, gray, gutterlike channels. In some places, the clay is so pure that nothing will grow on it, and it looks poisonous. Under the strong sun, the clay bakes and cracks the way a statue that hasn't been hollowed cracks when it is fired and becomes terra cotta. Layer upon layer, wave after wave, the pale clay has molded itself into ridges and mounds. Looking at it, one is tempted to say that this isn't earth but a sort of white lava.
>
> ("Radicofani")

In the gullies like flawed statuary, over earth like volcanic tufa, the clay "poisonous" (an apt term) yet also (what is even more apt) "so pure that nothing will grow on it," Vivante's protagonist traces the invisible history of journeys, stretching back into the Renaissance, by northern Europeans heading south. He not only remembers his own trips over the barren mountain with his family, but can recall how, after the War, the road to Radicofani was more visibly gouged with the tracks, and often littered with the remnants, of German tanks disabled as they retreated north. But it is the remoter prospect that most interests him: "Shelley had probably stopped here, and . . . Milton. . . . Charlemagne had probably stamped his feet here, and . . . Cassius the consul, before Julius Caesar was born."

A story like "Radicofani" is as much a meditation on cultural history as it is a work of fiction, and it is this quality of cultural imbeddedness that one finds so attractive. For Vivante is *at home* in the world in a way few American writers can boast, Henry James being the exception who proves the rule. I do not mean at home in merely artificial contexts like museums, salons, or historic "sites," but also at home in the present time, at ease whether in company or solitude, engaged, observant, happy to gossip, subject to serious "moods" in large part attributable to what is happening outside the self—all traits of any individual-of-culture. And although James and Vivante are utterly unlike in *manner* and in social aspiration—for James was ever the climber, while Vivante one suspects of being wilfully part peasant—yet in the thesis of an eager and automatic immersion in a social *donnée,* approached with almost rigorous reserve, they are arguably akin.

Alongside Vivante's fresh scenes and kindly attachments, however, two spectral presences appear. The first is Fascism, which drove Vivante's part-Jewish family to England during the War. Vivante touches this experience with some indirection; the only tale much occupied with the Fascists is "The Sound of the Cicadas." This is the story of an aggressive boys's-school instructor who realizes there is one youth (the narrator) who will resist the gymnastics drill and flub the "sixty movements" on the day of the government rally. So he releases the boy from the compulsory class. It is in this story that we encounter, beside the splendidly controlled irritabilities of the two main characters, the brief snapshot of the Anglican minister whose chapel (never well attended to begin with) is boarded up: Vivante's mother sees him praying in the Catholic cathedral.

The second spectral presence haunting Vivante's *oeuvre* is, more surprisingly, Eros, which has produced a peculiar yet fascinating dislocation in the fiction that treats of marriage and American life. I have not chosen more from this category because the soil here seems (to adapt the author's own metaphors) too pure and resistant. Vivante's *personae* often remind me of Vladimir Nabokov's in this respect: that they have fallen in love with what cannot satisfy the soul. But while the flight to America was restricting as a substitute theme, the removal seems to have been liberating in other respects—once Vivante returns to persons and things Italian. It is as if, in order to appropriate the themes of his life in Italy, he had to abandon those settings (and the people that gave them substance), until fleeing *from* home could allow him to flee *back*.

Hence dislocation, exile, and abandonment constantly play, in their minor key, throughout Arturo Vivante's work. Although fluent in English from an early age, for example, his choice of this medium for his tales meant the *leaving* of the Italian language. Vivante's best work as a result is made ineffably more wistful by his attempt to recapture, at one remove, in English, the rivery music of Italian intonation. It is also worth noting that Vivante carried out many of his relinquishments at once, leaving language, country, and finally his first major vocation at one and the same moment. Trained as a physician, and with a modest medical practice in Rome, he closed the door on an entire way of life when he decided to bring his young American wife back to the United States and try to make his living as a writer. (This he did, teaching writing for some years as well, notably at Bennington—he is now retired.)

Writing as a calling can emerge like a mysterious postscript in the lives of some exiles (Joseph Conrad and even Nabokov come to mind).

With Vivante, what exile there was, was imposed from within rather than from without. As a precondition for the maturing of his artistic gift, therefore, the "exile" he has accommodated in his career is more strange and perhaps ultimately less bearable than theirs. He resembles the person Wordsworth thought *he* was when young, "more like a man/ Flying from something that he dreads than one/ Who sought the thing he loved." For at the same time as the exilic condition's primary emotion, *Sehnsucht,* or yearning, has remained at the core of Vivante's very best work, little from the new environment to which he transplanted himself has flourished long in his imagination. In a moving way, over time, his great storytelling authority also withdraws from any thematic endeavor other than the retreating past, rather like the footsteps of Astraea.

As one might expect, in the first part of *The Tales of Arturo Vivante,* in which appear the tales about home, the paradisiacal element is strong. Even the derailments from this ideal reveal its strong hold. One story, "Fioretta," which originates in the stasis of that early domestic milieu, takes a turn that unsettles the brooding young medical student who narrates it. Although we meet the young man in the quasi-enchanted Tuscan villa where every branch is numbered by childhood memory, the story *tries* to be about the central character's plan to find a girl to lose his innocence to. But, after starting out on a headlong cycling jaunt to Rome, he is distracted from this urge by the pathetic radiance of a half-witted beggar, Fioretta, who at the end of the War had been left behind in the panic before the troops of savage French-Moroccan soldiers, pursuing the Germans, swept through her mountain village. One of the women explains to the narrator Lorenzo:

> "After two days, they cleared out.... We returned here and found her sitting outside, here in the *piazzetta.* We gathered around her and took her in our arms. 'What did they do to you, Fioretta?' we asked her. 'Tell us, what did they do?' 'Oh, nothing,' she said. 'We played and then we slept.' Because we kept looking at her without a word, she repeated, as if to reassure us, 'We played and then we slept.' "

Lorenzo is more or less stopped in his tracks by the delicate, loyal spirit of this poor abandoned girl, who wears a tiny charm, a horn of silver, around her neck—a gift from a sergeant named "Jamal" whom Fioretta lovingly calls " 'A terror. They were all scared of him. But I wasn't. He and I....' 'What?' " asks the narrator. "A look of inexpressible joy lit her eyes. 'Tell me.' 'No,' she said bashfully.... Minutes later, I was speeding down the mountain, south, toward Rome." When he returns to his parents' home, his mother asks whether he met anyone nice. Despite the amorous adventures we know (from the original setting of this tale in the novel *Doctor Giovanni*) were not insignificant, in the tale he has forgotten everyone but Fioretta. He and his parents share the following muted yet kindly—and beautifully paced— exchange:

> "I met a girl," I said.
>
> "You met a girl? Lorenzo met a girl," she said, and my father looked pleased.
>
> "A girl in Battistrada."
>
> "Bravo, *cocchetto,*" she said. "Imagine, a girl in Battistrada, my Lorenzino."
>
> "It's not what you think."
>
> "Tell us, tell us about her."
>
> But I was afraid they'd laugh. "No," I said softly.
>
> "Battistrada," my father said. "There must be some wonderful sunsets up there."

Like Lorenzo, most of Vivante's quasi-autobiographical protagonists deflect the stories from expanding very dramatically—though it is not only in "Fioretta" that the self-identification also brings with it a reticence that has some of the tension of taboo. (Cesare Pavese's work has this quality as well.) Held inscrutably in abeyance, the majority of Vivante's fictions perforce elaborate and develop themselves in the area usually occupied by descriptive interlude and secondary character. What in many tales—even those of digressive writers like Isak Dinesen—is transient, namely setting and atmospheric flourish, can become in Vivante chronic and obsessive, while plot and event are here diminished by the very qualities it has also been Vivante's gift to make engaging—reticence, nostalgia, and the want of reflective palette. We see Vivante's avoidances in his deft recoil from the implication, for example, in "A Gallery of Women," that he is soliciting favors for his father; or in his leniency toward the son's advocacy, in "Of Love and Friendship," of the infidelity his mother refused to commit; or in the opportunity—evaded—in "The Bell" and "The Soft Core," for the narrator to cease defending his own entrenched limitations and failures of sympathy.

But while the son never quite shoulders his independence from them, the other members of his family—especially his mother and father, also the proud and flamboyant younger sister—stand out strongly in all their piquancy. The tales about them are perfections of an attitude of mingled affection and piety that can boast few embodiments as touching as Vivante's. These are the kinds of family portraits you *expect* to find in the memoirs of certain blessed writers, like Kathleen Raine—and then you are startled by how dour and almost empty her childhood was. Or you might open the autobiography of Edwin Muir in anticipation of a world of love, only to discover that Muir's parents, kind and curiously soft, were still miles away from him, as if kept off by a kind of optical enchantment. Next to these, Vivante's childhood world is infinitely rich and sweet and *close*. His parents were always where the children unconsciously monitored and needed them to be, the father in his study or pacing the terrace as he calculated the coming yield of the orchard, the mother painting small watercolors in the few still hours when her large brood and punctilious, self-absorbed, yet decidedly noble husband let her be.

Not that the household was unruffled, indeed mild uproar seemed its leading humor; there was sometimes a hateful petulance from husband to wife: "I remember the silence with which she bore his anger. And rarely, perhaps stretching her arms down and back disconsolately, her replies, in a small voice: 'Oh, but listen. . . . What can I say? I'm sorry.' She didn't like people to make scenes, and for this reason, I think, she never left the room." In this same story, "Of Love and Friendship," the family friend Millo (the collector of lichens) gladdens them all with his friendly peculiarity and, by making the mother happy, seems to save the marriage. The world to which Millo's avocation introduces the family is quite magical:

> Pale green and yellow, orange and gray, tenuous blue, silver, and almost white, spread by the wind or growing by contiguity, [the lichens] improved the looks of almost anything they stuck to. . . . They made the tile roofs golden. They grew on ugly walls and monuments until their ugliness quite faded. . . . They were the hand of time . . . and if you looked at them closely you saw the marvel of their structure: lacework, filigree, touch-me-not golden curls. . . . [Under a microscope] one could get lost in the leafy and branchlike maze. Another world . . . with shadows of its own, a place where hanging gardens mixed with orange goblets and gossamer strands.

It will not escape the careful reader's notice that the descriptions of the lichens are in the way of being the love-poem the son never unearthed from Millo to Vivante's mother.

Apparently, the family took frequent jaunts—every Christmas, to Rome; in summers, to the tower near Ancona on the eastern seaboard in Le Marche. In a large open American convertible over steep roads with hairpin turns, the father liberally using the horn, the family began the journeying that seems to have sedimented itself in the quirky, gentle, nostalgic rhythm of Vivante's fiction. More even than these qualities, there is a sort of intense pleasurableness and preternatural accuracy to all the perceptions that accrue to family experiences. Even in their fearful exile in England and Canada during the War, Vivante's family appear to have enjoyed a remarkable solidarity, owing to the pluck and dignity, in almost equal measure, of the mother and father. In "The Holborn," for example, during a London blackout in 1939, the family warily pick their way along an unfamiliar street, trying to find a place to eat. They press against every door along the street until one of them gives, and then they seem to *fall* into a cave of light, "Light refracted by crystal chandeliers. . . . Rivulets of light. . . . a glow from a fire—a robust flame that rose from an open burner in full view of the tables. . . . A white-bonneted cook busied himself about it [among] copper pans so highly polished they brought the shield of Achilles to mind." In this startling, enchanted world, lit by a forge-light, where the classical allusion seems perfectly apt, the father moves with astonishing, "nimble" command:

> We stood at the threshold, looking at my father. Would he really let us eat here? Wasn't this a bit too good for us? He didn't seem to think so—without the slightest hesitancy, he brought us in toward the headwaiter, who was coming over.
>
> Waiters, especially headwaiters in black ties and dinner jackets, have always made me feel uneasy. . . . Not so my father. He was quite rich when he was a young man—went to the Ritz in Paris, climbed the Alps, took private dancing lessons. He seemed perfectly at home here. A slightly built man in a blue suit, he moved nimbly, and the waiter didn't so much lead as accompany him to a table—the one my father wanted, central, near the fire.

This is a fine cameo tribute to the almost choreographic grace of Vivante senior—grace the narrator can only admire from afar and never hope to duplicate in his own deportment. In addition, the cameo takes on lustre from another source—the relief, awe, and currents of unambiguous love that flow from person to person around the table.

In "The Soft Core," Vivante returns to the War years in a conversation with his father, who has had a succession of minor strokes that have affected his memory. The father has become unbearably curmudgeonly since the death of his wife three years previously—or it may be that the children now simply lack the mother's benign temperamental filter, which shaded them from the intense glare of his singlemindedness. But at the same time, the father's illness is what makes it possible for Giacomo to converse with him, now that he is weakened, in touch with death. The father is lying in the same bed where the son had come to lie down, as a child, while his father read to him from the *Iliad.* Now they laugh as they recall the way, after the War, the bailiff met them at the harbor in Naples with all their money stuffed into his socks. Then the son shows the father the latter's books.

> "This one you wrote," Giacomo said.
>
> His father looked at it closely. "This one I know. But the others. . . ." He stroked his head as if to scold it. "And these are your poems," he said, seeing a flimsy little book with his son's name. "I remember the first one you wrote, about the stars, when you were ten. . . ."
>
> "You see, you remember a lot."
>
> "About the distant past. Such a long time . . . for you, too." He smiled, then, looking at him warmly, said, "Our Giacomo," and it was as it had been when Giacomo was a boy and his father used to look at him and say "Ajax," because he considered him generous and strong.

Earlier in the story, Giacomo has been chafing at the very lexicon his father uses, " 'Negative possibility,' *'causa sui,'* 'psychic reality,' 'primal active' . . . He knew they were full of meaning for his father, but [they] weren't in his language." Now, son and father share the language of the former's childhood and the latter's teaching, when the roles of taking and giving were perfectly adjusted—if not a golden age, then at least one in which greater spirits moved in the background.

II. The Figure of the Fool

The second part of *The Tales of Arturo Vivante* is composed of works that involve the author in a subtle form of caricature. If one were to view the matter psychoanalytically, one might make the case that, once he leaves the enclave of his family, the typical Vivante protagonist can barely sustain interest in his own mental processes, in his moral or imaginative growth, even, oddly enough, in his amours. His typical narrator is a naive construction psychologically, given to sustained and perceptive *flânerie.* Frequently these tales involve travel and change of place—in some measure, I would guess, as compensation for the deflection of other energies from the narrating persona.

Several things are of interest here. One is that, unlike most American fiction writers, Vivante is far more interested in other people than he is in himself. Whereas it does not seem that many American writers can prevent themselves from creating obsessive artifices in which to shine (or glower), Vivante prefers to abstain from exercising power over others. Most American story writers are, so to speak, besotted with self—even minimalists know well the trick of exploiting passivity for the opposite ends, falsifying it, and turning it hungry.

But in Vivante's best work, the passivity of the projected self is authentic in its modesty. Thus its moments of "high purpose" are fragile. Both moral outrage and blundering courage appear at once spontaneous and short-lived. We accordingly experience a keen wistfulness as the young husband in "Fisherman's Terrace" grows indignant at what the poor fisherman has lost, or as we see the Sienese gentleman worrying over the blind man in "A Game of Light and Shade;" we are touched too, when the son of the house in "The Nightingale" attempts to aid the ageing, half-deaf woman to hear this bird's heartbreaking song, which she had so longed to do before her death (and we, too, are chagrined that all she hears is his own instructional whistling).

Most of these outbreakings of empathy "resolve" into a slight pathos; nothing changes for either object or subject. But at the same time, this recessive characteristic—a temperamental moratorium—makes other features of the narrative self, like sexual appetite, mental lassitude, fondness for jaunts, exercise, and creature comforts, seem the more unwitting. Vivante as narrator enacts *l'homme moyen sensuel*—the man of middling sensibilities—without conflict and without demurral. What distinguishes his *personae* from, say, Guy de Maupassant's is a correlative wish to be generous. So even as Vivante's Ferruccio disappoints the dreamy prostitute Beppa, who wanted to act the chaste young wife to him on their holiday, he does so in part because he wants to be lavish, to buy her things, to go dancing and see her wear the presents he has spent his whole income to buy her. De Maupassant (however seamy) never fails to show a human world in which pain is endemic; however exposed and debased they are, we *feel with* his characters because he draws to the life the malicious work of chance. Vivante does not descend to such depths. If Maupassant confesses his penchant for *certaines petites choses navrantes,* for Vivante the appeal of storytelling lies not in certain small distressing scenes but in certain small touching ones. Scenes, moreover, in which his narrator-figures subside in prominence relative to the greater weight and finer flavor of the scenes and beings that surround him.

The difference toward which he tends might almost be like that between Turgenev, say, and Chekhov, for in Turgenev the narrators are always perfectly attentive to the world, and themselves perfectly inert. But it was Turgenev's sketches, after all, in which readers found the crystalline pathos that is reputed to have moved the czar toward freeing the serfs. Never mind the relative moral inertia of the narrating consciousness: The images and conversations of the peasants are rendered with a piercing effectuality.

Correcting for the modesty of Vivante's influence, much the same can be said of his fictional sketches—that they touch us in proportion as they maintain their reticence. Unlike Turgenev, it should also be said, Vivante is unable to quell with any consistency the intrusions of the self; the sketches in the second half of this collection, therefore, remain torn—or rather, blurred—between the two kinds of tale. The one kind is a descriptive, poetic survey of place with a light shadowing of additional actors, a sort of "landscape with figures;" the second type is a contest between a disappointing or comic social-domestic reality on the one hand, and on the other an ancient, laconic, often beautiful European milieu.

Examples of the former type are "A Game of Light and Shade," "Fisherman's Terrace," "The Short Cut," and "A Place in Italy." In the last named, the narrator wants to invest the income from the sale of his dead parents' house in a piece of the country that bore them. Every place he investigates seems wrong; his wife and family are uncooperative (here the "landscape" grades off into the "fool's portrait": "'You'll never get me there,'" his wife says about one lovely stone house near Orvieto, "and I withdraw to my room . . . and pull the bedspread over my head"). But the narrator is also permitted his moments of pure admiration:

> The heat seemed to express from the flowers all their scent and disperse it in the warm air. I took great breaths of it and started up the little road, hardly able to walk, because in my eagerness I felt an urge to run. . . . I came across the pretty town of Panicale. On its outskirts there is the little church of St. Sebastian. . . . there, at one end, taking up the whole wall, was Perugino's fresco, *The Martyrdom of St. Sebastian*—the calm faces of the archers and of the saint, the faded gentle colors, the serene Umbrian countryside. In Spoleto, a real-estate lady who quoted Leopardi and Horace showed me around.

Vivante's narrator, driven by superstitious longing ("I don't want to leave Italy without owning something in it"), at last finds an old stone house in the middle of a village, which he buys. He discusses with the caretaker Cimitella and a mason how the structure will be restored; he spins his favorite fantasies about harmony, which, if not altogether warranted by the behavior of the wife and children thus far, is powerfully supported by the final "naming" of both near hill and distant planet in one embracing cosmos:

> And I'll have our things moved in. Someday, I hope, my children will laugh with the children of the village, and my wife will sleep with me there. Nearby is Monte Cimino, and a lake, and the old town of Viterbo, and the villages on the tops of the hills. Cimitella points them out: "Orte, Attigliano, Chia, Giove," he says. One of them is actually called Giove—Jupiter—and it is as if he were pointing to the planets and stars, naming them one by one.

The second kind of tale, which explores an episode of domestic confusion or chagrin, is well represented by the companion story to "A Place in Italy," "Night in the Piazza." The narrator is made to play the fool not only by the unreality of his fantasies but by the almost exaggerated reality of the actual woman who comes to satisfy them. The wealthy journalist Rebecca is almost completely deaf to the music and meaning of words; her Italian is execrable (though she insists on speaking it for practice); her English is flatly commercial ("'I got quite a story,'" she tells him as she leaves). Vivante's Rebecca is an amusing reminder of one of Henry James's most withering satiric portraits, that of the liberated journalist Henrietta Stackpole, the friend of Isabel Archer in *The Portrait of a Lady.* When the narrator asks her not to make a fuss about all the noise in the piazza, she hits the ceiling. "'Take some aspirin . . . or maybe plug your ears,'" he tells her:

> 'I certainly will not—I hate those things. I'll tell them to stop it.'
> 'Oh please don't. You *can't.* I won't let you.'
> 'What do you mean? You are talking to an American girl.'

Elsewhere in the second part of *The Tales of Arturo Vivante,* the reader will encounter works that vary the landscape-with-figures type by putting greater pressure on the "figures." In these we read tellingly lifelike portraits of curious persons, "The Prince," "Luca," "Mrs. Lee," Julia in "The Last Kiss," a woman we recognize as Vivante's mother in "The Art Teacher," but in a recital proffered with unusual authorial indirection. These portraits illustrate Vivante's great distinction as a writer, his ability to take a representative of what is, in fact, only a "type"—a character well within the range of the "minor" or "secondary"—and turn him or her into someone sympathetic and, while adhering to the small compass of the cameo, peculiarly complete. One example may serve:

> We go into a bar. He offers me a cognac, which we drink standing up, Italian style, then leave. He's looking absolutely delighted after this. That stuff keeps him alive. He reminds me of a sparrow just come out of a cherry tree, with the juice fresh in its beak.
>
> ("The Prince")

This ability to render the affect of a person in and on a moment by means of apt metaphors is at the heart of the storyteller's art, which must usually create the sensation of depth with none of the features of extent.

III. A Word About Style

There are in these tales many classical allusions. Those to Ajax and the shield of Achilles have already been mentioned. In a story not included here, Vivante leans his head out the window of a train, and as the wind blows his hair he says he feels "like Notus"—and one imagines an engraving of the South Wind with distended cheeks and furious hair in the margins of an old map. In "Fioretta," the village women were "like Parcae" as they clustered around the beggar-girl to hear of her rape. Something old and forbidding enters the scene with this metaphor. In a general way, Vivante is quite comfortable with culture. He understands art, and has a great liking for artisans and even mechanics. In the last piece in the volume, he describes how the Roman knife-grinders set up their equipment: "The grinder trestled his bike, and, still pedaling, turned the vertical chain connected to a whetstone wheel, on which he sharpened scissors and knives." He enjoys describing (and climbing) ruins, towers, hills, trees, and steep, spiraling streets. He is also just as much at home observing blacksmiths and potters at work as he is discussing Robert Lowell or revisiting a Perugino fresco.

Vivante often quotes Leopardi, whom he has translated into English—the bonds of predilection tightened by the fact that Leopardi was also one of his father's favorite poets. We are also apt to encounter references to poetry by Horace, Petrarch, and Gozzano; more recognizably, to poems by Shelley, Keats, and Shakespeare, amid a myriad more fleeting allusions to "notables" like Byron, Galileo, Foscolo, Stendhal, Raphael, Rossini, and Dante, of course—but never very prominently. In fact, Vivante is more apt to cite works by Theodore Dreiser and Emily Brontë than by this most universal of Italian poets. The restraint may have to do as much with his family's anglophilia as with the fact that Dante is often forbidding and dire. Vivante can rattle off impressive rosters of obscure authors, too, as he does to illustrate his father's reading habits in "A Gallery of Women."

Even more crucial than allusion as an index of the temperature and texture of Vivante's prose style are the fastidious turns and ceremonious parallels that maintain the surface tension. On occasion he seems to exploit a deliberate awkwardness of address: "This of Luca's is a spectacular town." The discursive effect can be comic: "Except for a flat and a consequent crack in the wheel rim at Dieppe . . . the car had given them no trouble whatever" ("The Shortcut"). He will almost never fail to complete a likeness or an antithesis; the connective tissue of English is carefully adhered to; dependent clauses are especially favored; word-order is flexed in a mildly Italianate way:

> Though of a white variety, the grapes were so ripe that they looked almost red, and matched some of the colors of the leaves about them.
>
> ("Fisherman's Terrace")

> Then, late one evening, the flag-shaped, rusty weathervanes over the house were heard distinctly turning on the roof—a grating, creaking sound. Slowly they turned, taking what seemed a long time about it, opposing as they did a fair amount of resistance to the wind and indicating a marked change in its direction. It was the north wind.
>
> ("The Orchard")

> Olga had strong opinions, and the subject was one that could make her forget her present state.
>
> ("The Angel")

> She came to an end . . . not slowly, like a train arriving at a station, but swiftly and convulsively, like a train derailing.
>
> ("Last Rites")

Vivante is also very clever at catching the sweet waves of Italian emphasis, and of a contrastive American flatness:

"She certainly flourished there," I would remark.

"There you have it, flourished, bravo, that's it exactly. Eh, America," he would nod, "you can't put down America, I've always said so."

("Luca")

". . . they wouldn't come . . . Why? I don't understand."

"Because they are true gypsies," her mother said. "You see, it's different with them."

The cook and the maid were quite happy now. "Ha, no, ha? They didn't want to come, eh?"

"No, they just wouldn't."

. . . .

The girl's father appeared in the kitchen. "Well?"

"They wouldn't come."

"Ah, you see," he said, as if giving them credit.

("Gypsies")

Alongside these gems of dialogue, the speech of the Americans in Vivante's work seems self-consciously bland; see the brilliant counterpoint between the two styles, flat and melodious, in the dialogues between Rebecca and the narrator, in "Night in the Piazza," also in the excerpts from *A Goodly Babe* and in the new story "The Last Kiss."

So although there are moments when one is conscious of him playing the studious and bemused outsider as he carefully scans the terrain of English prose and American dialogue, for the most part one relishes Arturo Vivante's great descriptive clarity, of which the style is—unobtrusive, decorous, restrained—properly expressive.

*

I would like to take this occasion to thank Arturo Vivante for his permission to reprint the tales included here, for his unfailing patience in responding to editorial queries, and for his generous response to requests for clarification; in some cases, these resulted in emendations, all of which have Mr. Vivante's approval.

Evanston
February 1990

I

The Lighthouse

Where the boardwalk ended and the pier began stood the old lighthouse, white and round, with a little door, a circular window at the top, and the huge lantern. The door was usually half open, and one could see a spiral staircase. It was so inviting that one day I couldn't resist venturing inside, and, once inside, going up. I was thirteen, a cheerful, black-haired boy; my step carried half my present weight in every sense, and I could enter places then that I can't enter now, slip into them lightly and without qualms about my not being welcome.

The town—a seaside resort with a good harbor, in South Wales—was foreign to me. My home was a long way from the sea, in an Italian hill town, and I had been sent to Wales by my parents for the summer, to stay with friends and to improve my English. I had never been out of Italy before. The outlandish town, the sea, the holidays, the summer, all added to my gaiety. The year, too. It was 1937, and England had begun rearming; there was a sense of awakening in the air. "In Bristol," I remember the head of the family I was staying with saying in a quiet voice and with a subdued smile, "they are building over a hundred aeroplanes a month." The threats and taunts and boastings of the Fascists were fresh in my ears, so it made me very happy to hear this. Everything made me happy. I watched the seagulls wheeling, wild even as the robins on the lawn seemed tame. In Italy, except for the pigeons in the public squares, birds didn't come close. I watched the waves thunder against the pier with a violence I had never witnessed, then rebound to meet and quell the onslaught of the next. And I did many things I had never done before—flew kites, went roller-skating, explored caves draped with stalactites, paddled in the pools left by the tide, visited a lighthouse.

Visited a lighthouse. I climbed the spiral staircase and knocked on the door up at the top. A man came to open who seemed the image of what a lighthouse-keeper ought to be. He smoked a pipe and had a grayish-white beard. Like a seaman, he wore a thick navy-blue jacket with gold buttons, trousers to match, and boots. Yet he had also something of the land about him—a well-set look, a firmly planted look, and his boots could have been a farmer's. Bathed by the ocean and buttressed by the rock, the lighthouse and its keeper stood in between, upon the thin, long fringe of land and sea, belonging to both and neither.

"Come in, come in," he said, and immediately, with that strange power some people have to put you at ease, he made me feel at home. He seemed to consider it most natural that a boy should come and visit his lighthouse. Of course a boy my age would want to see it, his whole manner seemed to say—there should be more people interested in it, and more visits. He practically made me feel he was there to show the place to strangers, almost as if that lighthouse were a museum or a tower of historical importance.

Well, it was nothing of the sort. There were the boats, and they depended on it. Their masts were level with us. Seagulls cut across the window on every side. Outside the harbor was the Bristol Channel, and opposite, barely visible, some thirty miles away, the coast of Somerset, like a bank of clouds. Back of us, there was the town, with its slate roofs, and the boardwalk, with its pedestrians unaware of being looked down on from above.

He had a large telescope—its brass well polished—set on a pedestal and pointed at the sea. He said I could look through it. I watched a ship going down the Bristol Channel, a wave breaking far away—the splash it made, the spray—and distant cliffs, and seagulls flying. Some were so close they were swift shadows over the field of vision; others, far away, seemed hardly to be moving, as though they were resting in the air. I rested with them. Still others, flying a straight course, winging their way steadfastly, made scarcely any progress across the little circle, so wide was the circle of sky that it encompassed.

"And this," he said, "is a barometer. When the hand dips, a storm is in the air. Small boats better take heed. Now it points to 'Variable.' That means it doesn't really know what is going to happen—just like us. And that," he added, like someone who is leaving the best thing for the last,"is the lantern."

I looked up at the immense lens with its many-thousand-candle-power bulb inside.

"And this is how I switch it on, at dusk." He went to a control box near the wall and put his hand on a lever.

I didn't think he'd really switch it on just for me, but he did, and the light came on, slowly and powerfully, as strong lights do. I could feel its heat above me, like the sun's. I glowed appreciatively, and he looked satisfied. "I say! That's jolly good. Super!" I exclaimed, and I strung out all the new laudatory words that I had learned—the old ones, too, of course, like "beautiful" and "lovely."

"It stays on for three seconds, then off for two. One, two, three; one, two," he said, timing it, like a teacher giving a piano lesson, and the light seemed to obey. He certainly knew just how long it stayed lit. "One, two, three," he said, and his hand went down, like a conductor's. Then with both hands, like the Creator, he seemed to ask for light, and the light came.

I watched, enchanted.

He switched the lamp off. Slowly, it went out. "Where are you from?" he asked me.

"Italy."

"Well, all the lights in different parts of the world have a different rhythm. A ship's captain, seeing this one and timing it, would know which one it was."

I nodded.

"Now, would you like a cup of tea?" he said. He took a blue-and-white cup and saucer out of a cupboard and poured the tea. Then he gave me a biscuit. "You must come and see the light after dark sometime," he said.

Late one evening, I went there again. The lantern's flash lit up a vast stretch of the sea, the boats, the boardwalk, and the dark that followed seemed more than ever dark. So dark, so all pervading, and so everlasting that the lantern's flashing, powerful as it was, seemed not much stronger than a firefly's, and almost as ephemeral.

At the end of the summer, I went home to Italy. For Christmas, I bought a *panforte*—a sort of fruitcake, the specialty of the town I lived in—and sent it to the lighthouse-keeper. I didn't think I would see him again, but the very next year I was back in Wales—not on a holiday this time but as a refugee. One morning soon after I arrived, I went to the lighthouse, only to find that the old man had retired.

"He still comes, though," the much younger man who had taken over said. "You'll find him sitting outside here every afternoon, weather permitting."

I returned after lunch, and there, sitting on a ledge of the lighthouse beside the door, smoking his pipe, was my lighthouse-keeper, with a little dog. He seemed heavier than the year before, not because he had gained weight but because he looked as though he had been set on the ledge and would not easily get off it without help.

"Hello," I said. "Do you remember me? I came to see you last year."

"Where are you from?"

"From Italy."

"Oh, I used to know a boy from Italy. An awfully nice boy. Sent me a fruitcake for Christmas."

"That was me."

"Oh, he was a fine boy."

"I was the one who sent it."

"Yes, he came from Italy—an awfully nice boy."

"Me, me, that was me," I insisted.

He looked straight into my eyes for a moment. His eyes discounted me. I felt like an intruder, someone who was trying to take somebody else's place without having a right to it. "Ay, he was an awfully nice boy," he repeated, as though the visitor he saw now could never match last year's.

And seeing that he had such a nice memory of me, I didn't insist further; I didn't want to spoil the picture. I was at that time of life when suddenly boys turn gauche, lose what can never be regained—a budding look, a certain early freshness—and enter an unwonted stage in which a hundred things contrive to mar the grace of their performance. I couldn't see this change, this awkward period in myself, of course, but, standing before him, I felt I never could—never could possibly—be as nice as I had been a year before.

"Ay, he was an awfully nice boy," the lighthouse-keeper said again, and he looked lost in thought.

"Was he?" I said, as if I were talking of someone whom I didn't know.

[1968]

The Sound of the Cicadas

In the early thirties, when my brothers and I were children, if we saw an airplane flying over our house in the country near Siena we would wave, then run into the house to tell my mother about it. "It was flying really low," we would say, hoping to stir her. "Perhaps it was our uncle." We would watch her. But her face wouldn't brighten. Her eyes, which we had known to be so lively, looked at us dully. The Fascists had done this to her, we told ourselves, and we hated them with a rich, deep hate.

In October 1931, her youngest brother had taken off from the Côte d'Azur in a small airplane and scattered anti-Fascist leaflets over Rome. From the terrace of his home on the top of an apartment house near the Piazza di Spagna, his mother had watched the plane flying around and around, and the leaflets showering down from it. She had seen people on the street below eagerly picking them up, reading them, folding them, and putting them in their pockets. Some had fallen on her terrace. Then the plane, in the twilight, had headed west, toward Corsica, and no one had ever seen it or my uncle again.

I came on my mother in the kitchen the day she heard that he was missing. Leaning against a table there, she told me about it. It was late evening. We remained silent in the gloom. Slowly, we began to weep.

She became dejected. And the house had depended on her mirth. A fervent talker, now she hardly said a word and barely changed expression. We waited for a guest to show up at the front door so she would smile. She seemed physically hurt, and my father took her to many doctors—in Siena, in Florence, in Rome. They all prescribed tonics and recommended spas. Finally, after a year, she went to one who would have had her stay in bed for months in a cast—a suggestion so extreme that she reacted by saying she wasn't all that sick, and left the office feeling better than she had in a whole year. Back home, she told us about the visit to this doctor the way one tells a story. She laughed with us about it. We knew that she was well.

My brothers and I were going to a small country school near Siena. For children under ten—I wasn't quite eight at the time of my uncle's death—we were sharply aware of politics. My uncle had written a half-dozen pages in French, under the title "The Story of My Death," the night before his flight, and sent them to a friend with the request that they be published if he should not come back. "Tomorrow," the document began, "at three o'clock, on a meadow of the Côte d'Azur, I have an appointment with Pegasus. Pegasus—it is the name of my airplane—has a russet body and white wings. Though he's as strong as eighty horses, he's as nimble as a swallow. Drunk with gasoline, he bounds through the skies like his brother of old, but if he wants to, at night, he can glide in the air like a phantom. I found him in the Hercynian Forest, and his old master is going to bring him to me on the coast of the Tyrrhenian Sea, believing in good faith that he will serve the pleasures of an idle young Englishman. My bad accent hasn't awakened his suspicions: may he pardon my deception. All the same, we are not going to hunt chimeras, but to bring a message of freedom to an enslaved people across the sea. To do away with metaphors (which I had to use to leave discreetly vague the origins of my airplane), we are going to Rome to scatter in the open air these words of freedom which for seven years have been forbidden like a crime. . . ."

I knew parts of it by heart, and for me the words were a purification from the sodden propaganda I saw on the walls and had to hear at school. They made me indignant, too; I remember tearing to pieces the registration card I got at the beginning of the term, because it had a picture of the fasces on it.

Our classmates were the children of neighboring farmers, who, like my family, had no use for Fascism. The only Fascist I remember at that school, and the first one I think I ever met, was an inspector who came from Siena to sell us party bonds. They cost ten lire each, or about half a dollar, which was a laborer's day's pay at the time. The inspector told us that when we were twenty-one we would get a dividend from the bonds, and that we each had to buy one. He would come back the next day for the money. The next day, he returned, and he collected from everyone except a strong, freckled boy who said his father had refused to give him the ten lire. For minutes, in front of the whole class, the man swore and shouted at him in a ruthless way. It gave me an excellent idea of the kind of people Fascists were. The boy—he must have been eight or nine years old—stood by his desk without saying a word. He didn't cry. He only flushed a little.

The next school we went to—a junior high school—was in Siena.

We had a bay horse, Graziella, or Gracie. A smart young farmer who entertained my brothers and me with stories of his sentimental conquests and plots of films that he had seen drove us into town each morning and brought us back home in time for lunch. There were plenty of Fascists in Siena. The town was theirs as the countryside never was. The moment we entered the city gate in our calèche and saw the dignified old walls pasted over with sheets of paper—usually pink and printed in block letters—we felt as though we had crossed into enemy territory. Our horse would trot fiercely over the paving stones, up a winding street, past a newsstand with the sad headlines of the thirties on a rack, past a small Anglican church, to a stable, where we left her.

There were few tourists, and the Anglican church, which had been built before the First World War, was shut. Its minister was still in Siena, though. We used to see him, in his black suit and clerical collar, wandering about the town, a shepherd looking for a flock. Then his church was boarded up. One day, my mother saw him, still wearing his Protestant minister's clothes, in the cathedral, praying.

From the stable we would walk across the center of Siena to the school—formerly a convent—at the south end of town, then through two very long corridors, the remodeled sides of a cloister, to the classrooms. Though the school was a state and not a church school, my professor was a swarthy, thunder-browed priest who lived alone in an apartment up the street. In the three years I had him, he became very attached to his class. He knew not just our names and capabilities but our nicknames, characters, moods, and dispositions. Sometimes he became furious with us and shouted. When he had finished, a deathly silence would settle on the class. Once, he was so impressed by what he had achieved that he seemed awed. He looked at us for a moment and said, "What tension!"

I didn't think he was a Fascist, but in the Ethiopian War, when Addis Ababa fell, he rushed into the classroom with the news, his cassock flying and his long underwear showing around his ankles. The class rose and cheered. I watched with scorn, kept quiet, and felt disappointed in the man.

The government was trying to turn Italians into warlike people, and soon military training was added to our curriculum, already burdened by two periods of gymnastics. As though this weren't enough, the authorities tried to ingratiate themselves and at the same time indoctrinate us by getting us out of classes right in the middle of a lesson. We might be translating a passage of Italian into Latin when suddenly the bell would ring, the class would be dismissed, and we would hurriedly assemble in the halls. There the head boys would arrange us in threes and march us out of the school, with the professor of gymnastics, who by now had become very important, in the lead. On these occasions, our priest wouldn't come with us. He seemed almost offended by the interruptions. Hands clasped behind his back and his hat on, he would go off on his own at a quick pace. We never knew where we would be led. If we were lucky, we would just march down the main street, march back, and be disbanded. More often, though, there was some surprise—like a speech broadcast from Rome. Then, in a square in which not just our school but all the schools of Siena had assembled, after a long wait we would have to listen to a mixture of voice and static carried at an incredible volume over the loudspeakers. Packed so tight we weren't able to sit, we would await the end with aching feet. Sometimes a Fascist official would clap his hands in the middle of a phrase, or chuckle as though something funny had been said.

It wasn't easy to leave the formation or to get out of these shows. But one morning—we had started on a march and were heading toward the center of town down a narrow street—I found myself so close to an ice-cream store that I just made a sharp left turn and went inside. There was a woman serving at the counter. "You've got some sense," she said to me.

For the gymnastics, my brothers and I had to return to town in the afternoon. The classes were held in what had been the lower church of the convent. There was no getting out of them. Not that we didn't try. Regularly at the beginning of each school year, hoping to be exempted, we would go to a doctor appointed by the school. "We come from a long way out of town," we would tell him in plaintive voices. But there was nothing wrong with us, and after a brief examination he would shake his head.

These gymnastics were a futile thing. A drill. We would have to march in step, stop, about-face, salute. There was no fun. The professor of gymnastics was a small young man with a face that he kept poking at you. When you least expected it, it would be in front of you, so close you could hardly see it, protruding from a taut, long neck. Or he would rush at you on his thick, soft rubber soles as though he wanted to kick you. You cringed instinctively to guard yourself from the blow that didn't come. He wore a big sports coat with padded shoulders and kept a whistle in between his lips. He would blow it with a sudden bloating of his cheeks that was even more striking than the blast it made. He was a true child of the regime. Sometimes, however, he would drop the whistle, which hung from a little chain around his neck, and replace it with a cigarette; then, leaning against the wall with his weight on one leg, the other crossed or bent, he would talk to his favorite pupils and seem as though he were a complete sport—the most regular fellow who ever existed. He always looked at me as if I were an oddity. I was the only boy in my class who did not live in the city. I had longish hair cut in bangs; I wore a homemade sweater and trousers that, because they reached the knee, he considered far too long. The other boys brilliantined their hair and combed it back; they wore jackets, and trousers that left their thighs almost completely bare. At some point or other, I had my bangs cut. He congratulated me as though I had recovered from a serious illness.

Once, I invited some of my classmates to my home. I was surprised to see how frightened they were of jumping across a ditch or sliding down a haystack. I could do both with ease, and could ride horseback, climb trees, and swim almost indefinitely, but no skill at country sports was of any use in the gymnasium. What was needed there was to be able to march in step and to be alert to rapidly changed orders. Because I wasn't snappy enough to suit his taste, and because he thought he could change me, the professor of gymnastics would sometimes let the class rest and make me perform his orders—run twenty paces, come back running, stop, and salute him—over and over, perhaps twenty times. I had the honor of being his worst student.

At the beginning of my third year at the school, the professor of gymnastics, holding a large scroll under his arm, lined us up and told us there was something new in the program—calisthenics. He unrolled the scroll, stretched it out, and showed it to us. From where we were, we saw a series of little stick figures. "An exercise in sixty movements," he said rather nervously. "You have the whole year to learn it. In June there'll be a big rally, and I want you to know it perfectly by then." He added that all the schools of Siena would take part in this monster demonstration, and that it would be held, in front of the mayor of Siena and an authority who would come especially from Rome, in the Piazza d'Armi—a huge, unpaved square outside the city walls, a place once used as an animal fair.

After pleading with us not to let him down, he had us try the first few movements. They were so complicated that even the professor had trouble and had to stop from time to time and consult the master sheet. I found them nearly impossible. I was continually falling a second or two behind the others, comparing my position with theirs and trying to correct it. When I thought I had it right, the professor would come at me and grip my arms to straighten them or flex them, or pull at my ankles to shift my feet. I felt like a marionette. I had always had trouble marching in step. Now these movements were beyond me. I saw no rhythm in them. Like formulas—unlike poetry—I couldn't seem to memorize them. And yet the constant repetition couldn't help but have its effect on me. By the end of April, I could do the sixty movements in my fashion. I didn't know them well enough to do them alone, but in the middle of the class, with all the others doing them, I could do them, too. I had to watch carefully, though. The moment I looked at the ground or for any reason was distracted—sometimes also if I tried too hard—I lost the sequence. There was a moment of hesitation then before I caught up with the others, during which all I could do was hope that the professor hadn't seen me.

As the drill continued into May, my mistakes became less and less frequent. I wasn't proud of this. Sometimes I would see myself, one of a crowd, performing like the rest, indistinguishable from them, and be disgusted. Then I would wish I were out in the fields and had never been sent to school at all. I wished I were illiterate, or at least that, like my country friends, I hadn't gone beyond elementary school. I hated gymnastics also because they spelled Fascism and the Fascists to me. How could I have let them get such a hold on me that they could twist my body this way and that according to their schemes.

Yet, with all my hating, there I was, improving with each rehearsal, an almost perfect marionette—one made to order. The day of the rally, I told myself, I wouldn't go to school; I'd stay home. But that seemed a weak kind of protest. I thought of my uncle, who had given his life. So far, the only thing I'd done against the Fascists' will was eat an ice-cream cone. I had to do something more, and I resolved to go and spoil the exercise with a mistake. I pictured the scene—three or four thousand boys, arranged three steps apart, moving like one. No, two, for at a certain point I planned to get muddled up, make some movements of my own, my very own, then stop and walk away, zigzagging from one boy to another, out, to the exit.

For weeks, I thought about it—at odd moments of the day and night, through tedious lessons, or when up steep hills our horse slowed down to a walk. The thought possessed me; I saw the Piazza d'Armi, heard the band and, when the band stopped playing, the swish of limbs. My fixed, charmed look made people ask what I was thinking of. "Nothing," I said, and held on to my secret. The thought even sustained me through the drills. I did them better than I had ever done them before.

The day was near. There were only four lessons left. I could do the whole exercise perfectly now, or so I thought. Suddenly, in the middle of a rehearsal, the professor blew his whistle. The class froze in their positions. I checked mine. It seemed right to me, but he called my name out with all the anger he had reserved for me in the past, and, like a man who has lost his patience, told me to step out. I went to stand beside him. "Should I do the exercise from here?" I asked, with an eagerness that wasn't like me. He didn't even answer. From a corner of the room, I watched the class resume their numbered movements. At the end of the hour, when he dismissed the class, I started to leave, but he motioned to me to stay where I was. I waited for him to say something to me. My classmates, one after the other, ran toward the exit, dangling their gym shoes. At last, he ambled over. "Don't come back again," he said.

"Aren't you going back for gymnastics?" my mother asked me two days later, after lunch.

"No," I said. "The professor told me not to."

"Why? What did you do?"

"Nothing."

"You must have done something."

"No."

"Goodness, have you been expelled?"

"He just told me not to go back there again."

"But why?"

"I don't know."

Whenever my parents asked me "How did school go today?" it was my custom to answer "Well," even if I'd got a zero. This time, my mother thought something dreadful must have happened. That very afternoon, dressed in city clothes, she went to see the professor of gymnastics and took me along.

I felt very embarrassed and self-conscious going with my mother to the school. Some of the boys said hello to me, or called out my name. I answered shyly, wishing I were miles away. Then the professor appeared. I pointed him out to my mother. "Come along," she said.

"No, I'll wait here."

"No, come."

While the class waited, I went and introduced her to him, then backed away a few steps and stood, my toes curled inside my shoes.

My mother spoke to the professor as though to a boy. With curiosity, a smile, and considerable grace, she asked him what I had done and why he didn't want me to come back.

He was very polite to her. "He hasn't done anything wrong," he said. “It’s just that he spoils the effect I want to produce.”

“Is that all? I thought something really bad had happened.”

“Oh, no. He’s a very good boy, but he just isn’t cut out for this.”

They said good-bye to one another very nicely, and I left with her.

Two weeks later, from my home, I heard bells ringing and sirens screaming, announcing that the rally had begun; the Fascists always made a lot of noise on these occasions. I turned my back to the city and went for a long walk in the woods. It was a comfort to hear the sound of the cicadas.

[1963]

The Holborn

On a moonless, starless night in London in December, 1939, my father, my mother, my two brothers, my sister, and I advanced along the sidewalk warily, a tight-knit little group. No chink of light showed from door or window. Sometimes a car went by with covered, slitted headlights. We grazed the walls and shop-windows, and groped at each doorway, hoping one might open into a restaurant.

We were staying in a hotel near Russell Square, in three little rooms at the end of a long, long corridor. The hotel was so huge one could nearly always get a room. That, I think, was its main advantage, and the reason we had gone there. Murky and dimly lit, it provided little contrast to the blackout outside. Rather, it seemed to partake of it. The lampshades in the lobby were like hoods. Only directly under them was there sufficient light to read a paper by. The darkness from the street entered as you entered, weaved its way around the heavy lampshades, and, hardly mitigated, spread along corridors and halls into the rooms. It was the sort of hotel refugees go to, and that was what we were. We had left Italy earlier that year at different times. My younger brother and I were going to one boarding school, my sister to another, my elder brother was living in the home of an old friend, my parents, who had spent the summer and fall in a country cottage, were looking for a house in which to settle, and now we had all convened in London for a family reunion.

The hotel must have had a restaurant, but we certainly didn't want to eat there, so we had gone out. We had walked around a great deal. I think we were quite lost. But we weren't so much trying to find our way as a place to eat. How different this town was from Rome, where practically every other doorway was a café or a *trattoria* that, war or no war, stayed open late into the night. Here everything was closed, or seemed to be. We stopped a passerby and asked him if he knew of a restaurant.

"I'm afraid you won't find anything open at this time here," he said.

My father drew a tiny flashlight and a watch from his pocket. It wasn't even eight. My God, there must be something. We moved along from door to door. Suddenly one gave. I remember the feel of it. It was a leather-covered door, fat and cushiony. It swung open as we pressed it, and it disclosed light. Light refracted by crystal chandeliers. Light broken up and shining. Rivulets of light. It lit us up. It bathed us. We looked at each other and felt we were really seeing each other now. We were in a restaurant—The Holborn.

I don't think I have ever seen a restaurant quite like it. The place had a glow the chandeliers couldn't account for. It came from a fire—a robust flame that rose from an open burner in full view of the tables. With its wavering light, it lit our faces orange and made the shadows dance. A white-bonneted cook busied himself about it. And there were copper pans so highly polished they brought the shield of Achilles to my mind. The tables were beautifully laid with white linen cloths, fine dishes, long-stemmed slender goblets, silver, napkins folded in the shape of cones. The waiters plied between the tables, carrying full platters high on their palms. Although the room did not appear crowded, there were a great many guests, some of them lovely women with bare shoulders, long gowns, and hats with sweeping curves. And there were wreaths of smoke, like lightest clouds unfolding, and a mingled sound of voices—almost tuneful—and warmth, and softness, and an undefinable perfume in the air. The atmosphere was dreadfully inviting. So inviting it seemed almost forbidden.

We stood at the threshold, looking at my father. Would he really let us eat here? Wasn't this a bit too good for us? He didn't seem to think so—without the slightest hesitancy, he brought us in toward the headwaiter, who was coming over.

Waiters, especially headwaiters in black ties and dinner jackets, have always made me feel uneasy. As they come to meet me, I half expect them either to refuse to seat me or to seat me at a table near the door. Once seated and presented with a menu, lest my choice meet with a supercilious frown I often find myself ordering an expensive dish—one that will meet with their approval and not one I really want, like eggs fried in olive oil or a Welsh rabbit. Not so my father. He was quite rich when he was a young man—went to the Ritz in Paris, climbed the Alps, took private dancing lessons. He seemed perfectly at home here. A slightly built man in a blue suit, he moved nimbly, and the waiter didn't so much lead as accompany him to the table—the one father wanted, central, near the fire. He ordered wine with our meal, and soon it was being poured from a bottle wrapped in a napkin and resting in a wicker cradle. My brothers and I had never seen such niceties. We laughed. Our table was round—about the size and shape of the one we had at home in Italy. The wine, too, was about the same—Chianti. It might have been from our own vineyard. As for the food, it seemed perfectly grand to me, used as I was at school to eating only bread, margarine, and jam for supper.

"When the English set themselves to it, they can cook as well as anybody," one of us said.

"Better," my younger brother said, finishing his Yorkshire pudding.

"And you get dessert every day," I said.

The waiter, who kept refilling our water glasses, suggested plum pudding, and soon, with a flaming blue halo and the smell of spirits hovering around it, a plum pudding was brought in.

Later, after coffee, the check came. We felt apprehensive round the table. Did my father have enough money? He had. He produced a strange white bill such as I have never seen before—a five-pound note—and got some change, which he left on the table. He made no comment on the price. He just smoked a cigarette and watched the smoke, contemplatively. When we left, the headwaiter gave us good directions. It wasn't very far to Russell Square.

Soon after that, the war, suddenly flaring, scattered us, and not till many years later, when we had all returned home to Italy, did we sit together again around a table. I mentioned the restaurant to my family then, but the memory of it had faded from their minds. "Don't you remember?" I said. "We were groping our way along the sidewalk in the dark, when we came into this place all brightly lit and glowing. A flame was blazing on a grill; the chef wore a white bonnet; they served the wine from a bottle in a wicker cradle. . . . Surely you remember."

No, they didn't. Obviously, the Holborn hadn't made the impression on them it had made on me—the night not seemed so dark, the lights so bright.

"Strange," I said. "For me it was the best restaurant, ever."

"Poor boy," my father said, quite touched.

[1968]

A Gift of Joy

A little thing—an incident, a chance encounter, something someone said—could make her so happy her children became happy, too. Arriving home and telling them about it, her warmth, her radiance were transmitted to them.

She was an Italian refugee, living in London, and worked as a cook in one of those government places set up during the war to feed large numbers of people at low prices. Once, she told of a thin, undernourished man—the sort of person who never gets a break. When she was at the counter, she always gave him an extra large helping of pudding. This was usually tapioca. She marvelled that the customers should like it. The poor old fellow would always look for her from the entrance. Their eyes would meet in an understanding that brought a smile to both. His smile would broaden into a delighted grin as she laid an extra spoonful of the pudding on his plate. He would nod thankfully, a little like a horse to whom a lump of sugar has been given. As she described it to the children, she would imitate the nods.

At the kitchen, she soon got the reputation for being smart and strong. Any hard job would go to her. "Ask Helen; she has brains," "Ask Helen to unscrew that jar; she's strong." She wasn't heavy or big, but she had a spare, strong frame, and keen, bright eyes.

It was tiring work at the kitchen, but she liked that job better than the next one she got, as typist and Italian translator at the B.B.C. There she had a boss—like herself, an Italian refugee—who was a pretentious and exacting person. Though she earned more money than at the kitchen, she often came home in a dejected mood. It spread to the children as quickly as her gladness. She seemed to have no more stories to tell. No little incidents to brighten her life and theirs seemed ever to take place.

But then, one day, just by looking at her—no, even before that; just by the light, gay sound of her steps and the brisk way she opened the front door—the children knew something had given her a lift.

She had worked after hours in her office, as she often did. It was a wet, cold, misty day. She said she had done a little shopping, and, coming home, inexplicably, her sense of direction had failed her in the Underground. By some odd circumstance, she had taken the wrong line. She had finally got off, at a station she had never heard of. In East London, was she? She walked down the deserted platform, distraught. A sense of loss seized her. As she related her experience, she brought her fingers to her forehead and her face took on a disoriented look. The tunnel, the ads, she said, began to appear disproportionate, unreal, the platform so long she couldn't hope to walk the length of it. She had a feeling that this was perhaps death, that, without knowing it, she had died and never again would she regain the surface of the world. The wet streets, the mist, the gray sky seemed infinitely desirable. Halfway along, she came to a flight of stairs. She climbed up eagerly, but it brought her to another platform. There, too, there was no one around. She waited, trying to collect herself. Suddenly, a train rushed in and came to a stop. The doors opened. Should she get on? She hesitated. In a moment, the doors slid shut. Immediately, she wished she had stepped in—anything was better than this station. To her amazement, the train did not move on. Instead, it slowly backed up till the head car was near her. Then it stopped, and the trainman, leaning out the window, called to her, "Girl! Come here!" Quickly she went over. He shook hands with her. "Where do you want to go?" he asked. She said to Kensington Church Street. Calling her "dear" and taking his time about it, as if he had plenty to spare, he told her that this was her train, opened the doors for her, and gave her full directions. Following them, heartened by them, she had absolutely no trouble reaching home.

"Imagine, the train backing up and stopping just for me, and that kind man calling me 'girl'—at my age!—talking to me slowly, softly, surely. I felt completely safe, taken in hand. And he certainly knew the way as well as anybody could possibly know it."

To her children, her story—the way she had arrived, the way she told it—seemed like a precious present that she unwrapped before them as she spoke.

[1968]

Fioretta

I was on vacation, after finishing my second year of medical school. A trip seemed in order, but day after day I stayed home, getting up late in the morning and passing the little that was left of it sitting in the garden, with my back against the wall of the house, and a cup of coffee—my breakfast—beside me.

Beyond the garden wall people weren't being quite so lazy. It was 1946, and Italy was recovering from the war. Nearly all the bridges had been destroyed. A great many were still broken down. But more often than not they were being rebuilt. Even from where I was sitting I could hear—down on the main road at the end of our drive a few miles outside of Siena, where a stone bridge had been blown up by the Germans retreating—men unloading, hammering, shouting, and swearing. They evoked Christ and the Madonna so often that they seemed their constant companions. "Swearing," my father said, as if to excuse them, "is the only way some people have of being in touch with the divine." Along with all the repairing there was a sense of regeneration, of healing. More than that, with the fall of Fascism and the advent of the republic, there was an air of freedom—freedom just born, freedom much awaited. No more did the stamps on letters have the faces of the king, or Mussolini, but smashed chains.

My home—an airy, sunny country house to which we had returned from England where we had gone as refugees in 1938—hadn't suffered much during the war. German and Allied troops had used it as barracks, but the farmers around had put away all our valuable things—hidden the silver, buried a statue, put antiques and books in their own houses. Now everything was back in place, and the only traces left by the war were a gate-post which a tank had knocked down, a black patch in the tiled floor of the drawing room where the Germans had set up a stove, and bits of coal strewn over the front yard. Sitting in the garden on this beautiful June day, it was hard to believe that only a few years before the place had been clicking with boots, resounding with orders.

I looked at the giant cypresses off to the front of the house, as they slowly, majestically waved in the wind. They had thick branches, but not so thick that you couldn't climb them. Then you came on openings here and there—spaces over beds of dense, fallen foliage, perfect hiding places where you could lie comfortably and sway in the wind. This side of the cypresses were orange and lemon-trees in pots so huge it took four men to lift them when the time came to move them to the orangery for the winter. And there was an abundance of flowers—geraniums, roses, oleanders, beds of petunias, pansies, marigolds. A wistaria grappled the garden wall with its sinewy branches. The sweet smell of its clustered blossoms in the spring drew you to them like a bee, and you pressed your nose into their cool, soft and yet resilient blossoms. The strong sun, the fertile earth made everything luxuriant. Some plants wouldn't be contained; trumpet vines sprouted through the garden wall, opened their way through clefts in the brickwork and came out in the sun. A rose, planted by the corner of the house below a ten-foot clump of ivy, had climbed right through it, gained the upper air, and blossomed. Way below and beyond the cypresses were the vineyards with their grapes, at this time of year still green and small. As a child, I used to tread them, laughing, in the vats. Scattered in between the vines were fig trees that would soon bear rich, dark purple fruit; there were the olive trees; there were the walnuts and the almonds. Before long they would all be ripe. The cherries were ripe now.

But I had other pleasures in mind, pleasures I had barely tasted. It seemed to me at this moment that life had no other purpose, and certainly nothing better to offer, than meeting a girl, and loving her and knowing her.

While I sat with my coffee, my mother was near the garden wall, working with a trowel, tending the flowers. This was what she liked to do, but she was never long at it before someone called her. Now it was my father. He came out into the garden and asked her to go somewhere with him. Reluctantly she dropped the trowel and gloves and followed him indoors. I stayed in the garden, beside the cup of coffee. No one was about to call *me*. Though it was morning, it seemed like afternoon—three o'clock, the slowest time of day. I passed the days between bed, dining room, and garden, as if waiting for something—September perhaps. It was hardly the way to spend a vacation. I remembered a verse: "Too soon, too soon/The noon will be the afternoon." And I stirred, but only for a moment.

"Why don't you go somewhere, dear?" my mother said, returning and seeing me sitting there miserably, looking like a beggar. "Take a nice trip."

"Yes. . . ." I said, and lingered on, and watched her tending the flowers, going from one plant to the other. I knew I should go, yet I could hardly remove myself from where I was. Such inertia, like a drug. And after coffee, not after wine. Go, but where? Go alone? If not alone, with whom? With a girl. But I didn't know any girls. That was the trouble. I should go and look for a girl, take a trip for this purpose. Here in Siena I didn't have any friends. I had lost them all. Been away too long. I looked at the grass in front of me, and thought of days when I playfully wrestled with a country girl and tumbled with her, taking care to fall under her so I would feel her weight on me. Of the days at the elementary school, halfway into town, when, during recess, I would try to take part in a game in which the girls, lifting their skirts, danced in a circle around you. Of the odor of chalk and perfume that clung to my teacher. Of when I serenaded a girl from a farm nearby and took her dancing and walked hand in hand with her on the ridge of the hill, there on the horizon. But then other horizons—foreign, distant—had come under my gaze, and I had lost my touch.

My mother seemed to see right through me. "You are ten years younger than you are. Consider yourself ten years younger." It was a comforting thought. I have repeated those words to myself many times, even lately.

After a while, around eleven-thirty, my father called my mother again—to have an espresso this time. They always had a cup of coffee together late in the morning. My mother went into the house, leaving the gardening gloves on the brickwork near where I was sitting. I watched them intently lying there on the bricks. Like casts, they retained the shape of her hands, but unlike casts they were pliable and soft. They did not lie straight or flat: the fingers curled, the index finger least, the little finger most; the thumb was flexed and adducted, the palm cupped. There was life—action—in those gloves if ever I had seen it. It made me get up and go into the house, into my father's study, where he was sipping coffee with my mother. This was the time they looked best, comfortable one with the other. My father always made a lot of a cup of coffee; it had to be just right, with not a trace of grounds in it—which, he claimed, confused his thoughts—good and hot, and preferably brewed in glass or earthen-ware. My mother sat in an armchair under one of her own paintings—a landscape, radiant in the sun. My father was at his desk, beside his typewriter, some passing thoughts—philosophical notes—typed on a very thin sheet of paper.

"I think I'll go to Rome," I said.

"Ah, bravo," my mother said.

"That's a good idea," my father said. "Rome is always worth going to. Do you have a Baedeker?"

"Yes, the nineteen-ten edition."

"It's still the best. I used to go and study for my exams in the Palatine, and in the Baths of Caracalla. They are the most monumental of ruins. And have you seen the mosaics at Santa Costanza?"

"No."

"They are among the best."

"I think I'll go by bicycle."

"By bicycle?" my mother said, then turned to my father. "Lorenzo has always been adventurous."

My father looked at me brightly and nodded. "It's 226 kilometers," he said.

They loomed in front of me, the kilometers, in the form of a long row of carved stone posts, weathered, lichened, dusty. For a moment only they counted, not the land between them. "I'll take them two at a time," I said, and laughed.

As a boy I had made a name for myself by cycling up the hill of Bagnolone, which everyone said had never been done by bicycle before, and once, during a bicycle race, I had dashed out of our drive and for a mile ridden wheel to wheel with Italy's champion—Guerra—ahead of all the rest. People used to look at me and call me Samson or Maciste, a character in an early movie. A man scrutinized me, measured the length of my arms, then shook his head. "Too bad," he said. "You don't have the reach or you'd make a great boxer."

"I don't want to be a boxer," I said.

I set out after lunch, in the hot sun, and soon was skirting the walls of Siena, taking the road to Rome. The road curved around the clay hills like a ribbon, then straightened out in the valleys. Some thirty miles from Siena, past San Quirico, the hills became steeper, the country more barren. The road runs along the margins of ravines and deep gorges, zigzagging to avoid them. Broom, the *ginestra,* turns much of Italy golden in May and June. Great clumps of it bordered the road, waving in the wind, beckoning me on. I breathed in its heady, sweet fragrance. There was little traffic—few people had cars in those days. Up the steeper hills I dismounted. I was out of practice and in no particular hurry. Here and there along the road I saw grim reminders of the war—the remains of German tanks, for instance, rusting in the fields, and, not so grim because they had turned into springs, some bomb craters near a bridge. At dusk, and feeling very tired after reaching the top of a hill so high it could have earned for itself the name of mountain, I got on the bicycle again, looking forward to the long descent. Almost immediately, I hit a rock, and I knew I had a flat front tire. I stopped. Tire and inner tube were not just punctured—ripped. Beyond repair. After the long climb, walking downhill was too depressing. I got on the bike and went clattering all the rest of the way down to the valley.

High above me, on the next hill or mountain, I could see the village of Battistrada. At first it was just a cluster of lights, and seemed not very different and no nearer than a constellation. It was so dark now that all I could see were the lights up high and the bicycle lamp, fed by a generator, waxing and waning with each step I took, making about as much light as a firefly. Once in a while I came to a milepost, but there was no reading it in that light. Though tired, I walked along quite comfortably. I was thinking that very soon I'd be at a trattoria with a glass of wine in front of me and a plate of pasta coming up. And that I'd find a bed. I needed that even more than food or wine. My mind provided the rough, thick, cool, locally woven sheets I liked, and I was between them, naked. My eyes closed at the thought, and I stumbled. But it is one thing to be tired when there is no place in sight where one can rest, another when lights beckon in the distance.

I followed the road that spiralled up toward the village lights as irresistibly as a moth. I felt just as attracted, and I hurried to the top, away from the dark valley to the lighted peak. I approached the first, the outermost street light. A friendly thing. There were no houses yet. It seemed to shine only for me, to have been put there to extend the little town's welcome to the stranger. It made a halo of red, yellow and blue-green minute darts as in a Van Gogh painting. Near it, a sign gave the name of the village: Battistrada. I came to a second or third street light, and now there were houses on each side. I asked a young man who looked just about my age (strange relationship this of two boys the same age meeting at night, a feeling of kinship and distrust) if there were a hotel and a restaurant. He pointed down the main street. "See where that light is?" he said. "You can eat and sleep there."

"Oh good," I said, and went on toward it. The narrow street opened into a tiny square. There were a few trees and shrubs—an attempt at a public garden—and a wall which looked down on the valley. At the corner the square made with the street, there was a lighted bulb over a doorway and a lunette with a glass pane—opaque except for where it read, "Albergo-Trattoria." I leaned the bicycle against the wall. It slid a little, but did not fall. Opening the door, I saw a middle-aged, energetic-looking woman with taut black hair parted in the middle, a chignon, and golden earrings, wiping glasses by a counter. A boy, about twelve, stood beside her.

"Could I have some supper and a room?" I asked her.

"Yes, come in," she replied.

I crossed the threshold. At the same time, the bicycle fell with a clatter on the sidewalk. "Hm, that's my bicycle. I'll go and pick it up."

"You stay here and sit down," she said. "Let him bring it in."

Before I had so much as turned, the boy had slipped out the door and hauled the bicycle in.

"Otherwise you'll find two of them in the morning out there!" she added sarcastically.

"A flat!" the boy said, and I explained it. Vehicles were always good for a bit of conversation.

The place was unpretentious—a small whitewashed room, four tables with white tablecloths, no customers, geraniums on the high window sill, and a bare overhead light. I sat down. The woman laid the table for me, and soon brought what I asked for—bread, wine, cheese and an artichoke omelet. Not pasta—it would take too long; the water was probably not boiling. She had just set the glazed brown earthenware dish with the omelet before me when a big, plain girl in a dun drab dress appeared at the door. She must have been about twenty-two; yet she looked older and younger—had about her something both infantile and wizened. Her hair was straight and cut short without care. There was a helpless look in her eyes. She stood by the door with her hands—pudgy, red hands—clasped in front of her as though in expectation of something. Her legs were red and bruised. She wore an old pair of men's shoes.

When the woman turned and saw the girl, she didn't say a word but went into the kitchen and returned with a half loaf of bread for her. The girl thanked her; then, looking satisfied, she slowly opened the door and left.

"Poor girl," the woman said with a sigh, "she's a little touched in the head, always has been. But she's good, would never harm anybody. And she works, too, but you have to tell her everything—everything. It's all in the head." She knocked on her forehead with her knuckles. "When that doesn't function," she added, shaking her head to express hopelessness, "there's nothing to be done." She saw that I was listening attentively, and she went on, "Do you know that when the battlefront passed here, she was the only one to remain in the village? And the *Marocchini* were here, the *Marocchini*. . . ." She brought the palms of her hands together in a gesture of prayer. For a moment she might have been a woman of three or four centuries ago talking of the pirates, the dreaded Saracens.

The *Marocchini* were the soldiers from what was then French Morocco. In 1944, after the Allies entered Rome, the Germans made a rapid retreat north. The van of the Allied troops pursuing them was here made up of Moroccans. They were brave, but very wild and unbridled, and especially the women were afraid of them. Indeed, at least in the province of Siena, many were more afraid of them than they were of the Germans. The inhabitants of Battistrada were at that time women, children, old men, and invalids. The other men had all gone and were either soldiers or partisans or prisoners of war somewhere.

"When we heard that the *Marocchini* were coming," she continued, "those of us who hadn't left the village because of the Germans, fled now and hid in the barns and farms as far away as we could from the main road. But *she* didn't leave. She had no one, and in the confusion and hurry, somehow she got left behind. She's a bit slow, as I said." The word "slow" didn't seem to satisfy her, so she put in, as if to appear modern and up-to-date, "Her reflexes aren't quick. Anyhow, when we realized she'd been left behind, it was too late—the *Marocchini* were already in the village. After two days, they cleared out to continue advancing north and chase the Germans before them. We returned here and found her sitting outside, here in the *piazzetta.* We gathered around her and took her in our arms. 'What did they do to you, Fioretta?' we asked her. 'Tell us, what did they do?' 'Oh, nothing,' she said. 'We played and then we slept.' Because we kept looking at her without a word, she repeated, as if to reassure us, 'We played and then we slept.' Do you understand?"

"Yes, I understand," I said.

" '*S'è ruzzato e poi s'è dormito,*' " the woman repeated, and ended her account with heartfelt, long, significant nods.

I said the words over to myself when she went into the kitchen, and pictured it all—the *Marocchini* entering the village, and later the faces of the women in their black shawls, with their somber countenances, like Parcae, listening to her, and she contentedly telling them of her experience, perhaps the nearest one to love she ever had or would have in her life.

After supper I was shown to my room. The sheets were thick, coarse and cool as I had wished them. In the morning, while strolling along the main street, waiting for the bicycle to be repaired—the wheel rim had got bent; the bumps in it had to be pounded out and a new tire and tube put in—I saw Fioretta standing by the wall of the little square. She was staring into space, facing not the valley but the village. I ambled over. "We are pretty high up here, aren't we?" I said, looking at the view from the wall.

She didn't answer.

"The air is good up here, isn't it?" I continued.

Still she made no reply.

I turned and looked the way she was looking—at the village. "This place must have seen many armies go by," I said. "You must have seen some yourself—the Germans, the *Marocchini*. . . ."

For a moment a flicker of response lit her face—her mouth closed, her eyes turned. But I waited in vain for a word. I took a few steps away from the wall, and then she came toward me, "Excuse me," she said, "but are you a *Marocchino*?"

I have a rather swarthy complexion and have on occasion been taken for an African. I don't know if it was this or my mention of the Moroccans that prompted her to ask this question. She asked it so hopefully that for a moment I felt like saying that yes, I did come from Morocco, but then I said the truth. "I'm from Siena," I answered.

The light of hope that I had seen in her eyes was put out by my reply. Her mouth fell open again, and I turned in the direction of the repair shop. Immediately I did so, I heard her say, "I knew a *Marocchino.* A sergeant. His name was Jamal. A terror. They were all scared of him. But I wasn't. He and I. . . ."

"What?"

A look of inexpressible joy lit her eyes.

"Tell me."

"No," she said bashfully, and looked down at the ground. She brought a hand up to her collar and, not without difficulty, fumbling around her breast, got out a thin chain with a pendant—a studded silver horn. "He gave me this," she said. "Someone wanted to buy it off me, but I value it more than my life."

"It's very beautiful," I said.

For a moment her eyes flashed, brighter than silver, then back the pendant sank, into the darkness of her bosom, next to her heart.

I went to the repair shop. The dour, taciturn man there was more of a blacksmith than a mechanic—there were carts, bellows, tongs, horseshoes, bicycles, as well as a tractor. At least for Italy it was a time in between—horses and oxen hadn't quite been supplanted by machines. The bicycle was almost ready. I said something about Fioretta and the Moroccans. He was so absorbed in his work he didn't say anything, but when he had pumped the tire up and pinched it and found it hard, he looked up at me and said slowly, "Some lose their love in war, and some find it."

Minutes later, I was speeding down the mountain, south, toward Rome.

In the city I stayed in a hotel, dutifully visited the Palatine, the Baths of Caracalla, Santa Costanza, and in less than a week returned home, by train, with the bicycle in the baggage car.

"Did you meet anyone nice?" my mother said.

I retraced in my mind the trip to Rome and back, and the boy my age, the cook, the child, the girl, the repairman, the hotel doorman in Rome, bus drivers, ticket men, museum guards, trainmen filed past me—an anonymous queue, but for Fioretta. "I met a girl," I said.

"You met a girl? Lorenzo met a girl," she said, and my father looked pleased.

"A girl in Battistrada."

"Bravo, *cocchetto,*" she said. "Imagine, a girl in Battistrada, my Lorenzino."

"It's not what you think."

"Tell us, tell us about her."

But I was afraid they'd laugh. "No," I said softly.

"Battistrada," my father said. "There must be some wonderful sunsets up there."

[1969; 1988]

The Conversationalist

I won't try to reproduce her conversations. I couldn't do it. Even if I had a tape recording of them, I could not. They wouldn't come alive again in all their vigor. For how could one forget the time that has intervened, ignore the gap, the knowledge that she and others who took part in them are no more, that the house they took place in is sold, changed almost beyond recognition? Their immediacy would be lost. For they were not meant to be recorded, or even remembered. They just happened, spontaneously, for their own sake only, not to prove anything or to score a point, but as an end in themselves. And then how could one conjure up the many things they depended on—the Tuscan breezes that came in through the open windows, perfumed with flowers and foliage, like a greater breath to mix with ours? Sometimes a firefly wandered in as on a visit. And the flavor of the wine; the warm orange light from the little silk lampshades that illumined us and cast a thousand shadows from above; the hand-painted terracotta plates; the homemade bread; the produce of the farm; and, more than anything else, the company—including the maid, who quite often lingered by the table to overhear or join in the conversation, and the smiling cook, who sometimes came in, proud of her dishes. The house, too, its age, its breadth, its weathered, solid walls.

It was three or four hundred years old, the house. Originally, it might have been a monastery. Later, until the time we bought it, it was in one family for two hundred years. We were there for forty-five. Compared to those who had it for two hundred, we were only sojourners there. But we left our mark, indelible. Perhaps it belonged to us and we to it more than we knew. Perhaps we were more firmly rooted there than anybody else. Whether in my family or in another, life and love were born and died there again and again, yet I cannot help but think that our life was more intensely lived, that our experience made a deeper mark there than other people's. I might be deceiving myself, but I don't think so. It is no empty vaunt. In some ways, I wish that our sojourn had left only a superficial mark, had only scratched the surface, and that we had passed lightheartedly as in a vain, brittle, fickle dance. But frivolous our sojourn had certainly not been. The Second World War was at the center of our stay, astride it, and the dramatis personae themselves were anything but fickle. On that stage, in that house, my mother was the best actress. And, in our forty-five years there, it was during the nineteen-fifties that the conversations around the dinner table reached their peak. My mother was in great spirits then, looked better, more alive than ever. In 1950, to make ends meet, we had started taking in paying guests—most of them friends or friends of friends from America and from England. It was a cheerful venture. Her animation grew with the company, the audience. And taking paying guests certainly improved our difficult financial situation. Until that time, what money we had came from the land we owned, which we kept selling, acre after acre.

We had continued sinking into debt because none of us had much business sense. We were none of us careerists or at all aggressive. In fact, I can remember my mother saying to us once, as if to console herself about the straits we were in, "Well, at least no one can say you are pushy."

My father was a philosopher who didn't teach but simply wrote at home. Oh, he tried his best to make the estate pay for itself—planted thousands of fruit trees, for instance—but it was an unequal task. More than for anything else, he cared for his philosophy. The self-sustaining, the underived, was what he had at heart, what moved him to walk up and down his room, deep in thought, through the long nights. The *causa sui,* an original, active principle, the principle of indeterminacy, the concept of potentiality. In the house, the words had a familiar ring from his constant repetition of them. He wanted to get to the kernel, the node of the problem life posed, the problem of thought and of matter, their relation, their inextricable, intimate kinship or union. And he had to promote his ideas. He thought the questions were vital. His books and articles came out, but his work never obtained the recognition that he hoped for and that perhaps was its due. To expound his philosophy he went on a lecture tour in America and England for a year, then returned home and continued his work, little known, neglected, and even ignored by most philosophers, but unperturbed, undiscouraged.

I had studied medicine, and I did research and practiced for a time, but I was more interested in drawing sketches of people and of places than in the condition of my patients, and it was hardly fair to them. After some years, I quit.

My elder brother was the most single-minded of us. He had taken up Greek and Latin at an early age. At school, he outshone his professor of classics, spent long hours studying, and filled his room with books. He won a scholarship to Oxford, but he, too, wasn't ambitious in a worldly way. He taught here and there, as a replacement, in various high schools in Tuscany and in Umbria. He hadn't the patience, or was too proud, to be a teaching assistant in a university and start the long career of a professor. He preferred to be free, and when he didn't teach, he lived at home, sheltered by his books. Once in a while, he took a trip to see a town, its galleries, its churches, or a girl.

My younger brother had got a scholarship to Cambridge, and, following my father's advice, had begun to study physics there. But he, again, had more an artistic than a scientific bent, and soon, exhausted from undernourishment and overwork, he changed to literature and history. In Rome, he studied architecture for a short time, then gave it up for acting. A Russian director gave him a tryout. The director shook his head but, patting him heavily on the shoulder, said, "Never mind. You, too, are a Karamazov!" After that, he was at home for a while; then he got a job in the Olivetti factory in Ivrea, in Piedmont. Soon he left that, too, and struck out on his own in Milan, importing British goods, and writing poetry now and then.

My sister, the youngest in the family, was rather gypsylike. Gypsies had an inimitable way of dressing, but she came close to it. Sometimes she would doff her gypsy clothes and don a golden Persian dress or an elegant Italian one. She was quite beautiful—tall and sinuous—and could look most striking. Like gypsies, she often went barefoot, and she loved to lounge about the house in the most restful poses. Whenever gypsies came to the house, she insisted on giving them all sorts of food, and once—to the consternation of the cook and maid—she asked them to spend the night there. She also liked to tell people's fortunes, reading their palms, or cards, or tea leaves. And she travelled a lot—even out of Italy, as far away as the Gold Coast—on very little money. She had a gift for portrait painting, and had a show in Rome. Then, all of a sudden, she stopped painting the human form and painted, instead, patches of color with sharp, straight contours. To guide her through them, there was no mark or point save in her mind. Most of her paintings were huge, and she worked them and reworked them, sometimes taking more than a year over one canvas. She had a rather exalted view of them, and when they didn't get the praise she thought they deserved she lavished it on them herself. She made little effort to sell them, sold them only rarely, but she didn't seem to care.

My mother painted, too, but never had an exhibition. Her paintings—landscapes and flowers—were hung here and there about the house, or kept in cupboards. A few she gave to friends. She didn't often paint, but when a bright, happy moment came she was moved to. Then quickly, almost slyly—so no one should stop her—she would get out her colors and her brushes, a canvas and a chair, and go off into the fields. To pay the bills, with a typewriter in front of her and the Shorter Oxford English Dictionary at her side, she typed for long hours of the day and night, translating Thomas Wolfe for Mondadori. But she only got a thousand lire—less than two dollars—a page, and the bills the estate received were crushing. She worked steadily on. For a year, she even took a job teaching art in a village school twenty miles away, and every morning she set off walking to the railroad station.

Then, in 1950, someone had the idea of taking the paying guests. The house had a dozen bedrooms, and across the courtyard and the chicken yard there were two other buildings with more rooms. The paying guests were young Fulbright Scholars from Rome, as well as artists, musicians, writers, critics. Old friendships were renewed and new ones made. With usual guests in the past—and there had been many—the vexing question often came up: How much longer are they going to stay? But not with paying guests. They didn't mind paying the modest prices. They had breakfast in the garden here and there, and lunch and dinner round the huge oval table with the family. Many of the guests were amusing. Some were brilliant. There was plenty of wine—an endless supply of it in the cellar—and wonderful fruit from my father's orchard. The cook, who had grown up in the Chianti hills, worked with extraordinary skill in the kitchen, and sent in the tastiest dishes. Everyone loved her, and they loved the maid, small and smart, as well as other women from the neighborhood who came to help. The meals seemed not so much meals as dinner parties. Now that my mother had money, she could buy linens, pottery, and all kinds of badly needed things. With the maid and the cook, she would sometimes happily go shopping in Siena or, better still, in Florence. She liked especially buying dishes at the market in Montelupo—hand-painted dishes, with flowers, fruit, vegetables, leaves, sometimes a bird or a landscape, done always with a flair, the brushstrokes free, the colors fresh. She loved, too, baskets—the strong, thickly woven ones—and homespun sheets and towels. She embroidered napkin holders with various flowers, sitting out in the garden where these flowers grew, and using the needle and thread as if the needle were a brush, the thread the pigment. She filled the house with a warm radiancy, and could impart her enthusiasms and gladness. Many of the paying guests, particularly some of the younger ones, really loved her.

But the best thing of all, almost everyone agreed, was to hear my mother speak or tell a little story—as about an elderly woman who helped in the kitchen and who had a daughter, a girl of about twenty, who had been working in town as a maid for a family. Once, my mother heard the woman telephoning the family to say that her girl wasn't going to be working for them anymore. Though the lady wanted to know why, she gave no reasons and made up no excuses, but simply said quite cheerfully, "My daughter isn't coming anymore . . . she just won't be coming any longer . . . she isn't going to come. . . ." And no matter how much the lady pressed her for a reason, she just stuck to those few words. Or when my mother told of a woman called Giuseppina, who once said to her, "Oh, I was supposed to've had a beautiful name—Solange—if my mother had had her will. But when my father got to the town hall, which was a long way from home, he forgot it. So the clerk said, 'Yesterday was San Giuseppe. Why don't you call her Giuseppina?' " Little things like that, but my mother could make them zesty. They had the unadulterated flavor of the countryside. From her one got it whole, authentic. And she knew the farmers' special, rare words for the wheat's first greening and for its later stages, their adjectives for wine, the words with which they described the underground struggle of the seed. Sometimes my mother would get very excited, especially when talking about political intrigues and scandals—as when she told of Pius XII, deathly ill, at the mercy of a quack doctor he trusted, and the hubbub at the Vatican about it. To some such sad thing, the way she told it, the guests would listen with delight, for she conjured up most vividly the world of whispering nuns and cardinals and priests, as well as the angry doctors who had been excluded.

She liked to sit on at the table long after the meal was over, with a crust of bread and a glass of wine. Often my sister would try to get the guests to move to the sofa and more comfortable chairs in the next room, which was separated from the dining room by an open arch, but she couldn't take them away from my mother. My sister would get up and go to lie down on the sofa, and, seeing that no one followed her, she would sometimes return and again suggest that they come over. But still she couldn't budge them. They would hardly even notice her. I would look at the absorbed expression on their faces, and at my mother speaking—unself-conscious, unrhetorical, striving for no effect, heart and soul in what she said, her identity completely taken up by the persons, the places, the situation she was telling us about, her eyes keen, and the lines of her face admirably serving to convey all her impressions. And the guests sitting there listening to her seemed the tribute to her power of conversation: the chairs around the table weren't very comfortable, the sofa and the armchairs *were*, my sister *was* attractive, but—boys though some of them were—there they sat, oblivious to all of that.

[1975]

The Orchard

"They all have this prejudice against fruit trees," he keeps saying.

Though no one wishes to remind him, there is some reason for it. Thirty-five years ago, when he was forty-three and a novice to agriculture—philosophy until that time had been his only field—soon after moving to the Tuscan estate his father bought him, with extraordinary energy he set himself to looking for spring water, of which the house was till then deprived, found it, ("It was there," he said), ordered two hundred peach trees from a nursery in Pistoia, and had them planted down on a fertile plain below the spring. Peaches, he claimed, would fetch far more than wine, wheat, or olive oil—the produce that the farmers in this, the Chianti, region prized. In the nearby town, he argued, much of the fruit had to be brought in from far away, so that there surely was a market here for perishable fruit like peaches, plums, apricots, and cherries—but especially for peaches. Peach trees grew fast. "In three years, they begin to bear," he said, and started counting, though when not on the subject of fruit trees he was fond of quoting the Latin dictum that he who begins to count begins to err. The figures he came to! Two hundred trees by twenty kilos by two lire. Eight thousand lire from just two hundred trees. Walking the fields, looking at the ground, hands clasped behind his back, he had his sons excited. Only the farmers remained skeptical. They understood vines, olive trees, and wheat. Anything else they rather distrusted. Their attitude didn't daunt him. It only made him bolder.

In the moist soil of the plain, the trees grew well, and in the fall he ordered more—three hundred this time. "Five hundred trees by twenty kilos by two lire," he now said. In the spring of their second year, the little trees had their first blossoms—the most delicate pink, a few to each plant. One or two became peaches—tiny slips of substance with a silvery, soft fuzz ending in a cowlick. At first the faintest green, they swelled, they reddened, they were ripe. And at the same time the price of wine was falling. It cost less than a lira a bottle—hardly a dime. He joked about it. "Please, *please* have another glass and help us drink it." Wheat, too, was low, and so was olive oil. Only the taxes rose.

But in the plain the five hundred trees, growing up and florid, promised harvests that would once and for all solve what he called the "disastrous financial situation." In the house, one heard a lot about it. "The water is level with our throats," he'd say, creating a feeling that made everyone uneasy and drew long sighs from his wife. "But oh, dear me, what can we do?" she'd say, stretching her arms down in a helpless gesture. Any big new purchase was put off till the peach trees would start producing. And in the meantime, to save on electricity, he bought weak light bulbs. The house grew dim. Never mind, his eyes were on the trees.

Every day, wearing over his shoulders the threadbare charcoal-gray mantle he had worn since his young days when he had climbed Mont Blanc, the Matterhorn, the Giant's Tooth, Monte Rosa, and a hundred lesser peaks both of the Alps and of the Apennines, he would go down to the plain to look at his peach trees.

The next March, there weren't just one or two blossoms to each tree but myriads. Each flower a peach. Well, perhaps not quite. Say three to one—three blossoms to one peach. Say even four to one. He counted the blossoms on a branch, and then the branches; he divided by four to be on the safe side; again he divided, to get the weight in kilos; then he started multiplying. It was like coasting on a bicycle down a mountain road and having the horizon at one's feet. He looked at the plain, only a portion of which had trees. "If all goes well," he said, "we'll plant some more."

All *did* go well. When the wind blew away the petals of the blossoms, there remained the greenish-white, tiny, rounded mass. A little bead of fluff it seemed at first, but if you squeezed it you felt it was pulpy even then, and if you squashed it there was a green smear left on your thumb. That downy light green was alive, and it clung hard by its minuscule stem. It was not about to drop or to come off at the least touch. And it seemed as though there was no blossom that did not turn into a fruit. The peaches were so thick that here and there the trees had to be thinned. When the peaches ripened, he hired some help—mainly girls from nearby farms—to pick them. Into the barn came the full baskets and the crates, filling it with fragrance.

"They are as beautiful as flowers," he said, watching the fruit being put in rows and layers inside the boxes.

From town, the buyers came with their wallets bulging, and the trucks left with heavy loads. There were so many peaches they tempted thieves. After some had been stolen, a barbed-wire fence was set up around the orchard, and a big white shepherd dog put there to guard it. Signs claiming the peaches were from his farm appeared on the pushcarts in the squares. He beamed. He saw the world peach-colored. So he ordered more trees—a thousand this time—and since the water of the spring wasn't sufficient to irrigate them all, some workmen who specialized in building wells dug a trench, spectacularly deep and long. Enough water was found to irrigate three or four thousand trees. To him agriculture was irrigation and fruit trees. Even as a child he had had a passion for water and watercourses. Once, he ran away from home and was found with a bundle on his back, walking along a stream, trying to trace it to its source. And now nothing was nicer than in a summer drought seeing water gushing out and making mud of the dry, the brittle earth—nothing more beautiful than fruit or than girls picking the fruit.

The blooming that took place the following spring! The bees seemed driven crazy. They buzzed from one blossom to the other, gathering pollen, bringing it around. Again the blossoms blew away petal after petal, leaving the tiny, almond-shaped, thin, fuzzy peaches that by and by swelled and captured color from the sun, except where the leaves cast their sharp, sleek shadows on them, and, swelling more and more, became so heavy some of the branches had to be sustained. Again the girls came, and the buyers. Again the trucks left laden. Again the farm's name appeared on the pushcarts. And before winter two thousand more peach trees were planted.

That made thirty-five hundred on the plain, and there were other fruit trees near the house—apricot, cherry, plum, persimmon, apple, fig, and pear. The peach trees were of several varieties, from the early kind, which ripened in June, to some that got ripe in November. Foreign-sounding names like Hale, Crawford, and Late Elberta became household words. In the next season, he said, there would be at least fifteen hundred trees producing. Winter came. Now the peach trees stood, bare of their foliage, in long, stern rows down in the plain, asleep and silent except when the wind blew strong, and then it whistled through them and they seemed to stir. They stood naked, yet so far from dead: each tiny twig intact, waiting and ready—heedful almost. Then in March a softening of the air, and very quickly, as if they could wait no longer, the first buds, the blossoms, and their petals falling to disclose the velvet of the newborn peach. Still March. Mist and gentle showers, and the sun shining out of speckled clouds; then clouds fringed with silver, followed by skies completely overcast. For days there was no sun, no stars, but under the dim days and the black nights the peach trees were safe, as though under a cover. Then, late one evening, the two flag-shaped, rusty weathervanes over the house were heard distinctly turning on the roof—a grating, creaking sound. Slowly they turned, taking what seemed a long time about it, opposing as they did a fair amount of resistance to the wind and indicating a marked change in its direction. It was the north wind. Quickly it cleared the sky. Over the house now, the stars were shining in all their wintry brightness. One couldn't help but admire them. But to the not so different blossoms on the plain this change of wind, this polished starlit sky was baneful, and all the members of the household knew it. In the morning, when they woke up, the sun was shining, the fields down in the valleys were hoary and stiff with frost. A workman who had got up at dawn reported that in the plain the frost had "burned" all of the peaches.

"All of them?"

"Hardly any left, you'll see. Why, it was like crunching through snow down there this morning," he said, and swore, impressed—no, almost awed by what nature could work when it put its mind to it. A robust frost, no doubt.

In the next few days, its full effect became apparent. The tiny, beadlike peaches, as you could readily see if you cut into them with your thumbnail, were black inside, had lost their firmness, had a shriveled feel, and they came off at the slightest touch, without a sound, as if they were bits of matter that had got there by chance. On tree after tree, one looked in vain for a whole peach, for one that wasn't black and wizened.

The leaves came out of the buds, deep green and thick, so thick sometimes that you parted them to see if by chance they weren't hiding a peach. But you would never find one.

"Still the trees are growing," he said, unperturbed. "Without fruit they may develop more, and next spring we'll try and protect them."

In the late fall, he bought an extraordinary number of cane mats, put up tall poles along the rows of peach trees, strung wires from pole to pole, and in March, just before blossomtime, hoisted the mats up. At the same time, he had piles of kindling, brambles, and moist straw placed here and there ready to be burned if a cold night should come. A cold night came—frosty, sparkling with stars. The fires were lit. The smoke rose, hiding the stars. And the mats hung like magic carpets over the three thousand five hundred trees. But in the morning, when the sun rose in the blue sky, the little peaches had fared no better than the previous year.

Another summer without fruit. Though fruitless, the trees still had to be pruned, the ground around them hoed and irrigated. It was discouraging; the workmen clipped and dug without believing in their work.

The following March, the mats went up again. They could be seen from the main road—a tented army. Some passersby wondered what they were. And those who knew laughed or made remarks like "The good money he wasted on that place!"

"Two good seasons and two bad ones," he said. "We have an even chance."

In March, there was no frost. No frost in April. The peaches, tens of thousands of them, were fair-sized. "They are out of danger now," everyone confidently said. Then, on May 2nd, the frost. The spectacle this time was worse than it had ever been. The peaches withered, and grew as black as mushrooms rotting, then fell from their branches. The workmen shook their heads. "That plain is lethal," his wife said, but he—he took it in his stride, like the philosopher he was, and continued hoping.

It was clear, though, that those first two good years had been exceptional, for the following spring, too, there came a deadly frost. The land—valuable, fertile land—could not be kept unproductive. The older peach trees were cut down; the younger ones were left in the hope that there might be a crop. There wasn't. Not for two more years was there a good season. By then, however, the Second World War had broken out, and he, being Jewish and alert to what might happen, had taken the family out of Italy to England, leaving the estate in the care of a bailiff. For the duration of the war, the peach trees were forgotten. For so long they had been the subject of so much conversation, and now suddenly they didn't matter anymore.

After the war, in 1946, when the family returned, of the three thousand five hundred peach trees only two trees were left. They stood by the barn, old and barren, many of their branches without leaves. Why they had been spared nobody knew. Perhaps because they weren't in anybody's way, perhaps to stretch a clothesline to—there was a font nearby where women did the washing. Or perhaps just as souvenirs.

But if the trees were gone, his passion for them wasn't. He read an American pamphlet on peach trees, which one of his sons had sent for and given to him. It was one of those booklets that the American government prints and sends out free upon request as a public service—a plainly written, informative thing. The choice of location for an orchard, it said, was crucial; since warm air tends to rise and cold air fall, in hilly country where there's danger of frost peach trees ought never to be planted at the foot of hills or on a plain, no matter how fertile and rich in water that low ground might be. Scarcity of water, it stressed, was far less dangerous than frost, since very little could be done to save the peaches on a frosty night, while in a drought the trees could be irrigated wherever they might be. These remarks were so pertinent that they seemed a comment on what had happened, and read as though they had been written for him. "Not one of those agricultural experts I consulted ever told me," he said.

He began again, went right ahead and planted a batch of peach trees high on the slope of a hill above the plain. People cautioned him. Irritated, he said, "Everyone is against fruit trees," and he complained about this "hostile attitude" as though it were absurd. If someone mentioned the word "frost" to him, he patiently explained that since warm air rises and cold air falls, up on the hill where the new orchard was, frost wasn't a danger anymore. And he repeated his old arguments in favor of peach trees—about the good market for perishable fruit in the hill town, about the low price of wine and wheat. People looked at him. They knew better than to contradict him. They knew that if they did he would come looking for them wherever they were—in their bedrooms, even—and bring up the subject almost as though they were heathens who had to be converted. One knew his step approaching, knew what was on his mind, knew what he would say, and either one didn't answer or was reduced to saying, "Oh, well, maybe you are right."

He certainly planted the trees with conviction; they were a sort of cause. It was as if some future need, hardly surmised or suspected, were directing the course of his actions. And there was no dissuading him. He went straight on putting all his savings into the new orchard, selling his shares, keeping workmen on it. They brought water to the new plants in a barrel on an oxcart. And he himself, though frail and aging, was often seen going up to the orchard in the heat, his arms stretched by two full pails. Finally, as the trees grew in size and number, he piped the water up to them. To increase its volume, he even repaired an ancient, leaking cistern into which rainwater drained from the roofs of the house.

"Sink money into that hole!" one of his sons said, without considering that his father led a very frugal life indeed and that the money he spent on the orchard was his only outlay of any size.

"What about men who have mistresses, go to Paris, bet on horses, drive expensive cars, drink the best cognacs, or, hypochondriacs, fill the house with drugs?" another of his sons retorted.

"There are those, too."

"He—he smokes Alfas, goes into town by bus, buys a book or takes in a movie once in a while. Why shouldn't he spend money on fruit trees if he wants to?"

"It's all right to say that. But when you see those deep new trenches he has dug—more than three feet deep, you know—"

"After all, the land is his, isn't it?"

Was it his land? Just before the war, in 1938, when the Fascists threatened to confiscate Jewish property, he transferred it to his sons, who, because his wife wasn't Jewish, were exempt from expropriation. In name, at least, the land was theirs. Morally, though, it was still his, for the transfer had been no more than a temporary expedient made necessary by an evil government for an evil reason. Those circumstances were now conveniently forgotten, and when a piece of land was up for sale, as his signature was not required, no one asked for his approval. He became more and more removed from the running of the estate. He cared only for his orchard and his books, went from one to the other, over his shoulders still wearing the cape, as threadbare as an ancient flag, darned many times over.

And now the peach trees on the hill were in their third year, the year in which they were supposed to start producing. He waited confidently. No cane mats or piles of straw and kindling up here. No need. The warm air rises from the plain, the cold air sinks. The stars can shine unutterably bright, the north wind blow, the frost fall. It won't affect them. Not up here, unless, of course, it is one of those exceptionally cold years that come once, and maybe not even once, in a decade, and we all hope it won't be one of those.

A frost came that made the plain and all the low ground white. But the hilltops were green, and so was the slope on which the peach trees stood, all clothed in pink. The cold persisted; sometimes the fringe of white—the frost coating with a silver edge the blades of grass—rose almost to the level of the orchard, skirting it like a tide. Each day, a workman, now become a real expert in fruit trees, disclosed the tiny peaches in their blossoms, and assayed them. They were still whole, still firm, still whitish-green and pulpy, their skin still fuzzy. "So far it hasn't touched them," he reported.

"If they'd been down in the plain . . ."

"Down there, there wouldn't have been one left; you can be sure of that."

The peaches ripened. The girls came to pick them. Girls picking fruit—the way he watched them, the way he spoke about them, sometimes it seemed he wanted nothing more in return for all his labors. Oh, the peaches weren't as large as they had been down in the fertile plain, but perhaps they had more taste. Nor were there truckfuls of them, but every day a station wagon left, loaded.

Each summer, there's a crop. Though he has high hopes and keeps planting peaches, cherries, figs, the orchard hasn't solved the estate's heavy financial situation—but it has solved *his*. At a time when, to pay the taxes, the land has to be sold bit after bit and two of his sons have left to go and live elsewhere—one in Milan, the other in America—he, without having to ask anything from anybody, earns from his orchard enough money for his books, the bus fare into town, the cup of coffee, the movie, the Alfas that he smokes, the little gifts he buys once in a while, and new fruit trees. The orchard fills his needs. Year after year, he watches the trees blossom in the spring, the girls gathering the peaches in the summer.

[1968]

Gypsies

At the corner where the two limbs of the L-shaped, elmed drive met, down some five hundred yards from the house and a hundred or so from the main road, there was a grassy plot bordered by a dozen cypresses interrupting the drive's outer row of elms. This tree-protected plot of green made an inviting resting place, and though it belonged to the house—a country house in Tuscany, near Siena—strangers would often leave the road and stop there for a rest.

In the hot summer, it might be a workman who would lean his bicycle against a cypress and sit in the shade to have a bite to eat and to drink some watered wine from an old fiasco. At night, a car with lovers might slowly drive there and the lovers would park and switch off its lights. In the spring, when the shepherds walked their flocks up from the pasturelands by the sea toward the mountains, or in autumn, walking down from the mountains to the sea, they would sometimes stop there for the night, and a hundred and more sheep, the sheepdogs, and the shepherds themselves would sleep on the grass. The shepherds would usually come up to the house and give the owners a drum or two of sheep's cheese—*pecorino*—as a present. And sometimes gypsies would stop there.

Then a certain wakefulness, a certain uneasiness would take hold of the house. The cook was nervous; so were the maid and the women from the farm next door to the main house. They would try to pass on their apprehension to the owners. But the owners, who were rather worldly people and not originally from this part of the country, would pay little heed to what was said. Nevertheless, the maid and the cook would make sure that the outside doors were bolted, barred, and double-locked, and would even lock the gates to the chicken run and the back courtyard. The owner's family would listen, faintly amused, to the stories about gypsies that the cook told. The owner's daughter, in particular, was skeptical of any stories with gypsies as the villains and critical of anything said against them. As she grew to be a teen-ager, and then into her early twenties, this sympathy for gypsies became more and more pronounced.

Her mother, laughing, often said she was a "little gypsy." Gypsies had an inimitable way of dressing, but she came close to it. Like them, she wore frayed black shawls, long skirts, unpressed and ragged, of a flowered, soft cotton, and much jewelry. She was very good-looking, even striking, slim and fairly tall. Her profile, her features were contoured in bold and sweeping lines, lines such as any artist would have liked to capture, but which if they were to be done justice had to be drawn quickly the first time and not cancelled or retraced. She had brown, almond-shaped eyes; her hair was black and long; she frequently went barefoot, and, rather than use a chair, she would sit on the floor or lie down wherever she could, assuming the most restful poses. She liked to tell friends' fortunes, reading their palms, or cards, or tea leaves. And she travelled a great deal and was often away for months at a time, even out of the country—as far as Egypt, Turkey, or the West African coast—taking little money with her. Indeed, she often said that she despised money and that it ought to be abolished, along with bureaucracy, passports, and all frontiers.

Though she had had a sketchy education, she read a lot, spoke French and English, had a good memory for poetry and names, and was fond of arguing about politics, art, and religion, with whomever she met, no matter how expert he was in his field; she was quite unimpressed by position, titles, degrees, or erudition. She delighted in sharing her enthusiasms—for the works of such disparate people as Lao-tzu and Kandinski—with anyone at all willing to listen, whether they were scholars or workmen. And some would nod gravely and others smile. But always she found someone who admired her, befriended her, and helped her—to carry her luggage, get her out of a tight spot, or find a lodging. She sometimes would have trouble with officials because her passport had expired, or because she needed a visa, or because she had run out of funds in some strange city. And always she would find a way out of her troubles: she made friends easily (and as easily made enemies, usually the Italian consuls), for she had something childlike, open, and innocent about her that soon made the police realize they were faced with no one dangerous. She would laugh, and they would laugh with her and let her go.

One cold and windy winter afternoon, not long after the daughter of the house had returned from Egypt, a caravan of gypsies stopped for the night on the green by the cypresses. Two thin, swarthy women shivering in their flowery rags came up with empty knotted kerchiefs to the kitchen door, and with outstretched arms asked the cook for food. The cook—a buxom woman in her late fifties, who had been at the house nearly thirty years and partaken of its ups and downs as though they were her own—went into the pantry and returned with a large chunk of bread, the usual fare for beggars.

"Bread alone?" one of the visitors said, taking it and dropping it inside her dark, capacious kerchief and stretching an arm out greedily for more.

"Eh, what did you want?" said the cook. "Isn't bread enough? These are hard times. The others are content." By others she meant the ordinary hoboes. "Why are you so special?" she added. But going into the pantry again she came back with the heel of a salami. "Here. I'm not giving you anything else. Go on, now."

Undaunted, the second visitor produced an empty two-litre fiasco, as if from nowhere, and bade her fill it up.

"Fill it? With what?"

"Wine."

"Ah, wine, too, you want now." She took the fiasco. "But I won't fill it," she said. Yet one saw that even though with the changing times she had outgrown some of her fears she still wasn't indifferent to the gypsies' putting a curse on her if they didn't get at least part of what they asked for. And at the same time she didn't want to give in to them. Why didn't they work the way she did for their food? Oh, they were vicious people. She had to strike a nice balance, and her calm, unruffled face was flushed. She returned with the half-filled fiasco, and still the curse came, not crushing but muddled—a grumble of a curse—as the two women left, fast and sly in the half-light.

"Go away! You can't put a curse on me any more than I can put one on you!" the cook shouted in a rage from the kitchen door.

And upstairs, where she was painting in her studio, the owner's daughter heard her. Down she came, like lightning. "Didn't you give them anything?"

"Bread, salami, and wine I gave them, and plenty of it. But were they satisfied? No, they are never satisfied. A curse, that's all I got back from them, and not a word of thanks."

"You didn't give them enough," the girl said, and she rushed into the pantry.

"What are you doing?" the cook said, seeing her take the best part of a salami.

"I'm cutting this," the girl said fiercely.

"What are you going to do? Give them all that? You can't."

But the girl went on cutting. From a shelf she took a loaf of bread, and then, with the bread and salami, she shot out of the house and down the drive.

"A whole loaf of bread and most of a new salami," the cook said aloud to herself. "But what can you do? She is herself one of them."

Soon the girl was back, her hands empty.

"You gave it to them?"

"Yes."

"Well, they'll have a good meal tonight for sure."

"Why shouldn't they?"

"Oh, as far as I'm concerned . . . It's nothing of mine," the cook said sulkily.

"It's so cold down there," the girl said, "and windy."

"Eh, but they've got their blankets and their coach."

For a moment, the girl seemed to ponder some difficult question. Then she said, "I'm going to ask them to dinner and to sleep here."

"What?"

"I'm going to go down and ask them to eat and sleep here."

"Eat and sleep here? Here you want them! But you must be joking."

"No, I'm not joking."

"Oh, I'm not going to make the beds, you'll see, or cook for them, after what they said to me."

"I'm not, either," said the maid, a short, unassuming woman, who had joined the girl and the cook in the pantry and was even more scared of gypsies than the cook was.

"I'll cook and make the beds," said the girl, who never helped with the housework.

"At least, first ask your mother."

"But no, absolutely not," said the girl's mother, brought down to the kitchen by the maid.

The girl, however, had a terrific will.

Her father was called. He, too, sided with the cook and the maid. "Don't even dream of it," he said. "You won't, because I don't want you to—do you hear me?"

"Yes, I'm going to invite them. They can sleep in my studio and in the *fattoría*." This was a wing of the house next to her studio.

"No."

"Bigots," she sneered, and with a dark, determined look she went upstairs to her studio. Minutes later, she could be heard vigorously moving furniture.

"You can't tell her anything when she gets into these furies," the mother said.

But the father, slight and old, started toward the stairs.

"No, please," his wife said to him. "Let her. Anything's better than these scenes. Let her. Please. For my sake. I'll stay up. We can lock an inside door, and then what can they do?" She knew her daughter well: she could become violent, especially about something like this, when she thought—when she was convinced—that she was right; then it became a cause with her. And deep down she admired her daughter, so flamboyant and unlike her. It was so bleak here in the winter. Perhaps the house could do with company, with music and gypsy dancing. Things like that might keep their daughter home.

In the kitchen, the cook and the maid spoke in undertones. And then they saw the girl leave by the front door of the house and walk toward the drive—it was getting dark now—down to the green where the gypsies camped.

As night fell, the cook, the maid, and the girl's mother waited. The father had gone back to his room. Long they waited. At last, they heard a ring at the front door. Her mother went to unlatch the door while cook and maid watched from the kitchen. It was the girl, alone.

"They won't come," she said to her mother. "They won't come," she repeated to the cook and the maid in the kitchen. "I told them I had beds for them, the fire lit, and that soon I'd have dinner ready, but they wouldn't come; though I begged them to, they wouldn't. Why? I don't understand."

"Because they are true gypsies," her mother said. "You see, it's different with them."

The cook and the maid were quite happy now. "Ha, no, ha? They didn't want to come, eh?"

"No, they just wouldn't."

"They are happy where they are," the mother said. "A grassy spot near a road is what they want, and to be left alone. They can do without beds, walls, furniture—everything but freedom."

The girl's father appeared in the kitchen. "Well?"

"They wouldn't come."

"Ah, you see," he said, as if giving them credit.

[1979]

The Angel

"It is a time-proven rule of fiction never to introduce an important character toward the end of a story," says a well known author in one of his books. But life has no such rules, so why should fiction, its reflection, have them?

It was 1946, and Olga had come back with her family to Italy from England, where they had spent the war years as refugees. She was sixteen, an unruly, impetuous girl. Spoiled, some said of her, placing the blame on those who had brought her up. But her parents objected to the term, reasoning that they had done no more, no less, for her than for her three brothers—Piero, Damiano, and Sergio—who were comparatively tame, quiet, and rather shy. Heredity and environment, her father—a philosopher—tended to discount, stressing instead an underived, spontaneous quality at work in any human being. They spoke of her as capricious, wild, inconstant, but not as spoiled. They were even apt to admire her wildness, seeing in it an element of individuality not attributable to any cause. Only sometimes, when she got insulting and swept her frail father out of the way with a strong push, did they have second thoughts and wonder. But they couldn't control her. Scolding her was useless. Physical punishment, even if they had been able to administer it, was quite alien to them. They deplored her bad behavior and implored her to be good, but she would not heed, never having any doubt that she was right.

If she was looking for something in the house and couldn't find it, she would go from room to room, pull drawers out of chests, dump their contents on the floor, refuse to pick them up, expect the maids to do it, scream, order them about, and, unmindful of the hypocrisy of it, sit down at the dinner table and speak as if she were the champion of the downtrodden people of the world. Locked doors infuriated her, and she would rattle them till they gave, or rouse the household till the key was found. She would appropriate any object she fancied and often, as if possessed by a destructive urge, leave it in unusable condition. At meals her greed was astonishing. To get more of the icing she would ruin the looks and shape of any cake, and turn insolent if one made a remark. Years later, thinking about his sister, sometimes Damiano almost laughed in disbelief, her behavior was so bad. And yet, despite her behavior, he felt close to her—closer than to his brothers. Was it her physical resemblance to him—the shape of her nose (a little rounded), the straight brown hair? Was it her artistic temperament?—she painted, he wrote poems. Was it just that she was a girl? Or was it that her outward display of force might cover a weakness, shield a vulnerable nature deep within her? Weakness was such a human trait. Though he wrote, he was going to be a doctor, and weakness, and sickness, interested him more than perfect health. And so, while critical and disapproving of her, he watched her with a certain fascination, as one watches a curious phenomenon.

She hardly ever cried or said that she was sorry. Rather, in a sudden change of course, to make up for her faults, almost as if tired of them, she would get over her rages and turn endearing—hug, kiss, laugh, dance. Her parents soon forgot her mischief. "She was made to bruise and bless," said her poor father, and smiled. At some cost, he had found in her someone who was absolutely familiar with him—far more so than any of his sons or than his wife, who all respected him too much to be effusive toward him. He delighted in the showers of kisses that she gave him, or suddenly to find her sitting on his lap, fondly hugging his shoulders, jostling him about and calling him "*papaino.*"

Why were people so ready to forgive her? Partly because she had a way of making you laugh. Certain persons struck her as funny, and when she talked about them you saw them as she saw them—wry caricatures—and you laughed with her. You laughed and you forgot. One had to admit she wasn't boring. She had more life than most. Though no great dancer or singer, when she danced or sang one watched her, astonished by her grand and sweeping movements, and by her voluptuous voice. Perhaps it was the enormous change taking place—the petulance turned pleasing, her better nature coming to the fore, the manifestation of indubitable grace, sunshine after a storm, the contrast. The relief one felt! The transformation seemed a miracle, and like fair weather it gave you the illusion of permanence. One then remembered amusing things about her—of how once, for instance, at elementary school, she had found the toilet messy, and, according to her teacher, had swept it up and cleaned it and polished all its fixtures till they shone; or of how the geese, craning their necks and hissing, chased her, and she came running toward you in the long frock her mother had made her; of how fearlessly she rode Turbo, their fiery horse, bareback, and climbed cherry trees to pick the ripest cherries on the topmost branches, branches such as only the birds reached; of how she would return from the woods with bunches of cyclamens and from the riverbank with violets, enough to make several little bouquets, which she would put in pots even in her brothers' rooms; and of how once at a hotel by the sea, hearing the waves break, she asked if someone was turning a flour sifter—"You're a real country girl," her mother had said.

The maids and the cook, too—who had taken care of her from birth and through her childhood—were willing to overlook her excesses. The maids found excuses for her. "She's still a child," they said to her mother, who kept apologizing to them. Then, remembering that as a child she had been sweet and gentle, they tried to account for her change. "It's that illness when she was little," they said, referring to a low-grade fever that she had when she was six or seven. Or, "It's her age." And the cook, who was very superstitious, whispered, "Someone put a hex on her. It's not her fault, Signora." The cook even claimed she knew who to blame—a friend of the family, a woman who had taken part in séances in the house: "She was jealous because she had no children—only cats." But Olga's mother recalled that, even as a baby, if Olga didn't get what she wanted, she would turn white with rage, quite unlike her brothers. At times, she would get into long, hearty discussions with the cook and with the maids, show them her paintings, take seriously their comments, even alter her work, ask them up to her studio again, and be altogether as nice to them as she had been mean. Oh yes, she could be quite engaging.

"You see, when you are good there is nothing we wouldn't do for you; you could have everything."

Immediately, she might turn resentful at the implication that she had been bad, and leave them with a frown.

Sometimes, they were quite proud of her—when, for instance, in a new, elegant dress, she would twirl in front of them with a flourish. Slim, tall, smooth-complexioned, almond-eyed, and with her straight dark hair down to her shoulders, she had something Gauguinesque about her. Showy, flamboyant, haughty, never shy, her awareness of being good-looking didn't help. It made her more proud and more demanding. She must have one new dress after another, and her mother, perhaps seeing in her the dashing self she had missed being, did not begrudge them. Though not exactly vain, Olga wasn't modest. She praised her own work lavishly. And, scattering names and quoting, she displayed what knowledge she had of art and other matters, never admitting ignorance on any subject. She denied the value of money, said that she despised it, sounded absolutely disinterested in all worldly possessions, and argued for a brotherhood of man. Her brothers smiled, but strangers were impressed.

Gratitude wasn't her strong point. If you asked for it, she would immediately accuse you of trying to ingratiate yourself. Once, she and her brothers went to the sea, and, shoving herself off a rock, she had accidentally kicked a sea urchin. Damiano painstakingly picked out all the spines that had stuck to the ball of her foot. She didn't thank him. In a moment she was inveighing against him for using her towel. Often, her effrontery made him wish she had never been born—or worse. And still, getting over his bitterness, he wondered about her. When they were children he had once asked her to close her eyes and handed her a red-hot chestnut and slightly burned her. Had she lost faith in him from that moment?

The high school in the hill town, with its strict curriculum, wasn't suited to her. Though fairly well-read and fluent in English and French, there were certain subjects she would just not take. Her parents decided to send her to Florence, two hours away by train, to an art school whose director they knew, and got her a room in a pensione. Let her have the independence she was seeking, and give everybody a rest. Piero, her elder brother, was doing graduate work in classics at Oxford; Damiano was a medical student in Rome, and Sergio was studying architecture in Milan. Damiano heard from home that she was happy in Florence, had made great friends with a girl her age, and that the two often visited and filled the house with their giddy laughter.

And then, a few months later, on the eve of an exam, Damiano got news that Olga had fallen seriously ill with tuberculosis. "They found a cavity in her right lung," his mother said. "She has a fever, too."

That night, he couldn't sleep. All her faults vanished. She was a saint, an angel. He was a fool ever to have thought otherwise. Her recovery was the only thing that mattered, urgent, crucial—and unlikely. It was one thing when a weak person got sick, but my God, she had been so very vital, so vivacious. Life itself, bobbing, exuberant, ebullient, seething. And now she was prostrate, in bed, sweating, with a fever, and a cavity in her right lung. He could visualize the germs, that so often he had looked at through a microscope, multiplying in her precious tissue, pullulating, a myriad crowd, and her defenses pathetically drawn up against them in an effort to circumscribe them, isolate them, check them. And he thought of Keats dying only a few blocks away, in Piazza di Spagna, and of Modigliani, Chekhov, Katherine Mansfield, Lawrence, and Gozzano. "They die young," he had read, "those who are dear to heaven." He thought of a friend of his, a girl he had gone to school with in the hill town, dying—dead now—and the deceptively florid look of her face, a rosiness in the cheeks that had something clammy, humid, about it, that tended ever so slightly to the violet—a cyclamen pink—and that betrayed a deficiency in the oxygenation of her blood. He thought of their hill town and of Florence, both of which had such a high morbidity and mortality, especially as regards tuberculosis, and of the ads and posters on the school walls about the fight against TB, the pictures of flies and of the sun—enemy of germs—and of the warnings about the dangers of spitting and coughing in public places. All those hideous cartoons and signs came back to him, and he could see the polished smooth walls of the hospital corridors. The hill town with its narrow dark streets and unwholesome grimy corners came back to him, and the death notices and the funeral processions and the men in black hoods leading the processions. His home was outside town, in the country, in a sunny place, in a house that—it seemed ironic now—was called Solatia, sunny. But what good did that do? She was sick, in danger. And not so long ago he had wished she had never been born, or worse. He couldn't sleep. All night he sat up staring at his books, not reading, deep in thought, and so alert that sleep held no sway over him, any more than wakefulness over a person deeply drugged. So alert was he still in the morning, that when the exam came, he passed it with full marks, easily, though it was unusual for him. And, after the exam, he took the train to Florence.

She had been taken by her mother, on the advice of the doctor and of friends, to a nursing home in Fiesole, overlooking Florence. The nursing home had one of those names that are supposed to suggest serenity, or green pastures, or beautiful views outside, but that give no inkling about the inside, and for that reason one immediately becomes suspicious of them. One wing had patients with nervous breakdowns, the other served as a sanatorium. And there was his little sister, in bed, in a single room. She smiled at him and he kissed her, the way one kisses a rose. "You'll see, you'll get better in no time," he said and felt the vainness of his words.

"She has already broken two thermometers," said their mother, who was sitting on a cot beside her.

He laughed. They'd forgive her anything now—anything. It was her right to break them.

"Well, how is it here?" he asked.

"Oh, these nursing homes," his mother replied. "You know. But it's the best that we could find."

"I'm going to die anyway," his sister said.

"What are you saying?"

"She's always saying that."

They X-rayed her and made many tests, which all confirmed what the doctor who first saw her had diagnosed, then gave her, every day, injections of calcium chloride (in the hope of calcifying the lesion), and vitamins, and began artificial pneumothorax—the introduction of air into the pleural cavity to induce a partial collapse of the lung, something that was supposed to promote its healing by putting it to rest. It was a procedure that, at that time, before effective drugs came into use, was practiced widely, especially in Italy, ever since it had been conceived by Forlanini, an Italian chest specialist, in the 1920s. A large sanatorium in Rome was named after him—The Forlanini—and the name in the city had taken on a dismal connotation. Many years later, Damiano read in a medical manual, "Such collapse procedures as pneumothorax . . . have no role in the treatment program [of TB]."

She was in the nursing home for a few months, but her condition didn't improve. From there she went with her mother to a sanatorium in the Alps, near Cortina, for the fresh, cool air. And, in Rome, Damiano thought of the hostile peaks of the Dolomites, and the frozen air, and balconies and terraces and chaises longues and beautiful young women in shawls, and of *The Magic Mountain.* She didn't improve there either, and finally it was decided to take her back home, where she wanted to be.

She was given the guest room—a large, airy room with a terrace and a double bed, the bed on which she was born. Soon, Damiano went home for a weekend. Her beauty, from her loss of weight, was even more apparent. Her eyes had a luminous quality, new to him.

"We've found a good doctor," his mother said, "the director of the sanatorium here. Very serious, but also a dear. A real medical man. Sardinian. A man you can rely on. You'll meet him—he'll be here at four. He was very interested to hear that you are studying medicine."

He came, the doctor, a short unassuming man with gold-rimmed glasses, a reddish face, and slightly protruding yellowish teeth. He played the pitifully cheerful role doctors often play when they come into a patient's room, especially a young patient's. His smile seemed genuine and it made you forget his homely look. As they shook hands, Damiano felt his gentle, pudgy hand. He was shy, and Olga had already grown familiar with him. "But when are you going to cure me?" she said. "I feel no better. I feel worse. Why don't you cure me *now*?"

"Eh, signorina, you must be patient."

"Patient? I'm tired of being a patient."

"*Calma, calma.* I know. You'll see that little by little you'll get well. It takes time. You can't get over it like that," he said, and flicked his thumb, then, turning to Damiano, added, "We are going on with the pneumothorax," and talked about it in detail—the amount of air that he introduced each time, its purpose, and so forth. Damiano nodded at everything he said, as behooved a student. Then the doctor showed him some X-ray pictures, and he saw the cavity quite clearly. "Little by little," he said, "it will get smaller and smaller, and finally close up and calcify. I've seen so many cases."

"But mine won't."

"And why shouldn't it? Why is yours so special?"

"Because I have bad luck."

"Oh, but how superstitious we are today, signorina. You must be cheerful. You've got to fight the thing. It helps to be cheerful."

"I want to die," she said. Why did she say it? Why such fatalism? Did she think of herself as one of those unlucky poets or painters whom she loved? Or to make herself dramatic? Did she have pangs of conscience and see death as her due? Or did she view it as a kind of liberation? Or was it simply said to evoke reassurance? Probably all of these to some degree.

"What? Why so pessimistic?" the doctor said.

"What is there to be optimistic about?"

"You. This. You'll see," he said, and turned to open his bulging leather bag.

"What do you ever carry in that bag? Empty hopes. Lies. You come to me with lies."

"Olga!" her mother said. "Be a little quiet. Forgive us, doctor."

The kindly doctor smiled. He swabbed a small area of her chest with iodine, then with a large needle and syringe slowly pushed air into her pleural space. She winced, but stood the pain better than Damiano expected, and he remembered a professor in the classroom saying that women faced pain more bravely than did men.

"*Brava,*" her mother said to her when the ordeal was over, and kissed her, and affectionately called her "Olgussi."

Coffee was brought, Olga's father came in, and they began talking about politics, for the general elections were coming up. Olga had strong opinions, and the subject was one that could make her forget her present state.

When it came time for the doctor to leave, Damiano accompanied him to his car. He was as hopeful as he had been in the room. When Damiano asked him about the effectiveness of artificial pneumothorax, he reconfirmed his belief in it. With it, calcium, and bed rest, he thought she would recover.

But the fever continued and the cavity would not heal. Weekends, Damiano would come home. One day, he found his sister crying, weeping on and on, with tears and a soft moan that would not cease, and her mother quite unable to console her. "See what you can do," she said to Damiano with despair, and Damiano, who was fond of movies and who had seen an American one about cops and zoot-suiters, imitated them. And soon his sister was laughing so loud he got worried about the lung that the pneumothorax was supposed to give rest to.

The next day, her despondent mood returned. She was reading a poem of Gozzano, who had died of TB in 1916, a poem about his illness, "At the Threshhold."

"Listen to this," she said, and read it aloud to him.

> My heart, playful child who laughs even when sad,
> my heart, you who are so glad to exist in the world,
> enclosed in your shell, do you not often hear outside
> someone who is knocking, who is knocking? . . . They are
> the doctors.
> They percuss me in their varied measure spying out I know not
> what signs,
> they listen with their stethoscopes to my chest in front
> and behind. . . .

And so, following such melancholy tunes, the days passed, and the weeks, gloomy and wan, though the doctor wasn't discouraged. "It is a chronic ailment," he said. "The healing is gradual."

"What healing?" she said. "There is no healing."

It was true, the measures that he and the others had taken did not work. And she grew weak and pale, consumed by the fever that would not remit.

But in America, in New Jersey, at Rutgers University, Abraham Waksman—a Russian émigré, expert on the molds within the soil—found one that no microbe seemed able to destroy, and from it, with his assistants, he obtained a substance—streptomycin—active against the tubercle bacillus. Now it was being tested in America with good results. Damiano had read about it in *The Journal of the American Medical Association* and in *The Lancet,* to which he subscribed. Olga's doctor, too, knew of it. Indeed, articles about it were appearing in the newspapers. When the subject came up in Olga's room, the doctor's eyes lit up at mention of the new wonder drug. Everyone's interest was stirred.

"But who is this man who discovered it?"

"His name is Abraham Waksman."

"But what a wonderful man! *Che simpatico, che caro,* what a dear! I love him. Oh, I love him. I want to hug him. Does he have a beard?"

"I don't know."

"And this stuff—this streptomycin—really kills these little creatures that are trying to kill me?"

"Yes," the doctor said.

"What are they like, these little creatures?"

"They are tiny rods. Under the microscope, dyed, they show up red."

"Damn them. And you can't get it here?"

"Not yet," the doctor said, and raised his hands in a gesture of frustration.

"But in America you can?"

"There is a limited quantity of it, so far."

"I know I'll die before it's available here."

"Signorina, your pessimism really . . ."

"In America," her mother said, "we have relatives. Catherine, a very rich woman."

"A millionaire," Damiano said.

"We could write to her. We could," her mother said, looking around at them all.

"We could send a telegram now," her father put in. "And we could send her the money, whatever it costs."

"How much does it cost?" Olga said.

"I think it is very expensive," the doctor said. "They talk of thousands of dollars for a course. A course—a full course—would be perhaps 300 vials. Each vial a gram. A vial a day. It has to be given over a long period of time."

"By injection?" Olga said.

"Yes, by injection."

"Oh, dear, what pain! But it wouldn't be any worse than what you have given me so far."

"No, no worse."

"Then shall we try to get it?"

"If you can, there's no harm in trying."

Her father had already got a piece of paper and a pen. He wrote the telegram, his wife and the doctor helping him. The doctor looked bright with anticipation at the prospect of being the first to try out streptomycin in his district, perhaps the first in Italy. The telegram was longer than any Damiano had ever seen. He went into town that very day and sent it off.

Within twenty-four hours a cable came back. "Streptomycin available. Will send it airmail care of American Embassy in Rome."

Damiano picked it up there and brought it home. They opened the tightly packed cardboard box in the presence of the doctor. It had several layers of little bottles, each with a white powder at the bottom and a rubber cap under an aluminum seal. And there were as many vials of diluent as there were bottles. The doctor gave the first injection.

And soon, very soon—in a matter of weeks—almost miraculously, the fever disappeared. She gained weight. The doctor took X-rays. The cavity had shrunk.

"Healing," she said, "I can hear, feel, the cells healing. It's almost worth having been sick, this feeling."

She was up and about the house. Her appetite returned and her old vigor. But she still had to take the injections and keep a temperature chart. Then, one evening, around Christmas, when Damiano was home, the doctor came to the house with an X-ray picture that showed no cavity. In her enthusiasm, Olga dropped the thermometer and it broke.

"What a silly," her mother said, picking up the pieces. "I don't know how many she has smashed. Now we'll have to buy another."

"No need," the doctor said.

"Really?" Olga said, and shrilly laughed and hugged him. She took the picture and held it against the light. "It's true. It was there and now I can't see it. What is that scientist's name? The one who discovered streptomycin?"

"Abraham Waksman."

"*Simpaticissimo!*" she said.

"A kind of deus ex machina," Damiano said.

"An angel," said her father.

"Really."

The doctor smiled. "Olga, do you remember how pessimistic you were? So sure that you were going to die?"

"If it weren't for that medicine I would have."

"She's always got an answer," her mother said. "Why don't you thank the doctor, instead?"

"Thank you," she said, in a slightly affected tone, though looking into his eyes.

He smiled modestly.

A moth was flitting around a lamp.

"Whatever did moths do," she asked, "before man came along with fire and electricity? Did they dance to the moonlight?"

"That's a good question," the doctor said.

"Something absolutely artificial and unforeseen comes along—a drug, in my case; electricity in the case of that moth—and I live though I would have died, and it dies though it would have lived."

"She's philosophical, Olga."

"Let's just thank God things went the way they did," her mother said.

"God? If you left it to God I'd be dead already."

"Here we go again," the doctor said.

"You and Waksman, not God, I have to thank."

[1982]

Of Love and Friendship

My father was a philosopher, who, right to the end of his life, thought he would make a living from his books. My grandfather, a law professor in Rome, soon saw this wasn't likely to happen and, in the hope that his son could become self-supporting, bought him a country estate in Tuscany, a few miles outside of Siena.

The place was rather remote, and Siena, though a pretty town, wasn't the lively center it once had been. It was, in fact, dormant. Tourism, which before the First World War had livened the town up and which was to liven it up again after the Second, was—with Fascism and the Depression—down in the thirties. The university, though one of the world's oldest, had only the faculties of medicine and law. The hospital, also ancient, was the single busy place except for the market on market days. The schools, most of them converted from monasteries and convents, retained their original bare, ascetic look. On winter evenings the town was positively grim. Stark, too, with its narrow, windy streets. As if the cold and frozen Middle Ages weren't enough, the walls were pasted with death notices, and you were quite likely to meet men in black hoods—members of the medieval confraternity of the Misericordia—leading a funeral procession. The morbidity rate in Siena was among the highest in the nation. Owners of the nearby villas—stodgy, titled people—for the most part passed their time in a club, playing bridge or billiards. My mother would have preferred Florence. Much. But she wasn't used to having her own way, and raised no objections to the choice of Siena.

To make up for its lacks, she and my father—both of whom had grown up in Rome and liked company—invited friends, old and new, to come and stay. There was an eccentric English painter of moonlight scenes. Once, she arrived from Rome sometime during the night, set up her easel in the middle of the drive, and at dawn, her painting finished, rang our doorbell. There was a lanky, clever, spectacled French poet and illustrator in plus fours with the energy of an electric eel.

And there was a young woman writer from Florence with long bleached-blond hair and plenty of makeup, a hypochondriac, insanely in love, often in tears. She was supersensitive, had mediumistic powers, and sometimes in her bedroom late at night she, my parents, and another friend would have séances, from which my two brothers, my little sister, and I were always excluded.

My mother was apt to change her mind about company and claim she wanted to be alone. The guests, she said, were fine—very dear, congenial, and all that—but everyone had the right to a bit of solitude. "Soon they'll go and we'll be alone, *cocchino*," she would tell me, and pat my knee. But when they finally did go—and sometimes they stayed for months—she would often fall into a silent, sombre mood. And we looked forward to a visitor, for then—at least at the front door—she would be forced to smile. We depended on her smile. Guests brought it on, and a hundred other things, of course—a brood of newborn chicks, fluffy and golden in a basket, looking up at her in unison, or the sun shining on a newborn leaf, or perhaps a letter. Not my father's jokes, I'm afraid, or his attentions. But a newborn leaf! An urge to draw it, or paint it, or embroider it (she said threads came in a greater variety of colors than did pigments) would assail her, and for a happy day it was a love affair between her and the leaf. She was a painter born. She never had an exhibition, though. She didn't care. She was too modest and at the same time too proud. Beyond worldly contest. A woman busy with the children and the house, and with her husband, who kept calling her—to read a paragraph he had written, to accompany him somewhere, to ask her for advice. She was never too busy to listen, never resentful of being interrupted, always ready to put away her work, though with a sigh. Most of her canvases were hidden in closets when they should have been hung not just in the house but in a gallery, for everyone to admire.

The relationship between her and my father: the hardest to imagine, the hardest to describe. Affectionate, loving even, but not passionate, not voluptuous—at least not on her part. Guests sometimes told me what a wonderful marriage my parents' was, that they'd never seen one that fared so well. Oh, they had the highest praise for it, and all the time I knew they were way off. She admired him for his being uninterested in a career, for his taste, for his liberal political opinions, for his tremendous dedication to his work. She believed in his philosophy. He was an extreme idealist, and most of the time she saw him as unassailably right. But she strained to understand his concepts. She was ready to agree with them, but they usually were beyond her grasp, just beyond her grasp; or, if she understood them, she wasn't able to argue with him about them, discuss them with him—only question them, ask questions, which he would answer affably but never in her language. An elusive element ran through his words, which in vain she tried to seize. She admired him, surely, but his thinking was beyond her. He encouraged her; he told her she had a very philosophical mind indeed, for there was no understanding a concept fully—everything needed to be deepened. She said he told her he'd married her because she didn't go by conventional values. Now, she asked, what kind of a reason was that for marrying you?

Did she love him? Or, rather, how did she love him? Almost like a son, like someone who had to be helped, comforted, humored, and consoled. But not quite like a son, either. He was more exacting than a son—irritable, willful, and so determined. At times, if she didn't take notice of something he was saying or misinterpreted something he had said or interrupted him, he would turn against her in a rage. I remember his sharp, hateful, self-righteous tone of voice—no swearing, insults, threats, or even shouts; just the tone. His lips taut. The words that seemed to be uttered by nothing soft, like lips or tongue, but only by the teeth. Words that came out rattling like small shot, propelled against her. I remember the silence with which she bore his anger. And rarely, perhaps stretching her arms down and back disconsolately, her replies, in a small voice: "Oh, but listen. . . . What can I say? I'm sorry." She didn't like people to make scenes, and for this reason, I think, she never left the room. I remember the stony silence that would follow, and her gloom.

Sometimes she couldn't stand it anymore. She seemed exhausted, at her wits' end. She wanted to be far away, alone. Once, wistfully, she told me that in her young days a workman had paid her some attention. "He talked to me as I walked along the Tiber. A bricklayer. I wonder what life would have been like with him. Simpler, perhaps. But then I wouldn't have had my little boys, my *ragazzini,*" she said, and brushed her palm down my face lightly. And sometimes she would say, "I'll pack a small bag and leave; I feel like leaving; I'm going to leave; oh, yes, I am leaving." But she always stayed. She and he slept in separate rooms, as far apart as the big house would allow. But often he would be heard calling her, calling her, calling her. . . .

And then about 1936, to save the situation, there came a guest who, especially in my mother's view, wasn't like any other guest we'd had—a complete original, and one for whose departure she never hoped. He would stay with us for a week or two, and come perhaps three or four times a year. No, he wasn't like anybody we had ever seen. Millo, that's what my mother called him. In Siena, he didn't go to the museums or the cathedral but, with a big old leather briefcase and a penknife, he went to the public park. His business was with the trees. He would be seen chipping away at the bark as if he had really come on something. A policeman or other public-spirited citizen would amble over to see just what he was up to. Everyone was curious about him. "Are you after mushrooms? Snails?" Smiling, and in a Genoese accent that sounded strange and worldly-wise to Tuscan ears, he would explain that he was collecting lichens, that this little thing he was cutting off the bark was, in fact, a lichen, and tell them its Latin name. Immediately they would start calling him "*Professore*." If they failed to be impressed, he would go on to say that some lichens had medicinal properties; this was almost certain to rouse their appreciation. Lichens, he told them, weren't parasites. The way he talked about them, they seemed to be possessed of all qualities. The little cut he made on the bark was insignificant, almost invisible, and he would be allowed to continue his pursuit. He had a scalpel and a hammer, too, and sometimes he chipped at a rock—for lichens, like moss, and perhaps more than moss, grew on practically anything and in just about any part of the world, even in the polar regions and the desert. This extraordinary interest, he explained, took him not just to parks and gardens but to deep woods and remote mountains. Ah, he was a cunning one for sure, or mad, and in either case they let him chip away.

Why such a passion for lichens? Well, for their beauty, mainly. Pale green and yellow, orange and gray, tenuous blue, silver, and almost white, spread by the wind or growing by contiguity, they improved the looks of almost anything they stuck to. Nor did they interfere with the host, except to give it cover. They made the tile roofs golden. They grew on ugly walls and monuments until their ugliness quite faded. They contributed to the ruins part of their weathered look. They were the hand of time, its patina, its gift, or an instrument it wielded. And if you looked at them closely you saw the marvel of their structure: lacework, filigree, touch-me-not golden curls. Always an adornment on the bare. How did nature manage to be so unerringly tasteful? Was it, as with the clouds, the magic hand of chance?

Soon Millo had most of us enthusiastic about lichens. My younger brother even started a collection of them. My parents bought him a small microscope. With it, one could get lost in the leafy and branchlike maze. Another world, it seemed. Not flat, as in a slide, but three-dimensional, with shadows of its own, a place where hanging gardens mixed with orange goblets and gossamer strands. Millo himself had discovered several new species of lichens. Some bore his name. He had sold collections to Harvard, Columbia, and a number of other universities. We were most impressed.

"I've given them the discards," he would say. He was only joking; according to my mother, he sent excellent specimens, beautifully packed. "You should see those boxes," she said after she and my father had driven to Genoa to call on him. His own collection was in a state of flux—he was continuously exchanging samples with lichenologists in Sweden and other countries. In Italy he had the field to himself.

"Is this rare?" my younger brother and I would ask him, running in from the woods to the house, and always he would look at the samples with joy and encouraging exclamations. "Oh, oh, look what they've found!"

My mother seemed rejuvenated. It was as if he had borne into the house a gift that brought new life. My father, too, looked through the microscope and marvelled, going as far as to say—I have it from a letter—that the *Cladonia verticillata* had the pureness and beauty of a Donatello. And the cook, who also looked through the microscope, went into praises of nature that sounded something like those of the chorus in Greek tragedy. We went for drives, and now there was more purpose in our outings. "Oh, we've found some rare ones," he would say, and, putting a hand on my younger brother's shoulder once, he added, "And Sandro found one that may be quite new—a new species altogether. Of this I am sure. I've never seen it before; I just don't know it."

Was he serious?

Millo was friendly with my father, listened to him and read his work, agreed with it and praised it, but no more than my mother could he discuss it at length. And with my elder brother, who was very studious and not as fond of lichens as the rest of us, he read Greek—Homer, Aeschylus, and Sophocles. Giving Greek lessons was something he did in Genoa to supplement his income from the lichens, but, as with them, you had the feeling he would have done it quite apart from the money—for pleasure. The thing is, he was a poet. As a very young man, he had written a book of verse, *Thistledown,* which had been well received and was still remembered. Now he was about to bring out a new one, *Atiptoe.* Brief poems, crisp as his lichens—indeed, so terse that at first it was hard to understand them.

He would often invite my parents out to dinner. "We are going to the notary public," he would say to us, trying to look serious but unable to look more than half serious. He was a friend of the whole family—of the cook and the maids, too, and of the curate who came to have dinner with us every Monday. But particularly of my mother.

They went for walks together, or, sitting on the garden brickwork, sipped coffee in the sun. Those, I think, were my mother's halcyon days. There was a joy in her conversation that was absent when she talked with my father. The reason was, in part, the subject matter. With my father, philosophy—perhaps some word he was looking for or some problem connected with the publication of a book—or a letter he had received no reply to, his hopes for a huge peach orchard he had planted, the heavy financial burden of running the estate. And with Millo the lustre of a leaf, some comic scene in town that morning, how "inconceivably bad" an article was by a writer whom they knew.

My mother, really, did most of the talking. She had this extraordinary verve, which the wine helped, and which someone who listened as he did brought out. He listened with glee. He appreciated her sense of humor infinitely—as if he could listen forever and never have enough. He had the brightest eyes, and the glasses that he wore intensified not just his vision but his looks, added to him rather than detracted; one missed them if he took them off. He was chubby and not tall—shorter than my mother, who was spare and strong. His rounded face tended to the red, perhaps because of his fondness for wine. My father was slim and pale, with large, thoughtful eyes, and was considered very good-looking. As a boy, he had won a prize as the prettiest child in town. So at first I never thought of our friend as a rival to my father. He didn't seem the sort of person to rouse a passion. And then my mother, though she didn't seem as happy with my father as with Millo, had for my father such a strong attachment, such a deep affection, and respect and admiration. Perhaps these feelings—even put together and taken at their height—didn't amount to love, but at that time I was too young to make the distinction. Anyway, except during their tiffs, which I was quite prepared to disregard, I thought my mother loved my father thoroughly, loved him as much as he did her, though in a different way. My father paid a great many compliments to women and said silly things to them—even, and especially, in my mother's presence—but I don't think he was ever unfaithful to her. He had a puritanical streak, an austere control, and an intellectual nature that kept him above gossip or interest in petty things, and took him into a rather remote world crowded with hypotheses.

Still, though I wasn't drawing any distinction between love and admiration, my brother was. Older than I by two years, he began to view the relationship between my mother and Millo with circumspection. He became morose, silent, and reluctant to read further Greek texts with him. He withdrew even more into his room and books. "They're always together," he said to me in a worried tone.

Poor boy, he loved my mother so much, had spent such a lot of time near her, had grown up amid her kisses and caresses, and now he felt the presence of someone else edging, intruding into his place, someone other than my father. My father's love, maybe because of its very nature, had never disturbed him, in the same way that my mother's affection for me, my younger brother, and my sister had never made him jealous. But this did. Perhaps it was that he felt protective toward my father, saw my father rather than himself as left out. At any rate, he began to resent the guest. Oh, not deeply or rudely—if anything, rather pitifully. My mother understood, of course, and I can see her kissing my brother on the forehead and stroking his curls, saying, "What is it, darling? Don't be sad." It wasn't easy to be sad in the house if she was happy, and, indeed, she could not really be happy if anyone in the house was sad. There was something in her of the nurse, the angel. Except, unlike angels, who are ever in a state of bliss, there was no paradise for her as long as anyone was in hell. And so, although my brother could hardly be described as being in hell, his state of mind disturbed her. "Come on, *cocchetto,* come with us to Florence. You need a change. You are always in your books. Let's go. We'll have fun. You and me, Papa, and Millo."

Millo would stand next to him and smile at him amiably. My brother would be persuaded to take the trip, and they would go to Florence, with my father driving his blue, open Chevrolet. And certainly the trip helped my brother's spirits. He would come back with a rare edition of Sophocles, perhaps, wrapped in tissue paper, and treat it as if he were handling a butterfly and barely let me touch it.

"I remember once they went to Rome together," my brother told me quite recently, by "they" meaning my mother and Millo, of course. *I* don't remember, or remember only vaguely. That *he* remembers shows how concerned he was.

Certainly I remember many trips, but most or all of them were with my father, in his car. We went to the sea, and Millo stayed with us there. And there were trips to the neighboring hill towns, and to Pisa, Lucca, and Pistoia, where my father bought fruit trees in the nurseries, and sometimes even to Genoa, Millo's home town. He always carried his old leather briefcase with him, for his lichens, and took more pleasure in strolling around the public parks than following us into the museums.

Often he would repair to a bar or coffee shop. These were his havens. He was a gourmet. In a restaurant he could become almost fierce with the chef if the cooking disappointed him. His usual mild, sweet countenance could turn an angry red. That was about the only aspect of him my mother had difficulty with. It was rare, though. He knew the best restaurants—especially in Genoa. There he would usually take you to the grottolike establishments near the harbor. The kitchen was near the entrance, so the fumes and steam could escape up through the open door. The cooks, usually women, greeted him by name. They would serve him well. They liked him—a real *intenditore* of their art.

He lived with his sister, who was unmarried. She worked in an office and looked after him. Recently, in an anthology, I've seen a poem of his in which she appears as a little girl. The poem is addressed to his father. "Father," it says, in rough translation, "even if you weren't my father I would have loved you, not only because one winter morning, glad, you gave us news of the first violet growing outside the window by the wall, and because you counted for us the lights of the houses as they went on up the mountain one by one, but also because once, as you were about to spank my little sister, you saw her cringing from you and, immediately stopping, you picked her up and kissed her and held her in your arms as if to protect her from the wicked fellow you'd been a moment before that."

My mother was forever writing to Millo, and often there was a letter from him in the mail. Both had the clearest writing, though there was nothing slow or childish about it. She wrote her letters on light, pale-blue stationery that she bought at Pineider, in Florence—one of the few luxuries she indulged in. She used not a fountain pen but a little wooden pen and nib that she dipped in a brass inkwell. Sometimes she would enclose a leaf, or a small drawing of it, or a sketch—perhaps the profile of one of us or of a guest—the thin line of her sharp pencil supplementing her description in quick, strong, black pen strokes. Sometimes I would watch her as she wrote, and in her face there was a reflection of the pleasure it showed when he was present; as she paused between one phrase and another, I could see that her eyes weren't on me or on the room but on whatever she was thinking of, and if I interrupted her she would say, "Be quiet a little now, love."

One could see she put her best effort into her letters to him. All her letters were spirited and spontaneous, but those to him had something more—a certain brilliance.

After her death in 1963, Millo put together excerpts from them into a small book and published it. The letters spanned almost thirty years—from 1936 to 1963. "Reading them," one critic wrote, "it occurred to me that many of us ought to throw away the pen, which in our hands is a hoe and in hers a little April branch." They were full of quick flashes, impressions, vivid touches, thoughts about people, plants, places, books, her work, her mood, the war. Some of them were written to him from England, where we spent seven years as refugees during the war and where for a while he had even thought of coming to join us; a few from Africa, where she had gone after my sister had a baby there; most of them from the house in Siena; and one or two from the Rome clinic, a month before her death.

They were quite innocent, these letters, but my father, who in thirty years had never appeared jealous, now in his old age—he was in his late seventies—seemed to view the book with suspicion. Perhaps it was its form that troubled him—not whole letters but excerpts. The excerpts in themselves weren't compromising, but what about the rest? What had been left out? Why hadn't the opening and closing words or lines been included? No, he didn't altogether approve of the publication. He thanked Millo for the inscribed copy he received, but not with the cordiality of old times, and a word or two he used (which I never saw) upset Millo so much that he wrote assuring me that his relations with my mother had never been anything more than a strong friendship—that, in other words, they had not been lovers.

I thought of my mother's life, of how unreasonably and hatefully angry my father would get with her, of her silences, her patience, her impatience, and her gloom, of the many long winters in the lonely house, and I wrote to him that I was sorry to learn that they had not been lovers, that I wished they had been, for in that case my mother's life would have been richer, happier.

A few years later he died without answering that letter of mine. Now I think I know why: It didn't deserve an answer—if ever there was a relationship one didn't have to feel sorry about, it was theirs.

[1973]

A Moment

Once in a while, toward the end of a meal, sitting at the table on which the children had completely disarranged the well-laid pattern of dishes, glasses, and silver, as one bounced on a chair, the other played on the floor, and his wife tried to feed the baby, he would do something which at that table seemed utterly out of place—like eating a pear with a fork and knife. The effort wouldn't last long. Before he had half finished, he would have to divert it to something else, like breaking up a fight. Still, the effort did give him a little satisfaction. It removed him from this table; for a moment he was far away, alone, at some peaceful inn, with a white tablecloth not spotted by ketchup or jam but on which the only color was the wine's reflection.

Peace and quiet—they seemed outside his range now, things he thought about but didn't experience anymore. Even when his children were asleep, his wife reading in the next room, and he had a cigarette between his fingers and a glass beside him, he wasn't really at rest. No, the feeling eluded him. It seemed to come to him only in his sleep. But was sleep peace and quiet? Not exactly. You needed to be awake to savor peace and quiet. They weren't just a void, a passive, inert state. They were a rich experience.

Love gave you a certain respite, he thought, and he remembered the long kisses, lips never parting, and a heavy calm, akin to sleep, falling upon him. Well, that couldn't happen with his wife; for one thing, she couldn't breathe through her nose and had to keep her mouth open at all times. And then, she thought they were past kissing. She always increased his age by at least five years. "There you are, going on to fifty," she would say, though he was only forty-three.

While working—painting, sketching—he had come on some of the brightest, clearest, serenest moments of his life. But one couldn't go and paint just because it promised calm. One needed a little calm—especially inward calm—to begin with. It wasn't any good to just sit and wait for inspiration, either, like some phony mystic. To work he had to feel alert and, if not happy, at least a little removed from troubles, so that he might have some perspective of them.

Sleep, love, work—they were conducive to calm, but why couldn't one have a true, self-sustaining moment that didn't need the support of other things? Why couldn't he just sit and draw peace from a cigarette, for instance, or, better still, just sit doing nothing, not even smoking, and be content—savor time, pure time, soar in it like a bird in space, still for a moment. Not easy; not for him—or rarely. It was hard to gain that moment because it depended on abstracting oneself from all the little harrowing things that the day presented and that clung, stuck to you with a sort of love. Yet it could be done, and when it was, it was each time a triumph.

He looked at the light of sunset that through gaps in the foliage of the maple trees came in through the window and lit up the antique rose of the wall into something very live and changing—a wavering, small oval blushing, metamorphosing into a circle, and then into an ellipse, and almost fading; then returning to what it was, an oval, again fading: a subtle, consummate dancer on the wall. For a moment as he watched that dance, he was happy, he was content. Effortlessly he watched it till, reviving, flaring up at odd times by surprise, it waned little by little.

Well, there it was—a moment. He felt, as he did after some intensely happy experience, almost like weeping. He got up from his chair; the sun had set. He looked at the sky. No cloud caught the sun as well as the wall had caught it. A dingy thing, that wall, compared to clouds and flowers, but it had its moments. Not every day, not even every week (and sometimes more than a month went by), but sooner or later it lit up, it shone, it lost its dullness; you almost forgot it was a wall.

[1968]

The Soft Core

It was suppertime. The bell had rung. Everyone was around the table except his father, nearly eighty. Sometimes he didn't hear the bell. So Giacomo went and knocked at his bedroom door.

No answer came. Going in, he found his father lying on the bed with his shoes on. His eyes were open, but they didn't seem to recognize Giacomo.

"Papa, dinner is ready."

"What? What is it?"

"Dinner," Giacomo said, without any hope now that he would come to it.

"Dinner," his father echoed feebly, making no effort to get up but rather trying to connect the word. Dinner where, when, his eyes seemed to be saying.

"You are not feeling well?"

"Yes, I'm well," he said, almost inaudibly. "I am well, but . . . you . . . you are . . . ?" His father could not quite place him.

"Giacomo. I am Giacomo," the son said.

His name seemed to make little or no impression on his father. Indeed, he seemed to have forgotten it already and to be groping for some point of reference, something familiar to sustain his mind, which was wavering without hold in space and time.

Quickly Giacomo stepped out of the room, through an anteroom, and opened the dining-room door. His wife, his sister, their children, and a guest were round the table eating, talking. He called his wife.

She rose and hurried over. "Is he all right?"

"No."

"Like last time?"

"No, no, not as bad."

They had in mind a time five or six months before, when Giacomo's sister had called from Rome for a phone number that their father had in his address book. Giacomo, then as now, had gone to call him in his room, and found him on his bed, unconscious, breathing thickly, and in a sort of spasm. A stroke, he thought. Thoroughly alarmed, he rushed back to the phone, hung up after a few hurried words of explanation, and called the doctor. In a few minutes, everyone in the house was round his father's bed. It seemed to Giacomo that the end had come. Its suddenness appalled him. He wasn't prepared for it. He had been so unfriendly to his father lately—almost rude. Why, only the day before, when his father had asked him to drive him into town, as he often did, Giacomo told him that he couldn't, that he was too busy, which wasn't really true. And other things came to mind—his curt replies to his father's questions, the long silences at table, and when there was some conversation, his father's being left out of it, ignored; his not laughing at his father's little jokes; not complimenting him on the fruit that came from trees he had planted, and for which he so much expected a word of praise when it was served at table. If Giacomo had only had some warning, to make up for his behavior—oh, he would have been his father's chauffeur, if he had known, talked with him about his books, his philosophy, his fruit trees, laughed at his jokes, listened keenly to the things he said and pretended it was the first time he heard him saying them. With a sense of anguish, he watched his father, unconscious, on the bed. He couldn't die just yet; he must talk again. The prospect that he mightn't—that he might live on paralyzed and speechless on that bed—was even worse.

They waited for the doctor. Yet, even before the doctor came, something might be done. He couldn't just wait and watch his father die in this awful, sunken state. To ease his breathing, Giacomo took out the dentures, which seemed to lock his father's mouth, and opened the window, because the radiator, going full steam, had made the room stiflingly hot. Then he hurried upstairs. In the drug cabinet, there were some phials of a relaxant—papaverine—that had once been prescribed for his father to help his circulation. Giacomo gave him two, by injection—a certain knowledge of medicine having remained from when he had studied it, and even practiced it, long ago—then waited for the effect. But even before the drug could possibly have had one, his father seemed to improve, to rise from his prostration. The breathing was easier. His limbs were slowly relaxing. It seemed that whatever had commanded them to stiffen was easing its hold, loosening up. His eyes began to look and not just gaze; the sounds coming from his mouth were not just moans but language, or the beginnings of it—monosyllables, bits with which words and phrases could be made. And the improvement was continuous. By the time the doctor arrived, he was moving his limbs and uttering words, though the words were disconnected. As the doctor examined him and prescribed treatment, his voice gained strength. He answered questions; he sat up; he even asked for food. An hour or two later, he was reading, making notes, pencil in hand and postcard on the page, in case he should want to underline a word or a sentence that had struck him. And he looked very sweet there on the bed in his pajamas, reading under the light, thin and ethereal, all involved in that spiritual form of exercise. His body—the material aspect of it, his physique—which had been so much in the foreground and had so preoccupied them a few hours before, now seemed quite forgotten, back where it should be, something one is hardly aware of, that works better when one's mind is off it.

So his father had been given back to life, and Giacomo had another chance to be warm and friendly to him. At intervals that night, he slipped into the room to see how he was doing, or, if the light was out, afraid to wake him, listened outside with his ear to the door. Oh, this was easy enough to do, and it was easy to be solicitous the next day—ask how he was, and help him with the half-dozen drugs the doctor had prescribed, and with the diet. But when his father—well again, his usual self, full of the same old preoccupations and requests—resumed getting about and Giacomo heard his aged yet determined step coming toward his room, something in him stiffened as if in defense, and he waited for the door to open.

His father came in without a knock, as was his custom. "After all, cars now are pleasingly designed," he said in a slightly plaintive, slightly polemical voice, from just inside the doorway.

For a moment, Giacomo wondered what he was talking about. Then he remembered his father's arguing a few days before against an ordinance barring cars from the main street of the town. Giacomo had disagreed, and now his father was bringing the subject up again, bothered as always by anyone's disputing his viewpoint. "You like them?" Giacomo said.

"Well, they are certainly more pleasant to watch than were carriages drawn by panting, weary horses. Besides, people put up with much more disturbing things than cars without complaining."

His father had his own peculiar ideas about traffic, about where Giacomo should park his car, about driving—about practically everything, in fact. He insisted on the frequent use of the horn, and if the person driving didn't blow it and he thought there was danger of a collision, he would shout to let the other party know that the car he was riding in was coming. It was almost as irritating as his bringing up an old argument and wanting to prove his point though a long time had passed. For him an argument was never closed. He went on pondering over it, debating it in his mind. One saw him doing it—wandering in the garden, pausing, starting to walk again, a true peripatetic—and if some new thought came to him he didn't hesitate to let you know it, wherever you might be.

About this matter of the ordinance, in the end Giacomo just nodded. Appeased, his father asked him for a favor. It was a way of showing he was on good terms with him. "Are you going into town tomorrow afternoon?"

Giacomo never planned his days ahead if he could help it. "Well, yes, I can go in, if you like."

"Would you? I need to buy some brown paper to line the crates of cherries with."

The cherries weren't ripe yet.

"Ah, yes, yes, I'll take you," Giacomo said.

"At about three o'clock?"

"The shops, you know, don't open until four."

"Say at half past three."

It took ten minutes to drive into town.

"Ah, yes, yes, all right."

Two or three times the next day, his father would remind him of the trip, and at a few minutes past three be at his door, ready to go. Giacomo would prevent himself from making any comments, but the very effort not to make them would keep him silent. "You are so silent," his father would observe in the car. "What is it?"

"Nothing. I am sorry."

"You have such a long face."

It was the hardest thing for Giacomo to look cheerful when he wasn't. He had no more control over his face than over his mood, and felt there was no poorer dissembler in the world than he. "I'm sorry if I can't be gayer," he would reply.

Sometimes his father would come into his room to ask him for advice on where to send an article he had written. But it seemed to Giacomo that he was asking for advice only in order to discard it. "I would send it to Wyatt, if I were you," Giacomo would suggest. But his father had already made up his mind whom to send it to, and it wasn't to Wyatt.

Speaking of his works, his father would say to him, "It is a *new* philosophy."

"Yes," Giacomo would reply, and be quite unable to elaborate. It was a pity, because his father yearned for articulate assent and recognition. People found his work difficult; some said they couldn't understand it. Nothing irked him more than to hear this. "Even Sylvia," he would say, referring to a guest, a pretty girl with a ready smile and pleasant manner, "who I don't think is very widely read in philosophy, found it clear." He never doubted that praise was offered in earnest. And no praise seemed more important to him than that which came from girls, from pretty women. Then a blissful smile would light his face and linger in his eyes.

With the single-mindedness of someone who has devoted his whole life to a cause, he gave or sent his articles around. He was so surely entrenched in his ideas that nothing could budge him from them. Each problem, each concept he came on had to be thrashed out and made known. Intent on it, if he met you—no matter where—he might stop and, pronouncing each word as if he were grinding it out, say without preamble, "Creativity is an underived, active, original, powerfully present, intrinsic, self-sustaining principle—something that cannot be resolved or broken up into preëxistent, predetermined data, and that is fraught with a negative possibility."

Giacomo would nod. He had been brought up to the tune of phrases such as these, had grown up with them, and though he had only begun to understand them he had finished by believing in them. At any rate, he was convinced there was a good measure of truth in what his father said. And yet he couldn't make it his own. "Negative possibility," "*causa sui*," "psychic reality," "primal active"—these terms perplexed him. He knew they were full of meaning, for his father, but he couldn't grasp what lay beneath. They weren't in his language, and he looked on them with the detachment of one who is given instruments he can never use.

The extraordinary importance his father gave his work! One had the feeling that nothing—not his wife, not his children—mattered to him quite so much as the vindication of certain principles. He probably saw his family, house, fruit trees, and philosophy as a whole—he had a unified view of everything—and felt that one could never damage the other; he probably even thought that his work was the key, the solution, to a host of problems, financial ones not excluded. Since he didn't teach and lived isolated in the country, to advance his views he tirelessly went to the post office to send off his manuscripts and books, as well as reprints of his articles, which he ordered by the hundreds. He sent them assiduously, and impatiently he waited for acknowledgments and answers that often failed to come.

It was all very admirable, but Giacomo couldn't really admire it.

He was more inclined to admire his mother, who painted and often hid her paintings in a cupboard. He thought of some of the landscapes she had done, particularly one of a row of vines, a study of green done with such love of leaf and branch and sod and sky its value couldn't be mistaken, yet, because his father—perhaps with a slight frown or tilting of his head—told her it was not among her best, she had put it in a cupboard, and it had never been framed until after her death. Paintings, his father said, looked better unframed. "Let's wait till we have a bit more money before buying one," he would say, which meant never to everyone but him.

His father wrote and spoke about the value of spontaneity in art and literature and all things, but was he spontaneous? He seemed the opposite to Giacomo sometimes—very deliberate and willful. And how he wanted to escape his father's will. He still felt it upon him as he had when he was a child, a boy, a young man. His father's will shaping his life. His brother's life, too. At school, his brother had been good at all subjects, including mathematics, so his father must have a scientist in the family and had strongly advised him—and wasn't advice, especially the advice of someone whom you admired, harder to disobey than a command?—to study physics and mathematics at college, subjects for which he had no special gift. His brother hadn't, as a result, fared well at college. And as for Giacomo, when he was twenty-two and had been away from home, overseas, for seven years—it was wartime—his father had written, making it seem urgent that he come back immediately. "You are coming home to save your mother," one of his letters said. And Giacomo, who would have wished to delay his return another year—there was a girl, there were his studies, well begun—had gone back only to find that his father had exaggerated, sort of been carried away.

Then his father had a way of asking Giacomo to do things that instinctively made him wish to disobey. He seemed to like asking favors, to ask them for the sake of asking. Giacomo had never answered a flat no; he wasn't that familiar with his father. Recently, though, he had done something worse. His father had called to tell him once again about a cistern whose drainage had become a fixed idea with him. Giacomo had made the mistake of contradicting, and now his father, pencil and paper in hand, came after him so he would get a thorough understanding of his plan. But Giacomo, who had heard enough of it, went off, leaving his father in a rage. Never before had he refused to listen. Now, doing so, he experienced a strange sense of freedom, as though he had shaken off the bonds of childhood. For a moment, he felt almost snug and comfortable in his attitude toward his father. Perhaps it wasn't all unjustified, he thought, and old, childhood resentments came back to him. He remembered a fall from horseback when he was a boy: limping home, with a gaping wound about the knee that needed stitching, his father scolding him for it, and the words of his mother—soothing, like something cool upon a burn—and her taking him to the hospital, the doctor telling her it might be better if she left the room, her replying that she had once been a nurse, staying with him, holding him by the hand while the doctor put the stitches in. His father had scolded him, instead. No, he thought, perhaps I am not altogether in the wrong.

But seeing his father watch the sunset in the garden as he so often did, absorbed in light, a man whom beauty had always held in sway, or hearing him recite a poem—though now he rarely did—enunciating the words in all their clearness, slowly, in a voice that seemed ever on the verge of breaking yet never broke and that seemed to pick each nuance of rhythm and of meaning, Giacomo felt his old love, respect, and admiration come back full to overflowing as when he was a child and it seemed to him that his father never could be wrong—in the realm of the spirit, a man of mighty aims and wider grasp.

And chancing to meet him late at night going into the kitchen for food, looking so frail and thin in his pajamas and so old without his dentures, Giacomo felt ashamed of himself. Oh, his unfriendliness was revolting. That he should be distant and cold toward his father now when he was weak and wifeless, now when he was so old he had become almost childish in some ways—laughing and crying with ease. It was unforgivable, horrible, inhuman. If it hadn't been for his father, where would they be, Giacomo asked himself. If his father hadn't taken his family out of Italy in time, they might all have perished in a German concentration camp. And he had seen that his children learned English almost from babyhood. And he had never raised a hand against them. And he had been generous with those who needed money or lodging or employment.

Well, there was nothing for it but to change his attitude. He must make more of an effort. No week went by without Giacomo's telling himself this. He would talk to his father as to a friend, about any subject that came to his mind. "What this town needs, I think," he said to him at lunch one day, trying to be nice, "is a newspaper. I'd like to start one."

"It would be a very bad idea," his father said.

"Why?"

"But it's obvious why," his father snapped with irritation and perhaps even dislike.

"Well, I wish you would explain it."

"But anyone can see that if there were only one newspaper in the country it would have a better chance of being a good one."

This wasn't like his father at all. He seemed only to want to contradict.

"I thought that to encourage writers and the arts, as well as trade, a local paper . . ." Giacomo didn't finish his sentence. Why should he? His father's face seemed full of aversion, as though Giacomo were saying something blasphemous.

The meal went on in silence. Giacomo looked up at his father. The lines of his face were still set in anger, and he was looking down at his plate, the segment nearest to him, almost at his napkin. No, one could not change, Giacomo thought. His father could not change. He himself could not change. Perhaps if one could fall into a state of oblivion one could change, but otherwise?

And then came the evening when his father did not turn up for supper and Giacomo went to call him in his room. It wasn't nearly as bad as the earlier time, when he thought his father had had a stroke—after all, now he was conscious, his breathing was normal, he wasn't in a spasm, and he could speak. Yet Giacomo had the same feeling that the end had come. His father seemed so tenuously, so delicately attached to life, like down of a thistle in the wind. And when he spoke he was like a flame that wavered in the air this way and that, sometimes almost detached from the body that fed it.

It seemed as though he were living in another century and in another land. "We'll have to ask the Byzantine government," he said.

"What Byzantine government?" Giacomo asked.

"In Constantinople," his father replied, as if he found it odd for anyone to ask a question with such an obvious answer.

It was strange he should speak of the Byzantines. His father's ancestors were from Venice, and Giacomo sensed that his father was talking of the affairs of six or seven centuries ago.

To bring him back to this one, he began to speak to him, to explain just what had happened and to reassure him. He told his father that his memory would all come back to him in a little while, after he had drunk some coffee. And he went on to tell him who he was, and, when his wife appeared with a cup of coffee, who she was, and about the house, his fruit trees, his articles and books, the recent letters; he went over all his life with him, in a fashion.

Intent on reconnecting himself to the past and those around him, patiently, like someone threading beads, the present not quite with him, his father sat up on the bed and, speaking very gently, asked him questions. "Where is Mama?" he said, referring to his own wife.

For a second, Giacomo didn't answer. He had expected and feared the question. Then he said, "She died. You know, she died three years ago."

"Ah, yes," he said sadly, and for a moment father and son seemed not so much to look at one another as to survey the last days of her life.

"And you say we went to England?"

"Yes, do you remember, in 1938? You took us there."

"Yes. You children were so good on that crowded train."

"And when we got to England you saw a sign that read, 'Cross at your own risk,' and you said it was worth coming just to see that sign, and that in Italy it would have said, 'It is severely forbidden to cross.' "

His father smiled. "It was a sign of freedom."

"Yes."

"And then we came back here?"

"Yes, by boat, after the war. The bailiff met you in Naples, all the money he had for you stuffed under his garters, in his socks. He was afraid of thieves."

They laughed together. Laughter, it has the power to reconcile lost friends, to bridge the widest gaps.

"Your wife . . . tell me her name again."

"Jessie."

"Ah, yes, so dear," he said tenderly. He got up slowly and went to his desk for a pencil. He said he wanted to write the name down before he forgot it once more. He looked at the desk aimlessly, then pulled out the wrong drawer. "My little things," he said, "where are they?" He looked like a child whose toys a gust of wind has blown away.

Giacomo found a pencil for him, and his father wrote the name Jessie on a piece of paper. Next, he paused by the bookcase. All the books in it he had annotated, but now he looked at them as if for the first time.

"This one you wrote," Giacomo said.

His father looked at it closely. "This one I know. But the others . . ." He stroked his head as if to scold it. "And these are your poems," he said, seeing a flimsy little book with his son's name. "I remember the first one you wrote, about the stars, when you were ten. Strange, your mother's father, too, wrote one about the stars—his best one."

"You see, you remember a lot."

"About the distant past. Such a long time . . . for you, too." He smiled, then, looking at him warmly, said, "Our Giacomo," and it was as it had been when Giacomo was a boy and his father used to look at him and say "Ajax," because he considered him generous and strong.

Strangely, now, Giacomo found that he *could* talk to his father, easily, affably, and with pleasure, and that his voice was gentle. When his father was well, he couldn't, but now he was reaching the secret, soft core—the secret, gentle, tender core that is in each of us. And he thought, *This* is what my father is really like; the way he is now, this is his real, his naked self. For a moment it has been uncovered; he is young again. This was the young man his mother had met and fallen in love with; this was the man on whose knees he had played, who had carried him on his shoulders up the hills, who had read to him the poems he liked so much. His other manner was brought on by age, by a hundred preoccupations, by the years, by the hardening that comes with the turning of the years.

Already, with coffee, with their talk, his father was recovering his memory. Soon he would be up and about, and soon Giacomo wouldn't be able to talk to him as he did now. But though he wouldn't, he would think of his father in the way he had been given back to him, the way he had been and somewhere—deep and secret and only to be uncovered sometimes—still was.

[1972]

By the Bedside

She was in bed, the double bed in her room where, thirty years before, her daughter was born, where her father-in-law had died, and where she herself would die in a matter of months. Thin, pale, her eyes clear and lucid in contrast to her pallor, her hair tied back by ribbons, baring a neck still young and supple, she was sitting propped against two feather pillows. Beside her was her granddaughter Rita, six years old, just back from school. The child's mother, her own daughter, watched from a red velvet sofa at the foot of the bed, her arms resting on the sofa's back, her chin on her arms, her legs drawn up under her. An old family friend—a chubby, rubicund man—was sitting on a chair by the wall and was looking at the sick woman with bright, keen, compassionate eyes. He had admired her, loved her, for twenty-five years, and now he knew she wasn't going to live very much longer. Her eldest son, Guido, was sitting beside her, holding her hand. Another son, Bruno, was sitting in an armchair by the window.

Bruno was, or had been, a doctor. Four years before, he had given up medicine to devote himself to painting, only to become a doctor again, this year, for his mother, her own private doctor, one of three doctors who took care of her—there were two others in town, a surgeon and the family physician. Bruno followed their orders and consulted with them. Indeed, it seemed to him that now he was more a doctor than ever before, continually looking into textbooks, trying to devise ways to alleviate his mother's symptoms. Yes, now he was back in medicine with a vengeance. When he'd had an office, painting, sketching had claimed most of his energy—which seemed hardly fair to his patients. So often and so eagerly, when a patient left, he would clear his desk of his medical equipment and take up his sketches. Off the dreary instruments would go to make space for sharp pencils, soft brushes, bright colors. And how reluctantly he would replace them when patients came. No, it didn't seem fair not to devote more time to them. This and the unexpected sale of three paintings had induced him to abandon his medical practice.

He had painted since he was eleven but had decided to study medicine because he believed he could never make a living by painting. The public's, the gallery owners', and the critics' attitudes discouraged him. And medicine at one point—when he was nineteen or twenty—had seemed more humane than the humanities, more artful than art. And, besides, his parents—perhaps because his mother was herself a painter, his father a philosopher, and they knew from personal experience the hardships that artists were apt to meet—had always wanted him to be a doctor. Since his early boyhood, his mother, especially, had seen him as a physician. "Look at those hands," she would say. "Aren't those the hands of a doctor!" But had there been yet another reason, he wondered, now that he was devoting so much time to her, for his mother's wanting him to study medicine? Had she, subconsciously or superconsciously, known even then, years ago, in his youth, that someday she would fall sick, and had she hoped that he might be able to cure her? Had the future determined the past? Had some future illness, hardly suspected (except by some intuition), prompted her encouraging him to become a doctor? He wondered and he mused on the irony of it. For he was quite unable to treat her effectively or cure her. The problem was too large, much too large. Cancer. Nothing less. He felt unequal to it, and his degree and medical training were no reward for her wish of long ago. So he fretted there in his armchair. And he knew that she saw his preoccupied look, felt his pessimism, his lack of hope—just what he didn't want her to feel. "Bruno worries so," he had heard her say to others; "worries so about me."

A neighbor, a young woman from a nearby farm, plump, with a kerchief on her head and a smile that showed her gums and massive set of teeth, had come into the room for a moment.

"And how are things at home?" the sick woman asked her.

"Oh, everyone's well, thank you, Signora. We must be content—when there's health there's everything. Isn't it so?" The neighbor looked around her as if she had uttered something very profound. Then she said goodbye and left.

"Certain people have a real gift for *gaffes,*" the woman in the bed said. "Imagine saying to me 'When there's health there's everything.' "

The way she spoke the others couldn't help laughing, and her old friend exclaimed, "What a mentality!"

A maid who had been with the family for a generation, and who had brought the woman a cup of tea that lay untouched on a bedside table, lingered by the door. The sick woman's husband came in and asked her how she was feeling. With a slight tilt of her head, she brushed aside the question that was put to her much too often, and he left as softly as he had come.

"Won't you have some tea, Signora?" the maid asked.

"No, I'd rather have this," she replied, and, letting go of her son's hand, she reached to grasp from her bedside table a little glass with a brown mixture of water and laudanum. She took it and sipped from it the way one might sip a very potent liqueur. "I like it," she said. "It has a bitter taste, but I like it. No, it isn't altogether unpleasant. An opiate. I'm getting to like it."

"It's good?" the child Rita said with a smile.

"Yes, yes."

"Will you let me taste it?"

"It isn't for little girls."

"If I get sick, can I have some?"

"You wouldn't like it."

She took another, longer sip, commanded by the gnawing abdominal pain. Again and again she sipped of it, as if answering a call. And little by little she lapsed into a keen critical mood that had something euphoric about it, induced by the opiate. "How can he come and ask me how I am all the time?" she said. "Heavens, can't he see how I am? Can't he gather the plain, simple fact? Ah, these solicitous people. They do so want some good news. What am I expected to say? That I'm feeling better? But what pleasure is there in lying?"

"He meant well," the maid said, "the poor signorino."

"But that's exactly what irks me. This hopeful attitude. As if I were supposed to produce some surprise every minute."

The cook, a widow, pleasantly round and serene, came in, and, seeing that she was sitting in bed, alert and fondling the glass in her hands, said, "You see, the signora looks better. See what good color she has? Eh, you are looking better, Signora."

"I just finished saying—but what's the use?"

"You are not feeling better, Signora?"

"A little better, perhaps."

"God be thanked. You'll see how if you continue like this you'll get better in no time. Isn't it true she looks better?" The cook turned to the others, and when they didn't reply she said, "To me she looks a lot better." In the continuing silence, she looked at the teacup. She touched its side and said, "The tea's getting cold. Shall I get you another, Signora?"

"No, thank you. I'd rather drink this," she replied, looking at the glass in her hands.

"Then I'll take it out." She took the cup and left the room.

"God bless her," she said. "There's another. Such kindness, but kindness can smother. She's a dear woman, but she does not understand. While you, Rita"—turning to the little girl—"you understand how Nonna is feeling."

"Yes," the child said.

"You don't ask silly questions."

The little girl looked at her without a word.

"Silly questions are those that people ask when they know the answers to them all too well. Then why do they ask them? Because they want a different answer. But you are not like that."

"Rita, tell Nonna how you won't let me come fetch you at school tomorrow," the child's mother interrupted from the sofa.

The little girl shrugged her shoulders.

"Isn't it so? You don't want me to, do you?"

The child shrugged her shoulders again.

"Children," the sick woman said, "are often embarrassed by parents showing up at their schools."

"You are not embarrassed by me, Rita, are you?" Rita's mother said. She was a tall, exotic-looking young woman, and was wearing an African shawl over her shoulders.

"A little."

The others all laughed.

"I told you," Rita's grandmother said. "I remember when I went to see Bruno at his school in England. I thought my visit would please him, but it didn't, did it?"

"Yes, it did," Bruno said from his chair by the window.

"You don't remember, perhaps."

He did remember. With pain he remembered her coming to see him at his boarding school in England, where they had all gone from Italy as refugees, just before the Second World War. She had travelled by train from London to the Midlands town, and suddenly there she was at his school—in her best dress, slender, vigorous, striking, effusive, cheerful, and absolutely unself-conscious—hugging him, while he felt all sorts of constraints. Under the monitors' gaze, which of course didn't daunt her, he showed her around the common room, the dining room, the dormitories. He introduced her to the housemaster and the matron, forbidding characters to him but to her not in the least. Then they walked around the school grounds. He took her to the tennis and squash courts, where—he didn't tell her—the monitors had beaten him up for having appealed to the housemaster to be spared the six strokes of the cane that they had wanted to give him. As he and his mother walked, boys nodded to him and smiled, whereas had he been alone they would have ignored him. On their way, they met a few teachers. The teachers, too, he had to introduce. They, too, oddly, seemed very friendly. And little by little, as they walked, she saw his discomfort and that she was a burden to him—she, his mother, whom he loved more than all people—and she said with a laugh, "You are not ashamed of me, are you?" "No, no," he implored and clung close to her and hugged her, and, even as he did, he felt embarrassed to be seen hugging his mother. She took him to lunch in a restaurant on the main street of town—or High Street, as they called it—and there, too, he was quiet and subdued, and wished she didn't speak quite so loudly. As he accompanied her to the station, he could see she was sorry that she had not made him happy with her visit. He hated himself for not being made happy. He wanted to shrug off his stupid timidity, his awkwardness, as though it were a tight-fitting collar, but it clung to him; he could not shrug it off. He kissed her goodbye. Some of his sadness had worn off on her. "Cheer up," she said as she left. "Try to be happy." Smiling sadly, she waved to him from the train.

"Is it true, Bruno?" his sister asked, pointedly, accusingly.

He sighed and smiled wanly. "I don't know."

"They should be left alone," his mother continued. "Oh, those terrible schools. And not only in England. Here, too."

He remembered her coming to his school here, before they went to England. She was so much herself and so far from being part of a group that she always appeared distinct, different, and therefore noticeable. He cringed at his being embarrassed by her. For surely there had been nothing to be embarrassed about—she was beautiful, smart, and perfectly normal. In fact, as she walked, so free and sentient, looking at the landscape and the street scenes with the eyes of a painter, of an observer, sometimes with pity, sometimes with an amused smile, sometimes with wonder, he often thought she seemed the only normal person around, a true human being, one "born as at sunrise." Sometimes she stopped to contemplate a building and, full of admiration, pointed it out to him. Or pointed out the pigeons wheeling about the main square. Or the grace of a tree. Or stopped to play peekaboo with a baby—even once, he remembered, with the baby of a tourist couple: the child laughed while its parents looked on, condescending, suspicious, until they, too, were won over. People didn't quite know how to place her. She looked foreign in her own town. While the other mothers all went to the hairdresser, wore lipstick and rouge and the tailored suits that were the fashion, she wore her hair in a chignon, never any makeup at all, and sweaters and bright plaid skirts. Like a peasant girl out in the fields. Except that she wore these skirts and sweaters in town, which the peasant never did, and hers, perhaps, were finer, bought at stores like Old England, in Florence.

But, above all, she could not be intimidated—not by anyone. She treated his teachers, even the school principal, as equals, which of course was the right thing to do, but quite astonishing in a country where people paid great attention to rank. Also, she spoke her mind, said anything that came into her head, quite spontaneously. In the seventh grade, he had a teacher named Ricci—a priest in a black cassock, who if the class ever got unruly could create an awesome silence with one shout. Well, she thought the cassock was very chic and one day told Ricci so, making his dark brooding face suddenly lighten and take on some color. Later, she invited him to lunch to meet a friend from Florence—a Latinist, a celebrity, whose pupil Ricci had been. "Oh, the boy Ricci!" the professor from Florence said on greeting Bruno's teacher, and she laughed. Lunch went very smoothly, but Bruno didn't say a word and felt weary throughout. He was only thankful that the conversation didn't verge on politics, for she hated Fascists with a strong, almost visceral hatred, and God knows what would have happened then. In the classroom, Ricci often spoke in glowing terms about the war in Ethiopia, and his mother could get very emphatic.

Deference she had for the poor and the sick and the aged, not for the socially important and wealthy. She gave freely to beggars and left waiters large tips. Occasionally, she and his father fetched him from school in their car—a rare foreign make, almost an antique, with a funny-sounding horn, which they thought nothing of. His father, too, could embarrass him, making him read poetry aloud to him in a coffee shop, insisting on it.

She kept sipping the laudanum from the glass that now was almost empty. "No," she said, looking toward her old friend on the chair, "they didn't approve of me in public, my children." And Bruno felt as though she had guessed his every thought.

"We didn't?" he said.

"I did," his elder brother, who sat beside her, said.

"Perhaps Guido," she said, and, after a last sip, putting the empty glass on the table, she took his hand and held it tight.

"Oh, they were quite critical. I think they would have preferred a more conventional mother."

"No," they protested. "What are you saying!"

•

On one occasion that Bruno remembered with some displeasure, his mother *had* tried to be conventional, to please his younger brother, Sandro. Sandro's bride-to-be came from a very rich Milanese family. She had a stepfather who tried to make Sandro feel like a pauper because his family was always in debt. A brash and inquisitive man, not only did he ask brazen questions but went to the length of getting a private detective to look into the family accounts. "If you want to know about us," Sandro told him, working up some courage, "you should look in the Encyclopædia Britannica." He was referring to an ancestor—a linguist—who figured in the eleventh edition. But the man was interested in the family's present net worth in cash, not in past accomplishments—especially of a literary nature. With his wife he came to the house. Oh, he was friendly enough—indeed, very cordial—but the intent was obvious: he wanted to look things over. Sandro's family had some very good things—furniture and paintings far finer, in fact, than the man and his wife had in their various houses.

"I like these panels," the wife said of four carved white and gold-leafed eighteenth-century doors that were hung on opposite walls of the front hall. "And that desk and that painting." Off these were sent, together with the proceeds from the sale of a large chunk of land, as wedding gifts. For the wedding itself, Bruno's mother went to the hairdresser. She had always washed her hair herself with a pail of rainwater because the running water was hard. If she used tap water, she added a little vinegar to it, to dissolve the lime, and then in front of a beautiful old gilded mirror in her bedroom she combed the long, straight black hair that went halfway down her back. That day, she wore a new suit and even put on lipstick. Then they all drove to the bride's family's country house in the north. And she looked meek for the first time in her life, a little conventional, unlike herself, trying to please Sandro, for appearances' sake. But when she looked at Bruno she knew what he was thinking.

"It all seems so false around here," he said.

"Yes, but what can we do? We are making a little effort. Don't you see? You disapprove of me whatever I do."

"No," he said, and he hugged her and kissed her.

But she was right.

A year or two later, coming back from Africa, where she had gone to visit her daughter, who had just given birth to Rita, she was met by Bruno at the airport. The flight—she had never flown before going to Africa—had exhilarated her and she looked radiant, triumphant, as if she still had wings. Lean and sunburned, carrying two large baskets, she set them down and hugged him fervently. She had remembered how as a child he had longed for a pineapple—a fruit he had never seen, for it couldn't be bought in Italy before the war—and so now, there in the airport, she had a basket full of pineapples and mangoes for him. Enthusiastically she displayed them not just to him but to the porter. In her other basket was a crimson rug. She unfolded it right there and then. She gave a mango to the porter, and in a Roman accent (she was born and grew up in Rome) she spoke with the porter, a man after her own heart, full of exclamations and questions, and she was happy to answer them all. In Rome it was cold and it was raining, but she had brought the African sun—no, for a moment she *was* the sun. And people milled around her, curious to hear her descriptions. She brought more things out of the basket with the rug—strange, wonderful things—but Bruno was trying to hurry her out and as she looked at him some of her happiness faded.

"Let's go," he said.

Thinking back to it now in his mother's bedroom Bruno felt he had stifled a lovely theatrical scene.

She asked for and received a little more laudanum, but not without Bruno's feeling apprehensive about it; if she took it at this rate, she would need more and more—soon a whole bottle a day—and he knew its side effects. "I was born in the last century," she said, taking a sip from the glass. "Much better than this one. I had only five years of it, but they mean something." Her lips parted in amusement. "I remember my dear father meeting one of his best friends in the street and pretending he didn't know him, walking on with a straight face, and when this friend took hold of his arm and faced him and shook him, my father acted astonished, even offended, till this friend actually thought he must have made a mistake, and apologized profusely; at which point my father burst out laughing."

Rita, surprised by this incredible story, herself broke into peals of uncontrollable laughter. And the others laughed, too.

"But no, is it true?" Rita asked.

"Yes, I'm telling you. Of course it's true. They did things like that then; they were gayer." She turned sombre. "I have the faults of those who hang on and shouldn't hang on. Better put an end to them. I have the faults of the old."

"No, you have none," Guido said.

"Oh, heaven knows I do! But they may not be as bad as the faults of the young, though not of this darling here," she said, and she leaned over to take Rita in her arms.

"Oh, what darlings you all were when you were small—then nothing I did ever seemed wrong to you. And when I nursed you! Especially Bruno there!" She laughed and imitated, to his infinite embarrassment, the eager sucking sounds a baby makes at the breast. He closed his eyes. He inhaled deeply. "But then what happened? You grew up, you grew every year a little less pleased."

"No."

"Yes."

She looked past Bruno out the window, where the leaves of the Virginia creeper were waving, and an amused smile lit her face. "I knew a painter in Rome—Donghi his name was—who mainly did paintings of trees, the leaves one by one, very carefully. But on a day like this he couldn't paint. 'Did you get any work done today?' I asked him one time. 'Eh, no,' he complained—he had a very melancholy voice. 'The leaves are moving.' "

Rita laughed and the others smiled.

Though his mother was in bed with a glass of diluted laudanum in her hand, for a moment Bruno had the illusion she was at the dining-room table with a glass of red wine and that they were all there listening to her conversing.

The illusion didn't last long. The laudanum was affecting her respiration, upsetting her stomach. She coughed. She coughed so hard that she gagged, though when he moved to help her, she shook her head. If only he could get her some heroin. Heroin was the most effective painkiller and had the fewest side effects. But of course it was also a potent euphoriant, and because the addicts were after it its sale had been banned. He had tried to find some substitute, but none had worked very well. Maybe he could get the heroin illegally. He thought about it, and of the flights of fancy that might ensue.

Finally, the retching subsided. "What are you thinking of, Bruno?" she asked.

He tried to smile, he tried to look cheerful and wished he could tell some funny story. But if there was anyone in the room who could make people smile, who could make people laugh, even at this late stage, it was she.

[1980]

Last Rites

"Better to die like the ancients," she said. "A great high fever, and you are spirited away."

She must have had in mind the fever that had marked the beginning of her illness, and that, without surgery, would indeed have spirited her away in a few days. Instead, she had had all the "benefits" of modern medicine—two major operations, sickening tests, transfusions, a cabinetful of drugs—and after fourteen months she was still alive.

The first operation had broken the fever but not cured her. The second, to which she had submitted at the doctors' insistence almost exactly a year after the first, had revealed an incurable condition, and instead of seeing fulfilled their promise that she would "get really well" she had seen strange new medicines being brought into her room, medicines that were supposed to retard the wild proliferation of the cells, and that the doctors, unwilling to tell her what her illness was, tried to pass off as something else, until one night, her pain keeping her awake, her suspicions fully roused, and her questions becoming more and more pressing, one of her sons, himself a doctor, told her. All along, he had thought she should be told, believing that life might seem lighter to her and each moment of it have more meaning if she knew. Nor did it seem right that she, the most concerned, should be the least informed.

Fears confirmed will cause as much alarm as fears first stirred. Sitting up on her bed, leaning forward, her knees bent, she looked at him with eyes that welled with thought rather than with tears, and that her thinned, girlish look intensified so that they seemed even larger than they were. "Cancer . . . no less," she whispered. "Now let's just work on the pain—on the pain only—and never mind the rest."

It was April, in Siena, and outside in the garden a nightingale was singing. They listened in silence to the notes appealing, and he thought it would be good to die on such a night, and the verses of Keats came to his mind:

To cease upon the midnight with no pain,
While thou art pouring forth thy soul abroad
In such an ecstasy!

He eyed the little bottle of opium drops on her night table. He would not remove it. He would not touch it. He would leave it there—though many mingled voices told him not to—within her reach, for her to empty "to the drains," if she so wished. He almost hoped—yes, *hoped*—that she would drink it.

But in the morning the bottle was still there—full, or nearly. The maid counted out the prescribed number of drops. Forty. But forty drops had not relieved the pain last night. Should she count more, the maid asked her.

"Oh, my dear, I wouldn't count them at all. I would pour it all out, except that I don't want to hurt you." She took the drops, and five more, then lay perfectly still and resigned, with her eyes closed and her arms at her sides, waiting with composure for the pain to go.

And she continued what her doctors called the "cure"—the new medicine from Switzerland. But she looked on it with scorn, as on something weak and ineffectual—the way a wine drinker looks on water at table.

One of the doctors, a small, sweet unpretentious man about her age, who had become very attached to her, was hopeful. He sat beside her and tried to cheer her.

"How long more do you think this can go on?" she asked him. "It can't go on much longer, can it, Doctor?"

"But, Madam, why do you say that? You can live for years."

"Years?"

"But certainly—five, six, seven, and perhaps even more."

It was just what she didn't want to hear. "If it were a question of weeks or months, I could bear it, but you talk of years. Imagine, years . . ."

The old doctor was wrong. After a few days, there came a crisis. Now the doctors multiplied their efforts, and though she was too ill to know what they were doing, more than once, with her hands, she tried to ward them off.

She came to an end six days later—not slowly, like a train arriving at a station, but swiftly and convulsively, like a train derailing. She died hard, because her roots were strong, and much more still than if she had gone gently was the final stillness that ensued.

•

The house had been geared for sickness so long, and now there was no sickness anymore—no one to take care of, or stay up for, or worry about. Now she was someone only to be missed. They began putting things away—cumbersome, ugly things of glass and white enamel, and boxes full of drugs. "Throw them away," one could almost hear her saying. "Clear out the cupboards. Open all the windows. Air, air the house." She had always been one for keeping things uncluttered, one for spring cleaning, and this was now her day.

Two days later, four men—by a happy chance, her favorite farmers from nearby—lifted the bier, bore it out into the sunny air, and laid it on the open hearse. Fronds brushed it as it passed down under a tunnel-like drive of ilex trees. On the highway, hedges and ditches were crowded with spring flowers. From the highway, the procession, on foot, turned left along an unpaved country road, and now there were fields of clover on each side, and vines in tender leaf, and olive trees with tiny yellow blossoms, and ripening peas and broad beans in their pods, and the wheat undulated by the wind—all things she loved, things she had tried to capture with her brush. "How surprised they would be," she once had said, "those people who praise me as a mother, if they knew that in my lifetime perhaps my children never gave me so much pleasure as the reflection that the sky makes on the leaves." The road climbed up through a wood. At first, there were acacias and honeysuckle on each side, then chestnut trees—great, ancient chestnut trees with hollow trunks and branches sprouting with the newest leaves. The procession took an even smaller road, which led to the brow of the hill up on the right. The slope above the road was a rock garden of wild and flowering plants whose leaves vied in beauty with the blossoms. On top of the hill, they came to four cypresses and to the tiny country cemetery enclosed by lichened walls. Her grave had been dug next to that of an old farmer who had died eight or nine years before. Small, witty, graceful, and a little quaint, he was remembered by everyone with pleasure.

She was laid in her grave. Though the parish priest was present, there was no service, tribute, or any kind of benediction, for she had never been baptized and didn't go to church. A mason—a skillful man, who did his work with intense passion, and whom she had known well, for he had recently restored part of her house—quickly covered the vault with terra-cotta tiles, laying them side by side with mortar. As usual, he worked with care and concentration. She would have admired him. At the end, he flicked the mortar off his trowel. That quick flicking of the trowel seemed to her son a kind of benediction, and the mortar that was flung from it holy water. She had never been fond of prayers, ceremonies, sermons; she had always been fond of watching skilled artisans at work. And this flipping of the trowel seemed so much more fitting, so much more to her taste, than any kind of religious benediction. It seemed to lend a touch of joy and freshness to the burial.

Afterward, the parish priest—a nice, if somewhat colorless, young man—said how sorry and embarrassed he was not to have given such a kind lady a blessing. He would have given it, he added, even though she was not religious, except that he thought she would not really have wanted it.

The grave was to be bordered by four bars of travertine. A stonecutter in town—a gentle little man, at the end of his career—advised her sons that if they wanted truly fine travertine and good cornices, they should go to a village twenty-odd miles away, where there were quarries of it. And there they went, and it was like some of the trips they had taken with her in her good days when, one or the other of them at the wheel, they would go out for long drives to some old village or country church and stop for coffee in the village square. They came back with four heavy cornices of travertine. The stonecutter engraved her name in marble, her name and dates—no mournful inscription, nothing else. He did his work by hand. "You won't find anyone else who does it by hand now. I am the only one in town," he said.

Certainly, her son thought, had she had a chance, she would have chosen this gentle man to carve her name. And it struck him that all during her illness and till the moment of her death she had had no say about what was done to her, that she had more or less given in to, reluctantly agreed with, anything the doctors ordered for her, but that from the moment of her death on everything that happened appeared to fall in with her wishes, though she had left none, though she had let none be known. It was, after so much dreariness, a pleasant observation; at last, it seemed to him, she had taken things in hand, in her own strong hands, and he could almost see them, those admirable hands, come alive again, directing, doing.

[1965]

A Gallery of Women

My father died at eighty-three, crippled both in his body and in his mind. In 1969, six years after my mother died, he was approaching his death, uneasily, fitfully. Again and again, he was on the verge of it. But it was a pit he shied away from. "Life, the abyss of death makes you great," he wrote in a tremulous hand in the notebook he kept on a table at his bedside.

I wasn't with him when he finally died, in 1970. But the year before, in midwinter, when his condition suddenly worsened, I left my family in America and went to Italy to stay with him. He was bedridden, recovering from a badly set fracture of the hipbone. And he had other things wrong with him—hardening of the arteries, for one. I thought my presence would cheer him, but it didn't. I was never any good at dissembling, and, seeing the terrible state he was in, I was overcome by such a heavy cast of gloom that I felt I couldn't break out of it and that I was only adding to his burdens.

"Why do you look so dark?" he would ask me, using for "dark" the word "*oscuro*"—"obscure."

"I am sorry," I would say.

Propped up by pillows, in light pearl-white pajamas, he would look at me sternly. "Go, go," he would tell me, and with a slight motion of his hand wave me out of his bedroom.

He looked very frail, with that frailty of the sick that lends dignity. His face was spare to excess, as was his body. Only his eyes—large, mournful, searching—remained unchanged. On his better days, he might read me a poem. In my many years at universities and in the company of literary people, I have never met anyone who liked poetry more than my father, or, for that matter, knew more about it. So I listened with attention and pleasure, for the rhythm always seemed absolutely right. It was the only comfort I could bring him. But even as a listener I wasn't quite what he wanted.

What he wanted was the company of women. Even Assunta, the

maid—an elderly, illiterate woman, who listened to the poetry with composure, her hands clasped in front of her—was for him a better audience than I was. He had always liked women far better than men. A philosopher by nature and vocation, he saw them as the embodiment of tenderness and he thought they were more intelligent, in most ways superior. If challenged, before his memory had deteriorated, he would bring up the names of Emily Brontë, Elizabeth Browning, Anne de Noailles, the mystic Jeanne Marie Guyon, and Diotima. They struck certain notes, he said, which were not inferior to any man's. Among modern writers, he was fondest of Willa Cather and Carson McCullers. Also, with a smile he would mention Dorothy Parker, and Katherine Anne Porter, and, from an earlier period, Mary Wilkins Freeman. Of the Italians, he liked Ada Negri. Though in his library there were thousands of books by all sorts of authors, mainly classics, which here and there he had underlined neatly in pencil and annotated in shorthand at the back, now he preferred reading books by women. Also, in defense of women he would read these verses written by Keats to his sister-in-law:

> Imagine not that greatest mastery
> And kingdom over all the Realms of verse
> Nears more to heaven in aught than when we nurse
> And surety give to love and Brotherhood.

Sometimes that winter, old friends, hearing of my return, would come to my father's house to visit me. Often they stayed for lunch or tea. If the friend was a woman, I would bring her to my father's room. I would introduce her to him, and after a moment see that my presence disturbed him and that he wanted me to leave. If I stayed on, he would get restless and, again, his hand would wave me out. "Go now, go," he would tell me. And I would leave him alone with her.

"Your father's a darling," or "Your father's so gentle," the woman would tell me afterward.

"Not with me," I would say to myself, but to her I would say, "It was nice of you to talk to him."

"Oh, it was a pleasure. He's so sweet. He read me a poem of Petrarch."

I would know just which poem it was—the sonnet to Laura which begins, "I sang, now I weep; and weeping is as sweet as singing was, for, still fond of height, my senses are intent on the cause, not the effects." Years before, when he had been well and we had taken paying guests at the house, he would give Italian lessons free to any woman guest. Sometimes a man, seeing that my father was so willing to give lessons, would ask him for one and be surprised at his reluctance. He didn't understand that his being a man and not a woman could make such a difference to my father.

And yet, even in his younger days, I don't think he had any intention of having an affair. He was always faithful to my mother. His compliments—and some of them were surprising—were never a means to an end with him but an end in themselves. Never subordinate, never instrumental, they flared for a moment, not meant to light a fire, only to illumine, and often they were offered in the presence of others, my mother even, who knew his ways and didn't seem to mind.

He really delighted in the company of women. On the land that went with the house he had a peach orchard planted, and sometimes it seemed to me that the only reason he kept it was so he could employ girls or women to pick the fruit. He had me, my brothers, and my sister learn English from the time we were small children, not so much because of his love of the English language, though it certainly was a factor, but, I think, so he could have the company of the young English and American women who came to our house as tutors. Every summer, one would come and stay. Once, in her letter, a girl from Ipswich, England, enclosed her picture, and I remember him looking at it through a magnifying lens, with admiration.

In the car, driving through a strange town, he would always prefer asking the way of a woman, and often choose a handsome one. He also liked to help women, to be at their service. Sometimes it was almost embarrassing. As I think back on it, though, it never embarrassed me as a child. Once, I remember, we were at Viareggio, the seaside resort, and a young woman walking along the sidewalk stepped out of her shoe. Immediately he rushed to it and held it for her while she slipped it on. She thanked him graciously. Some people laughed.

Now, in his bed, sick and old though he was, he still retained that admiration. "If he admires them, if they cheer him up so, and since I am not a good companion," I said to myself, "why don't I invite someone who is?"

Except for the few visitors who came to the house for lunch or tea, and the maid, there weren't any women that I could think of. And then from the maid I learned by chance that a girl—the daughter of a farmer who lived nearby—was working as a manicurist in town. "Couldn't she come and do his hands once in a while?" I asked Assunta. "It would be a diversion for him."

"Oh, surely she would. She wouldn't mind making a little extra money. She's only an apprentice, you know, and they don't pay her much."

"Then would you ask her?"

"Yes, I'll talk to her and let you know."

The girl, Lisa, was very willing to come. I told my father. He looked at his hands. They were small, delicate hands; and his fingernails he had always groomed himself, very carefully with curved scissors. The slightest scratch worried him, and he took great pains to disinfect it. He had never been to a manicurist in his life.

"What a thought," he said. "I do it myself. This I can still do." And "There's the danger of tetanus." And "It's an expense."

"No, it won't cost much. And she's very pretty."

He looked at his nails again. "Well, if you like," he said.

Lisa came the next day. She was eighteen and brought an air of freshness into the room. She was unabashed and smiling as she stood before my father, her bleached-blond hair cut short, level with her earlobes.

"Ah," he said, and his gray old face seemed to regain some of its color. Was he blushing?

"Well, I'll leave you alone," I said, and left them.

A while later, Lisa came out. "So nice your father is," she said. "Yes, yes, it really went well."

"You didn't cut too much? He's afraid of getting tetanus," I said, and laughed.

"He told me. No, no, don't worry. I only clipped the tiniest bit off, and then I filed them."

"So you'll come back next week?"

"Yes, I'll be back in a week. On Thursday next."

I went in to see my father. "Well, how was it? Did she do a good job?"

"Yes, you see," he said, proudly showing me his hands. "Lisa," he said. "And when is she coming back?"

"Next week, on Thursday."

"Thursday," he said, and, taking out his notebook, which he kept on the bed table at his side, he wrote her name in it, and "Thursday," which I had to repeat for him more than once.

Then every day he would ask me, "And when is the manicurist—Lisa—coming?"

"On Thursday."

"Ah, yes, on Thursday. Wait a moment." He would take the notebook out and look through it carefully for her name. "Here it is—Lisa, on Thursday. Good."

But Thursday was such a long time coming for him, and he wished for her so much it was pitiful. When Sunday came, I asked the maid, "Do you think you could get Lisa to come twice a week?"

"But the nails, they won't have grown any, or hardly at all, eh?"

"Well, it's not so much a question of the nails, you know. It's that he needs the distraction."

"Yes, I understand. Well, I'll see if I can get her to come again tomorrow."

And so Lisa came on Monday. She knew that she was welcome and she entered my father's bedroom with a flourish. "*Come sta, Signorino?*" she said. In the Tuscan countryside, *Signorino,* the diminutive of *Signore,* was the usual form of address for a man in his position, no matter how old, for *Signore* meant not only Sir but also the Lord.

"Ah, dear, I—" he said, and took her hands in both of his, and would have knelt beside her if he could, like an admiring old saint in front of the young Madonna.

I was quick to leave them alone, and I thought, Well, if I can't comfort him I've certainly found someone who can. And I felt rather pleased with myself for the solution.

A barber came to cut my father's hair once a month, a surly old fellow. "Couldn't we find a woman hairdresser for him?" I said to the maid. "Do you see how he brightens when Lisa comes?"

"Yes, I see it, but a hairdresser for a man?"

"Why not? all he needs is a little clipping. A woman could do it just as well and better than a man."

"Oh, I don't know," the maid said. The thought of a women's hairdresser doing a man's job bothered her. "And what about Claudio?" she said. "How is he going to feel?"

"I'll talk to him. I'll have him cut my hair instead. And we'll have a woman cut my father's."

She nodded gravely. "In that case, I don't see why it could not be done."

I stalked about town looking into hairdressers' shops and beauty parlors. I inquired at three places before I found a pretty young woman in her twenties who seemed just right. She didn't have a car, she said. I said I'd pick her up in my car, or, when I couldn't, pay for a taxi. The price of the whole thing was paltry compared to doctors' bills. "And how often do you want me to come?" she asked.

"Oh, at least every two weeks," I replied. "Maybe even once a week.

You'll see the situation when you get there. Just cut very little at a time. It's mainly that his spirits are so low, and your visits will revive him."

"I've never cut men's hair, but in this case..."

So she came, too, Sunday. Her name was Virginia, and my father wrote it in his notebook. And he liked her as much as Lisa—almost. He had a great deal of trouble getting their names straight. For a long time, he seemed to think of nothing else. He waited for them; he prepared himself for them.

"You see how much he's improved?" the maid said. "Eh, you had a good idea."

"But there are so many hours, days, between their visits," I said.

"I know," she said with a sigh. "What can we do?" And her mouth fell open and she stretched her hands back, as if she had come to a dead end.

What about the women in fiction, I thought. Sometimes my father spoke of them as though they were real. My mother, too, at times was for him alive, in the next room, arranging the flowers. "Go and call her," he would say, and I would go from his room wondering what to bring to him. One day, looking for a book he might like, I found Theodore Dreiser's *A Gallery of Women*. I saw his little shorthand notes pencilled at the back, which to me were hieroglyphics but which had numbers opposite them referring to the pages he liked best. And I brought it to him and read him some of those stories, his hand from long ago guiding me from woman to woman. And I asked him about Diotima, and read him the dialogue of Plato in which she appears.

"She must have existed," he said. "There are truths that cannot be ascribed to her interpreters."

And then I read him Emily Brontë's "No Coward Soul Is Mine."

Slowly, gradually, my introducing woman after woman to him—fictional and real—became a role unforeseen, unexpected. I warmed to it. It reconciled us. He saw me, I think, no longer as obscure but as a stagehand who disclosed scenes and people to him he looked forward to seeing. I peopled his austere room with characters living and dead—for him all of them living—while I myself kept in the background.

Then, early that spring, he had a relapse that brought him near death. With it came a severe loss of memory. He couldn't remember my name, let alone Lisa's or Virginia's. And when he improved a little and he was able to see them again, they were quite new for him, and again he smiled and some of his color came back, once more as if he were blushing in their presence.

So it tided him over, this vision of fair women, off and on, during that last year. In May, my wife arrived with the children. He said she was an angel, though whether out of pity for her being married to me or in admiration of her looks and kindness I don't know. Our younger daughter, who was four, would bring him flowers or slowly hold up a candy to him, and stand by his bed and kiss him, unbothered by his sunken face, and smile, and call him *nonno*. For those smiles and visits, too, I thought I was in a way responsible, and took heart.

I had a teaching job in Boston starting in September, and in late August we left, my family and I, though not before I had succeeded in getting Erminia—a cook who had been with us for thirty years but who, two years before, had retired and had gone to live with her daughter—to stay with him. She was a very talkative woman, full of tales and anecdotes of long ago. "She has such a command of the language," he said to me, soon after she arrived. And after I left, from Erminia and from the maid, I heard that the two girls continued to come, even when he was too sick for them to work on him. They came, and they sat with him, and more than once they refused to be paid. In a letter Erminia described his last days.

I see my father in bed, beyond them, his hands under the covers, his head thrown back, and the two girls at his bedside, their voices quiet, their hands still, unable to do for him what they'd done. And the books are there on his table and his notebook, which I now have here. I open it and on a page toward the end I come to their names. "Lisa, Thursday, Monday," it says. "Virginia, Sunday." Two pages farther on the names reappear. And other names are there—my wife's, my children's with their birth dates, Erminia's, and Assunta's.

[1978]

The Bell

He thought, I must live like a poet, and at this moment that means bearing with him.

It was three o'clock in the morning, and his father—eighty-two, helpless, bedridden, and with his mind wandering—had rung the bell again.

"He was born with a bell in his hand," the son said to himself. It was what his mother used to say about some people, her husband and daughter not excluded. His mother was dead now—had been dead six years—but her son still saw her, still heard her. A thousand things in the house, an old country house in Tuscany, summoned her to his mind. His mind was always open to her, eager for her.

He groped for the light cord. The bell in his bedroom was on another cord, thinner, smoother, of fine, frayed cotton, and it ended in a wooden, pear-shaped switch, almost an antique. Like his mother, the son never rang a bell, and this perhaps accounted for its not having been replaced with a little plastic knob like those in most of the other rooms. Even if he did ring, there was no one to answer—no live-in maids or cook, as there had been. The huge house had a bell in almost every room, and downstairs, near the kitchen, a board on which different numbers popped up when the bells were rung. Only a few still worked—the front door, his father's, and two or three others, but no one knew for sure to which rooms they belonged. Erratically, these popped up like naughty marionettes, even when no one had rung, and when they were cancelled they could not be trusted to stay down.

He switched on the light and drew his legs out from the warm covers into the chilly air. It was winter, and though this part of the house was heated, it was never really warm. The coal fire in the furnace burned full blast for only a few hours after it was lighted. During the night it died down, to be relit the next day by a handyman who had been with them twenty years and who lived nearby with his family.

He got into his dressing gown and slippers, and undertook the small journey to his father's bedroom, directly beneath his own, along cold brick corridors, the stone staircase, through the tiled telephone room, the dining room, and an anteroom. The light was on under his father's door.

"What is it?" the son said, peeking in.

"How do you mean 'What is it?' You are so curt."

"You rang the bell."

"But most certainly I rang the bell."

"Well, what do you need?"

"What do I need!" his father said irritably. "Come in and shut the door. Close that shutter, will you?"

The son walked to the middle of the room. "But it's shut. The shutter's shut. It doesn't need closing."

"But it does—can't you see?" Frail, slight except in his bones and eyes, his father was sitting up in his bed, which was set in an alcove of the room, looking at him with brows knitted.

The son walked over to the window. It was closed tight, and so were the inside shutters that fitted into the casements. Only, on the right-hand shutter the little bolt hadn't been pushed all the way under its bracket. He moved it over. "Is that better?"

"Oh, bravo," his father said, and now he seemed perfectly happy. "Tell me, what time is it? I can't find my watch."

"It's right there beside you, on the table. It's just past three o'clock."

"Three o'clock?" his father said, aghast. "Three o'clock in the afternoon?"

"No, it's night. Three o'clock at night."

"Night?"

"Of course. See," the son said, opening the window wide. The perfumed night entered the lighted room, and a rectangular light was cast upon the garden. "It's dark."

"But that doesn't make it three o'clock."

Strange, the playful way he reasoned. "Your watch," the son said sternly, not acknowledging the joke.

His father put his glasses on and picked up the watch, as if he still was not convinced. "So it is," he said. "Three o'clock." After a moment's thought, he added, "But I must go to the ceremony."

"What ceremony?"

"How do you mean 'What ceremony?' " his father said sharply. "The ceremony, of course. . . . The funeral."

"Whose funeral?"

"My funeral."

"Why, you haven't died."

"I haven't died?" his father said, looking about the room as if following a bat's flight. "I haven't died, you say?"

"No, and you are not about to. You'll probably outlive me!"

"You may not reach my age, but I won't outlive you," his father said, surprising the son with his reasoning.

"Who knows!"

"But how can you say that when I am dead already?"

"You are speaking. Your heart is strong. You have a good appetite."

"I didn't eat anything."

"There's the tray with your empty dishes. You've eaten everything up."

"Is it possible? It's true it seems that way, but it isn't."

"Oh, Papa. You must try and sleep now. It's late. So late it's almost morning, and I am sleepy; I must go to bed."

"Yes, you go now."

"Good night."

"Good night."

Slowly the son made his way up the stairs back to his room.

In the room adjoining the son's bedroom, two of his children slept soundly, and, two rooms over, so did his wife with their youngest child. He slept in a room of his own because of his father's calls and in the hope of doing some work. From a distance he viewed the sketches on his desk, at which he didn't manage to work much anymore. He took off his dressing gown, slumped into bed, and put the light out. He waited for the bell to ring again. He was sure it was going to—positive. Yet if he waited perhaps it wouldn't ring. Perhaps his waiting for it, his expecting it to ring, was the one thing that kept it from ringing. So he hung on to wakefulness, sure that the moment he closed his eyes and fell asleep the bell would ring. And, indeed, it did, for sleep had stolen over him. He uncurled himself. He might just ignore this peal. But there came another—long, insistent. He rose and went down once more to his father's room.

"Yes?"

"Where am I?"

"Here in your home. Try not to ring the bell so often."

"There you are, rebuking me again."

"I am not rebuking you. You can't sleep. Let me give you something." He went to the medicine cabinet and took out a sleeping pill and a tranquillizer, then half filled a glass of water from a pitcher on the table. "Here, these will let you rest."

His father looked at the pills suspiciously. "What are they?"

The son told him.

Still his father gazed at them. Could he trust his son? He glanced up quickly, then back at the pills, seeming to weigh them. He had always been against sleeping pills. He didn't want to rely on them for sleep. But now he wasn't on his feet anymore, and the days went by listlessly, one after another, and he slept to make time pass—time that alone could bring the improvement he still hoped for.

"Take them, or you won't sleep."

His father put the pills in his mouth and swallowed them with the water, but not before he had caught a taste of them, as the son saw from the embittered face.

"Perhaps you'd like a little apricot brandy."

"Oh, that, yes."

He poured his father and himself each a tiny glassful from a bottle he took from a shelf in the bookcase, and watched his father drink it like a balm.

"A drop more?"

"Yes, yes. It's the best I've ever tasted."

The son told him it was Bols—Dutch—and his father tried to bring to the surface of his mind the names of his favorite liqueurs. With the son's help, he was able to recover one or two.

Carefully, his hand trembling, yet without spilling a drop, as if it were something very precious, after a few sips his father set the little glass on the bedside table.

"Good, well then, good night," the son said, and rose to go, pleased to leave his father in a better mood than he had found him in.

"Good night. Take care you shut both doors." His father meant the one of the anteroom, too.

"All right."

He had shut the bedroom door when the bell's ringing stopped him short, and he turned to open it again. "What now?" he said, unable to hide a note of irritation and destroying the mood the brandy had engendered.

"I'm sorry," his father said in a meek, small, embarrassed voice that put the son to shame. "I meant to switch the light off and pressed the bell instead."

"The bell is that one," the son said, pointing to it.

"That one?" his father said, pointing to the light switch.

"No, that one. The smaller of the two. It's much smaller, you see."

"So it is." His father switched the light off.

"Well, good night."

"Good night."

That night, there was no further call.

"He rang three times last night," the son told the maid in the morning. She was the wife of the handyman, very plain and quiet. At first sight, or when she answered the telephone, she seemed gruff, but the gruffness was just a coating—the more you knew her the more you admired her. She was absolutely reliable, patient, sensible, and always doing things, so that the children, especially his younger girl, followed her everywhere, helping her put the rooms in order, or shell peas, or gather grass for her rabbits.

"Now he's sleeping," she said. "I looked in."

She looked after his father during the day, but at night she went home.

Besides mistaking it for the light switch, sometimes his father forgot to ring the bell, forgot there *was* a bell, or could not find it, though it hung within easy reach by the wall. The son bought him one of a different kind—not a bulb hanging on a cord, like the light switch, but a disc with a button—and he attached it to the wall, hoping this measure would avoid confusion. It helped, but still his father had difficulty. At such times, after fumbling in the dark for God knows how long, he would give up and shout. His voice was so loud it would fill a good part of the house, and it seemed louder for the silence that reigned there during the night. They were a long way from town and quite a distance from the road—a minor one, at that. For the son, the volume of his father's voice was a pretty accurate indication of his health, and a weak voice worried him more than a loud one. Still, it was even more compelling than the bell, and eerie, too, this tearing of the silent night. He would rush down, hoping not to find his father on the floor.

"Oh, at last," he would be greeted in an angry voice.

"Why don't you ring the bell?"

"The bell . . . the bell," his father replied, trembling with irritation. "Where is it?"

"There!"

"You have all abandoned me. I am dying."

"With that voice?"

"Oh, heaven! You—who are you?"

"Your son," he replied, thinking his father had forgotten, but he had asked in anger, not in confusion.

"You don't behave like my son."

"It seems to me I come down when you call."

"Reluctantly."

"Well, you know, it's not exactly fun. What is it that you wanted?"

"What is it that I want indeed! Everything. I am in want of everything. I am left all alone." He seemed to have forgotten what he had called for. "Do me a favor," he said after a moment. "Get me Leopardi's poems. It should be there on the desk. I can't walk."

"Yes, of course; I know." On the desk there were three piles of books, mostly poetry. The son went through them hastily. "No, it's not there."

"But it must be."

He went through them again. Nothing. "I'll look in the bookcases." No, it wasn't in the bookcases, either.

"Look, there on the desk," his father said, his voice rising.

Why did his father always make him feel like a child with his orders, a child with none of childhood's advantages and all its disadvantages, as if nothing but submissiveness were expected of him? He expected the son to be so submissive. Yet why? He was only asking for a book. "I looked," he said.

"Oh, Lord! There in the first pile."

The son looked again, more carefully. Sure enough, the book was there, at the bottom. "Oh, yes, you're right. Here it is." It amazed him how often his father was right and he wrong.

"Thank you," his father said, and the son thought, He's never petty, never says "I told you so"; he never even says "You see." His father took a pencil, put his glasses on, and began reading.

The son watched him and felt he wasn't wanted anymore. He should ask his father to read a poem, for he loved reading aloud to people. And then perhaps he could read something to his father. But he felt unable to do either thing—unable to humor him. It was like an impediment. He remembered lying on that bed as a child, and his father reading poetry to him. Once, when his father was reading the *Iliad,* the stove in the corner of the room (it wasn't lit now, since there were radiators) had got hotter and hotter. Its red-hot pipe had ignited the ceiling and a flame had leaped out. From the bed he had seen it and given the alarm. His father had put the fire out with pails of water and then praised him for saving the house. And once, listening to him read Dante, the son had fallen asleep on that bed. Now the positions were pathetically reversed. Slowly, he left the room.

His father didn't like him—the son could sense it. Oh, he had loved him then, when he was a child, and again much later—fairly recently, in fact—when, away in America, he had translated some of his father's articles into English. But they had reached another stage. Though his father's memory was defective, his sensitivity was unimpaired, even heightened maybe. It was as if, having lost one faculty, the mind tried to rely more heavily on the others, or the others came to the help of the stricken one. His father resented the son's curt replies, his hurry to leave the room, his inability to be affable and keep him company. But his son couldn't change. It was the most difficult thing, he thought, to change one's attitude toward another person, or even to dissemble. He could only do it for a few minutes at a time by reminding himself constantly, constantly checking and controlling himself.

"Why so hostile?" his father would say. And, "You don't love me anymore? What have I done? Tell me."

The questions, often coming right after he had washed his father, changed him, or lifted him onto a chair, left the son nonplussed. "Why, why do you say that? Haven't I just . . ."

He felt powerfully that it was his duty to stay in the house and look after his father, but he couldn't do it graciously. He wasn't a good nurse. With an unlimited amount of money, he might have been able to hire one, but, as things were, no, he couldn't get the ideal nurse—not for twenty-four hours a day. For a time, he had had an old orderly. It had worked for only a matter of weeks. His father had grown more and more impatient with the poor old fellow, and finally he had left. The son's wife helped. Indeed, his father often said she was an angel. But she had her three small children to look after, and at night she was too tired to get up. So at night now the son was responsible, and often during the day, too, when the maid, who was over sixty, couldn't come. Just recently, she had been away for three weeks with a bad case of influenza. The idea of sending his father to a nursing home sometimes crossed the son's mind, but he wouldn't do it. Let him die in peace in his own house, where he wanted to be. He had had a bout with an old folks' rest home, and he had almost died there. It had happened a year before, when the son was in America. His father had fallen in his room at night and been found in the morning on the floor. At the hospital, they took one small X-ray, read it as negative, and dismissed him. Because he was unable to walk, he was put in the rest home, and there he stayed for three weeks, until the son flew back and took him home and called a specialist. There was a fracture indeed, but with his father in such critical condition an operation was thought inadvisable. Slowly, over a period of months, he had pulled out of that crisis.

Sometimes his father wouldn't call the son but would get up unaided and, if he didn't fall, would lift himself onto a chair—though not always the wheelchair—and, if he didn't get stuck, and if, in fact, he had got onto the wheelchair, would push himself along toward the door, open it, and cross the anteroom, the dining room, the telephone room, a corridor, and reach the kitchen, open the refrigerator, and then, if he didn't find what he wanted, shout.

The son, a light sleeper, would almost always hear him, and, hurrying down, ask his father why he hadn't rung the bell.

His father, convulsed with anger, would hardly be able to reply. But some words broke out. "Why, why, why! Isn't it obvious why?"

The vast house—practically empty, and with the old man in the bare kitchen, pale, in a wheelchair, chiding his son in the cold, still night—seemed a place to run away from. And it had been so happy once, when his mother was alive and he and his brothers were children. Later, too. It could be so now again—his wife, his children were upstairs—if only there was no sickness. If only his father could get well. But there was no chance of it. And, unworthy yet insistent, the thought came to his mind: if only his father were to die! But his father wouldn't die; he clung to life obscenely. The son hated himself for thinking so, for saying these words to himself, and yet he felt them. That's the way he felt deep down—not even so deep down; the feeling was all through him, and it frightened him.

To hear his father even if he didn't ring or call, the son set up an intercom between his father's room and his own. Now he could hear his father's breathing, his soliloquies, his endeavors to rise, his talking in his dreams, his groans—more than anything else, his groans—and he thought of the "Ode to a Nightingale":

> The weariness, the fever, and the fret
> Here, where men sit and hear each other groan.

Often a sigh would come through, a long sigh that seemed final, the end, but always it was followed by another.

Sometimes there would be a crisis. His father would take no food, his voice would thin, become a reed of a voice. Just enough of a voice to ask for a glass of water and announce in a prophetic tone, "Tonight I will die; this is my last night with you," and though the son had heard him say those words before, it was hard to disbelieve that thin reed of a voice and that prophetic tone. His father was so convinced of what he was saying, as though there were no question. Then the son would keep vigil in his father's room, and when he finally left he would go in the drawing room and sit alone on the yellow sofa and wait confidently. But when, hours later, on tiptoe, he would reach the bedroom door and, like a thief, open it without a sound and listen, he would hear his father breathing hard.

The crises came irregularly every few weeks. There were so many things wrong with his father: the fractured hipbone that hadn't been set, his mind that wandered, a cough, incontinence, and lately, as if that wasn't enough, a peptic ulcer. But his heart was strong, its beat regular, and it kept him alive. And his eyes were good—he could read; his hearing was perfect. There was this to be said for nature: it provided you with so many faculties that no matter how many were struck out some were left intact. He read poetry mainly, often aloud to visitors and to the maid. She sat with her hands clasped on her lap, looking at him, and listened, as at church, quite contentedly. The children would come to him. Not all of them—the oldest one didn't like going into a sick old man's room, but the smaller ones didn't mind, particularly the little girl; she would go and see him and give him her hand and stand beside his bed and not be afraid to kiss him.

Weathering each storm, still his father clung to life. "Is life worth living in that state? I say it is not," the maid would say, and dutifully bring him milk and soup, and tend him as if life were in fact very worth living, even in his case—in no matter whose case. But the son, sometimes—seeing his father restless, fretful, and not improving but rather worse in practically every sense—counting the drops of laudanum or picking out pills of a soporific, would add one or two to the usual dose. In three-quarters of an hour, his father would sink into a deep sleep. Late in the morning, the maid would come to ask if she should wake him up. "No, let him sleep," the son would answer, and secretly hope his father would not wake.

Always he would wake up, refreshed and feeling better, around noon.

To kill a man you had to give him five times the usual dose—not just one or two drops more but eighty or a hundred. It was easy enough to give a few drops more, but a hundred—it would be like pulling a trigger. Beyond him. Quite beyond him. Let his father die in his own time. As for himself, he could wait; he could leave.

But seeing his father losing hope in his improvement, dissatisfied with the doctors, and rising out of one crisis only to meet another, again the son would wonder.

"What is death like, I wonder," he asked his father one such time.

"I've seen it, death. I have," his father answered, his head reclining on the pillow and looking at the ceiling, as if speaking of someone he had met. "It is a dim gray ward in which your senses fade little by little."

And his son thought, This is the true picture. And, He's perfectly right not to want to die. He has seen death, knows it from close by, has seen its gorge. And the son thought of the orange eye of a cat gone opaque and dull, the eardrum become sodden, the tongue unwieldy, the skin numb, everything powerless, flaccid, or worse than flaccid—stiff. From that time on, he didn't increase the dosage, not even by one drop, and though before he had hoped for his father's death, he didn't now, and he remembered his father's saying long ago, "Better to be the last among the living than the first among the dead." No, let him live on, outlast the son if need be. He seemed a leaf of last year still hanging to the tree, a leaf that no wind could blow off. The storm would come that would take him, but it had to be a hurricane. The son waited for it, and hated himself.

It came, a great crisis. For days his father wouldn't eat; his voice weakened to a thread. "This time there's no return," the maid said, shaking her head. The son phoned his sister and one brother. They came. But by the time they arrived their father had begun taking a little milk. Soon he was talking again.

"He has this terrific resilience. I'm sorry I alarmed you," the son said to his brother and sister, and they left.

In the spring, the old cook came—not much younger than his father. She had been with the family for forty years. Recently she had spent the winters with her daughter and grandchildren some two hundred miles north. His father had asked for her again and again, and she had returned to be with him.

Heavy, buxom, talkative, her hair dyed black, each morning she knocked gently at his door or looked in if he was asleep, and answered cheerfully each of his calls, and cheerfully brought him breakfast, washed him, powdered him, joked with him, told him stories, held his hand. For a while, he seemed to improve; then there was another relapse. But in the summer he was often well enough to be wheeled out into the garden in his chair.

And now it was mid-August. September—the real beginning of the year, the month in which people move and take up new positions—was at hand. In the spring, the son had been offered a teaching job in America. He had accepted it, thinking that surely in September his father would not be alive. But he was, and should he leave him in the care of two old women? His father might live on and on. The son couldn't tie himself down indefinitely. He went.

In October, while he was in his office, he received a call from his wife. A telegram had come saying his father was in a coma. I won't fly over, he thought. There's nothing I can do. He waited. For two days there was no news. Perhaps he's got over it, he thought. Then, on the third day, he phoned home, and his little daughter answered. "Nonno died," she said.

"He did?"

"Yes, a telegram came; Nonno died."

"On Wednesday," his wife said. It was Friday now.

So it was all over. The hurricane had come. The leaf had been severed. The son thought of his mother and his father. He wanted to remember them as their lithe and graceful selves, and instead he remembered them mainly in their agonies. Why did death take such a giant toll of one's memories?

Days later, letters arrived from the two old women in Italy. "He went like a candle," one said. "We said good night to him, tucked him in, and he never woke up."

On the night from which his father did not wake, the night that for him was forever night—the son wasn't there. Did he wish he had been? He hardly knew. But he knew it was right, fitting, proper that he had been excluded. With the bitter taste of heartburn, his curt replies came back to him, his silences when affability was needed, his cheerless manner. They were far better company, those two old women. Long, long ago, he had ceased to be a poet, perhaps had been one only as a boy.

[1973]

II

Beppa

It's raining on the Piazza San Marco. The marble paving looks as clean as a floor washed over and over. Though he could walk under the porticoes he does not. He likes to see the wet slabs, likes the feel of their wholeness. "Whole as the marble, founded as the rock, / As broad and general as the casing air," he chants, for there is no one near, and he looks up at the sky and opens his mouth for the raindrops. From the Piazza he walks to the Piazzetta and the lagoon, where the Riva degli Schiavoni meets the Grand Canal. The water is level with the pavement. Each wave splashes over and sends a ripple, fanlike, that merges with the rainwater. Salt and fresh water mix and he's happy. Such wetness. The boats, moored to the quai, ride high and look as if they are about to move in on him, do something mad. He lingers on the edge, as if he would dive in. He has nothing to do. Venice isn't a military town, and he's in the military, a young doctor, doing a year's compulsory service.

For some months he was in the Alps, with the Alpini. He wasn't happy there. The mountains to the south seemed like a bastion that held him "cabin'd, cribb'd, confin'd, bound in," separated from the plains and the sea. Then, as if his wishes had something to do with it, the medical captain in Venice broke a leg, and he was transferred to take his place. He has been here two months. The captain's leg doesn't heal. They say he has bad blood. He feels almost guilty, as if his wish to stay in Venice kept the captain in bed or disabled. He is only a sublieutenant, but he has a speedboat at his service, three orderlies, a room in the palace, now turned barracks, where Petrarch lived, just a few hundred yards down from the Danieli, and very little to do. He is the only army doctor in town. There are a few soldiers, the *carabinieri,* the state police, the customs men—in all about two hundred people to look after. The navy is big here, not the army. He is in civilian clothes every evening. He's rather literary. He's had a little book of poems published. He visits galleries, churches, and from time to time a couple of elderly people—bluestockings—with whom he is acquainted. But mostly he walks, alone. He has come to know the town pretty well.

From the water's edge he walks up toward the Grand Canal, then to the Calle San Moisè and enters a cafè where the streetwalkers congregate.

"Here's the misanthrope," one says—*Ecco il misantropo.* She is a sultry looking woman about his age, soft and sinuous, handsome, with straight, black hair and violet-shaded almond eyes that look at him half-teasingly, blandishingly.

"I don't know why you call me a misanthrope. I don't hate anybody."

"You are always alone."

"That's not being a misanthrope. A loner, a wanderer—*un solitario, un girovago*—if you like, but not a misanthrope."

"Oh, well, I'm not a professor," she says.

"Oh yes you are," says another, in a throaty voice. "Or if not a professor, a professional."

"What of?"

The other women laugh. He smiles.

He comes here fairly often, one of the few cafés that has any life. The young woman, Beppa, seems to have taken to him, and he likes her, though he doesn't know her well, has never been alone with her—or with any of the others. He knows she regards him as an oddity, different from other men, but he doesn't mind. He has the feeling he intrigues her. A couple of times, seeing him on the street, she has softly come up behind him and whispered, "Where's the misanthrope going?" She is rather naive, despite her profession and sultry looks. Once, he heard her say to the others about a woman who wasn't present, "She's a real whore, that one." "And what do you think you are?" one of her companions said. "Me?" she said, and for a moment she seemed lost, and he thought she even blushed a little.

Alone at a table, he orders an apricot brandy and smokes a cigarette.

"Guess who I saw today—and in a gondola, mind you?" Zanze, a slender redhead, says.

"Who?" Gina, a girl with an easy laugh, says.

"Milano."

"Was she alone?"

"You fooling?"

"Why d'you call her Milano, if she's a woman?" he butts in. "A woman, Milano!"

"Hear him?" Zanze says. "Because she's from Milan, that's why. And then aren't names of cities feminine in Italian? See, now I'm giving *him* a lesson."

"Who was she with?" Gina asks.

"With a foreigner—an American, I think. Or a Russian! Ever made love to a Russian? No, he was from Luxemburg. I can tell!"

"Ever made love in a gondola?"

"Once," Zanze says. "Almost tipped over."

"Liar," Gina says.

"Who you calling a liar?" She rises to slap Gina.

"*Calma, calma, signorine,*" the waiter says.

"No, but Milano gets around," Gina says.

"Is it true your name is Ferruccio?" Zanze asks him, impishly.

"Yes, what's wrong with that?"

"Nothing."

"And your name—Zanze—I've never heard it before."

"It's short for Zelinda. Will you give me a cigarette, Ferruccio?"

They laugh at the languorous way she says his name. He offers her one. She refuses it brusquely. "Too strong!" she says. "I never see you in uniform."

"Mornings."

"I'm never up in the morning. Wake up at two. Beppa says you were in the Alpini and are a doctor."

"That's right."

"And you come here every evening."

"Not every evening."

"You like Beppa, don't you?"

"I like you all."

"But especially Beppa."

"Especially Beppa."

They laugh.

"And me, you don't love me?" Gina says.

"Leave him alone, don't you see he's shy?" Beppa says.

"He's not shy. Are you shy?"

He shrugs his shoulders.

"So you're a sublieutenant?" Zanze says.

"Yes, on compulsory service for a year. I'm a sublieutenant, but here it's as though I were a captain, except for the pay," he says and continues about the captain breaking his leg, and his being transferred from the Alps to Venice where he wanted to be all along, and his feeling almost bad about it.

"I wouldn't feel bad," Zanze says. "But, say, you *can* talk! That's the most I've heard him talk since I've seen him! So what d'you do when you are through, evenings?"

"He comes here."

"Let him talk. I like the way he answers every question and gives you straight answers. No wisecracks, like you."

"I'm having a book of poems published."

"Ah, so you are a poet. Will you write me a poem sometime?"

"If you are very good to me."

"And what else do you do?"

"I wander, I roam; all alone, as Beppa said."

"Don't you have any girl friends?"

He makes a gesture to include them all. "Only you," he says, but he ends up looking at Beppa.

"Look at him looking at Beppa," Gina says.

"You mean to say you never had any adventures?" Zanze asks him.

"Oh, I picked up a couple of girls some time ago, but they've both gone home now—one to the other side of the Atlantic; the other to Genoa, on the other side of the country."

"And I thought *I* was sad. Tell me, *caro,* why didn't you like the Alps?"

"All those sharp rocks."

"Were you in Cortina?"

"No, way east of there, in Tarvisio."

"Ever been in Cortina?" Gina says to the girls. "Now there's a place. All those grand hotels. De luxe. Do you know how to ski?" She rises and imitates a skier, and falls on a chair.

"How would you like to take me to Cortina, *misantropo*—no, *solitario, girovago;* do you see how nice I am to you?" Beppa says to him.

"Why do you want to go to Cortina? Venice is much better."

"There's nothing doing here in the winter. That's where the activity is now, in Cortina."

"Why don't you go?"

"I don't have the money, *tesoro.*"

"I wouldn't mind taking you, but—"

"No fee. We'll be just like a married couple. It'll cost you nothing."

"Can you believe it?" Gina says with a guffaw. "Won't cost him nothing. The way she spends."

"And what do I buy? A handbag, a silk scarf, gloves, a bottle of perfume. You won't mind buying me those, will you, *amore?*"

"No, I won't mind."

"You see, he's good, the misanthrope."

"When shall we go?"

"I'm ready. I'll just pack my little valise."

"Well, I'm not ready. I have to get a furlough."

"You can do that. Just tell them your father is sick."

"I don't want to lie to them. I don't really have to. I've got a furlough coming to me, even if it's only a weekend; I've been here two months steady. There are navy doctors in case anyone's sick. I can go."

He's so serious the women have all quieted down and listen. They seem a bit envious of Beppa. "Why don't you take me along too," Gina says.

"No, he likes Beppa; haven't you got it? Look how he's watching her."

"Is it true you love Beppa? And me, you don't love me a little?"

"Just Beppa," he says.

"Then when do we go?"

"How about the day after tomorrow?"

"Friday. *Benissimo.* Friday."

"You mean it? I know you girls. You make an appointment and then you don't show up. In Rome I went to a nightclub. A girl came to sit at my table and ordered a bottle of French champagne which cost me an outrageous price. 'This place closes at one—in a few minutes. Wait outside for me,' she said. I waited till two. She must have gone out the back door."

"You are full of sad stories. But I'm not like that. Not me."

"Aren't you going to take her in a gondola to the station?"

"I'll take her in a gondola if she wants me to."

"No. Costs too much. You see, I'm thrifty. I'm no spendthrift. I'll treat you well—not as a client. As a husband."

"Then when they get to Cortina, *caro mio!*" Gina says.

"What? And you be quiet, will you? Why, are you jealous?"

"No, I am not jealous. Of whom? Of him?"

"Why? He's handsome enough," Zanze says. "I find him handsome. Nice black hair. Lovely eyebrows. Raffaello couldn't have done better!"

He just sips at his apricot brandy as they go on talking about him.

"And then he's robust. Look at those shoulders."

"Eh, *piano*. You are making him shy."

"You leave him alone," Beppa says. "You leave him to me."

"And who's taking him from you?"

"Bunch of harpies."

"Listen to her! But you really do like him. You'd make a nice couple. A doctor and a— You are professional people!"

Again they burst into laughter.

"Then Friday," he says, unperturbed. "What time?"

"He means it, you know."

"I mean it too. A little vacation in Cortina is just what I need. In the snow. It's dry up there. Such rheumatism here in this moisture. Cold but dry up there. Crisp. And I love snow."

"So where shall we meet?"

"I'll meet you at the station. I live near there, Cannaregio."

Cannaregio, he thinks, and he's touched, because that's where his people, who were from Venice, used to live long ago. "What time?"

"When does the train leave?"

"I don't know."

"I don't care. I'll meet you there at ten, and if we have to wait we'll wait in the bar. That's what I do all day anyway. We'll take the first train after ten."

"Alright," he says. "I'll be there."

"Are you really going to go, Beppa?" Zanze says.

"Why not? What's doing here anyway? Don't you see it's like a funeral home? What have I got to lose? I've got nothing to lose."

"With him?"

"What's wrong with him? He's kind. Isn't it true that you are kind?"

"Very kind."

"You don't have a bad temper, do you? You don't get mad?"

"Can you imagine him getting mad?"

"I never get mad."

He rises and looks at them all. For the first time he feels a little self-conscious. He smiles. He raises his hand as if to wave them goodbye. "Well, good night." And looking at Beppa, "Don't forget now. Day after tomorrow, at ten, at the station. I'll be waiting for you at the bar. If they shouldn't give me the weekend I'll let you know. But they will. Friday at ten."

"Make it eleven," she says.

Her saying eleven gives him the feeling that maybe she will really be there. He pays the check and he's gone.

On the way, he thinks: She said she has nothing to lose. And: they are the most moral people, those who have nothing to lose. Divested of all interests. Absolutely disinterested and without bias. Theoretically, anyway. Like a judge or a political figure who has to make a decision on a certain case and divests himself of all he owns connected with that particular case. The most moral of people, streetwalkers. He smiles at the paradox. Or am I mistaken, he wonders.

At the barracks, he knocks at the door. The sentry looks out through a peephole, recognizes him, unlatches the door, clicks his heels and salutes him.

"At ease," he says. and "Good night." He goes up to his room.

At eleven on Friday, he's at the bar in the station. 11:05. 11:10. He buys a newspaper. 11:20. He has always been punctual, and wasted a lot of time because of it. He has another page or two to read. He looks at the time, at the newspaper again, at the door, at the clock, at the time. Then, breathless, she appears. She has a tweed overcoat on and a suit, low-heeled shoes, not much makeup and is carrying a valise. She looks as much a traveler as anyone there. A traveler, nothing more, nothing less. "I'm late," she says. "I—"

"Relax. There's no train till 1:20. Have a drink, and then we can go to the restaurant here. I thought you weren't going to come."

"And why wouldn't I come? I said I would."

"Yes, but—"

"I went to bed so late last night! I was so sleepy this morning I could hardly get up. But I made it."

She doesn't look sultry here. In a way he misses her look of the night before last—and every other time he has seen her. As farmers look best in their sun-bleached clothes in the field, coal miners in their black sooty clothes and boots, fishermen in their heavy sweaters and Levi's, nurses in their white uniforms, and scholars in their shabby garb in the library stacks, so she looked best in her gaudy thin dresses at the bar. But he tries hard to dissemble and says, "You look smart."

"My travel suit," she says, shrugging her shoulders.

"Do you do much traveling?"

"No. This is the first time I've gone anywhere in more than two years. I'm stuck in this place."

"Oh well, Venice isn't so bad."

"Sometimes I hate it," she says.

At the restaurant, she eats with great appetite, then, putting knife and fork down and touching her midriff, says, "*Basta,*" and sighs.

He buys two round-trip tickets, first class, hoping to find a compartment all to themselves. One is vacant, but soon other passengers enter. He is next to her by the window. She closes her eyes as the journey begins. He has the strange feeling he's married, married to her. With her eyes closed, he can look at her closely, the way he has never looked at her before. He scans her neck, her face and her hair, inch by inch. He looks at her hands, wrists, knees, ankles, feet. He wonders about her. Beppa, beside him on a train. He can hardly believe it. Yet she's here with him. And the train rushes on across the lagoon, to Mestre, and heads north over the plain, toward the Alps. The first foothills appear. The foothills get higher. They see the first snow.

"Oh, how hot it is in here," she says and fans herself with *Oggi*, a magazine she brought with her.

He opens the window a crack.

"No, no," she says. "I don't want to catch cold. It's bad for you when you are sweating."

He's amused. She sounds so much like his patients. And he closes the window.

Cortina. He has never been to Cortina, but he has made inquiries about the hotels and reserved a room. Not that he really believed they would use it. When he booked it, he thought—he was almost sure—he would have to cancel it later. But here they are, on their way to it, in a taxi.

The room has a fine view of the mountains, but she doesn't look out. She tests the bed. He gives the porter a tip. At last they are alone. Gently he strokes her arms.

"No," she says. "Be still," and she goes to the mirror. She unpacks, hangs her clothes very neatly. Finally she goes to the window. "*Quant'è bello,*" she says.

He stands next to her, his arm circling her waist, and looks out.

"Now I'll freshen up a bit," she says, and withdraws into the bathroom.

He can't help thinking she's very refined.

They go down to the lobby, then take a stroll about the center of town. The little streets and squares are crowded with skiers returning from their afternoon on the slopes. There are family groups—children, parents, grandparents—all well clad, some of them sporting Tirolean hats and other funny headgear. Sleek, athletic couples walk briskly with skis over their shoulders and pants that are pulled very taut. And there are the Alpini, the feather-hatted mountain soldiers, who remind him of the months he spent with them. The townspeople—more casual, hanging around—look at the assortment of people as if they were actors' troupes come here to amuse them.

They windowshop. "Oh, the prices," she says. "They are worse than in Venice."

"Why don't we go in?"

"No, no, don't tempt me. If I go in there I'll be lost."

Is she trying to stick to what she said about spending? He recalls her mentioning a few items. "Didn't you say you needed a scarf, perfume, a new pair of gloves?"

She gives him a short but vigorous shake of her head.

She treats him as if she had a stake in his bank account. Isn't she taking her married role a little too seriously? She's so proper and prim. He wishes she were what she was. How can he make her be herself once again? Or is this her real self, this picture of a young woman in a tweed suit and coat, carrying a far from showy pocketbook, and casually holding onto his arm as if she had known him or as if they'd been married for years? Couldn't she be a little more playful?

For dinner he takes her to an elegant place. She reads the menu, or *is* she reading it? She's holding it up to her face.

"Do you see anything you like?" he asks her.

"Sh! I know that man over there."

He looks to his side. A middle-aged man with dark glasses is sitting at a nearby table with a matronly-looking woman.

"So?"

"I know him," she says, and her meaning of the word dawns upon him.

He rises. "Let's move to another table," he says, and looking at the man in the face he stands behind her chair and helps her out. The man is inscrutable behind his tinted glasses. He has an opaque, leathery face.

After dinner they take a ride in a jingling horse-drawn sleigh. Under the lights her cheeks look flushed like some of the children's beside them.

Back in the hotel there's a dance. They have a drink. She won't dance. She likes to sit in the shadow, in the almost-dark.

Then it is time to sleep. Again, somehow, she manages to carry on her married act. She's strangely demure. She kisses him once, on the lips. An innocent kiss. And their love, their first love, has the pureness, and insipidity, of a bead in a necklace all of mother-of-pearl.

The next day they slide down a slope on a sled. She has never skied nor does she want to. They return to the little town. "I am more at home on the streets," she says. Again she's reluctant to go into the shops. Her thrifty, parsimonious, home-economist role, which perhaps is her way of endearing herself to him and which he found touching at first, bores him now. "Come on, let's buy you something," he says and leads her into a store.

He buys her a red slip and a lacy buttercup nightgown. Silk slippers. A scarf. In another shop, perfume. She resists every purchase, but less and less with each one, and she looks more and more as she used to when, tired of long walks, he went into the San Moisè bar and saw her at ease with her friends.

"Now let's go back to the room," she says.

"No, buy some more."

"You don't have to. I told you you don't."

"I know, but let me. Don't worry about money—I've got plenty."

"I know how little they pay you."

"I've got other resources."

"You *save* those."

"Ah, you are such a darling. But let's have a good time."

"We'll have a good time."

"Yes, but I miss the Beppa I knew. Stop playing this housewifely role."

She glances at him with a serious, hurt look. "You are different too; not like you were in Venice, walking so thoughtfully along. Here you act silly."

"Do I? We are on a holiday here. Here in the distance! Just for the sake of distance I would travel. There's a nice store; I want to buy you a dress, the most elegant dress in the town."

"No," she laughs and pulls him away.

"Come on," he says, holding onto her hand.

"No, you mustn't!"

"I've never done any shopping for a woman. Come on, let me do it. Enough of this misery scene."

Smiling, she takes a few tentative steps. He swings open the door and they enter. "The golden one there, do you like it? The green one? The velvety red?"

She chooses a white one.

He says, "The collar's too high."

"No, it isn't. Alright, if you want me to I'll take the velvety red."

"Whichever you want."

"The white one then. Oh, no, the red. I'll take the red."

He pays with a check. In the bank he has money that his grandfather, an eminent lawyer, left him. With it he paid his way through medical school, had his little book of poems published, and, without hesitation, bought stocks that have failed him. This is more tangible stuff.

"And now for a necklace. No, you look better without one. A ring or a bracelet perhaps."

"No," she says with a laugh.

"Yes. It doesn't have to be studded with diamonds and rubies. It doesn't have to be gold. It can be silver if that makes you feel better."

He's drunk with glitter and color. She chooses an octagonal bracelet of solid Mexican silver.

That night they drink champagne and they dance. Men turn as they pass. He sees or imagines their furtive glances, hears whispers. Never mind. All the more fun. Yes, now he has her the way he wants her. Now she's herself once again. No mockery of a virtuous housewife. Her perfume is heady. Her step is rapid and bold. More champagne and more dancing. He follows her in the lead of a conga line that's advancing. Provocative, that's what he wants her to be. And when the dance is finished and the lights go out he holds her to him as he dreamed he would hold her. In bed, she's nothing as she was the night before, for he has stirred witchcraft in her eyes.

There is a moment, he has read, in the morning, soon after one wakes, in which one's judgment is clearer than at any other time. And she asks him, "Why did you buy me these things? Couldn't we just have had dinner, like the other night? It was so nice playing husband and wife. But you wanted me . . . to be . . . a whore. You wanted to give me those things in payment. You didn't like the little part I was playing. You didn't want me to be somebody else for a change."

And he wants to kiss her now, kiss her for what she wants to be, kiss her for what she was, kiss her for the part she was playing.

"No," she says, "whores don't kiss, don't you know?"

And he remembers the kiss she gave him the first night, the innocent kiss, the loving kiss, the kiss that he did not appreciate, the kiss that he did not value, and her love. And there is nothing he can say or do.

[1979]

The Emergency

"Being an Army doctor isn't like anything else," the medical captain said to the new medical sublieutenant, a young man who had just arrived in a winter uniform, though it was June in Tolmezzo, a little town in a valley of the eastern Italian Alps. "Why, even a Frugoni might find himself in difficulty." (Frugoni was reputed to be Italy's top clinician.) "When you're in a camp up there with three hundred men, only an orderly to help you and all your equipment in a haversack, you need a special talent. And the trouble with you fellows is, you haven't had the training. No sooner do you get out of medical school than you're whisked into the Army. They won't even let you intern. That would be too good. They've deferred you from military service for six years, and they can't wait another minute. No, though a few months in a hospital would only make sense and be to their advantage. All they let you have is three months' training in Florence, and don't tell me anything about that, because I know. All theory and half of it useless. No practice. But when you come up here it's a different story. Ninety-nine days out of a hundred, nothing happens—it's just routine. Then one day comes. The emergency. The crisis. And what do you do?"

The young man smiled and nodded.

"You can't do much, I'll tell you. You do your best, of course, but you only know so much. Ah! It's a bad system."

Again the young man nodded. He didn't need to be told. What the captain said was the truth, and it certainly applied to him. He didn't feel at all competent. This incompetence seemed to be centered not in his head, which was full of facts and information—he had done fairly well in his exams—but in his hands. They felt slow, inexperienced, despite their willingness to do. And the worst of it was that these words of the captain had a prophetic tone, sounded not so much like an observation as a warning. They carried the weight of an announcement, a special message for him, and he could see himself, maybe a hundred days from now, hearing those words over again the day he would be confronted with a crisis. That some crisis would come he had no doubt whatever. It was certain. Positive. He already started hoping that it wouldn't, and this hoping, like an inane prayer, seemed proof of his lack of self-confidence. Right then, he began preparing for the crisis as for an exam, studying, cramming his brain with more theory, and setting aside, in a box marked "Emergency," vials of adrenaline, morphine, atropine; plasma, needles, catgut. The collection kept increasing.

A hundred and more days passed. The company went on maneuvers. They camped on mountaintops. There were long marches and steep climbs, on which he was the only doctor. All he saw was blisters, backaches, bruises, swollen ankles, little fevers, upset stomachs. And he took out of his haversack pills, Band-Aids, elastic bandages, and straps. Was this all there was to it—to being an Army medic? Why, there was nothing to it! The days went by smoothly. Everything routine. All minor ailments. Perhaps he was just lucky and would continue to be lucky. He almost forgot what the captain told him.

In October, he was transferred to an outpost near the Austrian border. Now he had not just a haversack of medical equipment and supplies to himself but a whole infirmary. Six beds—all of them empty when he arrived. He seemed to bring good health with him, the way some people are said to bring good weather. In the dispensary, there was a glass cabinet full of surgical instruments, another full of disinfectants, yet another full of drugs, and he had a key to the narcotics. There were two high, narrow white beds in the center of the room, and by the walls a bureau, a desk, and two chairs, besides the cabinets. He used the desk—used it every day, to write reports, to make a note of who had called, of the pills he had given out, the little cuts he had bandaged, and so forth. The infirmary served a battalion. So each day more soldiers came to see him than when he had had only a company to look after. Sometimes someone would have to stay in bed for a few days. At one point, five of the six beds were taken. But there was nothing serious. If anything looked even half serious, he sent the soldier off to Udine, to the large Army hospital. He had an ambulance at his disposal. All he had to do was fill out a slip. The ambulance driver loved to go to Udine. Yes, it was an easy job.

At intervals, he went to visit a detachment of soldiers stationed up in Tarvisio, a village on the border. There the Vienna–Rome trains made a long stop, and once in a while there was so little to do he would go to the station just to take a look at the passengers leaning out the windows.

One afternoon when he was up in Tarvisio, he went for a stroll down the village main street. It was such a peaceful little town. The way a little town should be, he thought—the shops well stocked and neat; the sidewalks washed clean, still moist; flowerpots on nearly every windowsill; an air of peace. Interrupting it, two policemen with high boots, helmets, goggles, and leather jackets came out of a store and mounted their motorcycles with a swagger, as though the vehicles were two stallions. With a flourish, they pushed the starter cranks and turned the accelerators. Instantly, the motors roared. They revved them up. The roar took on the character of a scream. He couldn't help feeling a certain dislike, even hate for them. Then they departed—shot out, one close behind the other. Soon the village was as quiet as it had been. After a while, he himself left Tarvisio to return to his village and the barracks. He looked into the infirmary. Everything was quiet there, too. Just as well, he thought.

At the village theatre—a few minutes' walk down from the barracks—they were showing a movie he hadn't seen. After a half hour at his desk, he thought he might as well go down. As he usually did when leaving the base, he told the medical orderly where he could find him, and went along to the theatre.

The movie was better than he expected—quite entertaining, in fact—and yet, halfway through, he felt an urge to leave. He kept himself seated, but the urge to leave grew. Hardly knowing why, or what he would do when he got out, he rose and slowly walked away. Without hurrying, he went up to the infirmary and looked around. There was nothing new. He sat down. Why had he left? No reason. He shook his head slowly. Perhaps he ought to go back. But somehow he felt he should remain where he was. He stayed on, looking vacantly at the sheet of green blotting paper on his desk. And then, a minute later, he heard the distant sound of a horn blowing without pause, and getting louder. He went to the window. A small truck was coming at full speed up the road, the sound of its horn increasing as it approached. It pulled up in front of the infirmary door, and he rushed out. So did the driver out of the cab. From the barracks several soldiers ran toward them.

"Are you the doctor?" the driver said.

"Yes."

"Two seriously injured men," he said, opening the back door of the truck. "Motorcycle police. They didn't make a curve."

The doctor looked at the two men. From their uniforms he had little doubt they were the same two he had seen earlier that afternoon up in Tarvisio. "Easy now," he said as he helped move them to two stretchers. They were carried to the dispensary and laid on the two high, narrow beds. He looked at them again. Seriously injured was an understatement, he thought. The two men were a shambles. He had never seen such injuries. Wherever he looked there was something wrong. Nothing seemed whole. Nothing seemed intact. And there he was, alone, the only doctor. His hands trembling, he opened the cabinet doors and rushed from one to the other in a mute frenzy. Adrenaline, morphine, plasma, syringe, and needles all seemed to be hidden. Cotton wool, bandages, tourniquet, forceps, catgut—he looked for all of them at one and the same time, and didn't seem to be able to find anything. And yet they were there. He knew they were all there.

"Calm, now, calm," he told himself, and tried steadying his hands. His head seemed to be swimming, and hot, hot. "Hemorrhage and shock," he told himself. "These are the two things a man can die of right away. Never mind the fractures. Never mind the danger of infections now. Just hemorrhage and shock." He found a tourniquet, and tied it round an arm. Another tourniquet he tied round a leg. He got the plasma. He readied a syringe. And then he looked at the men again.

"But Doctor," someone said, "I think they are dead."

"Dead?"

He hadn't thought of that. Life—he had only thought of life, and how it could be saved. The thought that they might be dead had not entered his mind.

"Dead?" he said again, and felt their pulses. There was no pulse in either. He felt shamefully relieved.

"You are right," he said. "From their head injuries, no doubt. They probably died on the spot. When did the accident happen?" he added, turning to the driver.

"Oh, it couldn't have been more than twenty minutes ago," the driver said. "They overtook me. 'Those two men are going too fast,' I said. 'They are not going to make that curve. . . .' Yes, twenty minutes I would say. Up on the Promollo road."

Twenty minutes—when he had left the movie. He looked at the two men again. They seemed so peaceful, lying there. So unconcerned about their frightful state. Quite without a worry. And there was nothing to be done. Absolutely nothing to be done except put the things he had taken out back in the cabinets. That was something he could do. One by one, his hands not trembling anymore, he put them back.

[1972]

The Last Kiss

The theater, a small and fragile building on a wharf, is no more, burned down, set on fire by two local kids for kicks one winter night, and, despite much fund raising, it has never been rebuilt. Gone with it are the letters from Eugene O'Neill, Tennessee Williams, and others that Julia Westcott had received and framed, gone their photographs and the posters of their plays that she had hung in the theater's lobby. She had played in these and in a hundred others, but that was in the past, long before Livio met her.

By that time she was in her seventies and acting was behind her. She had withdrawn backstage, to support the new actors with her enthusiasm and what was left of her resources. The theater didn't belong to her, though once she'd had a share in it. In a way, though, it was more hers than anyone else's. She tended and preserved it till the flames turned it into ashes.

So it, too, like the plays it housed, had a dramatic ending, one more frightening and more real than any playwright or actor would dare to have staged. Now the sea breezes fan the vacant lot.

But on an early September weekend twenty years ago it stood there on the wharf intact, its weathered shingles as silver as the breaking waves, its door waiting to be opened, its curtain to be raised.

The play, which Livio had written, and which was almost as ephemeral as a day lily—it ran for just three nights—was entitled *Live Well,* the words Eskimos greet each other with in meeting and in parting. It had to do with their extreme hospitality to strangers, especially those who have lost their way and are dying of cold. It was really a very secondary play, but Livio believed in it perhaps more than he should have, and was in a pathetic state of expectation, tension, and excitement. He had quite fallen for the young actress—the wife, the provider of the warmth; he admired the boy who played the stranger; and, though Livio would have spoken the lines quite differently, he was very forgiving of the actor who played the unjealous husband. He was good friends with the director, and felt great warmth for the spectators as they began streaming in and filling the theater till there wasn't a vacant chair left. He loved the town. He loved, in short, everyone, but most of all Julia, the factotum, the animator, the spirit of the place. The play itself could have been more subtle. Some of the spectators, while keenly interested at first, disapproved of it as it went on, or so it seemed to him. It was successful enough, though, for the company to feel quite festive at the end, especially on the third and last night.

After that performance, Livio invited Julia, the actors, the director, and other friends to a party at his house, fourteen miles away. The weather all that weekend was so good that you couldn't feel sad summer was coming to an end—the leaves, some already hemmed gold or crimson, shone out; the horizon was so clear that, in the daytime, you could see the outline of land forty miles across the bay, and, at night, its lights glittering. He drove alone with Julia in his old convertible. They had known each other for two years now, and she had put on two one-act plays of his the year before. They had met at a party given by a friend—Sheila—at a house not very far from his own. Julia and Livio had talked about Chekhov and especially about Keats (her favorite poet), and he felt almost as if Keats, and not Sheila, had introduced them. Julia had a graceful, frail, ethereal look about her, a poetic quality. When she told him she was past acting, he said, "But not playing," and they both laughed. Though married and in his mid-forties, there was a certain innocence about him. He had a trusting smile, could not dissemble and was quite unpretentious. Beauty he could not ignore. Perhaps these traits endeared him to her. She might also have been attracted by his being Italian—she had studied the language, been to Italy, and as a young woman, in Boston, during the Sacco and Vanzetti trial, she had been arrested and spent a night in jail for demonstrating in their favor.

Tonight they drove not along the highway but along a winding back road. The top was down, the sky starry, the air balmy, the moon full. It was so beautiful he went very slowly. The crickets made a portentous din. "Between crickets and stars," she said. The whole night seemed to be singing. The low ground cover of bearberry, bayberry, and beach plum gave them a wide view of the low hills and dunes, bathed in moonlight. In the moon's delicate light, the ridges blended into each other softly, wave after wave, east toward the ocean, west toward the bay, whose pearly ripple could here and there be seen. Then, in a valley, by a stream, the road went through a tall wood. The trees arched over the road, which became like a living tunnel. The sound of the motor and of the tires' tread mingled with the sound of the crickets. On a straight stretch of road, he stopped the car and switched off the engine. There was hardly any late traffic on the small road, and he put the lights out. The night seemed even more magical, and more tuneful. They turned to each other, and he took her up in his arms and he kissed her with passion. It was an ageless kiss—one in which age was forgotten, one in which they forgot themselves. Then they drove on. In his home at the party, again and again their eyes met, knowingly, rekindling the warmth of the kiss again and again in the fondest reflection.

His wife was there, but wasn't his play about free love? If it had a point at all, then it was that, the idea of no jealousy, of a love "that to divide is not to take away."

Winters Julia spent not in the little town by the sea where the theater was, but in the city, in the first-floor apartment of a nice old red-brick building she owned on a pretty street. Sometimes he went to see her there purely for the pleasure of her company, to be in the presence of the grace of an earlier generation. Charity had nothing to do with his visits, rather they were like a bee's descent to a flower, which may do the flower some good, though doing good isn't the bee's intention. And they corresponded. Her letters were written in a flowing, clear, but not *too* clear hand, with some crossed-out words, as he thought letters should be written.

With the passing of the years—she was now in her eighties—she rarely went out of her apartment. Though she could still read (and without glasses), her eyesight had weakened, so a friend had the idea of giving her a TV and asked others for contributions. Soon, enough money was collected for a large color set.

"Something is making everything much dimmer," she wrote Livio about the TV. Like city lights dimming the stars, he thought. Reading the letter, he could see her—an actress who had never had television, not because she couldn't afford it but because she regarded it as a brash and buzzing upstart that had put out the lights in many theaters, and silenced voices that were to her much dearer. Not to seem ungracious, she accepted the TV. And so, her letter continued, she would "try to like it for the sake of so many friends who insisted there were plays and wild animals to enjoy and talk about with them."

Giving her the set had certainly been a kind thing to do, and one could see why her friends thought she would appreciate the gift. Yet its introduction into her house seemed like a bad fifth act to a well wrought play. Less a gift than an unwitting corruption. It might help her pass the days and nights. She might become accustomed, even addicted to it, and miss it if it broke or was stolen. But it was sad, a little like bringing "the comforts of religion" to a dying heretic. Let people live and die according to their principles, Livio thought, and hadn't sent any money. He took her out to dinner and a play instead, taking great care to help her get down her doorstep and into his car which he had double-parked. They had dinner in a cozy little restaurant under candlelight. She looked at the white table cloth on which the wine cast red reflections. "Isn't it nice that these aren't stains," she said. "For a moment I thought I'd spilled some wine. Just scarlet lights."

The goblets were small, mere thimblefuls, but she got quite heady, and Livio had to hold her close as they climbed the marble staircase of the theater. Even so she almost stumbled. He held her closer still, his arm around her waist, and felt her warmth. After the play, taking her home, she found, to her delight, piled in a trash bin and sticking up like flowers, some gilded and quite unusual wooden decorations from an old house that was being remodelled, and she picked out a couple of them and carried them to her apartment, as joyful as could be. Perhaps it was the last time she would go to a theater. He felt it was a victory of sorts over television. Going back to his car, which he had parked very nearby, he found he had got a ticket, but that didn't dampen his mood.

How beautiful, he thought, "Something is making everything much dimmer." Said so well, the gift was almost worth giving, worth receiving. Her reaction gave the whole thing a final twist. She had turned the tables around. It made for a fitting finish after all. Let them give what they wanted—having said such words she was safe, whole, uncorrupted, on home ground. No matter what happened, no matter how much she watched TV, those words saved her, saved the situation—a little (did he dare say it?) like Galileo's "And yet it moves."

Was he making too much of her remark? Perhaps because he knew her apartment it seemed meaningful to him. The living room had a marble image of Keats on a pedestal, several antique chairs, tables, a chest, books in glass-panelled bookcases, some paintings. It was a room that went the length of the house. One window looked out on the street, the other on a small walled-in garden. There wasn't much light. The patina of time was everywhere. The plain, dark-brown linoleum under the Persian carpets had been there for fifty years; she was so light-footed that it wasn't worn, and, from the many coats of wax, had acquired a polish—an odd effect on such dull material.

The room seemed full of shadows, but if you looked closely, things emerged out of the penumbra, disclosing themselves as in a painting that time and coats of varnish and fumes of candles have made dark. And there she sat, each time he went to see her, pretty, serving the coffee in the finest cups, looking more and more graceful with the years. Her hair was like a little cloud. The imprint of time was on her face, yet she could have been a girl there in the half-light. Her eyes were large and pensive, deep pools reflecting time, and looking larger for the spareness of her face. She was not past blushing. And her hands were active; she wrote many letters, some of these trying to promote plays.

So imagine a color TV set before her, and watch her, restless, disoriented in her own house, Keats concealed, her books a blur, the paintings blotched out, the silence broken, and the shadow cancelled by this new-fangled brightness.

He remembered the last time he saw her. She had been very ill with a virus and had had a high fever. She was recovering, but looked very frail like a flower that the blade of the sickle has spared. She was sitting on a living room couch. A student nurse was looking after her. "And I didn't die," she said wistfully. "It seems such a waste. I was ready to die but death just passed me by, wouldn't have me, and now I'll have to wait some more, who knows how long. Viral pneumonia—it should have been enough, but it wasn't."

"Oh, don't say that," he told her, and held her by the hand as if to lead her back to life's central path. "The body knows best."

"It doesn't know when to quit." She looked at her cat. "Moonlight has been very good to me, lying close beside me, sometimes on my chest, as if to ease the pain and congestion."

She didn't live alone, but with this cat, Moonlight. He was given her by a friend as a small kitten, six years before, when her former cat—Moonmist—had died. Livio had known Moonmist also, though not from a kitten. Julia had had him for many years before Livio met her, but he didn't think he would ever see, not if he lived as long as she, a more beautiful relationship between a cat and her owner. Owner? The word seemed hardly appropriate. They owned each other. Moonmist was quite irreplaceable, and when he finally died of old age, a little too quickly her friend—the same one who had the idea of buying her the TV—gave her Moonlight. It was a thoughtful initiative, but clumsily timed. It gave the impression that Moonmist could be replaced, the way one replaces an appliance. Also Moonlight wasn't anything like Moonmist in character, though in appearance they were alike, both being Persian and very soft and silvery. The old cat had been wise and restful. The new one jumped all over the place and soon smashed a vase. It was difficult to keep Moonlight confined. But she did her best. And since each year that went by for her was like five for the cat, Moonlight was soon closer to her in age, nearly as close as Moonmist had been. So Livio was glad to hear that Moonlight had sort of nursed Julia in her crisis, and indeed he seemed the image of peace.

Julia, as if knowing this meeting would not recur, asked the student nurse to bring in a little package from another room. She gave it to Livio and he unwrapped it. It contained a very small, old, and rare edition of Petrarch's poems. Here, he thought, was a friend who knew what to give and when to give it. Poetry had knit their friendship, and he vowed it would never unravel.

Her fever was down and the nurse said something about her looking better.

"Have you been watching TV?" Livio asked her.

"Oh dear no!" she said shrugging with horror. "It's there behind the sofa on the floor. I never watch it." She seemed to resent the very presence of it and had it hidden from sight, disposed of, *banished.* He felt like cheering.

Soon he left, meaning to return, but never did. He heard about her from Sheila, who sometimes went to visit. Sheila told him that unfortunately Moonlight's good disposition didn't last; he had given Julia's hands, arms and face some deep scratches. Apparently the cat had developed an intense and unaccountable dislike for his mistress, and had finally become so dangerous he had to be taken away.

Not long after that, Julia herself was taken away from her apartment to a nursing home, and her nice old house sold. Still, death kept her waiting for some years.

"She is so listless, just a shadow of her former self," Sheila said to Livio one day. "She is in her nineties, you know. Close to a hundred, I think, and she didn't recognize me. Nor, I must confess, did I recognize her right away, one in a row of very old women in wheelchairs, all with the same expression, or rather lack of expression. She was so distinctive once, so very bright—and now she just didn't respond. Only when I mentioned you did her eyes light up, and she repeated your name, *Livio, Livio.* It was amazing. It was too touching! For a moment she was herself again. What was it between you two anyway? What went on? She really loves you. You should go to see her. It would be so good for her. It would revive her. I don't think anything else will. You must."

One day, in the city, he looked for the nursing home, but couldn't find it and soon gave up. Was it that he felt she didn't want to be seen in that place and in that state? He remembered going to Italy to visit his mother just a few months before she died. She was very ill, and a stupid doctor, unable to make a diagnosis, had recommended that her teeth be extracted, on the assumption that they harbored foci of infection. This was done. There was a delay in readying the dentures for her, and, seeing Livio, she brought both hands in front of her mouth and chin, not to be seen toothless by him.

He learned of Julia's death from a telephone message left in his mail box at the college where he taught. It didn't give the name of the person who had left it, just that she remembered him fondly.

Late in the summer, driving home from a party in the town by the sea where the theatre had been, on a night that was extraordinarily like that other night, he remembered the kiss, perhaps—no, probably—no, almost certainly—her last passionate kiss, and, for a moment, it all came together, life, under the full moon for whom twenty years are as nothing. Like a lover he left the highway for the back road, and, between crickets and stars, stopped the car and listened.

[1989]

The Prince

I see him—a tall, thin man, looking the taller for his thinness, in a Glen-plaid, double-breasted suit, and a silk, constricting looking tie—walking down the street, alone, as usual. One is apt to meet him any time, but especially at this hour of the night, when Verona begins to look deserted. Holding himself a little stiffly, as though there were some danger of his falling, he walks an undulating course. One hand stretches a trouser pocket. The other holds a cigarette—for elegance's sake. And he smiles. The smile is his most distinguishing feature. It is constant, unperturbed, contented. He wears it like his tie. He is looking straight in front of him, yet he could be looking at the sky. He hasn't seen me yet. I swear he hasn't, though we are awfully close. By turning sharply left down this narrow street, or perhaps even by crossing over to the other sidewalk, I could miss him. I know someone who ducks the moment he sees him. But I won't. I, too, am alone, as usual. Perhaps we have something in common. And he is one of the few people in this city who have ever invited me over to their house.

"Hello," I say.

He turns sharply toward me from a tiny, involuntary detour he has made, and I smell spirits. "Oh, what are you doing?" he says affably, in his soft, mild voice.

"Just going for a walk. And you?"

He never answers questions. "How are you?" he says.

"Fine. How are you?"

"And how is your cousin?" he says. I have a cousin who is in the diplomatic service, and he rather fancies that.

"I don't know—I haven't seen him for years."

"How much does he get? He makes a good salary, doesn't he?"

He is obsessed with the idea of money. He will talk about nothing else. No matter whom he is speaking of, it is always the man's salary he wants to know about—as if I could enlighten him. Sometimes I invent an answer. But he is only interested in his questions, not my answers. Often he repeats a question I have fully replied to. He goes on and on, touring the city. Sometimes he'll go into a bar and order a cognac. All considered, he stands his drinks very well. One is conscious that he has been drinking, but he's never drunk.

"And how much do you make?" he asks, with his impertinent smile. At last I leave him; I *have* to leave him.

He wasn't always like that. When I first knew him, in 1950, he used to talk about writing—an article for a newspaper, I think it was. I don't believe he ever actually wrote one, but he had the aspiration, which is something. And he used to answer questions, not just ask them, though admittedly he was never very good at it. During the war, he had been a fairly active anti-Fascist—active enough to have been rounded up as a suspect and put in jail for a few days. He was very proud of this. His smile would fade when he told me about it, and I nodded in admiration. A few years after the war, he had married an American girl, who left him after a couple of weeks. He told me this several times, as though I lacked a memory. I think perhaps he wanted to impress on me that at least one woman hadn't disdained him.

He is a prince. His house—a palace, really—is the most desirable in town. I used to go and visit him when I was stationed in the Army here.

"Come and see me sometime," he had said to me, after my brother (I don't know how they met) had introduced us on the street, thirteen years ago.

"Where? At the palace?" From where we were, we could see it gleaming in the distance—a colossal, many-terraced structure, a thing of another age, impossible nowadays.

"Yes," he said, and told me that the front entrance—a huge gate on the street named, like the palace, after his family—was kept permanently shut. The present access was from the back. He gave me the address; it could have been anybody's. I had entertained the idea of that great gate opening for me and my walking through a scented garden, perhaps skirting a statued fountain, to the hall. Still, when I did go and call on him, I was impressed with the back entrance, too. The door led into a beautiful old stone courtyard. When I mentioned the prince's name, a liveried janitor rang a bell and showed me up a red-carpeted staircase to the second floor. There a maid in frills was at the door. She led me down two or three salons to one that perhaps had a few more armchairs than the others. But I didn't sit down. I went to the window, which was on the façade, and looked down on the garden, and on the city, and at the sunset.

"You lucky man, to have this splendid view," I said as he appeared. I commented on the beauty of his home. How pleased he was! I had the feeling he didn't often capitalize on its advantages, and that this was one occasion. He gloated. With his long, close-shaven, reddish neck, which he sometimes stretched to ease the constriction of his collar, his small head, with its few wispy curls, his thin nose, his paper-thin, almost transparent ears and rather pouting lips, he seemed as delighted as a duck that has found water. He showed me a bit more of the house. But there were many doors that he didn't open. Whole sections seemed precluded to him. He said something about their being his mother's and his brothers'. He was the youngest brother—thirty then, but looking younger for the innocence apparent on his face.

On one of my last visits to his house, he showed me his bedroom, and I understood why he hadn't shown it to me before. It was at the back of the house, and rather small and dark, and to get to it one had to climb up a few steps. One had the impression of going into the attic. His mother and his brothers had put him there. His father, the old prince, was dead.

A few years later, his mother died, too, and he was left with his brothers to contend with. First thing, they urged him to get a divorce from the American girl, in case he should die and she should lay claim to his share of the property.

I met him in Rome when he had this tremendous task of getting a divorce in mind. I had left Verona two years before; I hadn't seen him in the interval, and I was shocked to see how he had deteriorated. He looked shriveled, pinched. He asked me if I could recommend a lawyer to him. I knew one, and gave him the name and address. But getting a divorce in Italy is not a simple matter. A law states that there is no divorce. You have to start from there. It was an unequal task for him, even with a good lawyer, and after a few days he gave it up and came to see me in my apartment to tell me so. He borrowed ten dollars from me. He was always short of money—he didn't work, and his brothers kept him on a very small allowance. He didn't seem at all unhappy to have failed in his efforts to get a divorce. I think he liked to consider himself a married man. And then, he wasn't going to die. And if he did, why should he worry about what happened after on this earth? He invited me to a villa his family owned on the seashore. But I was far too busy to leave Rome.

•

After his visit, I didn't see him for another three or four years. Now, though, I've returned to Verona—I am living there—and I meet him inevitably. We are both fond of walking late at night about the center of town. Often we are the only two people in sight on the main square. It seems like a large stage. If we only had some drama to enact! But we are just night wanderers. Again I am half tempted to avoid him, but again I don't. Is it his mildness? He is the mildest, the most harmless man I know. Or is it that he is the idlest, the most ineffectual, and that I feel quite accomplished beside him? I hope not—I hope it isn't for a practical reason at all. But I must admit that failure interests me more than success, a man who has lost a million dollars more than one who has made that much. I do know some successful people here, and I change direction fast to avoid them.

Somehow, he thinks I lead a brilliant life. "Whom do you see?" he keeps asking me, like a snob. At the same time, he is puzzled by my clothes. This is a dressy city. He points at my sweater, at my corduroy trousers, at my rather dusty shoes, and ridicules me. "Aren't you ashamed to go about like that?" he says.

"Don't be so conventional," I reply.

He tells me that he is not living at the palace any more. His brothers apparently have put him out. He's staying in a hotel I've never heard of. It sounds small and cheap. But it must have its advantages, because he doesn't seem to regret the move; he is not depressed about it.

We go into a bar. He offers me a cognac, which we drink standing up, Italian style, then leave. He's looking absolutely delighted after this. That stuff keeps him alive. He reminds me of a sparrow just come out of a cherry tree, with the juice fresh in its beak. How marvelous that he should feel so exhilarated. After all, most of the time he drinks alone; there is no company to cheer him except the city's—its lights, its bars. They are able to cheer him as they don't cheer me. There's no doubt about it, his smile is his redeeming feature. He would be impossible without it. It isn't a dopey smile; it isn't a fool's smile, either. It changes. It is alive.

Some days pass and I don't see him.

Then one morning he is at my apartment door. This is out of the ordinary—I've never seen him in the morning, and it's the first time he has come here. He stands on the threshold for a moment, and I see that he isn't smiling. Without his smile, he looks positively grim.

"Come in, come in," I say, and he steps in. He hasn't been drinking, either, I soon notice.

"Can you recommend a lawyer to me?" he says. He didn't look like this when he asked me the same question in Rome.

"No, I'm afraid I can't," I say. "I don't know any here. Why? what's the matter?"

"It's my brothers," he says, and I am again surprised; he answers my question. "They want to interdict me—have me declared mentally incompetent and placed under a restraint."

"Why? You are perfectly sane!"

"So I won't be able to sell my share of the family property, which I want to do. I want to make a judicial sale."

"Do you get any money from your property?"

"I get practically nothing from it—a few thousand lire, which I have to go and collect from their lawyer. One of my brothers, who is himself a lawyer, has set all the lawyers in this city against me. I haven't found one yet who will take my case. Yesterday a court official came to my hotel and asked me a great many questions. My brothers had sent him, as a first step in their efforts to interdict me."

I am astounded by this speech. I have never before seen him so alert, so sober, so serious, so sound, so concerned. He strikes me as a man in the fullest possession of his senses, one with his wits about him, cornered but not helpless, out to defend himself.

"You have nothing to fear," I tell him. "You talk to them as you've been talking to me and it will be clear to everyone that they have no case against you. They'll never win."

"I am not an irresponsible man, am I?"

"Of course not."

"But you don't know my brothers. They are powerful. Powerful."

"You'll beat them."

"But I need a lawyer. I must find a good lawyer."

"I wish I knew one," I say.

A similar case reported in the newspapers a few years ago, in which the person on trial won, comes to my mind, and I tell him about it. Perhaps he can trace the defense lawyer. But he doesn't take much note—my recollection is too vague. So I suggest that he go and see a good friend of mine with whom he is acquainted, a sculptor who lately has been ably defended in a civil suit.

"That's a good idea," he says, making immediate note of it, and goes toward the door.

I look at him, a man intent on defending his integrity. I would like to tell him that his brothers, without knowing it, have done him a great service—they have made him look like a man again; they have shaken him out of his torpor with their action. But, of course, they are not aware of it. They are thinking about his property, and they push the case against him.

A fiasco—the judge can't accept their recommendation. The prince their brother is in his right mind—see how he answers? I learn it from the sculptor. The prince I haven't seen.

Then, walking about town a few days after the hearing, I do meet him. "So you won the case, eh?"

He is smiling. He seems very pleased with himself. He smells of spirits. "Don't you ever wear a tie?" he says.

I grimace at his question, as at a fly. "Sometimes. Tell me how it all went."

"Your cousin Sandro," he says, "is he still in Paris?"

"Yes, yes, I think so. But tell me about the case. Were your brothers there? What was the judge like?"

He answers all my questions with a smile and not a word. And suddenly I am annoyed with that complacent smile, and I feel like giving him a shake. But, however vigorous, it would be nothing compared to the moral shaking he has received, and I don't try to. "Good-bye," I say.

But he doesn't answer good-byes either. He just walks away smiling, as though he hadn't met me.

[1963]

The Nightingale

"Come, you are going to hear a nightingale, Mother," the son said, speaking into her hearing aid and taking her gently by the arm. He was a very tall, very thin, willowy young man; she was an old lady, close to seventy, thin, too, and with a long, bony face and large, wild, searching eyes, which seemed to be trying to make up for the other, impaired sense. Together they advanced cautiously, as on a venture.

Somewhere in the darkness of the ilex trees, a nightingale was singing. The nightingales sang at night and in the early morning and through the day. But in the daytime they required a shady covert, like that which the ilex grove provided. One hardly ever saw them. They were shy and nearly always alone, and small enough that a few leaves obscured them. But they were very lively, and sometimes, if one stood still under the trees and peered up to where the branches became dark-leaved fronds, a movement would—at least, partially—disclose them: a play of gray and russet in the shadow.

In the middle of the grove, the mother and son stopped and listened. The sound was so clear it filled the garden and the fields around it and the wide stone house, but her eyes, looking to this side and to that alertly, and her neck, craning and turning as if to lend first one and then the other of her ears, showed that she couldn't hear it. In a minute, they returned to the long, low wall they had started from—a kind of parapet at the edge of the garden, on which the young man's wife and little girl, both of them as slender as himself, were sitting with me. They were an American family, living in Florence, and they had come for tea, driven thirty miles to my family's house in the Chianti Hills.

"Did she hear it?" I asked, though from the way she was shaking her head, discomfited, it was plain she hadn't.

"No," the young man said. "My mother has never heard a nightingale. I hoped she might hear this one."

"I couldn't hear it," the mother said. "I've always wanted to hear a nightingale. You know, in America we don't have them. I tried to hear them in England. I went into the woods and listened for them. But I never heard one. I should have come here when I was younger and my hearing was still good."

"My mother was a singer."

"Was she? I hear you were a singer," I said in a loud voice.

"Yes, yes, I sang."

"She was a very good singer—a concert singer."

"You know," the old lady said, not following, "all my life I've wanted to hear a nightingale, and never have. Came here too late. Is it still singing?"

"Yes, Mother."

The sustained, continued song enlivened the air.

My mother, who had met the guests briefly when they arrived, now came into the garden. "Ah, the nightingale," she said.

"Isn't it wonderful?" the young man said.

"Oh, this is nothing. They sing better and better as spring advances. Now it is April. You just wait till May."

"It sounds so perfect now," the daughter-in-law, a singer herself, said. "I can't imagine how it could improve."

"Oh, with practice."

"Do they need to practice? I don't believe *they* need to practice."

The old lady, left out of the conversation, gazed at the ilex trees, took a few steps toward them, then came back.

More members of the household appeared as tea was served. The conversation shifted to Florence. When asked how she liked living in that city, the old lady gave an unusual picture of it. Black clouds shrouded the moonlight there, she said. I had observed at night in Florence dense, silver-fringed clouds screening the moon, and had called them violet and deep blue. How much more effective, I thought, to say that they were black. I looked at her, taken with her.

After tea, the guests were shown around the house. I accompanied them a little way, then left them with my mother and went out into the garden and sat again on the low wall. Just beyond it, on an ancient olive tree that grew up to the level of the garden from the field below, a bird was singing. A nightingale. Less than twenty feet away and in full view. I could hardly believe it. It seemed to contradict all my notions about the bird. But there it was, russet and gray, about six inches long, its note distinct, unmistakable. The olive tree had been recently pruned, and the nightingale sang, unconcealed and unafraid, on the sparse branches. I could see the throat throbbing with the song, the beak, the feathers and the plumes ruffled by the wind. Was it lovesick? It didn't move; it just stood perched on the little branch and sang, looking forlorn. "Well!" I said to myself, and moved away and quickly went into the house and, running from room to room, looked for the old lady and at last found her in the kitchen. "There's a nightingale singing on an olive tree close to the wall," I told her. "Will you come?"

"Oh, a nightingale, you say?"

"Yes, come," I said, and quickly but with care led her through a passage, down two steps, into the drawing room, and, afraid that she might trip, yet anxious lest she miss the bird, gave her an arm and took her to the garden and the wall. The nightingale was still singing, on just about the same branch as before.

"You see him?" I said. "There," and I pointed to it.

But there was no need to point. The bird was right in front of us.

"Yes," she said.

"Do you hear him?"

There was no reply. She was shaking her head, trying to capture the sound.

"He is singing," I said. "Can't you hear him?" I looked at the old lady. She was deaf to it. "It goes like this," and I whistled an imitation of the song.

"I heard it," the woman said. "I heard it then." But obviously what she had heard was my whistling. Yet she seemed delighted, enraptured. Her eyes were aglow. "I must tell my son," she said, and as quickly as we had come out we went indoors again.

"I heard the nightingale," she said triumphantly.

"You did? Mother!"

"How wonderful," the daughter-in-law said.

"I'd never heard it before, and I thought I would die without hearing it. But I heard it. Just for a moment I heard it. Right by the wall. He took me there."

"And was it up to expectation?" her son asked her.

She stopped still. She hadn't considered that. "Well, no. I had imagined it more beautiful. It was fair."

And that was all it had been—a fair imitation. I wanted to tell her that she hadn't heard the nightingale, that the nightingale's song was much more beautiful. But I couldn't tell her, and I felt like a cheat, and, like a cheat, I tried to make up for it. "Sometimes," I said, "they sing much better. They go up to a crescendo; no, not a crescendo exactly, but still you wonder how high, how *far* they'll go, all in the same breath, before breaking. You expect the song to break, and it doesn't; it goes on and on, further and further, and when it finally does break, it breaks into another song. What you heard was really quite poor."

"Oh, don't say that. Don't spoil it for her," her son said. "After all, she may never hear one again."

"No," I agreed, despondently.

[1963]

The Art Teacher

Physical exertion was nothing to her compared with spiritual constraint, and when people commiserated her for, at her age—she was over fifty—having to walk two miles early in the morning to the Siena railroad station to go and teach, and two miles back in the afternoon, she simply laughed.

Spare and a little taller than average, bright-eyed, resolute and fearless, she walked at a good pace, taking a country path instead of the main road much of the way, and resting once or twice up a steep hill. For this was hilly country, Siena itself one of the Tuscan hill towns. The path went by a pretty farmhouse and a stream, which she had often drawn or painted from the height of the garden of her home. The road got less and less attractive as one approached town, and the station was a good example of architectural decline. Looking down on its concrete from a hill and almost smiling at it was a graceful eighteenth-century villa. But the train soon sped you back into the open country. The railroad line was narrow and the foliage so lush and thick at times it brushed the cars. In October, if the train went past a farmhouse, you might catch a whiff of grapes fermenting in the cellar. In the spring, the white blossoms of the acacias or the broom's golden clusters made the air heady with their scent. Then the smell of clover, and later hay. A few miles farther, the countryside became desolate and trees sparse; the raw-sienna color of the earth turned gray. You were in the *crete*—the clay district—a strange terrain of dune-like mounds and hillocks, cracked by the sun in summer, furrowed in the spring and in the autumn by torrential rains. Even this, except for a few steep slopes, was farmed—there was little in Italy that wasn't. A half hour from Siena, she got off the train at the small town of Asciano where she taught art at the junior high school.

A friend in Siena—the headmistress of a school for teachers—had found her the job. She had never taught before, and it seemed strange to most people that she should have decided to teach now, and stranger still that she, wife of a landowner, living in a large villa on an estate of ten farmhouses and four hundred acres of highly cultivated land, should have to walk such a long way. After all, she had an able-bodied husband, three sons in their twenties, and a daughter. There were two maids and a cook in the house. A bailiff and several other men, besides the farmers, worked on the estate. But her husband was an intellectual, a free-lance philosopher whose books, though well received, brought in no money. This year he was in America on a Fulbright travel grant, giving lectures here and there. Her eldest son was teaching classics in a high school in Cortona, her middle son was doing a year's compulsory military service in the army, the younger son had a low-paying job in northern Italy. Her daughter—the youngest of her children—had only recently got over a bad case of TB. The bailiff, whom her husband trusted, was in fact enriching himself at their expense, and though suspected had not yet been exposed. The workmen weren't all needed, but because of the high unemployment in Italy, they couldn't be laid off. It was 1951, a time of land reform. The farmers—working under the discredited and soon to be abolished system of *mezzadria,* a form of sharecropping—claimed an ever larger portion of the meager profits. The government, inept at collecting taxes from the rich, exacted them from those who had land, something that could not be hidden. To pay them, part of the property—two farms, a mill—had been sold, and soon more would have to be. Before the war, the family had owned a car, horses and two buggies. But the German troops had taken those when the front had passed through Siena. And so now there was nothing left but to economize—and, yes, teach.

As a girl, in Rome, she had studied art at the Accademia and got a teaching certificate which she had never used. Why not use it, now that her husband was away and she needed money? She hated to ask the bailiff for it. She longed to separate herself from the dratted finances of the estate, from the account books, always in the red, that he kept and she went over at the end of each month. This was her chance, now when her husband wasn't here, to be a little free, independent of this awful whirlpool that the *azienda* had turned into. Oh, she loved the trees, the wheat waving in the wind like a gentle sea of green. She loved the peeping newborn chicks, golden in a basket. She loved the farmers with their lovely accents and ways of describing nature, especially one of them, an old-timer, who had a special, unheard-of verb for every stage of the wheat growing: "*Il semino pinta, verzica, accestisce, apprata, imbionda . . .*—the seeds draw down the earth to hide, and heave after being sown—then their first pale green appears; early in the spring the little blades form clusters, then a lawn, and then . . . and then in May they ear, in June they yellow and are ripe for harvest." He made it all seem a surprising spectacle, renewed each year and never dated. And she loved to draw and paint the landscape and the flowers. But the business of the estate, that, no.

And so she was glad to venture out early in the morning and to be alone for once, and to taste of the life she might have lived had she not married. The miles meant little to her if she didn't have to hurry. Her father, dead nearly thirty years now, was from the Marche, that thin, long, central region of Italy that stretches north and south on the Adriatic sea, the region that perhaps Italy's greatest painter—Raphael—its greatest modern poet—Leopardi—and perhaps its greatest composer—Rossini—were born in. Her father too, though not well known, was a poet, and had lived in a tower at the foot of a mountain by the sea. She had grown up there and that's where she felt most at home. Whenever she went back, the peasant women hugged her and kissed her and treated her almost like a sister, never addressing her in the formal third person as here, but always in the familiar second. There was a little woman now in her sixties, who every day came to the tower to help. She came from a village out of sight, on the other side of the mountain, walking all the way, miles and miles, and never looking tired or complaining of her walk. If one said something to her about it, she'd reply, "*Eh, che me fa?*—eh, what's it to me?" Well, she was like her.

Nor was the school right by the station of Asciano. There was a way to walk there too, but just a short stretch, and pleasant, after the train ride. And Asciano was a pretty little town, rich in fourteenth-century paintings of the Sienese school. It had churches that Lorenzetti frescoed and a museum with paintings by that rare man, Sassetta. It was a very fitting town to teach art in.

Her mother—still alive, in her eighties and living in Rome with her eldest daughter—was American. She had come to Italy as a child of seven with her father, a Methodist minister, who, in the 1870s when the papal state lost hold of Rome and Protestant churches were permitted in the city, founded one. He lived in Rome for some fifteen years then returned to America, but she married the poet and stayed on in Italy all her life. So her children spoke English well, and she—the painter, the art teacher—was even more fluent in it than the others, having spent a year at school in York. She looked and felt Italian, but her Asciano students soon caught on that she wasn't like the other teachers, that there was something unusual about her, even foreign. And perhaps not so much for her origin, but because all original people look a little foreign, wherever they may be. Oh, they were very pleased with her, there was no hostility whatever; quite the contrary, but still they treated her differently, with a little wonder in their eyes and an amused smile as though they knew something about her that she didn't guess. With the natural curiosity of children, they began asking her questions and probably asking other teachers too, till soon they knew a whole lot—that she lived in a big villa outside of Siena, that she was half-American, that during the war she and her family had left Italy because of the Fascists and gone to England as refugees, and even—whom they could have got hold of that from she had no idea, unless it was from her friend the Siena headmistress indirectly—that she had no religion, or rather that she had never been baptized. They asked her this knowingly, point-blank, with infinite glee, and she would not deny it. "But how did you know?" she inquired, and they laughed joyfully. Perhaps they had the feeling that since she was unlike them, and since they didn't have a very high opinion of themselves, she must therefore be smarter than they were. It was quite true—this about her never having been baptized. Her father the poet, though brought up Catholic, had never been churchy, and since his wife had been brought up Protestant—but in a very liberal tradition—they had decided to let the children choose their own religion when they grew older if they wished. She had been perfectly content not to choose any.

And not only her background was different, the way she taught, too. She wasn't strong on discipline and regulations. And in painting she told them, as she had told her own children, that one detail, vividly portrayed, could bring a whole picture to life, and to look at the object and hardly ever at the paper, and to break loose, so your sensations will be unhindered. She asked them to bring flowers and plants to class to paint and draw from. Often, in good weather, she would take them out into the fields. They were delighted with her and brought her flowers as gifts—not just for them to paint. Once, on a gloomy day, she gave one of them money to go and buy ice cream for the class. They got the idea that she was very rich. Ah, if they only knew! And she would tell them stories and anecdotes of the great painters' lives, and take them to see paintings of their forebears—of Lorenzetti, Duccio, and Sassetta. The principal—a young man—didn't interfere. One or two of the other teachers tried to impress on her the importance of discipline and told her not to let "the little rascals" take advantage of her, but they too, like the students, regarded her as someone not like them, not a competitor, no one to fear or envy or undermine, but a disinterested outsider who had alighted there by chance. And so the months went by simply, smoothly, and it was good to have money in her pocket she had earned by her own wits.

Toward the end of school, in June, she asked her students to draw or paint anything they wanted for a home assignment, as long as it was something of their own and not a copy. And one of them, a little boy, brought in a bowl. He said there was a vein of pure clay in the bank of a stream that ran by his farm where the stream curved and the current stole the sand, leaving the clay. He had scooped it up, close to the water, and then, without a wheel, molded it at home, glazed it, painted it, and fired it in the brick oven of his farmyard where his mother once a week baked bread. He was afraid it might not do, since it wasn't a drawing or a painting. And right away two or three of the other students raised their hands and said so too—that the bowl was off the subject, not what she'd assigned. "But what's off the subject!" she said. "This bowl is beautiful, and isn't that all that matters? Besides, he did paint it, too. Look at those colors. Bravo."

"But it isn't on paper, cardboard, wood or canvas like you said," one of the girls insisted.

She laughed. "The important thing," she said, "is that he had an idea, and did his best, all by himself, to bring it to life, from his own clay, without a wheel or kiln. I call that art."

On the last day of school, he brought the bowl back, full of cherries, hand-picked, choice, the ripest that he had climbed the topmost branches of a tree for. "It's for you," he said.

In July her husband came back from America. With him home, in September she wouldn't go back to school. It would be too difficult. He would be too worried about her, seeing her leave, too anxious waiting for her to come back. She wouldn't be able to do it casually anymore—not just get dressed and take off after breakfast, not just return and rest. And he would probably feel guilty about letting her go, when there was nothing to feel guilty about. No, it would be sure to spoil her little pleasure. Still, sometimes she looked wistfully south toward the clay hills which she had gazed at from the train, week after week. From here they looked like a gray-blue sea of ridges in the distance. To pay the house bills she would have to find other ways—translate, take guests.

She began translating American novels into Italian for a Milan publisher. When they were well written, she took a certain pleasure in it. You could hear her typing all day long, sometimes late into the night. Then a young American pianist came as a paying guest, the first of a long line of friends from England and America. And with him in the house it wasn't so much the sound of typing that was heard as that of music. "I thought that someone practicing the piano would disturb me," she said, "but he sounds even better than the birds." Enthralled, she would listen to him from the window.

One day—with guests around the table, including a close friend from Genoa—fruit was served in a bowl, and immediately her eyes brightened. "That bowl was made by one of my students at Asciano," she said.

"Poor signora," the maid said, lingering by the table, "how many times you had to get up early in the morning while it was still dark outside."

"Oh I liked getting up early.

> *I used to get up early just to sit*
> *And watch the morning quicken in the grey,*
> *And hear the silence open like a flower*
> *Leaf after leaf.*"

But her friend from Genoa joined the maid in the commiseration and shook his head. "That was incredible your having to walk to the station. Awful. Such a hardship."

"What hardship?" she said. "Hearing all the complaints about this blessed estate is hardship. That was no hardship. None at all. I assure you."

But the maid repeated, "Poor signora, at that time of the morning."

"But why poor signora?"

"Eh, don't I know it," the maid went on, nodding gravely, as if she hadn't heard.

[1987]

Luca

"'The achieve of, the mastery of the thing!'" I tell myself as I look at one of his drawings of birds—a windhover, this one—and I think of him, Luca.

I don't suppose he weighs a hundred pounds or measures more than five feet one, but he is so well proportioned that unless there is something near him to compare him to one forgets his size. And even more one forgets his age. He is sixty, but he looks like a child. Not just externally—he has something of the innocence of the child. And that is his beauty, that unaffected innocence. When he looks at you with his penetrating blue eyes you feel he is seeing deep into you, down to the core of you, the way he sees a sea gull, the way he sees an olive tree, and that if he wanted to and had pencil and paper handy he could catch you in two or three strokes—he is at once innocent and disarming.

He is quite unassuming, disinterested, scornful of anything that might tie him down. He must be free as his birds. And because of this and perhaps the diminutiveness of his drawings and sculptures, most critics have overlooked him, and he is not famous. Nor is it in character for him to be. There is still something of the waif about him.

He has a small studio on the ground floor of one of those courtyards that are the best feature of Via Margutta, in Rome. From the street a huge doorway, made for coaches, opens into a gravel yard. Opposite is the cliff of the Pincio sheltering the street, giving it peace and a touch of green. There are studios right and left on a path and stairway up the cliff. One has the feeling of being in a village while in the center of the city. His studio is neat, spotless, and a variety of tools are there, all sharp and clean. If you go looking for one of the other artists the chances are you won't find him. But I've never been to see Luca that I haven't found him hard at work, yet always ready to drop everything and welcome you.

He is a wellspring of conversation, and yet everything he says seems seriously considered, as though in the loneliness of his work a headful of thoughts came to his mind and he poured them forth. It is art he usually speaks about, and often I wish I could record that nascent eloquence, but perhaps it wouldn't sound so meaningful the second time. In a way it would be a shame to fix it, to preserve it. It would kill it somehow, mar its freshness. A little like capturing a butterfly. An imperishable enthusiasm is in him. He never discourages you. Oh, perhaps he tends to agree with what you are saying a little too much, but he does it out of goodness, because he doesn't want to contradict you. There is an ancient civility there, a fetching modesty, a humility that is quite appealing.

I've known him for twenty-five years, and he has barely changed in that time. I think that he will never change and that only death will dim the light that not just his eyes but his whole face seems to shed.

When I first met him, in Rome, he didn't have a studio of his own, but worked in the loft of the studio of a sculptor who had befriended him a long time before, in the thirties, when he had arrived from his native Sicily almost without a penny. His parents were dead. For a few years he had also been in Argentina where he had lived with an uncle. The sculptor was a man of vast influence who needed help on his huge projects and who liked having people around while he worked, especially girls. They came and went, apprentices and just lookers on. That's how I happened to go there, not as a looker on or an apprentice, but as an admirer of one of the girls. I was a practicing physician then and had a nearby office which I would leave to go to the studio a little before suppertime. I loved this girl, got no love in return, and in that wretched-blessed state kept going there faithfully, hoping for a change. Luca worked in the shadow of the maestro, up in the loft, at a small table. Often his presence went unnoticed till the sculptor called him and he appeared at the top of the staircase. The sculptor, or maestro, or *professore,* called him the *professorino,* and diminutive he seemed against the huge studio below him. At about 9:30 we would all walk to a nearby trattoria—all except the maestro, that is, who had a wife waiting for him at home. Out of his orbit, Luca came into his own, emerged; small though he was, he became the central figure, began to talk, his hands in motion as if unraveling his thoughts, and the light from the street lamps playing on his face. He would go on and on, right through dinner, and never become boring.

He lived alone, in a rented room. As regards sex he gave the impression of being quite neutral, all absorbed as he was in his art, unsexed by it. He certainly was sensitive to women's beauty, but only, it seemed, from an artistic point of view. And then, one summer day, I invited him for a long weekend to my family's home, in Tuscany. There was a group of American college girls staying there for a month, studying art, art history, and Italian, and they simply doted on him. He would draw for them, model clay, carve wood, try to teach them all he knew, encourage them, laugh, play with them, give them little gifts of his own making. That he knew little English and they not much Italian didn't matter—he was so expressive he came through in a thousand ways. In their company he seemed to be experiencing something he had never experienced, a bliss that wasn't of the soul alone. One of the girls in particular, Clare, a charming, very pretty girl with a cascade of platinum-blond hair, slender, and almost as lively as he, making nothing of the gap in years between them, singled him out, took him in hand, *held* him by the hand, and off they went for walks together, into the fields and into town. They seemed the same age, grown up on the same lawns. A pair of doves. Oh, she was quite serious about him, under her laughter, that is, because they smiled and laughed a lot; yet sometimes, her face cupped by her palms, her elbows on a table, she would just look at him from up close with wonder, and he, seeing her, feeling himself being looked at like that, would burst into some joyful exclamation and say, as if he couldn't believe this was happening to him, "Oh, look how she's gazing at me." For another long moment she would continue gazing, and perhaps at the end say, "Luca, you know you are very cute."

"Cute?"

"*Carino,*" I would translate.

And he would raise his head and laugh looking at the sky.

The girls went to Rome for a week, and the romance or friendship or whatever it was went on. He continually talked about her to me, praising her, and in talking about her he seemed trebly bright. "Clare is an extraordinary girl, there's no doubt about it," he'd say as if he couldn't come to terms with his good luck, "smart, intelligent, pretty, young, what more do you want—imagine her making friends with me! It's incredible, but there it is, and why not? I ask myself why not?"

"There must be an affinity between you," I would say.

He would make capital of that word "affinity" and go on about her till I laughed.

He would inhale from his cigarette, cross his arms and look up. "Clare has something classical about her and yet she is so *real.* More than anything—even more than a work of art—she makes me think that civilization has shifted to New York. From Athens to Florence to Paris, and, now, to New York."

"She certainly flourished there," I would remark.

"There, you have it, flourished, bravo, that's it exactly. Eh, America," he would nod, "you can't put down America, I've always said so."

At a certain point, the girls left, went back across the ocean, but she wrote to him, and he replied, enclosing, as he told me, each time one or two drawings. "Do you think she'll like these? This one? That one?" he would ask me.

He went on talking about her for months, a year and more, though the letters became rarer. And then we heard she had got married. He wasn't crushed, or at least he didn't appear to be. He said he understood her and even approved her decision, that it had to happen, that it was as inevitable as her leaving had been, and that his feelings for her wouldn't change, that for him she would remain a bright moment. In art and life, he said, only such a moment mattered. All other embodiments of eternity were illusory. Even the stars would fade, but a moment, a revelation, never.

He would stop in the middle of the street as if to conjure up that moment again, the moment that was past, that had had its eternity. It sounded like a contradiction. "It lasts and it doesn't last," he said. "It has nothing to do with the calendar. It's all of time compressed in one point." Expanding on this theme he would be led away from her, and then, becoming aware of having strayed, he would return; to this tune we would walk to the trattoria for supper.

I left Rome. For some time we lost touch. Then someone told me he had married an American girl and gone with her to America. Even though it wasn't Clare, I felt that I'd had something to do with it, that somehow, by chance, not by design, I had shown him the way, introduced him to a world he had avoided or ignored. I, too, had married and I also had gone to live in America, though a long way from him. One day, unexpectedly, I got a letter. His writing, though more intricate, had the imprint of his drawings. It said that he and his wife, Judy, had had a daughter, Sara, and that we must all meet. He wrote the way he talked—I had the distinct feeling of his presence as I read. It was a joyful note, dashed off in a moment of happiness that clearly he wanted to share. I couldn't recall his ever being dejected. He was always animated, or at least serene, as though nothing could harm him. But now, I thought, he must be jubilant, bubbling with mirth. A baby daughter—Luca, who use to sit unnoticed up in the loft of the sculptor's studio. The change had come late, but it had come indeed.

•

Not till fourteen years passed did we meet again. It was quite recently, in Rome, where they had moved from America. I went to his present studio, opposite the sculptor's. Later he took me to his nice, large home. His daughter is taller than he, shapely, vivacious, with something of his spark in her eyes. She speaks both English and Italian, Italian with a slight Roman accent and a ringing voice, as clear a diction as I've ever heard. And his wife has a temperate, warm way about her that is quite affecting. She is not at all like Clare, but very comely and pleasant nonetheless. My God, he has certainly done well for himself, I can't help thinking. It seems a miracle to see him so well surrounded, a husband and a father, in a house full of fine things, especially when I consider the time I first knew him when he lived alone in a rented room so miserable he had never shown it to me. He is very protective toward the girl, perhaps a little too protective. He accompanies her to and from school. He worries about the Roman boys. She is like a filly that he has to keep in rein. "If they did anything to her," he says with a fierce look in his eyes, "I would kill them." And for a moment he seems to be wielding a gun, not a pencil. "Oh, yes," he adds in a slow, determined voice, his eyes wincing as if he were aiming, "I would kill them whoever and wherever they were, get a revolver and kill them." His words startle me but my mind flies to Sicily where he was born and grew up, and I believe him.

His native town he rarely mentions. He seems to want to avoid talking about it. He has shown Sicily to his wife, but only briefly. He has cut himself off from it, never lived there from the time he first left it. Oh yes, he admires it, he loves it even, perhaps, but in a mute sort of way. He has become a traveler; America, where he has now been several times, has given him a new life. Yet symbols of his native land recur in his drawings and his sculpture—the fish, the gnarled olive tree, the boats, the orange tree, the sea gull, women in shawls. "I was born by the sea," he says once in a while, "and I always have an urge to live near it. Here I miss hearing it, seeing it. But I know it's only twenty miles away and that if I wanted to I could be there very soon. And I like its seafood." Suddenly he looks like a child fishing off the pier.

One of the reasons I have come to Italy this year is to buy pottery which my wife sells. And on a trip, a few days after I've seen him, I go south, by train, down the coast to Calabria, and then across the Strait of Messina to Sicily. The train proceeds along the north coast of the island. The next station, I read in my time table, is Cefalù. I don't know it. Then I remember that it is the town where Luca was born and decide to stop there for the night.

There is a strong northwest wind blowing, raising the sea to a frenzy. The waves, which look as big as those on Cape Cod during a storm, batter the harbor wall. They seem enraged to find such an obstacle, artificial at that, and they pound against it with a vengeance. Some overwhelm it, vault over it, frothing. It is a wind that makes short work of umbrellas, that takes your breath away, which you struggle to walk against, or which lifts you along with it. A wind that makes the weather vanes tremble in obedience. Up high, a cloud like a cobweb sails across the overcast, gray-silver sky that to the south is lurid pewter blue. The sea on the horizon isn't level, but uneven due to massive waves peaking here and there. And far to the northwest the sun sends vertical rays down behind the clouds in a wide arc. Through the rays, beyond the clouds, eighty miles away the outline of the island of Ustica is discernible and becomes more so as the day advances.

This of Luca's is a spectacular town. Cefalù meant cape, headland, in Greek. The headland is a colossal rock which the railroad pierces through a tunnel. Sheltered by the rock is the cathedral, unusual, castle-like, with two towers and a simple, columned interior. Above the altar is a magnificent mosaic—a large, forbidding Christ among saints. There is a wonderful cloister, and behind the cathedral, between it and the rock, an orchard. I walk hesitantly to it, past the caretaker's cottage, attracted by the fruit trees and the peace that reigns there. The caretaker's wife appears at the door, not, as I feared, to tell me that the orchard is out of bounds but to tell me that it commands a fine view of the sea and that I might walk at my leisure. The cathedral square is alive with flags waving and shops displaying pottery made in the next town—Santo Stefano, which I intend to visit. Narrow, straight streets lead toward the harbor, a tight little place, protected by the breakwater I had seen from a distance on arriving. The fishing boats are all colors, a little like Sicilian carts. They have a stubby, wooden, crossed mast and lipped decks pouting from the bow and stern. Near the harbor, one row of houses removed from the sea, is a peculiar ramp that leads to a medieval washing place. It is fed by a stream channeled under the main street. The stream rushes through supplying fresh, clear water to a series of fountains. There are trees and ferns and arches, and no one is washing, and it is cool and silent, except for the sound of the water swishing by to an exit under the houses to find its final exit to the sea.

For someone coming from the north the south presents a luxury that one who has always lived there finds hard to understand. For one thing, the flowers. Hibiscus and geraniums and a variety of others that I have seen only rarely and never in such abundance. And the openness of the houses, the balconies, the terraces, the open air cafés that suggest the benignity of the climate. The unpotted lemon trees. The palms. The orange groves. Yes, this town is worth coming hundreds of miles to see, even if I should see nothing else. Or so I feel at this moment. The place has a strange vitality, life imparting. It is partly the wind, the storm that's blowing away. "Luca's town," I say to myself. Because of him I'm here.

Evening, sunset. A crimson wreath lights the clouds over the frothy, boiling sea. Then twilight. Night darkens the tempest. Enveloped by night, the sea seems calm. But you know it isn't, by its sound. I turn toward the town. Down a sidestreet walks a tall figure, larger than lifesize, at an inhuman gait. A man mounted on a donkey. A humble centaur.

I'm carrying only a canvas shopping bag. It is so light that I haven't even checked into a hotel. But I do now. My room looks out on a grove of lemon trees. Their fragrance enters the room with the night air. The hotel has a restaurant. I pick a table at random. Above me, on the wall, a few feet up, is a pen and ink drawing that intrigues me. It has an unusual, yet familiar look about it. I stand up to get a better view of it. It's Luca's. An illustration of the Paolo and Francesca canto of the *Divine Comedy* with the verses at the bottom in his handwriting, *Amor che a nullo amato amar perdona* (Love that spares no loved one from loving in return). He must have been here, perhaps got a free meal for it long ago. Now I feel profoundly at home, in his company, no longer alone.

And a few days later, back in Rome, I go to see him and tell him that I've been to Cefalù, stayed there overnight, and his drawing. He is touched that I should have stopped in his town.

"It's such a beautiful place," I tell him, "aren't you tempted to go back to live there?"

"Ah, so many memories," he says, "some of them sad."

"I know what you mean," I say. "I too would feel strange to go back to my old home town. So many memories there too."

He looks at me and he wonders. He seems on the verge of saying something to me, but he doesn't. He is silent a long time, and then in his lilting, high voice, the voice of a child, he suddenly says, "They murdered my father there."

"No!"

"Yes, when I was seven."

"When you were seven."

"Yes, for that I don't want to live there or go back too often. For that I came away as soon as I could."

Here, to Rome, and to America, South and North. Distance, he thirsted for it, to put the miles between him and the past, distance that to time is next of kin. And suddenly it all makes sense, or more sense, his life. Seven. Something had stopped when he was seven; his father's life had been taken, and his, too, for a moment, had stood still. Then it had gone on, but that moment, that stillness had affected all the years that followed, tingeing them like a potent dye. A child still. Innocent, bright-eyed and eager, alert, keen, frail. He is all of those things still, though sixty. And his wife beside him seems for a moment like his mother. His wife a mother to him, his daughter an elder sister, and I myself a brother, all there to protect him. But only for a moment. He has wrested himself free. He picks the pencil up and a paper tablet. A line is drawn, unerring, utterly unchild-like. Decades of experience in that line. A learned line. Subtle, cunning, given only to a very few to achieve, and immediately he is secure in a world that's free of hurt and clear of hate.

[1977]

from *A Goodly Babe*

I. Mrs. Lee

"What's that?" he asked Jessie, seeing a package on her lap, as they were driving home after having had dinner one night at some friends of theirs—Brigid and Sidney, a married couple.

"It's a present Brigid gave me."

"I didn't know you'd got a present," he said, gaily.

"She didn't want to tell you. She thought you might refuse it."

"Why? What on earth for? What is it?"

"Some things she knitted for her baby."

Brigid, they knew, had recently had a miscarriage.

"I wish she hadn't . . ." He bit his lip. "Given them to you."

"I know," Jessie said in a whisper though there was no one around. "I don't like to have them."

"Why couldn't she wait?" he said. He grabbed the package. The soft, hand-sized woolens shrank in his fist as he compressed them. They were driving across the park of Villa Borghese. He had an urge to throw the package out the window. It seemed imperative to do it, rid himself of bad luck. He almost did throw it out. But something seemed to prevent him. He didn't want to be a slave to prejudice or superstition. "Shall I throw them away?" he said.

"No, no, don't. They are very nice. She showed them to me."

"I know they are nice, but . . . we don't want them. Let me throw it away. Some poor people may pick it up."

"No, no," she said, and took the parcel back.

At home, she put them in a drawer. His aunt called. A long, inquisitive phone call. A few days later, she left a package for them. More baby clothes. "It's so early yet," he said. "Why can't they wait? As though we couldn't provide!"

In his career, in his life, he felt things were getting to a climax.

For so many years so little had happened, and now so much—marriage, a baby on the way, short stories being published. Even in his practice, though still not busy compared to many doctors, he was busier than he had ever been. It's getting hectic, he thought, hectic. More and more often he would hastily have to clear his desk of his writing, and make room for his medical instruments and forms, or pack his doctor's bag and rush away. If the doorbell or the telephone were not ringing it seemed they were always about to. In August, the ringing seemed to be working up to a crescendo. "Doctor," came the voice of Mr. Lund at the American Consulate, "would you go to International House. There's a Mrs. Lee there. We are trying to repatriate her. Now she's had a miscarriage. Could you send her to a city hospital where she can be treated without charge? She may not want to go; she's been giving us an awful lot of trouble, but see what you can do. Oh, Doctor, this one may not be able to pay you."

Cosimo prepared his bag, trying to put in it only the essentials, and still making it heavier than most doctors' bags; hastened out of his office; hurried in his shabby, little, old car along the Tiber; crossed it; arrived at International House; and asked for his patient.

On hearing her name, the porter called the manager—a stiff, tall man who told Cosimo they couldn't keep her there any longer.

"I know," Cosimo said, "she's sick and she doesn't have any money."

The manager looked at him speechless.

A rubicund nun slowly accompanied him upstairs. "She's in a pool of blood," she said on the way. In vain he tried to hurry her step. He found his patient huddled up in her bed. Her eyes were closed. She was silently weeping.

"I am the doctor," he said, touching her shoulder.

She opened her eyes and gave him a single, swift look, critical and comprehensive. Illness, though it sometimes dulls them, frequently sharpens the senses. They become subtler. The mind undergoes a certain refinement. She spoke English with a slight foreign accent; was about thirty, good-looking, with a halo of black hair, a tall, frowning forehead, a vehement glance, and a long, infantile upper lip, slightly disdainful. She wasn't as ill as he had expected, and when he had examined her, he looked at the nun as at another alarmist. Even so, he couldn't treat her there. He ordered an ambulance. Two orderlies lifted her like a child onto a stretcher, then carried her down. She drew a sheet over her head to hide from the people she met on the way. They paused and stared at the stretcher as though they thought someone had died.

After he reached home, a woman from the Consulate called him. Had Mrs. Lee been a lot of trouble, she wanted to know. They were so tired of her.

He saw the pretty woman silently weeping. Troubled she was, not troublesome; weary, not wearisome. All his sympathy was with the patient. Even when, a few hours later, a nurse called from the hospital to tell him that she wanted to leave; even when she herself came to the phone to reproach him for having sent her there, he couldn't really dislike her. He felt she was someone unruly, untamed, as he secretly wanted to be.

She was out of the hospital in less than two days, against doctor's orders; took a trolley to International House; was refused a room; went on to the Consulate, and from there to Cosimo's front door, in a taxi. He paid the fare. In the apartment, she lay down on a sofa, he made her some coffee, while Jessie got pastries and cigarettes. He looked at the two young women, at the deep, troubled glance of the one; at the mild, pensive gaze of the other. The reception surprised Mrs. Lee. She appreciated the atmosphere and the comfort. The nervous frown almost disappeared from her forehead. They gave her some money. Its feel again in her hand had the effect of a marvelous tonic. And it was probably in gratitude for that money that she agreed to go to the Arciospedale nearby for the night. "One more night in a hospital," he said, "just to be perfectly safe. You'll like this one better; it's right in the center." She left her coat with them—a black, elegant coat. He noticed its perfume. For a moment he stayed there, in the dark closet, and breathed it. He touched the coat with his face, leaned against it in the dark.

"It hasn't been much of a holiday for you, this trip, has it?" he said to her when she came back for her coat the next day.

She wasn't on a holiday, she said, but had come with a one-way ticket to see her mother, who was Italian and lived in Turin. She herself was born in Italy. She had gone to America as a war bride. In Turin, her brother-in-law, in whose house her mother lived, didn't want her around. Her husband wasn't sending any money. "I am trying to go back to my children," she said, the thought of them distorting the rather beautiful lines of her face. Cosimo looked at the stranded woman. "If I weren't married," he considered, "I wonder what I would do," and deep inside him something said, "I'd try and take her in." He gave her some money for a taxi, and for a few days didn't see her. Then she came over, quite agitated, one evening. She had been late getting back to a boardinghouse run by nuns that the Consulate had sent her to, and they didn't want her to stay there any longer. The Consulate wasn't going to pay for her passage home till they heard from her husband. A woman vice-consul had asked her why she went there with her dress all wrinkled. At the Church of Santa Susanna, the father had got rid of her by giving her the address of the person who had sent her.

"No one has funds," Jessie said. "They spend the money on parties."

Mrs. Lee had the name of a pensione. Could she borrow enough money for one night. Cosimo gave her some, and offered to drive her there.

"No, the walk will do me good. If someone follows me, I know what to do," she said, raising her arm and looking fierce.

An absurd thought came to his mind, and he felt like telling her not to chase anyone away, and that if she wanted to go home all she had to do was wink at a few men at the Excelsior. Was she too virtuous, he wondered, for her salvation?

The next morning, she phoned Jessie, and hesitatingly asked her for some underwear. Jessie was out when she came to pick it up, in the afternoon. The need for money, like need for food or water, was making her frantic. She couldn't understand why the Consulate didn't help her. Wasn't that what they were there for? Wasn't she a citizen? She looked dark and angry, tired after going from place to place asking for help, and more tired for not having got it. Nothing is more tiring than an unsuccessful errand. And the worst of it was she couldn't find rest; she couldn't even stay seated. For a moment she looked unable to reconcile herself with some thought. "Could I use your phone?" she said. "I'd like to call the Consulate once again."

She spoke for a long time with Mr. Lund about her troubles, then broke into tears and handed Cosimo the telephone. "I know this is going to be difficult for you, Doctor," Mr. Lund said, "but I am going to have to ask you not to see her any more, particularly not to give her any more money or help her in any way."

"Oh, why?"

"I must ask you this favor," Mr. Lund said, and left him wondering.

"You didn't say anything good about me," Mrs. Lee said, after the call.

"I am sorry if I didn't say what you wanted. Mr. Lund told me not to lend you any more money. And really I don't have very much. I am not like some doctors. I don't charge much. Some patients don't pay me. Others I seem to give money to. Perhaps you'll find some mail for you at the American Express."

"I went this morning."

"Well, I am sorry, but I don't see what more I can do. I can't lend you any more money."

She hadn't asked him for any, but she was generous enough not to say so. "Well," she said in a low, sad voice, mumbling almost, and going toward the door, "maybe I'll go to the post office." She took a step toward him. "Oh, I have this little something for the baby, when it comes," she said, and handed him a small package.

When Jessie came back, he gave it to her. It was a little baby doll made of soap with clothes pinned to it. A doll stuck with pins and needles. The pins had rusted in the soap. One pricked him, and drew blood. A dreadful little thing. He put it in the bathroom. He told Jessie about the telephone call. She was surprised at him.

"I can't go on supporting her," he said. "I've done enough for her. And besides, Mr. Lund—"

"You don't have to do what he says."

"He might have some good reason."

"If he has, he should tell it to you. You are her doctor."

"If I ignore what he says, he might not send me any more patients." Immediately, he felt like a fool, felt like a subordinate of Mr. Lund.

"I have some money of my own," Jessie said. "I'll give her some money."

He wished Jessie had been with him. She was a brave girl, Jessie. She was afraid of waves and high peaks and darkness, but confront her with a moral problem, put her in a social difficulty and she didn't "go soggy, like a wet meringue."

In the evening, Mrs. Lee telephoned. She wanted to speak to Jessie. "Don't invite her," he urged.

Jessie talked to her for a long time, with friendliness, patience and understanding; nonetheless he could see the effect of his words. She didn't invite her; she didn't offer to give her any money; she merely suggested a number of places, people to whom she might go. "I know your husband has spoken to you," she was told in the end.

For several days they didn't hear from her. Her silence made him feel guilty. Why had he obeyed Mr. Lund? Mr. Lund wasn't his boss. He had no bosses. He was an independent physician. Wasn't that one of the reasons he had studied medicine and was here now, not to have to take orders? He wished Mrs. Lee would give him a chance to help her once more.

And Mrs. Lee did give him a chance. Unexpectedly, one night, toward one o'clock, she rang up, and in a rather slurred voice—as though she had been drinking—she asked him if he would come and drive her home. To really help that woman I'd have to become her lover, he thought. For a moment he felt like going, then he looked at Jessie, in bed, not feeling too well, and he said that he couldn't. Mrs.

Lee insisted, but he repeated he couldn't. Then, in the high-pitched voice of a woman who is defending herself, she said, "I am not a criminal, Doctor," just before hanging up.

"I know you are not," he said.

He would have gone now, but he didn't know where she had called from; he didn't know her latest address. He held on to the telephone from which no human sound came, then slowly replaced it.

Errors he had made came to his mind, preventing rest. Quite recently, for instance, he had taken a fracture of the ankle for a sprain. Radiography was an almost miraculous invention; why hadn't he taken advantage of it? I should stop being a doctor, he thought, and looked at Jessie, big, in the double bed, as at another patient.

II. Thistledown

"Oh dear, Jessie, don't cry."

It was like telling a child not to cry. She only cried more. And did anyone ever look uglier than his pretty wife when she cried? He would clutch her by the wrist. "We'll go to America. You'll have a baby there. In Boston. Everything will be all right. You'll see."

More and more of his stories were being published. They would be able to live on the income. When they got married, they had planned just a visit to America, but now they thought they would go and live there for some time. The visa he had applied for in June (an immigrant's visa, the only kind they would give him) was ready at last. To get it, he had completed giant-sized application forms, gathered entire folders of documents, and gone to the visa office in Naples four times. He had been given a number, called by that number, made to undress, been examined, X-rayed, blood-tested, and, in the interview, asked by a woman vice-consul if he had ever engaged in prostitution, been a criminal, an addict, a Communist, a Socialist. A secretary—a snappy, stern Italian girl—had addressed some of the applicants, especially the older and more rustic ones—a few of them patriarchal-looking people—not by the respectful third person singular, but by the familiar second as though they were naughty schoolchildren. No matter—the visa was a half-pound sealed bundle of papers with a red ribbon around it. With it firmly in his hand, at the beginning of November, he went to Rome with Jessie, and boarded an intercontinental airplane.

It lifted them over brown fields, newly plowed. Suddenly, he felt a strong attachment to that brown earth, felt uprooted from it, and it was painful. Then the airplane crossed over the Tiber. He saw the outskirts of Rome, white and new, which meant so little to him, and the gray or apricot buildings of the center, which meant so much. He spotted the façade of Villa Medici, Piazza di Spagna, and three blocks from it the little street he knew so well. Perhaps he shouldn't be up here, he thought, but down there. He felt he was going away too lightly, like thistledown, leaving, giving up again . . . . He looked at Jessie angrily. But for her, he'd still be there, or going to America for a holiday, bachelor-light. He said something of this to her.

"What? You don't want to go?" she asked. "Well, you can always go back."

"Go back! Oh yes, so easy!" He felt he could no more go back to what he was than water could flow upward. There were more brown fields. The tip of the wing seemed to make little progress upon them. He had never experienced such stillness. Yet in twenty minutes they were over the Island of Giglio; in a few hours over the Alps—the Western Alps, those they had crossed in the old little green car. God, this flight seemed like a quick recapitulation of something they had gone through step by step. It was weird. They were going over everything quickly once more, as in a résumé before some terrible final exam. There was France, its trees gossamer-light, autumn-yellow, floating in the thin bluish November air. And there were the lights of London, scattered horizonwide by the hundreds of thousands, like confetti, orange, white, and sulfur—best in a fog. But now there was no fog. The sky was starry and the city was all lit up. Then Shannon, and the smell of grass and rain. The Atlantic. Storm after storm buffeting the plane. And between storms, miles below them, through gaps, the beaten silver sea, and, level with the wings, the crescent moon. A ship's light. A few scattered lights off the Newfoundland coast. Then dawn over Nova Scotia—a dawn such as he had never seen, a shimmering of blazing reds and violets. The islands and bays of New England. Highways, cars. Then Boston's airport, and his in-laws. Simple hearts; tears in their eyes. Jessie's mother, her youth's beauty still recognizable, but looking very pale and wan. Jessie's fine-featured elder sister, light and very expressive. Jessie's father, a mild, big, handsome man.

They drove through the somber business district, past the Old State House and the new one, to the Common where the trees were of that ethereal yellow that he had seen in France, and also, hard to imagine, incomparable reds. It was raining. Driving along a parkway, they suddenly came upon such brilliant scarlet it seemed the sun was out. Later, he saw the trees from close up. The long-stemmed leaves of the maples disengaged themselves from their sockets at a touch, gave without a sound, or with the faintest, but most satisfying, tick. They stayed in Jessie's sister's apartment, soft and warm, with wooden floors and panels, so different from their solid, stone, ancient place in Rome.

They went to see the obstetrician the professor had recommended. He seemed too optimistic to be reassuring. "One? One is nothing. It's like sowing grass seed. Try again. Of course, after a Caesarean section you should wait six months or so."

Jessie's father, Mr. Reynolds—an affable and patient sort of man, whom in Italy they call "*una buona pasta d'uomo*" "as good as bread"—drove them to Cape Cod, where the family had a summer home, a small, cedar-shingle house hidden among pines, close to the sea and the pale, glistening blades of grass on the sand dunes. The pappi of the milkweed were floating in the air. He knew thistledown, but this . . . this was even more beautiful if it was possible; this was its American cousin with fine, soft platinum hair. He picked a pod that hadn't yet released its seed, and put it in his suitcase. When, a few days later, they went to New York and opened the suitcase in a hotel room, the ripened, plumed pappi lifted like smoke toward the ceiling, dozens of them; some took to the window and spiraled upward, free.

They looked for an apartment, and found one near Riverside Drive. Cosimo was enthusiastic about it. They moved in. But after two days Jessie wanted to move out. Too many cockroaches, she said. He scrubbed and sprayed; but still they came, the roaches. Jessie found them everywhere.

"You are looking for them."

But this was the Kleenex age, and she very much belonged to it. She was dreadfully conscious of germs and bugs. After four days, they left, losing a month's rent.

Now they found an elegant one-room apartment up high in a hotel in the middle of the town. It was so expensive they would be able to stay there only a few months. "We'll winter in this nest like birds," he said. And it *was* like a nest, warm, cozy, and with a view. A few blocks north, a new skyscraper the color of gold; west, a stately bronze one. Others seemed made of ice. The golden one changed color with the time of day. Sometimes it seemed on fire, sometimes it reflected the sun like a polished shield. At twilight, its color deepened, became the color of old gold. Rockefeller Center looked mountain-blue—the color of distance, the color he liked best. Losing and finding his way again and again, he got to know the city. From the Cloisters, at night, the island seemed to wear a golden bracelet. The massive, step-like, many-terraced skyscrapers at Bryant Park reminded him of the succession of cliffs on the face of rocky mountains he had climbed in the Alps.

An icy, violent wind blew over Manhattan. The Hudson was nearly frozen. Great slabs of ice floated downstream. The Hoboken ferry cut its way across the river like an icebreaker. On one of his walks, down Third Avenue, a thin-faced man with a raincoat caught up with him then stopped him and showed him the badge of the Immigration Service. Was he Italian, did he have his alien's registration card, he asked Cosimo. Cosimo produced it. He hadn't entered illegally, the man could be sure of that. There weren't many things Cosimo was more certain of.

With Jessie, he went to several parties. At one, in Brooklyn, Nick, an American who owned a bar in Rome, was talking to them about Magda, a girl they knew. Nick had employed her as a cashier, and Cosimo had first met her in the bar. "I remember her so well," Cosimo said. "She was sitting on a high stool by the cash register, tall, her arms akimbo, looking at the figures perplexedly, with a little frown."

"I had to help her add them," Nick said.

"She couldn't do math, but she was beautiful. Vibrant."

"She was a glamour girl all right, but she couldn't add. I had to fire her. I'd have gone broke," Nick said, and went on to tell them about other people he had employed, or helped out, as he put it. His bar sounded like a haven for Americans stranded in Rome.

"Did you ever meet a Mrs. Lee, the stranded woman par excellence?"

"Yes, I met her. She needed help worse than any of them," Nick said.

"Oh, she came to you too. We saw quite a lot of her in Rome; in fact, she was one of my patients. I wonder what's happened to her."

"What, don't you know? She killed herself."

"What?"

"She killed herself; with sleeping pills. They found her on a train. She had thrown away her passport, and they didn't know who she was. They had a picture of her in all the newspapers. All they found on her was a note that said, 'It was all a mistake.'"

The conversation went on with Cosimo out of it. "I've done enough for her," he remembered saying to Jessie. But, especially if one was a doctor, he thought, one could never help a person enough. The moment one said, "I've done enough for this person," one had done nothing, one had done nothing at all. Somehow, drawing a line where no line could be drawn, he had ceased to consider her a patient, while of course she was that all along, sicker at the end than at the beginning.

Like a doctor of limited scope who cares for pain and disregards sorrow, he had not understood; he had joined those who failed her, that rather large group of people she had asked to help her. "It's just as well I quit medicine," he said to Jessie.

At night, while she slept, he sat at the table in front of the window, and traced his thoughts on paper. For a writer, he thought, next to knowing the value of a blank sheet of paper, the most important thing was to have a wastebasket beside him. In the daytime he couldn't work. He was continually taking the elevator; more frequently, he guessed, than anyone else in the hotel, and the elevator boys had begun to resent it. In the first few days, they had made remarks about the weather, and he had tried his best to reply appropriately. But now they understood the effort it took him, and they went up and down in silence, and it was a strain, almost as much of a strain as walking down eighteen flights, which he sometimes did. Once, though, one of the boys complimented him on a published story of his, and then he felt that this was his town, this more than any other. And he liked to see the piles of magazines with a story of his in them at the newsstands. It cheered him to see people buying them, reading them; to see, in a bus, the magazine opened to his story on a stranger's lap.

He walked, and rode, to the parks, to the bridges. Jessie didn't often go with him. She wasn't restless, physically. But he felt an urge to get up and go. "Let's go," he kept saying.

"Where?"

"Anywhere."

At times he meant somewhere in town, at other times somewhere faraway. Leave for the sake of leaving, go to Grand Central and take a train, any train. Why were they here in New York? They had seen it now. Why didn't they get a car and see the country, cross it, criss-cross it? No, she didn't want to travel. She didn't even want to go out. Uninterested, uninteresting, he thought, and went out, alone. Sometimes he went to the main medical library, up on Fifth Avenue, to look up articles on erythroblastosis, blast it. The statistics didn't seem encouraging. He could come to no conclusion about it. Sometimes, when he was searching in the catalogues and books, he felt that what he really wanted, what he secretly wanted, was to find that, yes, there existed an absolute incompatibility between them, and that they should never, never attempt having a second child . . . So he could leave her, so there would be, if not a reason, an excuse to leave each other, and he could say, "We are incompatible, Jessie; there's nothing we can do; good-bye." But they were momentary thoughts. In bed he would touch the scar of her operation, and feel the link of pain. It was stronger than the link of love. No, it *was* the link of love, and nothing could sever it, nothing could divide them. They went to one doctor and to another, had an expensive blood test taken, and still there seemed to be no definite answer. "You can only try." From his medical school days, when he subscribed to an American medical journal, he remembered that the journal had a letter answering service. He wrote to the journal, posing their problem. The answer came. There was no incompatibility, but their chances of having a normal baby were only relatively good, it said, and quoted some disturbing statistics on the subject. "Let's not think any more about it," she said, "and wait until late spring."

Perched up in their eighteenth-floor room, day after day, week after week, month after month, night and day, they would often get very irritated with each other. Sometimes, exasperated, she would leave, go to the floor below, the lobby or round the block. He would look for her, entreat her to come back. One day, she bought a navy blue suit, and he told her it made her look like a policewoman. She became venomous, she started packing, then, not finding what she wanted, stuffed a few things in her handbag and rushed toward the door. She was going home, she said, to Boston. He held her. "Jessie," he said, "I've only got you in this big country, in all the world."

At times he would come into the room and find her lying in bed, perfectly still, hardly breathing. She was trying to look dead and she succeeded in scaring him every time. Then, one night, she said, "I am going out to meet Cornelius in Bryant Park, behind the library."

"What?"

"Cornelius is waiting for me there." She looked at her watch.

"Who is Cornelius?"

"A friend."

"At this time? It's three o'clock." He looked at her. She seemed serious, serious and sort of listless, half in a trance. Had she gone mad? "Look, sit down. I'll get you a glass of water."

Suddenly she laughed. She had been pretending. Too relieved to be angry, too exhausted to smile, he sat down. There was no whiskey, only water, and the bars were closed. It took him a long time to recover.

"Let's go," he said. "Let's go to Cape Cod, to the summer house."

"It's too cold yet. The pipes may burst if the water freezes."

"When can we go?"

"The first of April."

One day, feeling rather dizzy, he measured his blood pressure with a sphygmomanometer, one of the few instruments he had brought with him. It had always been normal, but now it was very high, over two hundred. At his age! He could hardly believe it. The next day it was down, but far from normal. He wished he could write prescriptions. He missed that power. He had a prescription book with him, but it was no better than any old pad. In Rome, with it, he had felt like a magician. Some days later, there was another dizzy spell. "Let's go, let's go," he said.

[1966]

The Short Cut

But for the map, the incident wouldn't have happened. It was one of a series of road maps that a drug company had sent him; being a doctor, he received all sorts of unsolicited gifts. First had come a map of Italy (his practice was in Rome), then one of France. By the end of the year, he had maps of all Europe. They weren't very good, though. They gave the main roads, the towns, and the mileage, but no markings to tell a plain from a mountain, and no indication of heights.

It was the drug company's map he was using on the trip back to Italy from England, where they had gone for Christmas and New Year's. She was twenty-eight—a slender, pensive American girl with long, chestnut hair. He was a few years older, dark and broad-shouldered. Most people didn't think he looked like a doctor, but they were probably wrong. Once, in a train, a little girl about two, sitting opposite him on her mother's lap, had looked at him for a long time and then, pointing at him, had said, *"Dottore."*

He and the girl had met two summers before, when she had fallen ill while in Rome as a tourist. He had seen her a few times, and an attachment had developed between them that soon brought them to a relation different from that of doctor and patient. After much debate, she had left for New York on the day for which her passage was scheduled. But the next spring she had surprised him in Rome. She had looked for a job that would keep her in Italy, and at last she found one in Bologna. It was a long way from Rome, but once or twice a month, on weekends, she would come down for a visit.

His car was a small, green, twenty-year-old convertible Fiat, all nicks, patches, and crusts, which he had bought two years before for about fifty dollars from a second-hand dealer in Rome. She thought it was cute. Because of its smallness and age, it was out of the contest, out of the tedious fray that cars, especially in Italy, have with one another. It was only a match for bicycles. Uphill, the cyclists often raced with it in sport, and, more often than not, overtook it. Sometimes, on small country roads, big sheepdogs would chase it and keep barking alongside for hundreds of yards. It was the only car he had driven that spared butterflies—they nearly always had time to get out of its way—and this was one reason he kept it. It often broke down. Once, in Piazza di Spagna, during the afternoon rush hour, the front axle broke, and the car went down like a horse on its knee. Before leaving on the trip to England, however, he had had it checked and had bought two new tires. Except for a flat and a consequent crack in the wheel rim at Dieppe—they had had to buy a new wheel—the car had given them no touble whatever.

To cross the Alps on their way to England, they had loaded the car on a freight train and gone through the St. Gotthard tunnel. Now, coming back, they planned to avoid the Alps by driving down to the Côte d'Azur and the Italian Riviera. But at Lyon, instead of going south along the Rhone to the coast and then east to Nice, a love for short cuts induced him to drive directly southeast toward Grenoble and Nice. As a result, about thirty miles out of Lyon the Alps began to loom, their white crests hovering over the dim horizon in the east.

"Are we going to have to go over them?" she said.

"No, no," he reassured her. "We'll be skirting them."

The lacy white fringe of peaks became clearer and clearer, then disppeared behind a brown, wooded mountain that stood in the way. They began to climb this one, and for a long time the Alps remained hidden. When they reached the top, they saw them again, but now they weren't just to the east; they were also to the north and the south.

"We *are* going to have to go over them; they're on all sides of us. Look at those," she said, pointing at some particularly high peaks to the southeast, on the other side of the valley. "Do we have to go over those?"

He stopped the car and studied the map. "I thought we'd be able to skirt them," he said. "But now I don't know. This damn map—I wish I'd bought myself a good one."

"In America," she said, "you can get good maps at gas stations, free."

"Here you have to pay for anything decent," he said. "Well, we'll find out in Grenoble," he added, slapping the map down on the floor of the car.

Going down the mountain, they had a flat tire. He found that the rim of the wheel had cracked, as in Dieppe. Metal fatigue, he thought, and proceeded to change it. In Grenoble, he stopped at the first Fiat-Simca garage they came to, and they bought another new wheel. This left them with only about twenty dollars between them. He asked the mechanic who fixed the tire about the way, and the mechanic replied that if they were going to Italy they might as well cross the main chain of the Alps to Piedmont as drive to Nice. "To go to Nice," the mechanic said, "you have to go over the Alps, too, and that way they are higher."

"Oh," he said, and looked at her.

"Yes," the mechanic continued, "and with this car, I'm afraid . . ." He didn't finish his sentence, but just gave a second-hand dealer's disparaging kick to the bumper.

"Perhaps we could put the car on a train," he said. "Is there a railroad tunnel through this part of the Alps?"

"There's the Fréjus," the mechanic said. "But it's a long way from here—at Modane. If you want to avoid the Alps, you have to go back to the Rhone."

"We'd better," she said.

"I don't feel like driving back to the Rhone," he said. "I'm tired." Suddenly, all trace of weariness went out of his voice. "Let's go over the Alps."

"I knew you'd say that," she said. "I knew all along that what you really wanted was to cross the Alps!"

"Yes, let's cross them," he said. The thought made him feel buoyant. He saw the fringe of peaks, the many summits, fantastically white; he was almost level with them. "Let's!" he said. "The map didn't show them, and I thought we could drive to Nice and stay clear of them, but now—"

"That map!" she said. "Why don't you buy a good one?"

"There's not much use buying one now; the mistake's been made. Look, there's one," he said, pointing at a wall map in the office of the garage.

They both went over and looked at it. Grenoble was in a narrow valley. Its river, the Isère, flowed deviously southwest toward the Rhone, and the only mountain around that was a reasonably light shade of brown was the one they had come over. All the others were a disquieting dark brown. Here and there, whitish-blue streaks denoted glaciers.

He took her hand. "Let's go straight to Italy, over the Alps," he said.

"No," she said. "It's mad at this time of the year, in that car."

"Our back tires are good. We could get chains . . ."

He asked the mechanic how much chains cost, but found the price was more than they could afford.

They left the garage and called at the municipal tourist bureau to inquire about road and weather conditions.

"The Alpine passes are open," the clerk said. "Naturally, conditions may change from hour to hour."

"Let's go," he said enthusiastically.

"You've never driven over the Alps, have you?" she asked him.

"No, never," he said, as though that were a good reason for doing so now.

"I don't think we should go."

"We practically have to. It's the quickest and cheapest way, and we don't have much money left, or much time."

"I don't have to."

"No, you don't. But I feel as if I have to cross them if it's the last thing I do—I feel sort of committed to crossing them."

"Oh, all right," she said with a sigh. "I'll go with you."

It was rather late, and they decided to spend the night in Grenoble. They drove about the darkening town, along old, sombre streets and dim alleys that sometimes led to squares and sometimes had desolate endings one wanted to get quickly away from. Every once in a while, they would come to the river, like a wider street.

In the morning, they checked at the tourist office again.

"The passes are still open," the clerk said.

He rubbed his hands together with satisfaction. "At eight o'clock tonight we'll be in Turin and dine at the Cambio," he said, "near the table they still keep set for Cavour."

They hurried out of the office. On the sidewalk, she paused. First she looked at him, and then at the car.

"You don't have much confidence in it, do you?" he said.

"Yes, I do," she replied, and got in.

It was cloudy but not very cold as they left Grenoble and followed the course of the river Romanche toward the heart of the Alps. Very gradually the valley narrowed to a gully. Soon they met the first snow. At first it was just on the sides of the road, but later, as they continued to climb, it stole more and more of the surface, until soon there was only left a wavy, bare strip in the middle. Then this, too disappeared and the road was all white.

"We haven't met a car for quite a long while," she said. "Do you think the pass is open?"

"Well, there are still tracks," he replied, "and it isn't snowing."

They passed a cluster of abandoned, doorless, shutterless houses. "Open but not inviting," he said.

Below them, from time to time, they could hear the rushing of water. Notices posted along the road warned against walking down to the river or along its banks, as sudden floods took place when water was let out from a hydroelectric plant farther up. They came to the plant, a dam, and a reservoir. Higher up, the fir trees, which below had been thick and healthy, became more and more stunted. Soon there were no more trees, or bushes, or any form of vegetation that showed above the snow. The mountain looked bleak above and below. A few hundred yards away, it blended imperceptibly with the sky. They couldn't see farther, in any direction. Rare flakes of snow hit the windshield. The road was now a channel of hard-packed snow that zigzagged up the white slope. On either side were mounds of cleared snow, where the plow had gone through, but they were not conspicuous in all the whiteness, and it would have been difficult to keep to the road if some red dye hadn't been thrown here and there to mark its borders. The dye tinged the snow and kept them on the right path, but it was worrisome to be reminded that there was need for such a measure, especially since the flakes, which were falling faster now, threatened to cover it. Already it was hard to tell whether there were any recent tire tracks on the snow. They went up in first gear, at all the speed he could get from the worn, little motor, the arrow of the speedometer oscillating between five and fifteen miles an hour. From time to time, whenever the tires lost their traction, the arrow would dip and strike zero, the car would almost stop, the tires would whine, and they would look at each other, then breathe with relief as the spinning ceased and the car moved forward again. On one side—the left or the right, depending on the zigzag—there was the steep, white slope that seemed to have no top; on the other, the steep, white slope that seemed to have no bottom. The snow that had been cleared off the outer side of the road had been dumped or had fallen down the incline, and there was no mound to protect them from skidding over the edge. He steered to keep close to the inner side of the mountain. They came to a stretch where the slope below them was precipitous.

"If we go over," he said, "they'll find us next summer."

She refused to look.

They followed the red marks and were grateful for them. Without skidding or stalling, the car continued up. He wanted to say something about it, praise it, tell her what a good car it was, but he was superstitious enough not to do so. They just went on and on, up and up, zigzag after zigzag, until at last they reached the top.

"Col du Lautaret," a sign read, and gave the height. It was nearly seven thousand feet.

They started descending. "Briançon is only a few miles away," he said. "We'll be in Italy soon."

If he put the brake on, the car skidded, so he cautiously drove down in low gear. They came to a plateau, a stream, and then to the small town of Briançon. There they stopped at a gasoline station, near a café.

"How far is the Italian border?" he asked the man at the pump.

"Five miles, but I don't think the pass is open."

"What pass?"

"The Pass of the Montgenèvre."

"You mean to say there's another pass? I thought we had done all the climbing."

The man laughed. "No," he said. "You have only done half of it. There it is—the Montgenèvre," and he pointed east.

Faintly, one could see the wooded base of a mountain.

"And you say the pass is closed?"

"Yes, I think so."

Two men, in different cars, stopped at the gasoline station. One said the pass was open; the other said it was not. Both were vague.

He looked at her.

"I am not going over another pass," she said. "One is enough."

"Is there a train to Italy from here?" he asked the man at the pump.

"No. The train goes to Gap."

"Gap," he said. "That's way back inside France. It's no good taking a train."

"Yes," she said.

"I am going on."

"*I* am not."

"Oh, come with me," he said. "We've gone so far together, and now there's only this little stretch of five miles."

"No."

"Well, I'll go alone," he said, and looked east, at the mountain.

She stood, ready to leave, her mind divided; then at last she said, "I'll go with you."

They had a cup of coffee and hurried on. "We must reach the top before the temperature falls," he said, "or we'll never make it. It's almost three o'clock."

The Montgenèvre was easy compared to the Col du Lautaret. It wasn't bleak and deslate. There were trees all the way, and he had the feeling that if the car should skid off the road, the trees would hold them.

"This road's a cinch," he said.

"Oh," she said, disapproving. She didn't like to hear him use American slang.

Near the top, icicles bigger than he had ever seen hung from a rock. They had blue reflections.

"I didn't think blue ice really existed," she said, looking pleased.

At the top, on another rock, a huge inscription said that Napoleon had taken this route to invade Italy and Austria in 1796. For a moment, he could almost see the army trailing its cannon, Napoleon ready to swoop.

They crossed into Italy halfway down the mountain, at a place called Claviere, and found themselves in the midst of parked cars, buses, and people in ski clothes. There was a bakery and coffee shop. He parked the car and they went in and had a tangerine punch. The place was run by a Neapolitan couple. In a husky voice, the husband complained to them about the confinement and heights to which necessity had brought him. Yet the café seemed to be doing very well.

With cars in front and behind them, they descended the Montgenèvre. Night fell as they reached the foot. They crossed a river. And still there was another mountain, but it was low—no higher than the one they had gone over before Grenoble. At last they reached the plain. She was tired, and they drove in silence toward Turin. From time to time he looked at her and wondered if she were sleeping.

"Are you awake, Chestnut?" he said.

She stirred and looked at him.

He glanced at her, then resumed looking at the road in front of him, flat and smooth.

"What?" she said.

"I just wanted to know if you were sleeping."

"Oh," she murmured and sat back, bundling herself up in her blanket.

He looked at her again. It was good to have her beside him. He thought of the first time he saw her in his office; he thought of the way she had surprised him, coming back from America; of her journeys from Bologna to Rome; of her sitting beside him wrapped up in a blanket in the small seat of the shaky, cold car each day of this long journey; of her going with him into hotels that she would never have gone into alone; of her weathering his moods, his complaints, his impatience; of her agreeing to go over the Alps. "Chestnut," he couldn't help saying again.

"Yes?" she said, peeking out of her blanket.

"No, nothing; I'm sorry," he said.

By eight o'clock they were in Turin, at the Cambio, sitting near the table set for Cavour.

Not long after this trip, they were married.

"Who went over the Alps with me?" he would say to her sometimes.

"I did," she would reply.

[1966]

The Binoculars

"How I'd like to go to the Abruzzi to buy dishes!" his mother often said. It was the one trip she really had at heart. "Just you and I in your little car—with room for only the dishes in the back." From time to time, some friend with a big car offered to drive them. "Shall we go? Shall we go?" she would say and look ready to leave. But they hadn't got around to going.

Then she had fallen ill. She had improved, and again she spoke to him of the Abruzzi trip. Her illness was one of relapses and remissions. During the remissions, she would say something about going, wistfully—more wistfully, it seemed to him, after each of the relapses. Finally, one came from which she did not recover.

It was four months now since she had died. He and his wife were living in her house in Tuscany. The set of dishes there served to remind him of the trip not taken. Plain white, with a couple of green circles at the rim, they had been bought by his mother provisionally, to discard as soon as she could find what she was looking for. They had the merit of being unpretentious, but that was all; they didn't offend you. At the same time, like a canvas with a piece of stripping around it, their blankness was intriguing. You felt a constant urge for some kind of form to take place in that blankness.

The right form was not easy to find—not in the shops within reach, at any rate. Stuffed birds, stiff flowers, patterns so often used that they looked dusty, deliberate wriggles—that's what you got here. In the Abruzzi, it was different. There, in the town of Aquila, six years before, while walking down a narrow lane, he had found a small ceramics store. Each cup, vase, plate, and saucer had a painting—a landscape with trees, a brook, a little house, and mountains in the background, done with colors that held meaning: the blue of distance, the green of freshness, the brown of earth. They were earthy dishes—glazed clayware, terra cotta—not stamped, not out of a mold, not printed but made by hand. Each had a different landscape, reflecting a mood, a fancy, a moment in a person's life. And on the back of each, handwritten, like a signature, was the name of the Abruzzi mountain village they came from—Castelli. He had bought several and taken them home. His mother, who had an even greater passion than he had for dishes, had liked them very much, and for a long time—six years—he wanted to take her with him and go to Castelli to buy more, right in the place where they were made.

Now it was too late to take her. Still, he felt he should make the trip—felt it almost as a duty. Perhaps in some supernatural way she would be with him, partaking of his pleasure everywhere. He was in Rome with his wife and baby for a few days—he had come by car, they by train, to avoid the bumps and bends of the roads. They were getting ready to return home—again he by car, with the luggage, and they by train—when he said, "I think I'll go back by way of the Abruzzi and Umbria. I want to get some dishes. I may take two days. Don't worry about me if I'm late."

Out of Rome, he headed north along the Tiber for a way, then left its valley, climbed the Sabine Mountains, proceeded to Rieti, and turned east toward the Apennines. He crossed the great divide, descended to a plateau, only to begin climbing again up toward the watershed, northeast of where he had crossed it. He reached a high, saddlelike mountain pass. From it, between spectacular mountains, the road ran down along a deep and narrow gully carved by a river.

It was a good thing the car was open, he thought; from a closed one, unless he leaned out, he wouldn't have been able to see the mountaintops, they were so high and he was down so low—almost level with the river. The river glistened between fallen boulders, some so huge no flood could ever budge them, others precariously balanced on one end—colossal pillars the current continuously undermined and would someday topple over with a splash. He raced the river—always before him and behind him, like the road. From bridge to bridge, dazzled by its silver light, he raced it, joined it, left it, caught sight of it and lost it, came on it so close he felt he'd run it down, only to see it curving around the corner of the gully a mile away.

The gully got no sun, though it was late morning and September. But he could see the sun shining on the brow of the mountain high over the river, on the opposite side. Up there, several white objects caught his eye. Rocks, were they? But why so white, when everything around, and the rocky cliff itself, was gray? Puzzled, he stopped the car and reached for a pair of binoculars he had inside a basket on the back seat. He looked through them. Sheets—bedsheets laid out to dry in the sun—that's what they were. Shifting the binoculars slightly to the right, he saw what he hadn't noticed with the naked eye: a little row of houses, gray like the mountain—part of the mountain, really—an upward prolongation of the cliff, made of the same stone, but with windows and a slightly more geometric outline.

He drove on. He wasn't just sightseeing. Before midday, he must get to Castelli, to buy the plates there. It was a village, perhaps, like this one, perched up high, on the east—for him, the far side—of the Apennines' tallest mountain. It was bigger than this village, though, big enough to be on his road map. This one wasn't; it didn't make the 1:500.000 scale. But Castelli was more out of the way—so remote one either went there expressly or not at all. He had an idea that the Renaissance had taken refuge in it and its pottery works, taken refuge in plates, dishes, humble things, up there on the mountains away from the main roads, and that someday, when the time was ripe, it would blossom out from there, invade the plains and cities once again.

The gully he had been driving along widened. It was a valley now, and the huge boulders on the river had given way to stones and pebbles. He came to a fair-sized village, and a fork. His road was on the right—the smaller of the two, the unpaved one. Less than a mile away, it left the valley and began to climb. Up and down the foothills of the mountain it led him, across small stone bridges over streams, in between woods and fields, the woods gaining on the fields as he went on, and the mountain always looming in the distance to the right, its peak concealed by a uniformly gray curtain of mist.

He passed a village islanded by a stream, connected to the mainland by a stone bridge—a village whose five- or six-centuries-old castle looked, and perhaps was, its newest building. On the many-creviced brick structure, herbs and flowers sprouted tall and thin, waving in the wind, and here and there even a shrub and stunted tree—an olive, an oak, a cypress. He stopped to examine all these closely, brought eight times nearer to him by the lenses of his binoculars.

He came to another, smaller village. Past this one, two or three miles, the soil, which farther down had been a fertile brown, became ashen gray. Clay. "What their dishes are made of," he said to himself, and knew he must be near. The landscape was guttered by deep creeks. No grass, no plant whatever, grew here. But for that common clay, he thought, there'd be no village—or, at least, no potteries. Yet the clay was a mere condition: An intelligent hand had picked it up.

He came to the last corner that concealed the village; snail-shell-shaped, on a high hill across a deep ravine, it disclosed itself. The road descended the ravine to cross a stream, then sharply rose again to the first houses. It became a village street, flanked by a low wall on his left and by a curving row of houses on his right. He passed a small store with dishes and vases in the window. I am here all right, he thought. Twenty feet farther on, the street turned inward, between houses, and soon it opened into a square. He parked his car. There were no chimney stacks, no factory buildings or workshops in sight—just ancient little houses close together. One had a ceramics store, and he could see another up a narrow street. On the opposite side of the square, a wider street climbed in a curve toward a second, smaller square, where the town hall and parish church stood.

He had no watch. Hoping to do some shopping before the stores closed for lunch, he asked a man the time.

"It's twelve-twenty," the man said. "Were you looking for something? Maybe someplace I can direct you to?"

"Yes, I came here to buy plates."

"Plates," the man said, like an angler who had sighted a fish biting. "Dinner plates or plates to hang up on a wall?"

"Dinner plates."

"Then come with me. I'll take you to the best place for them. These stores here have more the decorative kind." The man led him down some steps into a steep alley, down the alley and to the right, through an arch, a vault, a narrow passage, into another alley on a lower level of the hill, then up a few steps, where he gave a push to a battered wooden door. It opened into a small workshop with walls blackened by smoke. A big young man turned slowly to look at them. "He wants to buy plates," the man said briskly, and left.

The young man looked at him as at a customer who won't buy much—a couple of things at most. An older man looked up at him from the shadow, the semi-darkness of the room, then went on working, his curiosity taken care of. "I'll show you what we have," the young man said, and took him down a staircase to the floor below, which, because the village was on a steep hill, was the basement on one side and the ground floor on the other. It had two rooms. One, a few steps below the other, was a storeroom, and it was piled with dishes.

They were just what he wanted. He hummed with satisfaction and crouched before each pile. "At least a dozen of these," he said, and picked them out. Each landscape, similar to the ones he had seen years before, was different from the next, though they were garlanded by more or less the same flowers. "And a dozen matching soup plates. Six cups, six saucers."

The young man looked at him with surprise. "Shall I get a box?"

"A good idea," he said, and walked around. "This ashtray, too, and this, and this, and this. The more I look around, the more I want to buy. They fascinate me."

"Ah, yes, that's the way it is," the young man said. Somewhat opaque, his expression held a certain admiration now.

"This pitcher, too. And this little box."

The young man had a hard time keeping up with him, packing the things in straw.

"This little vase, and this, and this." God, there was no ending. Well, I must really stop now, he thought. He wanted to see some of the other stores. "Could I have these taken to my car? A small green convertible parked there in the square. Oh, and let me pay you." He observed the young man handling the dishes, packing them, making up the bill. "Who painted them?" he asked. He would have wagered that it wasn't the young man—a good fellow, but shallow-eyed, a little dull. Nor, he thought, was it the old man he had seen. A sharper stroke, a quicker hand was needed than this young man possessed, but chiefly a brighter glance, eyes more perceptive.

"He isn't here now. He only comes once in a while."

When he feels like it, he thought. Yes, that sounded right. He paid the bill—about twenty-five dollars—and went back up to the square.

One of the stores was still open, and he entered. Contrary to what the man he had first met told him, the shop had a wide selection of dinnerware. Again he began choosing. I must have at least twenty of those beautiful blue anemones, he thought. He felt that he was buying flowers. "Twenty of these pale-blue ones. A dozen of these fruit plates. And a dozen of these teacups."

A girl, a young man, an older woman and her husband busied themselves around him, pleased to have business, especially at this time—the good season over. The husband, owner of the firm, was a roundish, bald man with a clear and happy face. He looked like an artist; there was curiosity in him, speculation in his eyes. He seemed to want to engage in a conversation. He rubbed his hands together, clasped them, let them go, and, almost too politely, very gently, asked if where he came from they made plates like these.

"No," he replied. "Just the conventional fashionable stuff. Nothing like this—nothing fresh. Coats of arms, emblems, artificial-looking flowers."

"Here we paint like our fathers, like out grandfathers. I paint myself, and my family here helps me, and seven workmen." He went to the window and looked out. "There, you see. They are unloading the firewood. Beechwood. We use beech because it makes a very hot, bright flame. Nine hundred degrees our dishes are fired to. That's why they don't easily break. We sell them even in foreign lands—Boston, Amsterdam. The man from Amsterdam drove here to see me recently. Oh, *simpaticissimo*. Over there is the mountain. It's clouded over, or you would see it."

The dishes were packed. He paid for them—twenty dollars—then left with his bundle and took it to the car.

He had lunch in a little trattoria in the square, and afterward he walked up to the small square on top of the hill, to see the town hall and the parish church. In the center of the upper square, there was a bust of a celebrated seventeenth-century Castelli ceramist, painter, and sculptor. It was he, apparently, who had begun—or given new impulse to—the works. On the outside walls of the town hall and the church, there were several reliefs he had done in terra cotta. The town hall was a massive building—a castle, really—whose base, on the left side and back, was set on the bare, steep, sloping hill, at least a hundred feet below the level of the square. The town hall seemed like the bulwark of the village, protecting its little houses from the north.

He went back down to the lower square, and into two more stores. He bought two salad bowls, egg cups, coffee cups, and three or four vases, spending all the money he had except for a few thousand lire—just enough to get home on, he hoped. He had given each store and workshop a little business, and at the same time had got a supply of dishes that would keep him well provided for years. In a way, he felt odd—he, a man, buying all these household things. But he wasn't doing it just for himself.

With the last bundle of dishes in his arms, he went to the car and set them in the back next to the other dishes and his basket. The car was full. Yet not quite—his basket had an empty space on top. The binoculars weren't there. He was sure he had left them in it. He should have locked the car—even if one door didn't lock, the other did. He had only pulled the top up. Maybe they had fallen on the floor. He looked under the seats, between the boxes. No, they hadn't.

"Have you lost something?"

He looked behind him. A man was leaning over his shoulder, an expression of concern on his face.

"Well, yes—a pair of binoculars."

"Had you left them in the car?"

"Yes, in the basket."

The man looked inside the basket, tousling the change of clothes there, then inspected the whole car thoroughly. Nothing.

By this time, a couple more men had come to the car, and several more were on their way, all asking questions, milling around. "Was it a good pair of binoculars?"

"Well, yes, fairly good. . . . But it doesn't matter."

"And you are sure you had them when you came?"

"I think so. . . . Yes, I had them."

They looked at one another. "Bernardo," somebody said.

"Bernardo," another man repeated.

"Who is Bernardo?"

"Hu! He is a foolish boy. I saw him strolling around the car before—snooping."

"I should have locked it. But it can't really be locked."

"This time he isn't going to get away with it, though," one of the men said.

"He needs a lesson," said another.

"It's once too often," the first man said.

Somebody started cursing. "There goes the honor of this village by it!" he said.

Halfheartedly, he was still looking inside the car, just to give himself something to do.

"You know," a man explained, "he's a bit odd, this Bernardo boy," and he dipped his hand to this side and to that next to his forehead.

A *carabiniere* came, and began asking tedious questions—questions no one would have thought of answering, except to a *carabiniere*.

"Come, let's go find Bernardo," someone said.

"No, look," he said. "I'd rather you did nothing about it. I don't mind about the binoculars. Anyway, they hurt my eyes."

They looked at him as if he were a little odd himself.

"He's a thief," a man said to him. "You came to buy dishes. You brought us good business. You mustn't be treated in this way. It isn't right."

"Come, let's go get him," the first man said, and in a moment he was off, with two or three others and the *carabiniere*. They seemed to know exactly where to go, as if this had happened before.

"Where are they going?"

"His home."

Soon they came back with a youth; at second glance, he looked to be in his late twenties—an overgrown, red-faced fellow with bad acne and very short hair. He was followed by a slender old woman with a black kerchief on her head, in black stockings and threadbare clothes—a woman who looked as if she had been in mourning half her life; she was probably his grandmother. Part of the time she was swearing at the boy, part of the time beseeching the *carabiniere* to forgive him. Two or three times she hit the boy on his back, hoping, perhaps, they might accept that as punishment enough for him. Each time, he ducked and raised an elbow. The old woman looked at the car and at the stranger, and began asking his forgiveness.

"Yes, yes, I forgive him," he said.

"No, he's in for it this time. He's stolen before," the *carabiniere* said. "Here—are these your binoculars?"

"Yes," he said, and took them. "Really, marshal, I don't want to press charges. Let him go. After all, the binoculars have been found. Everything's all right."

"It's out of your hands, I'm afraid. Everyone come to the police station with me."

They all went up to the town hall. There, in a dingy office that smelled of filthy paper and looked as dreary as every other police station in the world, he answered many questions. At last, after an hour, he went out the front door. Half an hour earlier, Bernardo had been led through another.

He walked slowly down the hill to the lower square, past the store where he had bought part of his dishes, to the car. Everywhere, he felt eyes looking at him. He got into his car, started the motor, and drove away—down to the creek, across it, and up to the top of the next hill. There he stopped, took his binoculars out of the basket, and looked through them at the castled structure of the town hall. On its left and tallest side, he could see many holes and a tiny window, barred. He wrested the binoculars from his eyes. Quickly, he resumed driving. He drove all evening, and reached his home that night.

A few days later, waiting for the food to be passed around, he stared into his empty plate. He looked at it intently. What he saw was not the open sky, the little silver cloud, the tree, the hut, the mountain the blue color of distance, and the flowers but a barred window.

"Aren't these plates lovely!" a guest said to him.

He looked up at her. "Yes," he said. "Yes. Lovely,"

He thought, The binoculars stolen, the boy in jail, and this woman here instead of my mother—they are all in keeping with each other.

[1964]

Radicofani

The Via Cassia—the ancient highway from Rome to Siena and Florence, named after Cassius, the consul—reaches its highest point about halfway along its course, at the village of Radicofani, twenty-nine hundred and forty feet above sea level. The road twists between hillocks and ridges of clay, up and up, to the summit. To motorists, the name denotes, more than the village, the bleak and desolate mountain—steepness, and horseshoe curves, the screeching of tires, and remoteness.

Most of the land is barren, but here and there, where the mountain isn't too steep, it is plowed for wheat. The harvests are scanty, for the clay sheds the rain, and, with no trees to hold it, the water rushes to the valley, carrying seeds with it and carving great, gray, gutterlike channels. In some places, the clay is so pure that nothing will grow on it, and it looks poisonous. Under the strong sun, the clay bakes and cracks the way a statue that hasn't been hollowed cracks when it is fired and becomes terra cotta. Layer upon layer, wave after wave, the pale clay has molded itself into ridges and mounds. Looking at it, one is tempted to say that this isn't earth but a sort of white lava.

A few hundred feet from the village, on the very top of the mountain, is Radicofani's medieval castle, gray as the mountain it stands on. It has outer walls and a tower, both in a state of disrepair. The walls are especially dilapidated; one has the impression that they have been used more than once as a quarry. The door to the tower hangs open, because the wood is so warped it doesn't fit the jamb any more. Inside, the wooden staircase, hugging the four walls and leaving a great chasm in the middle, is missing several steps. At some risk, one can still climb it. Then, from the terrace at the top of the tower, one has an unobstructed view of the farthest horizon—to the north, one can see the hills of Siena, over forty miles away. Sheltered by the castle walls are a few trees—a pale olive tree, a stubby mulberry—over-pruned, cut and recut, not given a chance. From the tower all that one sees of the village is the terra-cotta tiles. They cover two rows of about fifty houses. Between them is a narrow paved street—the Via Cassia as it originally went. Today, the through traffic doesn't enter the village but passes a little below it. Here on the bypass there are two gasoline stations and a couple of cafés. There is also an old, square, solid building with four open arches, a portico, and four large wooden doors. It is the old posthouse. Once, the stone floor of the portico must have rung with the sound of iron wheels and shod hoofs; now it is silent and the doors of the stables are shut. The gasoline stations, however, are quite busy, for this is still the main road between Florence and Rome.

Of all roads, the Via Cassia is the road I know best. It is the road of my childhood. From my home, near Siena, Radicofani could be seen as a blue, distant peak dominating the way to the south. Often I would point it out to travellers. "That's Radicofani. The road to Rome goes through it."

"You mean we have to go up there?"

"Yes, all the way up."

I knew it from having been there more than once. Every Christmas, my father would drive the whole family down to Rome for a visit. At various points along the way, Radicofani would be visible in the distance. It would become more and more awesome as we approached. It seemed almost incredible to me that a road should go like that to the top of what from a distance looked like a cone. Sometimes it was white with snow, and it was a question whether we would be able to get through. This made the trip very exciting. Once, the snow was so deep we had to drive back all the way to Siena and take the longer, coastal route through Grosseto. But even without snow the climb was dramatic—in those days the road was narrower and in some stretches steeper than it is now. When we reached the top, we usually gave my father a cheer.

I remember the Via Cassia just after the war, the sides of the road—especially at Radicofani—littered with the remains of German tanks. All along the way, the treads of war machines had left deep marks in the asphalt, and pits had formed where spilled gasoline had dissolved it.

But it was in the postwar years that I came to know the road best, and particularly the Radicofani part, for then I began to ride over it on a light motor scooter I had bought. I was studying at the University of Rome at the time, and one day in the winter of 1948, when I was going up to Siena for a holiday, the engine failed me about two miles below Radicofani. I had to push the scooter up to the village. There was no garage, and the men at the gasoline pumps directed me to a blacksmith, whose shop was at the northern end of the bypass, near where it was joined by the street that ran through the village. Even before I arrived there, the wind brought the sound of his hammering to me. From the open door I saw the blacksmith deep inside the shop, framed by red-spoked cart wheels, strings of horseshoes, tongs, and coils of wire—all hanging from the walls and ceiling. He was intently forging a piece of iron. His hammer would not so much strike the iron he held in his tongs as heavily fall on it. After each fall, the hammer would bounce and then fall on the iron again, very lightly, producing a musical sound and giving a moment of rest to his hand. I watched the incandescent iron in his tongs, blinked at each blow, listened to the hiss of the water, looked at his foot on the bellows, at the response of the brazier, at the iron resting in it becoming again incandescent, then reddening under the blows, then dimming as it lost more of its heat. I didn't want to interrupt. I wanted to see each step over and over. Pushing the motor scooter along, I went closer. There was a smell of rust and burning coal. He seemed to belong to the time of coaches, not of automobiles, and I wondered whether he would even look at my scooter.

I expected him to pause or at least glance my way, but he continued in what looked like an effortless rhythm. At last, I decided to speak. "Excuse me," I said. "Coming up the mountain my motor scooter broke down and I wonder if you could repair it."

He didn't stop hammering right away but kept me waiting till the bright red iron became dull. Then he laid his tongs and hammer aside.

Slowly—his arms were more agile than the rest of his frame—he turned toward me and crouched to examine the engine. He rattled something. "This piece is broken," he said, pointing at a part of the transmission.

"I don't suppose I can get a new one in Radicofani," I said.

"No, but I can make you one," he said.

He disassembled the motor till he could free the broken piece, then took it and looked at it, turning it around and around in his hands.

"Can it be welded?" I asked.

He shook his head. "Not this," he said.

He took from a box a length of metal. Metal, the way he handled it, seemed full of possibilities. But he discarded it. He took another piece. With the broken part in front of him for reference, he began forging the new one. Again I watched him, fascinated by the fire and his skill. After a few minutes, I asked him how long it would take him to finish. He seemed annoyed by my question—wasn't his work, no less than a work of art, full of imponderables? "An hour or two, maybe," he said.

I walked down to the posthouse. It looked massive. Beside it the gasoline stations seemed sheds. There it stood on the wayside—a relic, outmoded, used to store, not to shelter; perhaps not used at all. Inside the four wooden doors, there probably had been room for fifty horses. This must have been a very important posthouse indeed, I thought. The nearest villages—Acquapendente to the south and San Quirico to the north—were each nearly twenty miles away on the steep, winding road. In my mind I could see the teams of horses breathing hard up the mountain, the vaporous breath from their nostrils in winter, the sweat foaming on their haunches in summer, the passengers descending, stamping their feet, looking at the bleak mountainside below them, at the castle and at the rows of houses above them. Shelley had probably stopped here, and Byron, and in remoter times, Milton. I thought of Stendhal, of Foscolo and Galileo; of Leonardo, Michelangelo, and Raphael. I thought of Petrarch. Centuries before him, Charlemagne had probably stamped his feet here, and, two millennia ago, Julius Caesar, and Cassius the consul, before Julius Caesar was born.

I wondered how long the stagecoaches stopped here. Just long enough to unhitch the old team and hitch on the new? Or did the passengers have time for a meal? I knew that stagecoaches travelled about fifty miles in one day, and that, important a relay station as Radicofani must have been, it was too close to Siena to be an overnight stop—on their way from Florence to Rome, passengers usually passed the first night in Siena and the second in Acquapendente. At Acquapendente there was a well-known inn, and many famous people had signed its register. Poets were asked to write a verse. An English poet wrote: "I can think of *niente*/To rhyme with Acquapendente." And yet, in bad weather no coach could have reached Acquapendente from Siena in one day; it was a distance of nearly sixty miles. Of course bad weather, accidents, brigands, and other delays must have caused many travelers to stop here for the night. There was no question about it—many famous people of the past had slept in Radicofani, too.

I said to myself, "I have two hours; why don't I go and look for signatures at the local hotel? I might find something even better than what the English poet wrote at Acquapendente. Shakepeare's own signature might be in the attic!"

I don't know why I thought of Shakespeare—I didn't know whether Shakespeare had ever left England. Perhaps it was the extreme rarity of his signature that made me think of him. Or perhaps it was that so many of his plays are set in Italy. Anyway, the thought of Shakespeare's signature excited me. In my mind I was already in the attic in front of a pile of old registers that became older and older the nearer one got to the bottom. Already I was drawing out the very bottom book, opening it, and, after turning a few pages, seeing Shakespeare's signature staring at me—not the unsteady, tremulous hand that we know but a cursive, impatient one, followed by his Stratford on Avon address and a verse that made the one written in the hotel at Acquapendente seem like prose.

I was hurrying now—almost running—up to the center of the village. I found the inn (it was the only one in Radicofani) halfway along the street. The building was old—as old as any in Radicofani, I thought. Not old, I corrected myself—ancient. Its travertine, hard stone though it is, had lost its sharp edge at the corners. It was smooth everywhere. Here and there it was glossy. "This house is as old as the castle," I said to myself. "Perhaps even older. The castle was probably built later to defend these two rows of houses."

The front door of the inn—two thick boards of dark wood—was open, and I went up a few steps to a glass-paneled door with the word "*Locanda*" across it in old-style italic. A good sign, I thought. I went in. There was a narrow hall with a door on either side and a staircase at the end. The door on the left led into the dining room, which had a few bare wooden tables and a big brown stove of glazed terra cotta. I chose a table near the stove and sat down. A woman peered in at me from the kitchen, withdrew, and soon a chubby waiter came in. He began setting the table.

"Is this an old hotel?" I said.

His hand spiraled up, describing the vortex of time. "Very old," he said. After his gesture, the words were an anticlimax.

"How old?" I asked. "Do you know?"

"The present owner—no, what am I saying? His *father* bought it in nineteen hundred; but it was a hotel before that. It has always been here."

"The guests it must have seen!" I said. "Famous people must have stopped here. Who knows, perhaps even Garibaldi."

"It could be," he said.

I asked for a plate of spaghetti. He disappeared, and twenty minutes passed before he came back with the dish. During that time, my thoughts hadn't veered from the idea of the poets and Old Masters who might have stayed here. In my mind the hotel registers had taken on the splendor of illuminated medieval manuscripts; I was quite outside this age of passports and identity cards.

"Do you have any of the old registers?" I asked him.

"Registers?" he said.

"Yes, with the names of the people who have stayed here in the past."

"You want to see them?"

"It would be interesting," I said.

He left in the direction of the kitchen. A few minutes later, he appeared at the hall door, accompanied by a stocky, elderly man. They both looked anxious. The elderly man led the way. "You want to see the registers?" he said. "Are you an inspector?"

"No, no," I said. "Nothing of the sort," and I laughed, then explained to him what I meant. "I'm interested in them purely from a historical point of view," I said.

He looked relieved and turned to scold the waiter for having alarmed him. "The gentleman speaks plainly enough," he said to him.

"I should have made myself clearer," I said.

"Old registers," he said, turning back to me. "We don't have any."

I could see that he wanted to end the matter. "I thought that perhaps in your attic or somewhere you might have some." I spoke with the feeling one puts into lost causes. "Just one famous signature and you'd be rich. I know a lady in Rome, a certain Signora Rossini, who was able to buy a house with a signature of Shelley."

"A whole house?" he said.

"Yes. Who knows, perhaps Shelley came by here and stopped in this very hotel."

"Shell—" he said.

"An English poet. Or Byron, or Leopardi, or Foscolo," I said. The names didn't seem to make an impression. "Or Milton," I went on. "Or Shakespeare."

"Shake-a-spear," he said, his face at last lighting up. "I have seen *Giulietta e Romeo* in Acquapendente."

"With *his* signature you could buy the whole of Radicofani," I said. "Why don't we look? Perhaps you have some old books you've forgotten about. There may be a treasure in your attic."

"Really?" he said. "Up here in Radicofani?"

"This is a great route," I said. "The great thoroughfare between Florence and Rome—the Via Cassia, not just another road."

He seemed impressed. He seemed so impressed that for a moment

I was afraid I had said too much; he might become too jealous of his registers to want to show them to me, if indeed they did exist.

"I am not an expert," I said. "But if you have anything worthwhile, I think I would be able to tell you."

"I believe you," he said. He poured me another glass of wine. "You finish eating and then we'll go and see."

I ate the rest of the meal quickly and asked the waiter how much it was. But the owner laid his hand between us. He wouldn't let me pay. I was scarcely able to leave the waiter a tip.

The owner went into the kitchen for a candle; then I followed him up the stairs. At the third floor, the staircase became steep and narrow. At the top, he unlocked a door, lit the candle, and led the way into the attic.

It was a windowless room with a low ceiling, a water tank, and some broken furniture. I followed him, looking sharply at every object. He was already shaking his head when I saw under a table a pile of large, rather thin, album-like books. There must have been a dozen of them. "There they are," I said.

We went over and opened the top one. Page after page of numbers—it was an account book. I opened another. The same—more figures. Halfway down the pile, I began finding names and dates, where guests had registered. I looked at the dates. They were much too recent. Nervously, I drew out the bottom book and opened it. There were names and addresses, each written in a different hand. I turned a few pages.

"Oh!" I said, with such excitement that the old man started and the candle almost went out "I've found something! Here is the name of my father, my mother, and the names of my two brothers, and my own. December 23, 1928."

I closed the book. "My father used to drive us to Rome every Christmas. We must have stopped here that night. I was too small to remember. Perhaps you were here."

"Yes," he said. "I was here in 1928."

"We had a convertible—a blue Chevrolet."

I could see his eyes roving down the scale of the years. At last, they stopped roving—he couldn't remember.

We went downstairs.

"Let me pay you for my dinner," I said in the hall.

But he still wouldn't let me.

"I am sorry I couldn't find any valuable signatures for you," I said.

"You found yourself," he said. "What more do you want?"

•

At the blacksmith's, the motor scooter was ready—reassembled, waiting for me, leaning against a wall. The blacksmith came over and started the engine. It roared. I was enthusiastic and praised him, but he turned away from my praise back to his work.

I went on. The long descent, the night air exhilarated me. It seemed I would never reach the foot of the mountain. It seemed I was descending the spiral of time that the waiter had described, down the years, to my childhood that I had found locked up there in the attic. Around a curve I skidded and fell. It brought me back to the present. Picking myself up, unhurt, and the scooter, undamaged, I said to myself, "Now I really know Radicofani well."

[1960]

from *Doctor Giovanni:* The Tower

"It's south of Ancona, on the shore, below a mountain, and from up above it looks like a little castle in a game of chess. The tower is so close to the sea, during storms it is sprayed by the waves that break on the rocks. The beach is pebbly, and sandy in places, but the tower is protected by boulders. It was built in 1740 by one of the popes to ward off the pirates.

"My grandfather was from Ancona. When the tower still belonged to the town, he used to rent it from them, and write poems there. Then, in the twenties, my father bought it."

I was explaining all this to Daphne, hoping she would come with me there for a week or two.

"It's an old building with no electricity or water. Quite nice though—a tower with a small house attached. The rocks and the beach are white, and the tower, on a little mound, is yellow brick. It has small windows and a roofed terrace on top from which you can see the whole beach and the mountain."

"It sounds beautiful," Daphne said. She was an artist, widowed during the war.

The tower was on a lonely strand—half a mile wide at its widest—that ages ago, in prehistoric times, slid down from the mountain. This mountain, steep and high and huge, was all wooded, except for where landslides had made streaks of coral red, and the blue of the sea and the white of the shore went together like the blue and white in a Della Robbia. In May, the stretch of land below the mountain, and some of the mountain itself, was gold with broom—the *ginestra.* And in all seasons, there was a pungent smell of heather, myrtle, and thyme.

"But perhaps the nicest things," I said to Daphne, "are the stones, all colors, small, and rounded so they roll with the waves. They are such beautiful colors—white, pink, mauve, and amethyst—you feel like picking them up and taking them with you. But as soon as they dry out, their colors fade like flowers'. But why am I telling you all this? You'll see them.

"We used to go there often before the war, when we had a car, but we haven't been since. The Germans took our car when they retreated. We used to go down loaded with provisions. It was a long trip for us, from Siena—two hundred miles, and the Apennines in between."

We would cross them by a different pass each time. Some were dramatic; the walled road zigzagging up—from below it looked like a series of fortifications. At Bocca Trabaria, for instance. We would stop to drink at mountain springs, and spend the night in some nice old town, like Urbino, or Borgo San Sepolcro, or Sassoferrato.

"The other day, I thought of going there, but it's pretty lonely. Much nicer if two go. There are only a few inhabited places there—a couple of houses next to a church that isn't in use, a few fishermen's huts, and a tavern by a spring at the base of the mountain; each at least a quarter of a mile from the other. We get our water at the spring. It's half a mile from the tower."

The train had so far followed the Tiber, whose water was quite blue up here. It made little islands, and received pretty brooks that came down from the hills in deep, wooded gorges. On its right, for a while, it skirted Mount Soracte—an isolated mountain and extinct volcano—which from the train looked like a sail, and which, though a long way from the sea, gave the serene impression of being right on its edge, as if there couldn't possibly be anything but an expanse of blue water beyond it. No other part of Italy seemed to me more beautiful. Ancient Etruscan towns, built of gray stone like the crags on the river, rose on top of the hills, hardly distinguishable from them in winter. In early spring the banks of the streams were bedded with violets. Later on, the hollyhocks bloomed along the railroad. And all the time, the lone mountain reflected itself on the water, lending it stillness.

At Orte the train left the Tiber and turned east along the valley of the Nera. At Terni, a soldier got off; at Foligno, a student. We shifted to the window. Now we were skirting the Apennines. Soon we entered a murky tunnel, cold and moist. Once past it, the steep mountains jutted up, so high we had to bow low to see the sky. A river glittered below us. Soon the train noisily entered again into the bowels of the earth. Again we came out in the open as into a sea of light.

Suddenly, we saw the white foam of a wave, and in a moment there we were, right by the shore, with the waves advancing, retreating. The train jolted, sidetracked, and we got even closer. We had crossed Italy. A fresh sea smell, briny and bracing, came in through the open window. A wave fell heavily, its blue turning silver, then white, as it swept the shore.

"Fifteen miles down the coast," I said, "the sea is splashing on the rocks off the tower."

We could see Ancona across the bay, grayish-white in the distance. The long waterfront, the cranes of the harbor, and, beyond the harbor, white, on top of a cliff, Ancona's cathedral. We drew into the station. It was past four o'clock. Level with us were ships lying at anchor in the oily, scummy water that beyond the pier was so blue.

"By the tower, the water is crystal clear," I said.

"So if I drown you'll be able to find me," she said, and laughed.

Towns with a harbor have a welcoming air, an openness about them that inland towns lack. Is it the freedom that blows in from the sea? Is it the ships coming in and going out? Is it the sailors' appetites, which the town willy-nilly, rises to satisfy? Call it a looseness, call it a wantonness—there's something obliging about a town on the sea. An odor of spice and tea, of coffee, dried fruit, and wine comes out of the warehouses. Things are apt to be cheaper. Fish can be had at low prices. There's nothing stingy about a town on the sea.

We walked across the railroad tracks to the street. What a sensible station. Right in the center of town. On one side the ships, on the other the cars and pedestrians. It was a little like getting off a trolley instead of a train.

During the war Ancona was heavily bombed. Much of the waterfront was in ruins. The rubble of bricks, mortar, and stones hadn't all been cleared. Some of it was still there, arranged in neat piles, the bricks one on top of the other, lining the streets. We walked up, as one usually does from the water. Inland, even one block from the harbor, the damage wasn't so extensive. The main square seemed unscathed. Certainly it was full of life. So were the streets issuing from it. This part of Ancona seemed to want to make up for the other, in ruins. It did so with people, with traffic, with produce. It specialized in freshness as the other in desolation. We bought more supplies, among them watermelon, grapes—and bread so fresh, so crisp, so hot you could hardly hold it and felt like buying butter too and spreading it on and eating it right there and then. We ventured away from the sunny square up a narrow, dark lane in deep violet shadow. Here too there were shops, and one trattoria with a menu outside. The specialty was *vincisglas*—a sort of lasagna dish, only richer. At a wine shop, we bought a fiasco of Verdicchio, the wine of Le Marche.

"I think we are doing well," I said.

"Very well."

With this load and our other baggage Daphne and I went to Piazza Cavour and our bus. It was due to leave at five-thirty for Numana and Sirolo, two small towns down the coast. To get to the tower we would have to get off on the ridge of the mountain and walk down a secondary road. Only on Sundays was there a bus that took you all the way. Well, it wouldn't be a hard walk—about a mile, and for the most part downhill.

At five-thirty we began climbing out of Ancona, along a steep, dusty road with sharp turns. Two or three times, as the bus took the curves, we saw the town down below, and in the distance the shore along which we had come, stretching north, hazily. To the northeast, even more hazy, were the foothills of the same Apennines we had crossed. The climb got more gradual. We were in the open country now, between vineyards and olive trees. The road wound on, and now we could see the mountain—the Monte Conero—its ridge reared up in front of us like the powerful neck of a horse. Despite the many dips and rises that we covered, we didn't seem to be approaching it at all quickly, testifying to its breadth and grandeur. But at last we came to the base of the ridge, the start of the great rearing neck. Soon we reached the fork where the secondary road led down the mountain obliquely. Here the bus stopped and we got off and stood on the side of the road, which was soft with accumulated white dust, and watched the bus, raising a cloud of it, resume its twisty climb up the mountain before descending again to Sirolo and Numana, on the other side.

We took the little road. Hedged in between two fields of stubble, it went out, flat and easy, toward the face of the mountain. There was a little hump in the road, then a curve. "We'll see the tower in a second," I said.

And there it was, still there, small and alone, on the edge of the sea, on the edge of the land, about a mile away and a thousand feet down. At the same time, the odor of thyme greeted us, and with it memories of other trips here—childhood memories of when I used to come with my parents in an open blue 1928 Chevrolet. The road had been worse then than now. No bus could make it down, and almost no cars. We were among the few who dared. The road had no fences or parapets of any kind, and there was a dangerous, open, steep hairpin curve at which we would all get out but my father. The road was like an inclined shelf on the side of the mountain.

"My mother painted the tower, once, with the sea on one side and on the other the mountain; the sea rippled by the wind, streaked by currents; the sky a very light blue; and the coral red of the mountain. I remember that best."

It was easy walking down, but not so easy to stop. One step brought on the next. Soon, there was more land above us than below. "That's where the farm is," I said, pointing to a little road that led through the wood on the left.

We went over. In a minute we came to the end of the wood, and saw the farm. Two ducks wobbled toward us. We passed a haystack and came to the stone house, and there was the smell of bran and corn mush for the hens, the smell of mud mixed in with manure, and the smell of grass, too, and of fresh linen hanging on a clothesline. The old grandmother was sitting on a chair, under a trellised vine. When I told her who I was, she didn't respond, but her daughter—Anita—heard me and appeared at the window. She had grown up with my mother, played with her as a child. She immediately recognized me. "It's Giovanni!" she said. "Laura's son," she added, addressing herself to her mother.

She was downstairs in a moment, and in my arms, an armful of a woman with an open, heartwarming smile and the feel of something wholesome. We hadn't seen each other since before the war, but she hadn't changed. She was still attractive, a prize. Her husband—Guido—came out, too, from the stable, a man not half as impressive as his wife, but kindly, though quiet and uneffusive. In this part of the world it seemed to me that the women were always more commanding than the men. People never referred to this farm as Guido's, nor did they use his last name for it, but always said "Anita's." Guido was continually described as Anita's husband. And so it was with every family I knew near Ancona.

"And is this your bride?" Anita said, looking at Daphne.

"Not yet," I said, and introduced her to them.

A look came over them that seemed to say, "This is the modern world we haven't quite caught up with."

"Daphne's American," I said.

This made them very happy. *"Americana!"* they said, and looked at her the way one looks at a bright, newly minted coin.

"Sì," Daphne said.

They offered us some *vin santo*—a thick, white wine made from seared grapes—and gave us the key to the tower. I looked at it kindly. It was all rusty and so big it stuck out of my pocket. I took it out and looked at it again. Its bit had three notches, and each notch was notched in turn twice over. "They don't make them like this anymore," Anita said.

We went on, and soon we reached a crossroads at the bottom of the mountain. A hundred feet to the left, hidden by a dozen immense and luscious sycamores, was the spring we depended on for water, and, right next to it, the tavern—Letizia's.

"Letizia," I said to Daphne, "is even more important than Anita. She's big and brawny and she wears a kerchief like a pirate. She has a husband, too, but compared to her he's like a little errand boy."

We could see the tower—the top of it—beyond the green, brush-covered hillocks that stood between the mountain and the sea. "Fifteen minutes more," I said to Daphne, leaving the road for a rough, stony track that wound its way around the hillocks and mounds. Here and there the brambles had invaded it. It looked forsaken, and indeed few people used it. In the air, the smell of laurel, myrtle and heather persisted. Daphne stopped and sighed. "Let me take a little rest," she said, sitting down on the stones. I sat down too, in the middle of the track. "I'll give you a hand, if you want," I said. "I could even carry you."

She shook her head, smiling and looking at the ground. "That's just like you," she said. "Just be quiet a minute."

I sat quietly. My golden girl, I thought, looking at her hair; at her rounded, honey-colored shoulders, bare, under the loose, flimsy, sleeveless dress. She had her knees flexed, her feet together, and she had drawn the skirt back from her legs to cool herself. In a moment she got up and we went on, up and down and up again, along the billowy terrain, the bushes rising above us obscuring the view. In a little while we reached a clearing, and suddenly in front of us there it was, the tower, on top of a grassy, thistly mound, beautifully isolated, serene, its wind- and rain-worn yellow bricks still holding firm as they had for over two centuries. The grass and the thistles were long and untrampled. At each of the four corners of the tower some of the cement between one brick and another had been blown away by gales, but the walls were enormously thick; they could afford to lose bits of cement or even a brick here and there. Protected as it was from the waves by a semicircle of boulders, the tower was good for at least two centuries more. The water looked friendly, and as blue as Daphne's eyes, which, as she looked at the waves, seemed even bluer. Here and there, herbs and long-stemmed flowers waved on the walls from nooks and crannies where small amounts of earth had collected. A recess in the papal coat of arms on the front, below the second floor window, had become the home for a colony of wasps. Their buzzing, the lazy motion of the flowers, the sea's even lazier glutting on the rocks, the crinkly lichen underfoot lent the place a calm that couldn't but affect you.

I inserted the key into the lock of the massive, plated front door. Three turns, and the bolt was released. I slid it out, and the door swung open. I picked Daphne up and carried her in my arms across the threshold like a bride, into the huge hall. It had no windows, the better to be defended. With the door closed, it depended for light on two high and narrow, slitlike embrasures that revealed the great thickness of the walls. To close the door from the inside, there was another bolt; as an added precaution, a heavy wooden bar could be slid across the door from wall to wall. With that in, you really felt secure inside. But we left the door open, and went up a wooden staircase into the living room which was to the right, in the little house built onto the tower. I opened the windows, which looked out to sea.

A light breeze and the evening light filled the room which had been kept dark for a year. The sea air had corroded the walls, and bits of plaster had crumbled off onto the sofa, the tables, a bookcase, and the floor. I got sheets and pillowcases out of a cupboard and brought them and our baggage up into the best room, on the second floor of the tower, where we would sleep. Below the window was the papal coat of arms with keys of paradise. This seemed very auspicious. Then we went up two more flights of stairs to the top floor where there were two more rooms, and from there, up a steep, narrow staircase and through a trap door to the terrace, which had battlements and a tile roof supported by enormous beams artfully locked in place according to a time-honored pattern. The wood the beams were made of—cypress—had become a very light gray color with the weather. Its surface was soft, almost powdery—a patina which you could easily scrape off even with your fingernails, but only for a fraction of an inch. Underneath, it was whole and hard and solid. We looked out from the wall over the beach and mountain. About a quarter of a mile down the shore was an abandoned Romanesque church, and, next to it, a house inhabited by two customs officials. They had a boat, and kept a watch for smugglers of tobacco. These officials, along with Letizia at the tavern and a few fishermen who lived in some small huts at the north end of the beach, were our only permanent neighbors.

The sun had set behind the mountain. The breeze had subsided, and by the shore only a few waves—hardly more than ripples—managed to break into foam. The mountain, from a misty blue, had turned into a purple that seemed to deepen with each moment. A pink haze was gathering westward. And the sea was reflecting all these colors in turn, making them paler, more delicate, as well as keeping its own shade, far out, near the horizon. Now it seemed the wind and the waves had gone to sleep. The tower mirrored itself in the water, trembled, broke up, vanished, resurrected itself, intact, perfect for a moment. Not long ago there had been a shipwreck right in front of the tower—a Polish freighter had gone down. I had seen a picture of it in the paper, a picture of raging white seas with a dark hull, pitifully close to the shore. Yet now there was nothing but stillness.

We went back to the living room, and from there, down a little staircase, to the ground floor of the house where I showed Daphne the kitchen and the bathroom, and unbolted another door that led outside. In the kitchen there was a sink with a drain, but no faucets—two empty pails instead. And there was a raised brick stove with grates and a chimney. A little vault, under the stove, was half full of charcoal.

"Let's go and gather some driftwood," I said, "to start the fire for supper."

"I'll wait for you here, do you mind?"

"Are you tired?"

"A bit of a headache," she said and smiled.

"All right; I'll be back in a few minutes," I said, and went out.

I ran down to the shore. There were plenty of small, dry pieces of wood. I paused to look at the pebbles; they were of all colors, many pink with blue veins, and incredibly smooth; some were perforated, probably by weeds of a prehistoric age. I picked up a shell for Daphne, then returned to the tower with my bundle.

I picked up the two pails by the kitchen sink. One was a pretty ordinary galvanized pail. The other was copper, thin-necked and pot-bellied. I was sure they were the very same ones of long ago, and I remembered with the clearness of childhood how I had once come here alone with my mother, and how I used to go to the spring to fetch water every day, over the scorched track in the hot summer at noon, so the water would still be cold for our lunch. Going, the two pails would clatter as I held them both in one hand and swung them freely in the air, but coming back I walked slowly, taking a rest every once in a while, and setting the pails down on a stone. I knew the stones of the road almost one by one; some of them were sharp and cutting, others flat and smooth, some I would step on and use as a footing to push myself forward and bounce ahead a few feet; any help was a blessing over the scorching track at midday. At noon, with the sun overhead, the brush afforded no shade.

But at the spring there were the giant sycamores and an abundance of vegetation. The spring gave wonderfully fresh, light water. It formed a pool so transparent you hardly knew it was there till you touched it. After filling the pails, I would dip my fingers into it, then my arm, and watch the silver rings becoming a bracelet. Or I would kiss the water; little by little the surface would cover my chin and my cheeks; over my eyes it would rise, over the nape of my neck; I would almost go to sleep in that freshness. I would drink then, and feel its coolness descending into me to slake all my thirst. When I couldn't hold my breath anymore I would laugh and look at the bubbles ascending. It was the only fresh water for miles.

On my way back to the tower, one of the places where I would stop for a rest was a large, flat, pitted rock which lay in the middle of the road. Only the top of it showed; the rest of the stone was so deep-set and massive no one had been able to remove it. It was about halfway between the spring and the tower, and I always took a longer rest there than anywhere else. One day, after leaving the rock, I happened to look back, and I saw a snake winding across the road to the rock and sipping the little water that had spilt off my pails on setting them down and on picking them up again. The next day, I looked for the snake; but only on my way back, after I had set the pails on the rock, spilt a little water as usual, and left, did he appear. I watched him trailing across and drinking; his sly tongue flickered and then he returned into the bush. I realized then that every day he had done that same thing, that somewhere in the rubble at noontime he had been waiting for me to pass and supply him with water. This went on happening regularly; it was the event of the day. I looked forward to it more than to swimming, more than to the rides in the rowboat; it was the only unusual thing, this appointment. I came to think that he depended on me for water. A strange and secret attachment accordingly formed between me and the snake, and I took care to spill a little more water than usual on the stone midway between the spring and the tower.

One day, I asked my mother when we would leave, and I surprised myself wishing she would say, "Oh, not yet," and being quite disappointed when she said, "Next week we must go." The next day, I asked her if we couldn't stay a little longer, at least till the end of the month. Then, too, it was August, the sun blazing hot; the bush was parched and yellow—it looked as if it could catch fire even without the stroke of a match, blaze up, become stone and ashes, and all life disappear for a while.

"Maybe we shall stay a little longer," my mother said.

I remember how glad I was about it, because I knew then that I wouldn't have to miss the appointment I had with my silent companion. I had told my mother about the snake the first day I had seen him, but I hadn't told her that every day he continued to come and sip the water I spilt on the stone. It was almost as if I were ashamed of this strange friendship. As if it were something secret and delicate, I kept it from her. But then one day I told her the whole story and casually added, "I wonder what that old snake will do when we are gone? How will he ever find water?"

"Maybe he'll steal to the spring at night."

"But it gets cold at night, and can snakes come out in the open?" I asked with concern.

"He'll find some way," she said to console me. "Perhaps he'll go in the daytime, when there is no one there."

"But there's always someone around by the spring."

And I could see the snake approaching the spring and getting beaten to death and stoned and crushed, lying there miserably, a stinking remnant of life with flies about him, all the lustrous beauty of his life gone, the colors fading in putrefaction.

I kept hoping something might happen to postpone our departure, but there was no further delay. A telegram arrived from my father saying he would come by car the next day to pick us up. That last noon, I went to the spring as usual, and on my way back, after spilling a large quantity of water on the stone, I walked off and stood watching.

Slowly again the snake trailed across the road to the stone and lapped the water. I stood waiting a long while, and when he had finished and returned into the bush, I went back to the stone and poured another large quantity of water and left. I didn't look back; sooner or later I knew he would come, maybe not immediately like the other times, but again, toward evening, perhaps. But I couldn't stand the thought of his being disappointed the days that would follow. Off and on that afternoon, the thought of the snake would come to my mind. It was unbearably hot. Late that evening we saw, up on the ridge of the mountain, the lights of a car. It was my father's Chevrolet. Early the next morning we would be leaving. I went to bed, but I couldn't sleep. I kept sitting bolt upright in my bed, then forcing myself to lie down again and try all sorts of ways of falling asleep. I must have succeeded at some point, because late in the night I was awakened by thunder so sharp it seemed to crack the roof and the sky above me. A second later, lightning announced the coming of another clap of thunder, and then I heard large drops of rain pelting against the window. I got up and looked out; the thundering had become continuous and the sky was constantly being streaked by angry lightning that lit up the sea with an eerie green. It didn't seem night any longer, but fantastic daytime. I heard a single wave breaking on the rocks with great distinctness. A whiff of wind sent the shutters banging and made the bed sheets flutter. I stretched an arm out the window—the rain made it all wet in an instant, and I licked the water off my arm, fresh and insipid. That storm broke the summer. The next morning the bush seemed brought back to new life; the ground was full of little pools, and the road was so muddy the car could hardly pass. . . .

Yes, the rock was still there, and the spring water just as fresh and abundant. Jubilant it gushed out of the mountain. Filling the pails, I saw Letizia through the open kitchen door of her tavern. There she was, intent on cooking. She turned, holding a frying pan, and the firelight lit her face. She looked like a marvelous savage. I went over. A gold tooth gleamed in her mouth as she saw me. "If it isn't Giovanni!" she said, and with one hand pressed me to her. I felt the hairy upper lip, the mole, the cool straight hair, on my cheek. "So the war didn't kill us," she said. "Look who's here," she said to her husband and to her daughter, whom I remembered as a child and who now was as tall as her mother. We shook hands all around. They expected me to stay for supper, but I told them about my precious guest, my beautiful Daphne waiting there in the tower, and I left with my pails. I came to the rock. Like twelve years before, I stopped, and rested the pails, and some water spilled from them. And then I went on, and looked back, but no snake came, of course. There was only the mountain, dark now. I sensed that something was wrong under the mountain. "Only a little headache," I kept saying to myself. "When I get back she'll be all right." I repeated this in my mind, but I knew I was expressing a hope, not an opinion.

When I returned, she was sitting by the window, looking out to sea. There was still some light in the room—the sea emanated light as the mountain seemed to emanate darkness.

"How do you feel?" I asked her.

"A little better, thanks."

I knew it—I knew that the headache wouldn't have gone.

"I'll light the fire and heat up some soup," I said.

She did not move. "Isn't this silly of me? And I think I have a fever."

"It's the long trip," and I felt her hot forehead; "or perhaps you just need something to eat. You'll be all right after supper, you'll see."

Again I had the queer feeling that I was hoping, not evaluating facts.

When I came back from the kitchen with a bowl of steaming hot soup, she had set the table and lighted the candles. The glasses filled with red wine cast pretty reflections—polychrome shadows, violets fading to white and swaying with the flame of each candle. Everything was quiet all around, except for the occasional sound of a wave glutting small caverns or washing the rocks, and when we spoke it seemed strange. . . .

[1955; 1959; 1969]

A Place in Italy

The place exists. I see it, high over the valley, one of the highest points on the horizon—a jagged relevance, blue in the distance. We are in the car, going away from it, about ten miles off. I catch one last glimpse of it. Then it is gone.

"No, it isn't practical for you," the architect's wife says—as if that would cross it out of my mind forever. But it won't be crossed out. I continue to see it, though it is no longer in view. "It's beautiful, but it's not practical," she says, and the others agree. The architect himself, who is driving, has already had his say. He didn't approve of it, said that it should cost only half as much as it did, and that the extensive repairs it needed would double its price. In short, he made me feel as though I had flunked an exam. But it is as though the place were a new friend whom all my old ones are critical of, but whom, despite their adverse criticism, I continue to like. I like it more and more.

Even the children didn't take to it, the way I thought they would. I expected them to be on my side, to stare at it with marvel in their eyes, and shout, "Oh, let's buy it, Daddy." But they didn't. The little girl was feeling carsick from the many turns in the road going up to it, and the little boy was overwhelmed by the tall grass, the sheer loneliness of it. As for my wife, she said exactly what I might have foreseen she would say: "Someone's gone to the bathroom there." Those were her first words. I laughed to myself—there were no bathrooms, but what she saw plainly wasn't of human origin, and, glancing to one side, I saw a flock of sheep huddled against a wall, afraid of us. "It's the sheep," the architect's wife said to her sternly. My older girl wasn't there. I wonder what she would have thought of it.

Coming up to it, we had left the country road for a narrow, stony, curving track that led up around the steep, wooded hill to the house. Halfway up, we had to stop for a small tree that had fallen across the way. "Let's just leave the car here and walk," the architect said, and so we did. "Smell the broom, the *ginestra,*" I said, elated to get out of the car. It was May, the sun hot, and the heat seemed to express from the flowers all of their scent and disperse it in the warm air. I took great breaths of it and started up the little road, hardly able to walk, because in my eagerness I felt an urge to run. But I contained my enthusiasm, and kept only a short distance ahead of the others.

"Are you sure this is the right road?" my wife said.

"Yes, of course."

I had been there a few weeks before with a real-estate man from Orvieto, a kindly old fellow with a sparse gray mustache, a pipe, a narrow-brimmed soft sage-green hat, and a pair of binoculars—a handy thing for him to have, given the setting of his work. Orvieto is perhaps the most unusual town in Italy after Venice, being built high over the plain on a table mountain, an Italian mesa. The cliffs on all sides make it impregnable, or almost. A town with an aerial feel, it has been pictured as standing on the palm of a hand raised over the valley. A small town—about thirty thousand people—with an immense cathedral, possibly the finest in the country. The other buildings are of gray stone or brown tufa; the sides of the cathedral are striped like a zebra with white and black marble. Its windows are of stained glass or thin, transparent alabaster, and much of the façade is finely carved or laden with mosaics. One has the impression of having come upon an outsized jewel among the common stones. The town has a very large number of palaces and churches for its size, and—so that the people wouldn't go thirsty in case of siege, when the Roman aqueduct that fed it could be easily cut off—Orvieto has a well that is at least as deep as the cliffs around the town are high. Dug into the tufaceous rock, it has two spiral stairways down around the shaft. There is an old saying that if you look up at the sky at twilight from the bottom, you can see the stars before you can see them from the top.

Coming to the south edge of the town, the real-estate man showed me, through the binoculars, two farmhouses in the distance. Without having to go there, I decided they weren't for me. Not unusual enough, too close to a road.

"I'll take you to a farmhouse with a tower, near Castel Viscardo," he said.

On the way, we stopped at an old house he had bought for himself. It was set on a rocky mound, once an Etruscan burial ground. The outlines of some of the tombs, opened and filled in again, were still visible in the tufa. He said he was an amateur sculptor, and planned to carve the rocks, leaving them in place. I wondered if their original form could be improved upon. From his house we went to "mine." Rain was threatening. The sky was leaden and silver. It was near sunset. There was a strange light—eerie, ecliptic. And though the sky was overcast, the clouds were high, the visibility quite good. We went up the little road through the wood. The way was clear then; the tree hadn't fallen. Beyond the wood we came to a grove of olive trees that hadn't been pruned for a long time and had a wild, untended look, then to a row of mulberry and cherry trees leading up to the house. This was even better than his, I thought—grander, higher, more isolated. On the right was the old tower, of stone and with a roof. It had a beautiful arched doorway, framed, like the windows, by slabs of a darker, gray-blue stone. The door was locked and he didn't have the key. But, going round the back, I found that a ground-floor window gave when I pushed it, and we both clambered through. The room, empty of all furniture, had a large stone fireplace and an inviting stairway up. This branched—one branch led to the house and its two bedrooms, the other to the second then to the third, or top, floor of the tower. The room on the top floor was under the rafters of the roof. One of these was supported by a pole. The room had no windows, only narrow openings at each corner, and, set into the walls, many round, widemouthed, empty earthen vases—nests for pigeons. There were no pigeons anymore. The place had been uninhabited for years.

On the ground floor of the house were two stables, one with a long and handsome terra-cotta manger. At a right angle to them were more stables and barns and a porch. There, under the porch roof, I saw for a moment a table, set, with family and friends around it, wine on the table, a white tablecloth . . . a scene out of the past, or in the future? Desperately I wished that it might come to be. Dug into the rock of the steep slope some fifty feet back of the house was the wine cellar. You had the feeling that on a very clear day you could see for a hundred miles in all directions—a vast, almost limitless view of dawn and sunset. Below, to the east, a river valley; to the west, ridges, ranges, woods. And here and there in the wide landscape a distant village, a castle, an isolated farmhouse. Orvieto, too, lay below, eight miles away. Nearer, the roofs of the old village of Castel Viscardo. Nothing ugly in sight. The house's steep hill, or mound, was really the highest point of a grassy ridge. The yard extended southward into a broad sweep of grass combed by the wind. It was Italy as it might have looked a hundred years ago, pastoral, bucolic. Yes, I was enthusiastic about the place. That the roofs and some of the walls, doors, and windows needed extensive repairs, that there was no running water or bathrooms, that the electric wiring would all have to be redone meant little to me.

There was a spring nearby. I would build an aqueduct. I had always wanted to build one. I would get a mason and a carpenter to come and help me with the repairs, perhaps give work to someone unemployed. I would get to know the villagers this way. For a moment nothing daunted me. "Yes, I would like to buy it," I said. "I like it. I like it very much."

"It certainly is an original place," he said.

"Yes. My family had a country house near Siena which, unfortunately, we sold three years ago, after my parents died. It was a foolish thing to do, and I constantly regret it. This place would make up for it in part. It has some of its good qualities and none of its defects. Oh, I wouldn't live here all the time. Maybe a few months a year. I live in America, but I am free—I paint. Do you think it might be broken into while I was away?"

He tilted his head, not in a nod or a denial but as if to say that it could happen. "The worst are the hunters," he said. "You'd have to get someone to keep an eye on it. One of these shepherds maybe. And put a fence around it."

No, not a fence, I thought. It would interrupt the sweep of the landscape. But a neighbor to look after it, yes.

"Well, I'd certainly like to buy it, but first I'll have to show it to my wife," I said. And I left in buoyant spirits.

All the way to Rome, I felt euphoric, the way one feels when one has discovered something after a long search. Why, I thought, the place was so beautiful one would want to travel miles to see it, come and watch the sunset from it, have a picnic at the foot of the old tower under the cherry and olive trees. I could see myself returning with the car, the children cheering, and, all at the same time, the cherries ripe, friends sitting at the dinner table, the stables made into comfortable rooms, the fireplace in the tower lit, paintings and books around me, and music, the top room and every other room furnished, the garden blossoming. Yet no major changes made in the structure of the place, nothing demolished or torn down, everything left standing.

But it wasn't to be. Impractical. "I want to buy it," I tell my wife again and again, and she replies, "All right, go ahead, but you'll never get me there."

And I haven't the heart to do it alone. What is property to me anyway? Can you really own a piece of land, a house? Aren't we all sojourners, tenants in this world? And yet the place attracts me. I am almost on the point of going to Orvieto with my checkbook. The world is mine. I am in the driver's seat. But only for a moment. The words ring in my ear: "You'll never get me there." And I withdraw to my room and slump on the bed and pull the bedspread over my head and lie as a mummy until, short of air, I am forced to uncover my nose.

We have some money in the bank—the sale of the old family house. Inflation bites into it. The lira dips. We should invest it somehow. We've seen dozens of houses and apartments, and inquired about a hundred more. In this year in which I am in Italy, that's all I seem to do. But in Rome, where we are staying, what's for sale is either too expensive or too small, and none of the places we've seen outside of Rome can compare with that one near Orvieto. Oh, yes, there was a place on the Argentario I took my wife to. It had a full view of the sea, of the island of Giglio, of Montecristo, even of Corsica on the clearest days, but she said it was too small, and it wasn't a whole house, just a half house. It had its own garden, though, lemon trees, a portico. There was an old mill, too, between Pisa and Lucca, that we went to see. But that was too large, needed too much work, the view wasn't to her liking. She has seen several one- or two-room apartments in Rome. These you could rent, she says. But we could never live in one—not the five of us, I say. And so the weeks pass and the months, and our stay in Italy is almost at an end. But I won't give up.

On weekends I sally forth into the country, sometimes alone, sometimes with wife and children. Besides the places mentioned, I have been to Venice, Florence, Narni, Todi, Spoleto, the Circeo, the mountains of Tolfa, Subiaco, the Sabine Mountains, Viterbo, Arezzo, Bagnaia, Lake Trasimeno, San Gimignano, Bolsena. I have seen places I would never have seen otherwise, and met some unusual people in the process. In the Sabine Mountains, a parish priest, and real-estate agent in his spare time, showed us, among other things, what he described as a "terrific" buy—a onetime convent that was now an abandoned ruin. The cracks in the walls were indeed terrific; there were floors missing; through the roof not only would it rain in but you would see the stars. Might as well try to restore the Colosseum. In Subiaco, I saw a tiny house, unreachable by car, a tremendous walk from the main street. Perhaps when I was young. . . . Near Lake Trasimeno, I was shown an old farmhouse, fully restored, well worth its price. But every tile, door, window, step spoke out the owner's taste—it would remain his even after I had finished paying for it. Yet by going to see it I came across the pretty town of Panicale. On its outskirts there is the little Church of St. Sebastian. It was closed, but a boy came to unlock the door for me, and there, at one end, taking up the whole wall, was Perugino's fresco *The Martyrdom of St. Sebastian*—the calm faces of the archers and of the saint, the faded gentle colors, the serene Umbrian countryside. In Spoleto, a real-estate lady who quoted Leopardi and Horace showed me around. Near the Lake of Bolsena, a count drove me down an incredibly steep road in the woods to a little farmhouse he wanted to sell. The farmer and his wife were there. The man was ill, and told us his sad story. Toward the end of our visit, the wife went to get a bottle of wine from their cave cellar. She uncorked it. It fizzed almost like champagne, and like champagne it was light and very dry—and cold, having been "cool'd a long age in the deep-delvèd earth." In Bagnaia, it was market day, and a comedy atmosphere pervaded the little town. In the main square, I felt as if I were on a stage, an actor among actors, all perfectly unaware.

And still no house.

We have only ten days before we have to board a plane for Boston. It seems too late to try to buy anything now. A friend says, "It's mad for you to leave your money in the bank."

Money in the bank. In my youth, we were always short of money—lots of land, a big house, but very little cash. Therefore, keeping money in the bank doesn't seem mad to me. Not mad to have ready access to it, especially since I have no job, no salary, but only do free-lance work. But another consideration makes me go on one last errand for a house: I don't want to leave Italy without owning something in it, a place to repair to in case hotels and the houses of friends and relatives should suddenly all seem inhospitable to me, a place where I can leave a few of my things—some of my books, a desk, a chair, a bed, pots and pans and dishes, something familiar to return to. And so I rent a car and venture out again, in my pocket an address from a classified ad in the *Messaggero*. It's one that I saw weeks ago but ignored because the price seemed ridiculously low: twenty-three hundred dollars. A barn, I thought, or storeroom—no place that I could live in. But on the telephone I asked if it might be suitable as a studio, and the man said yes, it was, and he gave me good directions and the name of the caretaker. "His real name," he said, "is Anselmo Remi, but you'd better ask for Cimitella or you won't find him. Everyone knows him as Cimitella."

I follow the Autostrada del Sole up the Tiber Valley toward Orte. Here the Tiber isn't tawny, as in Rome, but green-blue. I know the valley well. Up to the right in the fields, below a hamlet, I see what from the road seems a speck but is a little farmhouse that an English writer friend of mine bought long ago. I am sure he is there typing, while his Italian wife is quietly painting in the room below. I won't go to see them this trip. I have no time. I go on up the river ten more miles, take a left, follow a stream along its gorge, then gradually drive up a craggy hillside. It's good to leave the expressway and be here on this curving, narrow road. I feel at home amid the olives and the vines. Up high, on top of a hill, across the stream, is a cluster of stone houses the color of the rocks below. Everything blends delightfully. It is the hand of time that makes it so. My village is the next one, on this side of the stream, and higher than that one. I come to the first houses and then to a central little square.

"Where can I find Cimitella?" I ask.

"Ah, Cimitella? Eh, you go up there, up to the very top, beyond the arch."

On up I drive. Just before the arch the road bends so sharply that my car, though it is a small Fiat, gets by only after some maneuvering. On my right I skirt a wall below which is a sheer drop, and I come to another square and a church and a castle. Here I leave the car and ask for Cimitella again. Somebody smiles and directs me higher still. I go up a lane in a zigzag. A bunch of small children peek and hide behind a corner and laugh uproariously. A dog barks playfully. I come to Cimitella's house. Everything is little here, except the castle and the church. Cimitella's wife—a pleasant, smiling, middle-aged woman—appears at the doorway, and calls her husband for me. He's talking to some neighbors in a lane. Spare, with an expressive, friendly face and bright eyes, he comes over, and down we go to see the "studio." It turns out that it's on the first little square I stopped at on arriving. The studio is on the second floor of a small house that juts out into the square. It has a medieval aspect. It's made of stone. It has an outside staircase, and it is buttressed by two chimneys. It must be seven or eight hundred years old. Yet it's not dilapidated. Simply worn. The stone steps are hollowed out by use through the centuries. On top of the staircase is a little terrace. Cimitella unlocks the door. There is a room with a beautiful ancient fireplace, and another little room. It has running water and a light. From two of the windows you can see the countryside; another window looks onto the square. Yes, it's much better than I expected. And the floor below, too, is for sale, for less than the second—for about a thousand dollars—so that by buying both I can have a little house.

I return to Rome quite enthusiastic about my find. But my wife won't go to see it. I am determined to buy it, though. And so, a few days before our departure, I sign a contract. Then I make one last visit to it, alone, for no one will come with me. I meet Cimitella again, and a mason. He is going to restore it for me—mend the floor and roof, put in a bathroom, replaster the inside walls. And I'll have our things moved in. Someday, I hope, my children will laugh with the children of the village, and my wife will sleep there with me. Nearby is Monte Cimino, and a lake, and the old town of Viterbo, and the villages on the tops of hills. Cimitella points them out: "Orte, Attigliano, Chia, Giove," he says. One of them is actually called Giove—Jupiter—and it is as if he were pointing at the planets and the stars, naming them one by one.

[1976]

Night in the Piazza

It was past midnight, and in the Piazza della Repubblica—the little square outside his studio—people were still engaged in endless *conversazione.* Other conversations were going on in another small piazza, outside his bedroom window. He shifted from one room to the other, depending on which of the two squares was momentarily less noisy. But there was really very little difference. And again he asked himself what had possessed him to buy a place in such a location. Why, this was the very hub of the village. His only excuse was that he had first seen the apartment in the afternoon, when everyone, including the children, were taking their siesta. Such a quiet, peaceful place it had seemed. He ought to have known that the silence couldn't last, that it would in fact set the stage for this wakefulness, this . . . this *baccano. Baccano, chiasso, rumore, caciara, cagnara*—what an abundance of words there were in Italian for noise! It seemed as significant as the Eskimos having an extraordinary number of words for snow, because it was such a constant for them.

Under the lights, children were scurrying about kicking a ball, their shrill voices octaves above the bellowing bass of the men, especially the older men, who to be heard relied on volume. Not to be outdone, the women chattered on steps and chairs and loggias, providing a cicada-like sound.

No, he had never imagined it could be this noisy. It was full summer, of course—July—very hot, and windless. Not a breath of air, the only breath human. No wonder they were all *al fresco,* to escape the rooms behind the thick old stone walls of their homes, which all day long had absorbed the blazing sun. The dog days, the *solleone.* This was the hottest summer on record. At a bus stop he had heard a man say that never, never had such and such a tree wilted before—not in his memory. And there were fires, all the way from Calabria to Tuscany, also in Sardinia—forest fires and brush fires, and fields of wheat going up in flames, set or not set a subject of heated debate here and in the newspapers. Arguments about spontaneous combustion. Endless, endless arguments on this and other topics that he didn't want to overhear, much less follow (but he had no choice).

And this was supposed to be his studio. No chance of study here, or sleep. All he could do was wait. The noise would subside after two o'clock, as it had last night, and the night before, and every night since he had come two weeks ago. If it would only rain. But none was forecast in the weather reports he consulted, oh so faithfully, each day in the newspaper. No rain, no thunder, no windstorms to clear this crowd from the piazzas.

Though he was born and had grown up in Italy, he was considered a foreigner here. He knew he was referred to as the *Americano.* He came from Tuscany, north of here, where people—he hadn't the slightest doubt at this moment—were far more civilized, infinitely more refined. Much of the conversation he caught was about eating. Food, food, food. They stuffed themselves, and with hatred in his eyes he peered through the windows at a huge old man, who was holding forth, vociferating like a king toad, about the merits of roast boar. Despicable people.

A foreigner, a stranger. The *Americano.* Well, he certainly didn't want to be anything else at this point. They stared at him every time he descended the old, footworn flight of stone stairs outside his front door. He had bought the apartment on the spur of the moment, to have a foothold in Italy, the year after his family house in Tuscany had been sold—bought this little place after seeing it advertised in the *Messaggero.* It was cheap and it was ancient and it had a fine stone fireplace, and, that one afternoon, it was quiet. He had it restored while in America, where he taught Italian in a college. Almost every year, as soon as classes were over, he had flown to Italy and spent a few weeks here. The first year it had been May, and too cold for people to sit outside at night. All he heard then was the nightingales singing in the valley, an owl hooting on a chimney top, and the wind carrying the sound of the hour from a bell that tolled it on a tower. But each year he had come a little later, and this year in full summer.

Though he rarely listened to radio or television, now he wished he had one of the two to drown out the noise. All he had to pass the time with was books, which required a quiet background. At the same time he resented the fact that, with so much conversation, none of it was directed at him. That was perhaps what made it so intolerable. He longed to go back to America, to the village he lived in, where people often greeted him on the street. Here, hardly a word.

Ah, but wait. Soon, day after tomorrow, a friend, Rebecca, was coming for an overnight visit, and he'd have his own conversation. *Una conversazione intima.* He might even be able to forget the crowd outside. Let them talk, let them. What did he care when he had her to talk to, her in his arms?

She was a journalist, though much more of a teacher of journalism than a journalist. He had met her at the university where she taught, in Chicago, the year he had gone there to teach for a couple of months, a term, or quarter as they called it. She was enthusiastic about Italy and had been there three or four times. Sometimes he suspected that all she wanted from him was some practice in speaking Italian. Even so their relation had gone beyond that. She was very self-possessed and took compliments as her due. "Yes, I have good legs," she said when he observed how sleek they were. Sleek she was, nimble, self-assured, energetic, and authoritative—he was fairly sure—in the classroom. Quite unlike him. Opposites, it is well known, are attracted, though perhaps not very deeply. A superficial relation, then. Her bedroom was cold; she kept the windows open, and her mattress was hard, and the bed not very wide.

They didn't have to quarrel to make leaving easier. They remained friends and wrote to each other from time to time—cards. In one of them she said she'd be in Italy in July. And since he was going to be in Italy too, he invited her to his studio. He had called her long-distance from a public phone, and now he was waiting for her.

It wasn't an easy place to get to. A hill-top village some sixty miles from Rome, ten miles from any railroad station. Few buses. But she was dauntless, enterprising, young-looking for her age—late thirties, maybe even early forties; she hadn't told him and he hadn't asked—and he had no doubt she'd find her way to him without too much trouble.

He waited. The bus arrived and she wasn't on it. The next bus, then; but that didn't come the whole way—it stopped at a junction two miles from here. Should he go and meet her there? No, perhaps she would take a taxi. She had plenty of money—tenure, a rich father, no dependents. (She had got married once, long ago, briefly.) Yes, she could easily afford a taxi. He didn't walk to meet her. He'd probably miss her if he did. He stayed put, and once in a while looked out the window. He had made supper, which he kept warm in the oven, and set the table. A bottle of wine cast red reflections on the white table cloth. The silver shot them back. It was late. Past eight o'clock. She was overdue. Must have missed the last bus. He looked out the window more and more often, almost uninterruptedly now, like someone in love.

And at last there she was, getting out of a car, not a taxi, a car driven by a brawny young man who very solicitously took her luggage out of the trunk and shook hands with her, clasping her right hand with both of his, and seeming not to want to let go of it. Meanwhile he went down the steps of his outside-staircase to meet her, though hesitant to interrupt that goodbye. Seeing him, the young man let her go, reluctantly. She had hitchhiked. Such a nice fellow, a real *cavaliere,* she said.

He carried her luggage up, everyone in the square staring at them, as if hardly able to believe that he, always so alone, should have a guest, and such a guest. Elegant, in a light green silken dress, a thin gold belt, and with expensive luggage never seen in this village. Her hair shook in unison, coil-like. And he so shabby. The city air—Rome, Florence, London, Paris—still clinging to her. He was glad to shut the door behind them.

She thought the apartment was cute, cozy. "Five-hundred years old," he said, and showed her the fireplace. "If it weren't quite so hot I would have lit it."

They had dinner. At her house, in Chicago, she always served the best French wines. Here he had the local red. Hardly a match, but drinkable. She still had the habit of answering in Italian anything he said in English, as though her Italian were better than his English, which was not the case. "I have to practice," she said, "and you correct me. *Devo esercitare me.*"

"*Devo esercitarmi,*" he corrected her.

"*Devo esercitarmi?*" she said, not without a little resentment, as if the language and not herself were at fault.

"*Sì,*" he said, and felt as if he were back in his classroom, doing Italian One.

Conversation with her in Italian was decidedly difficult. He had almost forgotten how difficult. Never mind. Soon dinner would be over and they would shift to the bedroom, where he had brought his twin beds together. Love needed no language, or made its own—kisses, more eloquent than words.

She had brought her typewriter along, an electric, battery-operated. "Oh, I've so much to write about," she said. "About this village, too, but not tonight—"

"But you've hardly seen it yet."

"Well, I get the feel of a place right away. The feel—that's what's important, and I feel I know it already. But not tonight. Tonight I want to sleep. Oh, I'm so sleepy," she said, with a yawn.

"Love and sleep," he said, as he accompanied her to the bedroom.

"No, just sleep."

"Sleep," he said wistfully. "Except it isn't easy here. They go on talking late into the night. I should have warned you. And if you shut the windows it gets stiflingly hot. Not that it would do much against the noise. Those flimsy shutters."

"Oh, I could sleep anywhere tonight, anywhere. A power drill wouldn't keep me awake."

"Good. But you wait, don't be too sure. The main force comes out later."

"Won't bother me, not tonight," she said. She turned over, and by her deep, slow breathing he knew she was asleep.

As for him, he couldn't possibly go to sleep this early—eleven o'clock. He had got up at eleven in the morning, to make up for the sleep he had missed the night before. He went back into the living room and looked out the window. The children—the first to leave the dinner tables—were at their most active, some even running up and down his staircase. Two benches outside the pensioners' association on the square were vacant. But when he looked again a while later, four or five elders were sitting on them. Soon the talking was as loud as ever. As if she were a baby, he went to the bedroom to take a look at her. She slept on. Such a serene, restful look on her face. A smile seemed to linger on her lips—as if she had fallen asleep smiling, bless her. Back in the living room, he sat in an armchair and opened a book, but snatches of the conversation outside distracted him, and he found himself listening, despite himself. He overheard the words "*Americana*" and "*Americano.*" Someone was obviously talking about her and him. He put down the book and went closer to the window. But the medley of voices was too confused for him to make out any other words. About an hour later, some children rushed up his staircase and pushed violently against his door, making it shake, before running down the steps.

"What was that?" she said from the bedroom.

"Oh, just some of these kids playing."

"Oh," she said sleepily. He resumed reading, then she appeared, rubbing her eyelids. "Hm, there *is* a lot of noise. I see what you mean."

"Those scamps, they pushed against the door."

"They are not the worst. Who's talking in that loud voice?"

"Stentor, I call him. One of the village elders. He's an enormous fellow." He led her to the window. "See him? He's talking to the little fellow right next to him, but he wants everyone to overhear. And it's like this every night."

"How long do they go on?"

"Till two o'clock, sometimes even later." A couple of men might stay on and keep talking till three, quite oblivious of all the open windows around them. "They just go on talking as if it were their perfect right. It's expected. They are out *al fresco.* In the fresh air. It's the custom."

"And no one complains?"

"Not in public. At least I've not heard anyone. Italians love noise—bells, motorcycles, loudspeakers, bands, fireworks, but more than anything else *conversazione, discussione.* Even in the old days Italians were called *populus clamorosus,* the clamorous people."

It was nearly one o'clock. The spectacle would last another hour—at least. "Pretend you are at the theater," he told her.

"Another hour? Well, I don't have to put up with it."

"How do you mean?"

"I'm going to tell them I want to sleep, that they are keeping me awake and to please shut up," she said, very matter-of-factly.

"Oh you can't do that. This is about the only entertainment they have here. There're no movies, no theater, no opera—nothing. There's hardly a café. This is the only thing they have to look forward to these hot days—their nightly *conversazione.*"

"But I can't sleep with this going on, and I have to sleep, or I won't be able to connect tomorrow."

"Oh, you'll connect. Let's just drink and stay up another hour or two. Wine will help you sleep. Or love."

"No, I'll get a headache if I drink anymore. And I don't feel like love."

"Well take some aspirin, or a sleeping pill, or maybe plug your ears."

"I certainly will not—I hate those things. I'll tell them to stop it."

"Oh please don't. You *can't.* I won't let you."

"What do you mean? You are talking to an American girl."

"They're pitiful, don't you see?"

"Misplaced pity—I can't think of a better example."

"Let them have their few hours' entertainment. Leave them be."

"It's one. There it goes—past one."

"Look—you are just a visitor. I have to stay here. It's difficult enough for me as it is. They'll turn against me. They'll hate me. And it won't be any use anyway. They won't take any notice of you."

"Oh, won't they!"

"No, so you can save yourself the trouble and be patient awhile."

"No, simply no. It's not right."

"I'll prevent you. I'll muffle your words."

"You'll do nothing of the sort."

Just as she was, in her white nightgown, she opened the door to the balcony at the top of the outside staircase and stood looking at them in silence. He watched from the window. Soon faces began turning toward her.

"Pe favor... silenzio... no possible dormir qui," she said in her appalling Italian and in a voice that carried in an extraordinary way over everyone else's.

He left the window and looked at her from the living room. In her nightgown, alone on the balcony, with her arms raised, she looked like a saint—a preacher-saint—addressing a crowd. Joan of Arc.

"Pe favor... silenzio... ohè silenzio pe favor," she repeated, and went on to tell them how early she had got up in the morning and what a long way she had come, and she had to *lavorare domani.*

People grumbled. Some voices could still be heard. But she had succeeded in damping things. It might have rained. Yes, it was as if it had begun raining on that hot, dry, clear, starry night. Soon there was a hush. But heavy, oppressive, dangerous. She returned inside and closed the door. There were a few rumbles, a few exchanges, but it was nothing like before. It was as if the party had been broken and couldn't be put together again.

"You see." she said.

Some people began leaving.

"Yes, I see."

"Now we can sleep."

"I hope they don't kill me tomorrow."

"They didn't seem to mind. They were probably tired, too. Time someone told them to go to bed. Now there's the other square. I'm going to tell them, too, from the bedroom window."

"Oh please, haven't you done enough?"

"No." She leaned out the window. *Pe favor io dormire,"* she said to these others, even though they had already quieted down considerably, obviously aware of what had occurred in Piazza della Repubblica, just around the corner.

There was a laugh. A young man was laughing at her. But she stared him down.

She left the window. It was over. He took a big breath, a long sigh.

"It's quiet on both fronts," she said.

"I don't know which I'd rather have, this kind of quiet or that other noise."

"This quiet," she said.

They went into the bedroom.

"I don't know how I'm going to face them tomorrow," he said, "I'm self-conscious enough as it is."

They heard the distant clock strike 1:30. An owl hooted, accenting the silence. "It might be a dove instead of an owl," he said, "it's so peaceful."

He drew nearer her on the bed. "Listen," she said.

A voice, even softer than the owl's and more discreet than the bell's toll, though far less distant, directly under the livingroom window, intoned her name, "Rebecca, Rebecca, Rebè . . ." A mandolin struck a cord, accompanying the voice. Then a deep low chorus, and the tenor rising with the mandolin:

> Rebecca, Rebecca, Rebè
> *Quante notti aggio perso per te* (How much sleep I've lost for you.)

"How do they know your name?" he whispered.

"Sh . . . The guy who gave me a ride."

On and on the song went, and when it was over, "Oh, the darlings," she said, "this has never happened to me before. I've always wanted a serenade—all my life. I love them I love them I love them. This is the real Italy I've been waiting for. Do you realize what this means to me? Do you have a hanky, a flower? No? Oh!"

She left the bed, went to the window, opened her arms and threw them kisses. They cheered her, they applauded. "Rebecca!" they called.

With the speed of a model she doffed her nightgown and donned a dress.

"I thought you were sleepy," he said.

Down the steps she went, into the crowd, among hugs, among kisses.

From the window he watched her, already a part of the crowd, as involved in conversation as any of the others. And there was that brawny young man who had given her a ride, with an arm around her waist. About the only one who wasn't taking part in the revelry was himself. He turned away from the window.

He didn't know when she got back—he was sleeping. When he woke up, she was typing. "When did you get back?" he asked her.

"Don't interrupt me," she said. "I got quite a story."

She finished it just in time to catch the Rome bus, which stopped right by the square. He accompanied her downstairs, carrying her luggage. A crowd milled around her and the bus. She was cheerfully shaking hands. A political candidate couldn't have done better.

Almost from the moment she left, someone on the streets or the square would stop him to ask, very friendly, "And Rebecca, when is she coming back?"

"Soon, I hope."

"Oh, she was a phenomenon, that one. No one will ever put *her* down. That't the kind of woman I like. Proud. A rocket. Dynamite. A *bersagliera*."

He laughed and thought of the *bersaglieri*—the Italian soldiers with a bunch of cock feathers in their hats who are noted for marching at the sound of a trumpet, on the double.

[1987]

Fisherman's Terrace

. . . I remember a terrace on a steep and rocky slope overlooking the sea. I came to it by chance one day early in October two years ago, after I had driven with my wife from Rome to Porto Santo Stefano, a small seaport on the north side of the Monte Argentario, the promontory on the coast of Tuscany, between Leghorn and Rome. The road that connects the mainland to this little town continues beyond it for a few miles, climbing steeply up the mountain but keeping always in sight of the sea. It is a new road, and they call it "*strada panoramica,*" scenic route. Someday it will follow the sea along to Porto Ercole, a small harbor on the south side of the mountain, and so complete the ring around the promontory, but for now, owing to lack of funds, it ends abruptly high above the shore, several miles short of its goal. I drove to the end of it the morning after we arrived in Porto Santo Stefano. My wife, who was convalescing, had stayed behind in the hotel.

There were no houses in sight, and, except for a field just below the road, the slope of the mountain all the way down to the sea, about a mile away, looked wild and untouched. I started to walk down. It was one of those clear October days on which one can't feel sad that the summer has ended—the mountain shone above me, and the sea below me; the grass I brushed through also shone, being light and dry, having lost all of its greenness, and being smooth and moved by the wind. On the field, ripe little tomatoes, too small for the farmer to bother with, shone here and there. I picked one and sucked its juice, and it was so tasty I picked another two. Farther down were some rows of vines. Their leaves were turning crimson. Some were crisp and brittle round the edges, others were still soft and green. The grapes had all been gathered, except at one corner of the vineyard, where I was surprised to find a vine from which several large, conspicuous bunches still hung. Though of a white variety, the grapes were so ripe that they looked almost red, and matched some of the colors of the leaves about them. I thought that perhaps they had been left on the plant to make some special wine, and I refrained from picking any.

The slope got steep and wild. I had to open a way with my arms through thick bushes of mountain laurel, or hunch up and walk backward through the brambles. Soon the bushes were so tall and thick I was quite hidden, and couldn't see the sun or the mountain or the sea. The ground was carpeted by moss, and I sat down. Sitting under that roof of foliage, in the silence of that wide green chamber, I felt as though I had disappeared, or sunk into oblivion, and that to find myself again I had to rise and go on. Almost regretfully, I did so. Suddenly a thin blacksnake glistened like a streak of oil on the ground in front of me and slid up the incline, a wonder of locomotion. Instantly, I became more alert; I picked up a stick and, slashing it about in front of me to scare away any more snakes that might lie on my path, I went on through the bushes, impatient to come to the end of them. Finding that the slope tended to be clearer on my left, I went that way along a horizontal shelf until I reached a creek. The water trickled down, almost hidden in the furrow it had created. It made a straight and smooth, if steep, path to the sea. I followed this, jumping down small, muddy waterfalls until I came to one that was too high to jump, and here, as I made a little detour to the right around the creek, I found myself among orange trees upon a terrace. It was a narrow shelf of level ground cleared of all bushes and carved into the slope. A stone wall supported it from below. Between the trees, some rocks too large to be removed rose from the ground like keels and prows. Besides the oranges, there were lemons, pomegranates set against the slope, a palm, a few olive trees, prickly pears, and, scattered here and there among the weeds, some hardy garden flowers—chrysanthemums in bloom, and amaranths. The oranges were still green, but the lemons were ripe, and the pomegranates were so ripe that some had fallen on the ground, and those that were still on their branches showed deep cracks. One was split open and had shed some of its seeds; a few of these lay—brown instead of crimson—straight below it. I picked a pomegranate, broke it, and bit into a cell of succulent and pulpy seeds. I wondered whose this terrace could be. And why the unpicked fruit? Was it forsaken? Were pomegranates worthless on the market? But what about the lemons? They were ripe. And those flowers—did they grow from seed, year after year?

With these questions in my mind, I followed a barely traceable zigzag path to the sea, which was only about a hundred feet down from the terrace. The creek formed a sandy inlet in the rocky shore. Its trickle of water was enough to keep the terrace fresh, its sand enough for a rowboat to land on safely, and I thought that a fisherman or a sailor with an inward longing for land had eyed the creek and the narrow shelf beside it, and built the terrace and planted fruit trees there. Certainly it was much more accessible from the sea than overland. Soon, I thought, perhaps in a few days, he will row over from Porto Santo Stefano in a little boat, land at the inlet, and climb up to his terrace with a basket. I could almost see him—an old man wearing a beret and blue jeans, tired of being tossed around by waves and stormy weather.

I returned to the terrace, picked another pomegranate, put it in my pocket, and then began to climb back up the slope along the creek. During rainstorms, it must become a wild and roaring torrent, but now it came down drop by drop and I found no pool deep enough to drink clear water from. The water became muddy at the slightest touch. When I saw the vineyard—way to my left—I was too thirsty to consider the special wine the farmer might have had in mind for the grapes left on the single vine, and I went over to them. I picked the rosiest-looking and ate them not with my fingers but thirstily, by holding the bunch against my mouth and biting into it as though it were an apple. It was sweet almost to excess, having had more than the usual time in which to ripen, and having drawn from earth and sun and air all the flavor they could give. I threw the bare bunch of stems into the air and picked another cluster. Not as thirsty now, I walked up the incline holding it in my hand and plucking the grapes slowly, one by one. I hadn't gone far when I saw an old man with a hoe coming toward me. He wore a shirt whose color, bleached by the sun, had faded to a light and rosy hue—similar to that of the grapes that I was eating. His trousers were the color of dry earth. He certainly looked as if he belonged here, and I felt timid with my stolen grapes.

He walked slowly, looking at the ground, and I thought I had better say something before he did. "I picked this bunch of grapes down there," I said, pointing at the corner of the vineyard. "There's a vine that still has all its grapes."

He nodded. "That's all right," he said, and from the way he spoke—with a kind smile—I knew that he wouldn't have said anything about the bunch of grapes.

"Why wasn't that vine picked?" I asked him.

He brought the hoe down from his shoulder to the ground and rested on it. "We always leave one vine unpicked," he said. "For the stranger. It is an ancient custom."

"Oh," I said.

"Yes, it's supposed to bring us luck for the next season."

"Well, I hope this brings you luck—here I am, a stranger," I said, raising the grapes as though they were already wine and I were toasting.

"Yes," he said, and he repeated, almost apologetically, "It is an ancient custom."

"I went all the way down to the sea," I said. "Whose is that terrace near the mouth of the creek with oranges, lemons, and pomegranates—all unpicked?"

"Oh, you've been down there," he said. "A fisherman from Porto Santo Stefano planted those trees when there was no road up here and all this slope was wild. He didn't buy the land, though. Until this road was built, nobody cared. But the value of land now has risen, and the owner here told him that it wasn't his."

"Not his?" I said. "And no one picks the fruit?"

"No," he replied. "It's too far down the slope for a few trees. *He* used to go there by boat, of course. It was all right for him."

I left the farmer and went up the slope, wishing I could buy the terrace and give it to the fisherman. I thought of him, of his carefully choosing the land near the mouth of the creek, of his clearing the bushes away and digging up all the rocks that weren't too deep-set and massive to be removed, of his building the supporting wall and planting the trees and the flowers, and then, when the trees had begun bearing fruit, being told to go. I pictured the man who had bought the land—probably some big-paunched contractor from Rome or Grosseto, who had got it from the government for very little. I had an idea it would be sold in lots as Porto Santo Stefano expanded and that coast became more and more fashionable. Already there were new little villas a mile or two from the town, and others were rising just around the corner from here. One could be sure that in a few years this uninhabited slope would have its own gleaming white little houses, and a serpentine road running all the way down to the sea. The fisherman, I was thinking, should have gone farther, around the next point, where perhaps he could have come to the end of his years undisturbed. Or had all this coast become so valuable that there was no ledge from which he wouldn't be ousted? Perhaps it was so, and he should have stuck to fishing and the sea, which belonged to no man and every man, and off which only stormy weather could sweep him.

With these thoughts in mind, I drove back to Porto Santo Stefano. Once or twice, as I thought of the terrace, I wished I could buy it for myself, for it corresponded in every detail with what I desired—oranges were my favorite trees; it was on the sea and was backed by a high mountain whose name (Argentario) suggested to me rocks streaked with silver; since it looked west, there would be a view of the sun setting over the Island of Giglio or the sea, depending on the time of the year; it was on a promontory (an island with an avenue of escape, my favorite land formation), and it was in Tuscany, almost equidistant from Siena and Rome; it had a creek, a stone wall, an inlet; there were olive trees. . . .

"Even if I could buy it, though," I said to myself, "I would feel like a trespasser, like a usurper—I would never be able to keep it."

That evening, strolling with my wife along the waterfront of one of the two crescent-shaped harbors of the little town, I saw many fishermen, some sitting on benches, others talking to one another and standing in little circles opposite a fleet of moored fishing boats and in between mounds of brown nets. I approached one who was alone, a dark and sinewy middle-aged man wearing a blue sweater and a beret tilted to cover most of his forehead. "Excuse me," I said to him. "A few miles around the coast, in the direction of Porto Ercole, I came to a little terrace on the sea with fruit trees on it. I wonder if you know who built it. I hear it was a fisherman from here."

"That one," he said, pointing to a man who was sitting alone two benches over—a big, brawny man with hoary hair, wide lips, and a sullen look.

We went over to him. "That fisherman over there," I said, "told me that you built the terrace on the sea I saw this morning down from where the new road ends."

His face, which at first had seemed opaque to me, lightened in all its features. "Have you been up there?" he asked, speaking as one would who was used to approaching it from below.

"Yes," I said. "It's a fine terrace, and those are beautiful trees that you planted. But is it true that they won't let you pick them?"

"That land doesn't belong to me," he said.

"So I've heard," I said. "I think it's an injustice."

"Why?" he said. "It isn't my property. I went there thinking no one would ever care. I recognize I made a mistake."

"They should let you pick the fruit you planted."

He shrugged his shoulders.

"That terrace belongs to you more than to anybody else."

He shook his head and looked out toward the sea, his face impassive. Then he turned to me. "When you work land that isn't yours," he said, "that's what you have to expect." He continued looking at me, as though to see if I could reply.

I couldn't. I could only nod. In my pocket I still had the pomegranate I had picked. "This is from your terrace," I said, offering it to him.

"Give it to the signora," he said, looking at my wife.

We thanked him and left.

"Surely," I said to my wife, "that land is his."

"He doesn't think so."

"But it's his, nonetheless—in a way altogether irrelevant to whoever has bought it."

"Irrelevant to him, too, I'm afraid."

"Oh, I don't know. I am sure he returns to it again and again in his thoughts—lands there, goes up and sits under a tree, gathers the fruit in his basket."

"I can see that *you* do," she said. "You are co-owners."

[1961]

A Game of Light and Shade

There was a time, before the conquerors came and razed them nearly all, when Siena had a skyline thick with towers. The steeple of the cathedral and the bell towers of the churches were left standing, and one other—the highest and the oldest, the tower of the town hall. It stems from the left corner of the communal palace and rises more than three hundred feet over the piazza. It stands erect. It is so old, so tall, it can't afford to lean. Especially if you look at it from below, you wonder how in the fourteenth century anyone dared build anything so high.

Visitors may climb to the top. A little door at the foot of the tower, in the courtyard of the town hall, opens into a small, zigzagging stone stairway. A short distance up, a passage leads from it into the palace and the ticket office. You go up a flight of steps to a terrace, where a door brings you back into the zigzagging stairway of the tower. Here there is even less room than below, and you hope you won't meet someone coming down. The walls are so thick and the space so scanty you feel you are inside the hollow core of a great tree. The stairway widens somewhat farther up. It changes as you climb. No step is like the next one. Only the thickness of the walls, seen through narrow openings that show the sky, seems constant. Within them you feel secure.

The tower was begun in 1325 and raised as the commune grew bolder. In 1345, at the peak of its glory, the tower reached its present height. From the piazza, if you look closely, you may see, marked by a slight but abrupt change in the color of the bricks, the outlines of former stages.

The stairs zigzag around a hollow shaft. This is the very core, the pith, of the tower. Through it run two big ropes, used to ring the bells that hang in the turret above. With them, in an emergency, the government of Siena could put the whole town and the countryside around it in a state of alarm. I've often heard their plangent, deep, dramatic tone, and almost felt the waves of sound. In Fascist times, they used to be rung whenever there was a parade. The sound carried me centuries back to when it meant something else and didn't just strike a hollow and empty note.

Slits in the walls, and at intervals narrow, tall windows with a pointed arch, bring air and light. Most other towers have dark, monotonous stairways that make you despair of ever coming to the top. Here, instead, you reach it sooner than you think.

The red bricks of the stem blossom into travertine, white machicolations, and the stairway opens onto a crenellated terrace. There is a view of hills and mountains, of the cathedral and the roofs of the town. If you lean over the crenels on one side, you see the red brick square below, radiated like an open fan.

A tall, arched stone bell tower rises from the terrace. You may climb this, too, past the bells it lodges, to a second terrace, and go still higher, up to a platform that supports a weather vane and yet another bell.

I have climbed the tower twice in my life—the first time in my childhood, the second recently. I should really say that I've been up three times, for when I recently climbed it something happened that made me go up again as soon as I had come down.

It was a sunny winter day. I had gone up and down the tower, and felt pleased with myself for having taken this initiative, when, outside the little door at the foot, a blind man came toward me. He was a pale, thin man, with sparse black hair and dark glasses that gave him an impenetrable look. He kept close to the inner wall of the courtyard, grazing it with his arm. On reaching the door, he touched the jamb and sharply turned inside. In a moment, he disappeared up the staircase. I stood still, looking at the empty space left by the open door, and at the little plaque that said "To the Tower" nailed to the wall. I felt compelled to follow.

I didn't follow closely. I caught up with him in the ticket office. There I was surprised to see the attendant selling him a ticket as though he were any other visitor. The man fumbled for it, sweeping a little space of desk with his hand until he had it, but the attendant didn't seem to take any notice. Then, with the ticket in one hand and touching the wall with the fingers of the other, he reached the staircase leading to the terrace.

I stood by the desk, watching him until he was out of earshot. "That man is blind," I said to the attendant, and expected him to show some concern, but he just looked at me with his sleepy eyes. He was a heavy man who seemed all one piece with his chair and desk. "He's blind," I repeated.

He looked at me vacantly.

"Why would a blind man want to climb up the tower?" I asked.

He didn't answer.

"Not for the view, certainly," I said. "Perhaps he wants to jump."

His mouth opened a little. Should he do something? The weight of things was against him. He didn't stir. "Well, let's hope not," he said, and looked down at a crossword puzzle he had begun.

The blind man was now out of sight. I turned toward the staircase.

"The ticket," the attendant said, rising from his chair. It seemed the only thing that could move him.

I handed him a fifty-lira piece, and he detached a ticket from his book. Then I hurried up the staircase.

The man hadn't gone as far as I imagined. Much less time had passed than I thought. A third of the way up the tower, I heard his step. I slowed down and followed him at a little distance. He went up slowly, and stopped from time to time. When he got to the terrace, I was a dozen steps behind. But as I reached it, he wasn't to be seen. I dashed to the first corner of the bell tower, around the next, and saw him.

He was facing the cathedral, and had I not known that he was blind I would have said he was enjoying the view. Soon he withdrew from the crenel and began walking toward me. He touched the wall, not like one who is groping in the dark but as the blind do. Their fingers touch objects lightly. If they use a cane, this seems alive, a part of them, as sensitive and sharp as a cat's whisker. I moved out of his way, and he passed by me. When I had seen him below, he had seemed eager, tense, and in a hurry. Now he looked as though he had found what he wanted. His gait was calm, and his face had lost its tautness. He ambled over to the other side of the terrace. I didn't feel anxious about him anymore, just mystified. Often he stopped, retraced a few steps, then went on again. Sometimes he seemed to expose himself to the light breeze, sometimes to take shelter behind a merlon. He climbed up to the second terrace. I went, too. We lingered there, he strolling about, I looking at the view.

At last, after ten minutes, I approached him. "Excuse me," I said with the greatest courtesy I could summon, "but I am very curious to know why you came up."

"You'd never guess," he said.

"Not the view, I take it, or the fresh air on this winter day."

"No," he said, and he assumed the amused expression of one who poses a puzzle.

"Tell me," I said.

He smiled. "Perhaps, coming up the stairs, you will have noticed—and yet, not being blind, perhaps you won't—how not just light but sun pours into the tower through the narrow, slitlike windows here and there, so that one can feel the change—the cool staircase suddenly becomes quite warm, even in winter—and how up here behind the merlons there is shade, but as soon as one goes opposite a crenel one finds the sun. In all of Siena there is no place so good as this for feeling the contrast between light and shade. It isn't the first time that I've come up."

He stepped into the shade. "I am in the shade," he said. "There is a merlon there." He moved into the sunlight. "Now I am opposite a crenel," he said. We went down the bell tower. "An arch is there," he said.

"You'll never miss. And the sun isn't even very strong," I said.

"Strong enough," he said, and added, "Now I'm behind a bell."

Coming back down onto the terrace, he went around it. "Light, shade, light, shade," he said, and seemed as pleased as a child who, in a game of hopscotch, jumps from square to square.

We went down the tower together. "A window there," he said, up near the top. "Another window," he said, when we were halfway down.

I left him, gladdened as one can only be by the sunlight.

[1962]

At the Caffè Greco

The summer before last was so hot in Rome I spent a good deal of it in the coolness of the Caffè Greco, sipping iced tea, reading, writing letters, using it as a sort of study. It's a charming old place, right on the Via Condotti, a block from the Piazza di Spagna and Keats's house, and even nearer to the building where Leopardi stayed in the 1820s. Elizabeth Browning also lived in the neighborhood, on Via Mario de' Fiori, and Shelley a five-minute walk away, on the Corso.

Yes, I felt very well there, close to my favorite poets. Time glided by. And the suave old waiters in tails—as unobtrusive as the portraits hanging on the walls—showed no signs of impatience with my continued presence. A few I recognized from when I used to come here as a student, 40 years ago. I remembered only one of them as being at all talkative, but he wasn't there anymore. A short, wispy man with straight white hair and bright little eyes, he was fond of pointing out a portrait of Buffalo Bill to the customers, saying that he had served him here, telling of how Buffalo Bill had met with the *vaccari*—the Roman cowboys—out in the campagna, entered a riding contest with them, and—his eyes more and more gleeful as he reached the punch line—lost.

Almost every day of that hot summer, a well-known poet in his 70's, whom I had met at a dinner party in a villa a few weeks earlier—I remember the way he suddenly strode in, half way through the meal, saying, "I'm very hungry"—would appear. Thin, pale, with a wild and weathered look, his hair yellow-white, in a light silk shirt and linen slacks, he cut a striking figure. He would walk from one room to the other and peer at whoever was sitting at the tables as if he were looking for someone he could never find. I would acknowledge his presence with a *buongiorno* or *buonasera* each time his icy eyes rested on mine, but, each time, he ignored me.

"Next time he comes I'm not going to say anything," I vowed, but when he arrived and peered at me I was unable to keep my resolve.

And then one day, he came in, saw me, and beaming walked straight over to me. "I'm going to America," he said, in Italian, of course.

So he had known who I was all along. At the dinner party I remembered telling him that I taught literature in a college in New England. He spoke of some translations he had done of Robert Lowell, and when I told him that I'd admired them, he scrutinized me. Apparently satisfied that I was not just trying to please him, he said, bitterly, "You are one of the few."

Now he stood in front of my table.

"To America," I said. "Oh, good!"

"Harvard," he said.

"I am not surprised," I said.

That pleased him. He sat down.

"In September," he said. "I'll be there four weeks."

"In the town of Robert Lowell," I said.

"Yes, I hope to see him."

"Oh but . . . he died."

"No, no," he said, very sure of himself, "he's living."

"Oh, but—,"

"Of course he's living," he said. "Robert Lowell, eh," and he shrugged his shoulders as if to dismiss anything I might have to say to the contrary.

"Oh, yes, he's alive," a man, evidently another man of letters—the place was frequented by them—said from a table near us. They greeted each other. Was the new man just taking his side, or did he really think that Robert Lowell was still alive? And at the same time a doubt came to my mind: could I possibly be wrong? But no, unfortunately Robert Lowell was dead. I had heard him read in Cambridge months before his death. He had surely died. I had read and heard about it. And yet this poet here and this other man . . . I felt like one of those characters in a movie whom everyone else pretends is mad.

"Yes, of course he's alive," the poet said with irritation and looked at me as at some ignorant student.

I didn't insist further. After all, he could have meant it figuratively: that Robert Lowell lived because of and through what he had written. And when he had said that he planned to see him or pay him a visit, he might have had in mind his grave. Besides, he left my table and went to sit next to the *letterato*.

Going by the U.S.I.A. library on Via Veneto a few days later, I looked up in an almanac the name of Robert Lowell. Indeed he had died. I made a mental note of the date.

I was back at the Caffè Greco the next day, reading, when the poet entered and was as cordial as he had been when he had first come over to my table. Again he spoke to me about the trip.

"What book have you there?" he said.

"I bought it at the Lion bookshop this morning. *Old Mortality* by Katherine Anne Porter."

"Katherine Anne Porter," he said. "There's no one I am more fond of. Oh, I know her very well. Our Miranda. She is a lively lady. *Bellissima. Simpaticissima.*"

I looked at him with astonishment. Did he think she was alive too? She had died in 1980. I knew the date without looking it up, because, as they say in colleges, "I taught her."

"I met her in Paris," he said. "I called her Miranda because of that charming character in the very book you are reading, which is herself, of course. Talk about liberated women—she is the prototype, the independent woman par excellence. A prima donna, too, and something of a dragon. But what a delightful dragon!"

This time I had no intention or even temptation to say that the person he was speaking of was dead. I was no spoilsport. To have said it would have made me feel like a vulture, some bird interested only in the dead. I told him instead something I knew firsthand about her. "She was giving a reading at a midwestern university I taught at, a very important reading, with lots of people, a huge audience, a multitude, a thousand or more, in a great big auditorium. Well, half way through the reading—after about 30 minutes—the dean, who had introduced her, fell asleep. Visibly, audibly asleep. Slowly she turned toward him, stared at him a moment and closed her manuscript. 'That'll be all,' she said."

"Fantastic," the poet said. "Memorable. Whatever they paid, they got their money's worth that day. Not just another reading. Something to talk and tell about for years to come, as you just did. Oh yes, she's a no-nonsense woman, as they say in English. A dragon and a darling. I must remind her and congratulate her."

"I like this place," I said, changing the subject. "Not just the locale, but the location too. So near all these poets—Leopardi, Elizabeth Browning, Keats."

"Keats," he picked up. "Last night, I was walking down the Spanish Steps and the moon was shining on his room. A ray of light gleamed through the window pane. The moon seeking Endymion, you understand?"

I nodded.

"The moon finding Endymion at his address—26 Piazza di Spagna—bathing him with light, with her own light, with herself, there, while he slept. There was love in that room last night. The full moon shone. A soft and balmy night, a night of love."

He looked at me while I nodded. A moment later, again without saying goodbye, he rose and left.

After a while, a waiter came by.

"I think I'd like a double whisky," I said.

The waiter, whom I'd never seen perturbed, raised his eyebrows the tiniest fraction of an inch. "No tea," he said.

"No tea," I repeated after him.

I drank the whisky, and ordered another, and drank that. I stared at the picture of Buffalo Bill who was staring at me. Soon, the image split in two, and one—or both—began to move.

"Hi, Bill," I said, "how are you, old sport? Don't let what happened today out in the campagna get you down—those *vaccari* are just a bunch of kids."

[1986]

“Tarocchi, Cavoli, Belle Cavolelle, Donne, Oh!”

Not the pleasantest moment in any move is waking up in a new bed and not knowing where you are, or thinking you are where you most decidedly aren’t—your home or the last place you slept in. This bit of disorientation was something I had learned to expect in all my travels, but I was spared it early one morning in a Rome hotel after a flight from Boston, for I was aroused in my sleep by the call of an itinerant broom seller on the street right outside my window. “*Scoparo!*” it went, or rather “*Scopaaa-ro!*” and I immediately knew where I was. Yes, the cry was quite unmistakable; the Roman accent and familiar enunciation of the word clearly told me I could be nowhere else. It was a call I had never heard except in Rome, but in Rome always. It had the unabashed boldness of a cock’s crow. There was also a certain sweep in the way the word was said, as if the very action of the broom were expressed. I got up and went to the window. There was the man, looking more like an exotic bird—a peacock perhaps—than a man, with several brooms on his shoulders, the handles all different colors and the straw pointing up to the sky, and whisks, and dusters made of soft real feathers and plumes, hanging from his forearms. What a load! How did he manage it? Myself, if I carried so much as an umbrella I felt encumbered.

The thought of an umbrella reminded me of the umbrella menders, who also roamed the city, though not so much in this season (it was late spring). No, they were mostly heard in November, and their call “*Ombrellatoooooh!*” had a melancholy note that spelled rain more effectively than drops of rain to me. Infinitely prolonged, the cry or, rather, mournful halloo fascinated me, and I would listen to it till—the man walking on—it became fainter and fainter and was finally too remote to be heard anymore.

I wondered: Perhaps I should make a recording of these calls, for sooner or later they will become rarer and rarer, then extinct; they will disappear and be heard no more; they don't really belong to the modern world; they will go the way of the chimney sweeps, the *spazzacamini* whose calls I can't remember ever having heard. But a recording—no, never the same as the real thing, and only there to serve notice that modernity had done or was doing away with them. And also, maybe I was being pessimistic, maybe the calls would last, maybe I didn't credit them with enough resistance, for, despite vacuum cleaners and raincoats, there would always be a need for brooms and umbrellas.

I looked at my watch. It was early—half-past seven—but I didn't mind having been awakened. Bless him, I thought, may his call never die out.

It occurred to me, in this city there was also the grinder—the man who rode about on a bicycle and here and there, usually in a piazza, stopped, trestled his bike, and, still pedaling, turned a vertical chain connected to a whetstone wheel, on which he sharpened knives and scissors. *"Arrotino!"* he cried, and the word meant sharpness to me, and grinding wheels spinning, and sparks flying, and water dripping from a can perched on the handlebars through a straw onto the whetstone, and the peculiar smell of the wet whetstone and steel, and the fricative sound that came as he applied the blade to the stone, alternating with the sound of the wheel spinning freely when he held the blade off it and wiped it and tested it on his thumb. Sometimes I wished I were an *arrotino* myself and could live that way, travel from square to square.

And there was the call of the ragman—the *stracciarolo*—who also collected used paper, and that of the fish and shellfish itinerant salesman—the *pescarolo*—and that of the fruit and produce peddler, his voice as fresh as what he sold, *"Tarocchi, cavoli, belle cavolelle, donne, oh!"* ("Oranges, cabbages, lovely sprouts, women, oh!"), and his vowels lengthened out of measure. And, of course, that of the newsboys, the *giornalai.* And I was sure there were others that either I couldn't remember or had missed. How long would they last? Into the eighties, the nineties, the new millennium?

I didn't know, but these sounds stayed in my mind. That morning as I went for a walk, I ignored or tried to ignore all the others. The sirens, the honks (they could hardly be called horn blowing—those to me were the shepherds') that grew to an exasperating crescendo because of some snarl in the traffic, and the staccatos of protest and rancor, I would simply avoid. I decided I would try to apprehend only the beautiful, and, shunning the large thoroughfares, listen to the weeping of fountains, watch the water run down mossy statues and rocks. I was not disappointed. From behind familiar street corners, I heard, as I hoped I would, the tinkling spray, sometimes a gurgle, a rush of water, or the sucking sound of a whirl. They were all spouting, the tritons.

[1979]

Biographical Note

"I was born in Rome in 1923 and grew up in the country near Siena where I went to school. My father was a philosopher, my mother a painter. Her brother, my uncle, was Lauro de Bosis, a poet, active in a movement to overthrow Fascism. In 1931 he flew over Rome scattering leaflets, and, like the hero of his play *Icarus,* was lost at sea. In 1938 we went to England as refugees. I spent the war years there and in Canada, where I began to study medicine at McGill University. We returned to Italy after the war. I became a doctor but soon gave up my practice to dedicate myself to writing. In 1951 I published a book of poems. My first short story appeared in *The Manchester Guardian* in 1955. In 1958 I began to contribute short stories to *The New Yorker* which has published seventy of them. Two novels—*A Goodly Babe* and *Doctor Giovanni* were published by Little, Brown who also published my first collection of short stories, *The French Girls of Killíni.* A second collection—*English Stories*—came out in 1975 (Street Fiction Press.) Scribner's in 1979 published a third collection of stories, *Run to the Waterfall.* From 1968 on I have been writer in residence in various American colleges and universities. In 1980 I published *Writing Fiction* (The Writer)—a series of essays on writing. I have also done translations: *Essays on Art and Ontology* by Leone Vivante (my father) published by Utah University Press in 1980, and *Giacomo Leopardi, Poems,* which Delphinium Press published in 1988. I was married to Nancy Bradish in 1958 and live with her in Wellfleet, Cape Cod. We have three children."